Lords of Oblivion

S.L. Luck

This is a work of fiction. Names, characters, places, and incidents are either the product of the author's imagination or are used fictitiously. Any resemblance to actual persons, living or dead, events, or locales is entirely coincidental.

Copyright © 2021 S.L. LUCK

All rights reserved. No part of this book may be reproduced or used in any manner without written permission of the author except for the use of quotations in a book review. For more information: info@authorsluck.com

FIRST EDITION

www.authorsluck.com

ISBN 9781777165277

E-Book ISBN 9781777165284

Cover design by 100covers.com

Edited by C.B. Moore

Other Novels by S.L. Luck

Redeemer

Interference

1

It was a chilly May evening when Kade Hart died. Six of them around the fire, blitzed out of their minds, one of them was bound to fall in.

When Cody's girl, Whitney, finally left him that morning after a faithless eleven-month relationship, they assembled around him like horseflies to dog shit. Edwin was liberal with the dope and the beer but it was Billy who brought the Oxy, courtesy of his cancer-ridden grandmother languishing in an underfunded nursing home in Florida. The first pill went to Cody, the second to Edwin's girlfriend, Charity. Edwin had to work in the morning so he declined Billy's outstretched palm, but Terry snatched three pills. Billy whipped his hand away and slapped Terry upside the head.

"The fuck, man," Billy grumbled, but it was too late. Terry was already crushing the Oxy between his teeth.

The kid, Billy's cousin Kade, was a first timer at Charity's trailer. At fifteen, Kade took the scene all in as Billy had those many years before. Much like Charity's make-up, the area was a collection of debris piled high and ugly.

The sun was still up when Kade kicked aside a rusty bucket and followed Billy over a ragged carpet embedded in the grass with his hands in his pockets, careful not to touch anything. Charity and her trailer had a reputation that Kade now realized was deserved, if not even a little under-reported. So he knew to expect the two grunting mutts and the mildewed couch and the cracked toilet with the plywood lid that Charity used to store things outside in the months when the fridge inside wasn't working. Kade nudged the lid open with the toe of his shoe. It snapped back and hit the side of the ceramic bowl.

"You want a sandwich?" Charity asked. "You can make one if you want it. There's peanut butter under the bread. I got plates in the house."

Kade's eyes fell to the bowl where, sure enough, there was a half a loaf of Wonder Bread, the white variety, with the green lid of something brown beneath it. The juxtaposition of the colors in the bowl did not appeal to him, and he politely declined. Billy gave him a sideways grin and handed him a beer.

Before Billy proffered the Oxy, the spell of beer and dope fixed them in the easy glow of quietude and they stared at the fire with glazed eyes, thinking of nothing until Terry stirred them up.

"I heard she fucked Jimmy in the can at Shooter's." Terry spat into the fire.

Billy shook his head. "It was behind the car wash."

"I heard it was in the back of the 214," Edwin said.

"The bus?" Charity raised a needle-thin eyebrow. Edwin nodded.

"You better get your pecker checked," Billy told Cody.

They all laughed so hard Terry's beer sprayed out of him. Kade bit the inside of his cheek to keep from doing the same. Cody pulled up the frayed collar of his sweater and used it to wipe his face, then he hunched further into the corner of the couch. He chugged the last half of his beer, brooding while the others hurled insults at his expense.

When Cody didn't return their abuse, Terry smacked his arm. "Come on, man. We're just having a little fun. She grabbed your balls so tight, you barely pissed without asking her permission. You're better off without her." There was a round of agreement amongst them.

Cody kicked the dirt at his feet where a spark fell, then his eyes swung from the extinguished speck of flame to Terry's vulgar excuse for a beard. In his half-bashed state, Cody wanted to run a razor over those pubic patches below Terry's chin, wanted to blade the bush off the neck that made Terry look like a giant, unkempt testicle. His face mottled from drug use, Terry might have been attractive once, but there had been no sign of that as long as Cody had known him. The night when they'd met in the Dorian (affectionately called the "Dory" by regulars) five years ago, Terry had a pocketful of money and was eager to spend it. Three rounds of shots for everyone in the bar, strangers and friends alike, brought Cody to shake the other man's hand. Even then, Terry was sporting that goddamned neck beard. Cody figured a guy that looked like that *had* to buy drinks if he was ever going to have a shot at a social life, but that idea changed when he realized that Terry was not only a small-time drug dealer but also a big-time drug *user,* and that Terry was so often whacked out of his mind that self-care was beyond his abilities.

Now, as Terry expounded all the possible diseases that Whitney might have passed to Cody, Cody focused not on Terry's words, but on his mouthful of broken teeth and his blistered lips, and whipped his can of beer at him. The empty can bounced off Terry's beard but a few drops of beer settled on the wiry hair like dew on a spiderweb.

Terry didn't wipe them away. Instead, he put his elbows on his knees and leaned low toward Cody, looking at him with one eye and pointing the mouth of his bottle at him. "Have I ever messed with you, man? Have I? You tell me a single time I screwed you. Tell me that."

Cody, in fact, could think of a hundred different times when Terry had screwed him. If he counted all the times Terry had borrowed five here, twenty there, then double that number. In one of Cody's more charitable moments, he had even lent Terry his grandmother's Buick for a so-called hospital visit to see his dying mother over in Fauville, only to have it impounded after Terry failed a roadside sobriety test outside of Toronto, two hours beyond where he had told Cody he'd be. It cost Cody nearly fifteen hundred bucks to get the car back, money he had to borrow (and was unable to repay) his grandmother. But because Terry was a beast when challenged, Cody didn't like reminding him of his indiscretions.

Terry leaned back, full of satisfaction. He said, "I thought so. You know I'm legit, man. I'm just telling it like it is. Real friends do that." He pointed the bottle again, then drank back the rest.

"Leave him alone, Terry." Charity snapped her gum. "They were together a long time."

"Eleven months of hell," Cody finally contributed.

"You're goddamn right it was hell," Terry agreed. "For us, too, man. Couldn't stand that whiny-ass voice of hers." He stuck a finger in his ear as though Whitney was still blasting him with her judgy mouth.

Cody snapped. "Shut the hell up, man, okay? Can you do that for one goddamn second?" A fleck of spittle erupted from the corner of his mouth, but he sucked it back before it could drip. He narrowed his eyes at the holes in Terry's mouth, knowing full well his own mouth wasn't that far off, and spit on the dirt near Terry's foot, where a leaf of red-hot ash had floated.

Terry slid the neck of his beer bottle across his beard. "You got a problem?"

It was Edwin who saw the trouble and he rushed to stop it before Terry's temper could gather steam. "Leave him alone, Ter," Edwin said. "He's had a tough day. Cut him some slack."

"I don't want any trouble," Charity said. "You want a sandwich, Terry? I can make you a sandwich." She stood and collected their empty cans and bottles and tossed them into a bush at the side of the house, then she pulled open the cooler Edwin brought and returned with fresh beers for everyone. Her over-sprayed hair crunched against Edwin's cheek as he kissed her, and he slapped her rear when she stood beside him with a hand on a jutted hip, waiting for Terry's order. "If you don't want a sandwich, how 'bout some chips, then?"

"You got any of that jerky your brother makes?" Billy asked from the other side of the fire. He said to Kade, "Her brother makes the best jerky. Spicy as shit. You have to try it."

Charity nodded and disappeared behind a creaky screen door, then reappeared a moment later with a grocery bag half full of dried meat. She passed it around. Terry dug into the bag and gnawed on a pepperoni stick, glaring at Cody.

Another beer down, then two, then three. The stubborn armor of indignation began to split, then crack, then completely fall away, and by the time Edwin's joints made their rounds, Terry's simmering rage had lost its heat and Cody's flaring resentment had fizzled to its obdurate resting place. Outside of the flame, the sky was now black and the air was becoming cool. Collars were drawn up and Charity's jacket was extracted from its hook inside the screen door, and still they sat while the flames imparted a symphony of light and shadow on their contemplative faces.

After a while, Cody took his phone from his pocket and checked the time. It was late, and though he had nowhere in particular to go and no one to go home to, Cody yawned and stretched, indicating to the others that he was done. Gifted with the height of a ten-year-old boy, Cody stood barely higher than the flames, which had just been stoked and built tall so they could roast midnight dogs and warm their cooling fingers.

Charity said, "You going, hun?"

"Sit your ass back down," Terry ordered before Cody could squeeze out of the circle.

Cody rubbed a dry spot on his eye and looked at Terry. "I'm tired and it's a long walk home. I'll call you tomorrow." He turned, and Terry's bottle instantly cracked on his left shoulder. A second one got him on the back of his neck. He spun around, touching his sore spots, glaring at Terry.

"I said sit your ass down," Terry demanded again and nudged Billy, who pulled from his jeans pocket a bag of pills. Kade squirmed as Billy shook the bag in front of his face. Terry jerked a thumb at Kade. "The baby here is going to get right fucked and I can't let you miss that, Cody. You want to take your mind off Whitney? There's no better cure than watching a newbie boil over. Impossible to think of your woman playing lap hockey with an entire goddamn team when you got to babysit, you know?" Billy laughed and hooked Kade's head with the crook of his arm and ruffled his hair. Kade pushed him away but grinned as though he was used to his older cousin's ribbing.

"Have at 'er. But I'm cutting out. See you tomorrow," Cody said and backed away from the fire. He was tired. He was drunk and high, and though there had been some good laughs tonight, the longer he was with Terry, the more he felt like punching him. In his current mood, the outcome was exceedingly likely, so he felt it best to call it a night while he still had the capacity to do so.

"C'mon, man," Billy begged him.

"You can sleep here tonight," Charity offered. "The couch is yours if you want it."

As kind as the offer was, Cody's skin tingled with the memory of bed bug bites from the last time he'd crashed on Charity's couch. He knew she did her best to keep the place tidy, but it was like working with an old suitcase; there was only so much you could stuff into it before it cracked and things got inside. He said, "I got to take my grandma to an appointment in the morning, otherwise I would. Thanks, though."

"Liar," Terry said.

"Whatever, man," Cody said, and slipped back onto the threadbare carpet between the junk heaps leading away from the property. Wind stirred the loose piles around him and there was such a tinkling and a rustling of all the metal and plastic that Cody felt that if he closed his eyes, it wouldn't be hard to imagine himself near a railroad track while all the freight in the world clicked on by.

Cody wasn't three steps on that carpet when Billy sprang from his cinder block, chased him down and threw a persuasive arm around his neck. "Don't listen to him, man. You know how he gets sometimes. Stay a bit, will you? An hour and we'll go with you." Billy's hair swayed along the top of his shoulders as he looked back at his cousin, who squirmed uncomfortably when Terry slumped onto the unoccupied cinder block next to him. "Just trying to give my little 'cous a good time. My bitch aunt kicked him out of the house today."

One of Cody's eyebrows went up and they regarded the youngest of their group with familiar sympathy. The boy was fair-haired and lean but had yet to develop any of the narcotic disfigurements the rest of the group presented not long after Kade's own age. His skin was smooth and still had the infantile radiance of youth. Clutching his long-nursed beer to his chest, Kade turned his head and wrinkled his nose when Terry thrust his face close enough for Kade to count Terry's remaining teeth if he wanted to.

"Let's go save him," Cody said heroically, and it was that deep sense of valor his grandma had embedded in him that spun him around and brought him back to the fire. Charity was on Edwin's lap with her lips crushed up against his, so they were ignorant of Cody's return, but Kade's relief was written all over his face.

Billy sidled in front of Terry and slapped Kade's knee. "One and done; just like losing your virginity, but this one won't make you a daddy come morning." He shook that powder-dusted bag of pills in front of Kade's face again.

"Not true," Charity corrected Billy.

"Are *you* going to fuck him?" Terry asked, pointing to the fidgeting fifteen-year-old.

"You know what I mean, Terry."

"She's right," Edwin said. "If you're tapping it, you gotta wrap it, but that's really easy to forget when you're high as fuck. That's a lesson for you, Kadester." Edwin circled a wise finger in Kade's direction while Charity nibbled on his ear lobe. "And if one slips by, don't you go AWOL on your kid, hear me? I respect no asshole who puts another kid on *No Daddy Alley*."

"He knows better than that," Billy said, and nudged Kade's knee.

The heat from his embarrassment flushing pink on his cheeks, Kade sat quiet as they imparted their intimate wisdom. He didn't feel the need to tell them he was still a virgin because none of them would believe it. An early-puberty growth spurt had bulked his miniscule frame with an impressive amount of lean muscle and lifted his clumsy frame high, until the tip of his skull fell just a few inches below every door he entered. Now, at a staggering six-foot-four and with a recent x-ray indicating his bones were not done growing, Kade was as much an impressive figure as he was attractive. His father's strong jaw, his mother's sharp cheeks, and the Hart family's wide blue eyes made him the ambition of most, if not all of Garrett High's young female assembly, and his known affiliation with Garrett's more shadowy elements made him damn near irresistible. Opportunity was as abundant in Kade's world as there was wheat in the prairies, but he didn't want the chaff. Kade considered the virulent relationships that were a predisposition for Billy and his friends and determined to wait until the time—and the girl—was right. In an effort to drown out their unsolicited advice, Kade threw back his beer and then burped the ABCs like the fifteen-year-old he was.

"We going to do that or what?" Terry poked the forgotten bag in Billy's hand. Billy snatched the bag away to keep it from Terry, then he obediently distributed the pills, instructing Kade to ignore the shit taste and quickly crush his own between his teeth.

Kade pinched the pill from Billy's hand, but he hesitated once he saw Billy, Terry, and Cody grimace when they bit down. Then Charity pinched her nose and clack-clack-clacked her pill expertly to a white sludge that bubbled at the corner of her lips. Edwin said to Kade, "I'll watch you, man. I'm sticking to beer and bud tonight, but I got your back. Nothing's going to happen." He tipped his chin to Kade and winked a bloodshot eye at him, then all of them—Billy, Terry, Cody, Edwin, and Charity—tracked the little pill from Kade's fingers to the side of his mouth, where he tightened his molars until the same white goo pervaded his mouth, releasing the entirety of the otherwise controlled-delivery drug.

What followed for Kade was the happiest forty-seven minutes of his life. He felt heaven in his veins, tranquility in his blood, and the greatest calm he'd ever known expanding from the pit of his stomach, painting its way outward until his insecurities and frustrations and fears were cloaked in wellbeing. Out from the beacons of his eyes, swinging left, right, left, over the swaying faces around the fire, Kade's consciousness was one of acceptance and forgiveness and peace. Even Terry, mean old

Terry, he wasn't so bad. In this moment, Kade remembered how Terry had sat beside him and kindly offered advice. That's what he saw if for now: kindness. That and nothing more. The boy, grinning wide and white, stretched a hand to Terry's shoulder and squeezed.

"People don't get you, bud, but I get you. I get you. You're all right. All right. All right. All. Alllll—"

The L would not leave Kade's lips. He tried to shake off that L, tried to flick it from his mouth, but it hung on there, clinging to the tip of his tongue like a burr.

"Cat got your tongue?" Terry smiled back at him and Kade saw how his teeth had grown back, so clean and straight and present they were almost beautiful. Edwin chuckled and nudged Billy in the ribs.

Billy said, "How are you feeling Kadester?"

Kade felt their many sets of eyes on him and grinned. "Lllll," he said, because the letter was still on his tongue. He brought his fingers to his mouth and took his tongue out as far as it would go. Cross-eyed, he looked down and saw the letter hanging on. It waved at him. He waved back.

Feeling comfortable himself, Cody plopped his heels on a short stump in front of the fire and let his knees splay out. Everyone but Edwin envisioned a jean-clad pair of frog legs extending from Cody's seat, and it drew a round of amphibian sounds that caused Charity to stand and hop clumsily behind their chairs. On her fourth attempt, she sprang too far and caught her knee on the top of the toilet and knocked it over. A squished bag of Wonder Bread spilled out, and the unsecured lid on the peanut butter jar came loose and fell away. The two sleepy mutts now came running and snatched the jar, dashing off behind the house. Laughing, rolling on the ground, Charity took the bread from the bag and began tossing the soft white slices in the direction of the dogs.

"Don't eat it plain!" she shouted into the darkness. "Take some bread, you assholes!"

More laughter. Despite the chill in the air, Kade grew so warm he took off his jacket, tying the sleeves around his neck like the capes on the superheroes he'd worshipped not so long before. He felt like he could fly, believed that if he tried he might never return to the ground, such was his euphoria.

"He's trippin'," Edwin said.

"There's nothing like your first time," Billy said enviously, watching his cousin puff out his chest and flex his muscles.

Terry sucked the filter of his cigarette into his mouth, pushed it out, watching the younger Hart play make believe. Then Terry rose from the cinder block. "You got power now, don't you?" he said to the boy. Kade wrapped his unblemished fingers around his biceps, his forearms, and nodded dreamily.

"Sit down, Terry," Edwin said, almost but not quite managing to conceal his inebriation.

The three pills Terry had stolen from Billy reacted with the beer and the pot to form something so noxious in him that the roots of his teeth stung. He pulled his beard to counteract the pain and yanked Kade to his feet by the jacket knotted snugly around his neck.

"Easy, Terry," Charity said, finding her place back on Edwin's lap.

"I just want to see the pretty boy up close," Terry said to Kade's whimsical face.

"He is pretty, isn't he?" Billy agreed. "He can thank the mailman for that." They laughed. Cody, happy to have Terry pick on someone else for once, laughed the hardest of them all.

"I'm invincib-a," Kade said confidently because there were no Ls.

"Me too," Terry said, and scooped Kade up in his arms and pretended to throw him in the fire. "Know what firewalking is, little Hart? It's what real men do."

"Put him down Terry!" Charity shrieked.

Billy flicked the back of Terry's leg. "Put him down, Ter. Don't fuck around the fire."

Kade felt the flames lick his rear, his legs that hung low in Terry's arms, but he felt no worry at all. The world was as it should be. All was fine and all was right. Terry began bouncing him up, down, up, stumbling under the weight of the overgrown child. Kade threw his head back and looked at the starless sky, where everything was black.

Edwin pushed Charity away and stood, swaying. "Leave him alone, Terry. He's going to get hurt."

"Don't fuck around, Terry," Cody said, emboldened by Edwin, but his words were slow and half-hearted. He sank deeper on the couch, and though Kade was flying above the fire, Cody's eyelids were too thick to lift them apart. Instead, he stared at the light flicking beyond his shoes and absently sucked back his beer.

Still in Terry's arms, Kade marveled at how fast he must have traveled without remembering as the bottom of his shoes began smoking.

"Want to see a Hart fly?" Terry asked the others.

"My heart flew away this morning," Cody said dreamily.

"Put him down, Terry." Billy slid his cigarette to the corner of his mouth and turned his Pilsner cap backward.

He got up, stumbled into Edwin and Charity, and recovered by grabbing Terry's jacket with the hand not holding his beer. Terry wobbled backward, almost dropped Kade, and then hoisted the boy over his shoulder so that Kade's face was free of the fire, but his feet were again hovering close to the flame.

"My feet," Kade said, though he did not know why.

Billy now took one of Kade's dangling arms and tried pulling him and Terry away. Terry planted his feet. Cody saw the tussle and closed his eyes, passing out frog-legged on the stump. His beer slipped from his hand and fell to the dirt, where it emptied and foamed in a divot dug earlier by one of the dogs.

With Billy behind Terry on his right, Edwin rounded the fire and came upon Terry from the other side. "That's enough, Terry. You've had your fun. We know you're strong, okay? You don't have to prove anything to us." His words were slurred, but still Edwin recognized his part as the responsible one in the group. He cleared the muck thickening his throat and approached Terry cautiously because he still had Kade on his shoulder. When Terry didn't move, Edwin smoothed back his prematurely thinning hair like a father about to have a difficult conversation with his wayward son. "Not tonight, Terry."

Terry huffed so hard his neck beard rippled down the middle. "Know what? I'm done. I thought this was our fucking night. He doesn't belong here," he said, hitching the dead weight on his shoulder up a few inches. Kade grunted. "You want to protect the pretty boy, you go ahead. But I'm not here for a kid's movie, understand? He wants to be here, he's got to take what he gets. This isn't a fucking daycare." He pushed past Billy and dropped Kade onto the couch beside Cody, who was now openmouthed and snoring. The foam from Cody's beer splashed up on Terry's shoes and he made a fuss kicking it away.

"I think it's time to call it a night," Charity yawned, stretching out dramatically.

"Whatever. I'm out of here," Terry grumbled.

Had the night stopped here, had Terry left like he said he would, the real trouble might never have happened. Hours before, they might have been able to foresee Terry's unpredictability, itself as predictable as gravity sucking them to the ground or self-righteousness chaining them to luckless circumstance in perpetuity, but now not even Edwin anticipated the ramming of Terry's hands against Charity's shoulders when she stood in front of him to pacify his anger. A squeak of pain erupted from the hundred-pound woman as she went sideways over the cinderblock and landed hard on her wrist.

Edwin threw his beer aside and faced Terry. He drew his hand back. One of Terry's teeth jutted over his lip as he, too, prepared to fight, but then Billy was between them, pushing them away from each other. Still conscious, Kade understood that something was happening and lumbered to his feet using Cody's unresponsive leg to right himself. He looked at Billy and saw him dancing, moving between Terry and Edwin with the Hart gracefulness imparted by their great-grandmother, who had been a professional dancer until she married their great-grandfather. With his long arms, Billy pushed out. Kade joined him now, one hand on Edwin's chest, one on Terry's and hummed a song he didn't quite remember while Edwin and Terry shouted at each other. Terry slapped Kade's hand away, but the boy thought it was funny and put a finger on an outcropping of chest hair springing from the scooped collar of Terry's exposed shirt.

"I'm going to have to wash my finger now," Kade mumbled, wrinkling up his nose.

"What's that supposed to mean? Huh?" Terry snatched Kade's finger and bent it more, more, until the dreamy boy with not a care in the world felt the edges of discomfort, then pain, then retreating numbness when Billy shoved Terry off him. Terry shoved Billy back. Nursing her wrist, Charity pleaded with them to stop, and Edwin stepped away to attend to her. Cody snored louder.

Billy grabbed the back of his cousin's jacket. "I'm taking you home, Kade," he said, but wasn't two steps away when Terry decked him.

Half-blinded with pain and with the rusty taste of blood seeping down his throat, Billy's hand went to his throbbing nose. Kade swung around to defend Billy, but then Terry pushed him backward and Cody's legs acted like a tripwire that sent Kade sprawling not forward, not backward, but in the very direction no person should fall—headfirst into the fire.

2

Bill Asket enjoyed the sunlight slicing through the windows of his convenience store as he sat behind the counter reading the *Garrett Gazette*. At forty-seven, Bill wasn't keen on his cell phone or his laptop for his daily dose of news. He didn't mind it a day late because his regular customers kept him informed of the happenings in the world whether Bill inquired or not. So world news rushed like wildfire into the So-Lo and *local* news spread even faster than light.

He turned the pages, still fighting down the terrible smoothie his eight-year-old, Maria, had made for him, but the tastes of spinach and Sugar Loops and apple juice made it a hard battle. Had it been a school day, Bill would have tossed the concoction out, but with Maria and Mrs. Panks upstairs in Mrs. Panks' apartment every Saturday, the two could surprise him any time. His only consolation was spitting the occasional sip into an empty cup plucked from the coffee station after Mrs. Panks whisked Maria away.

The bell above the door signaled an arriving customer, so Bill straightened and pushed the chunky smoothie aside.

"Morning Bill."

Martin Gimbel never failed to give his two-finger salute. He carried on with his arthritic limp to one of two small tables next to the front window near the deli counter. While the So-Lo was by no means a restaurant, Bill didn't mind waiting on the regulars who were as loyal to the So-Lo as they were to their own families. Bill went to the coffee station, poured Martin a medium black coffee and strode the few steps over to the deli, where with tongs he plucked thick slices of smoked meat and placed them between two slices of dark rye bread. He added a pickle for good measure before bringing the sandwich out to Martin, who clapped Bill appreciatively on the back.

"You're too good to me, Bill. Tell me why again no woman has scooped you up yet?"

Martin readjusted his cane on the back of his chair and gestured to the empty seat across from his own. Bill sat, unable to keep from smiling at the old man's age-old quip. The hair in Martin's ears glowed white when he bent his head into a ray of sunshine to bite into his sandwich.

"I know, I know," Martin said before Bill could answer, "because a good woman would keep you in bed so often you'd have to shut this place down." Meat fell onto Martin's plate as he laughed with his mouth open.

"I never said that." Bill shook his head, chuckling in spite of himself.

"Doesn't make it any less true."

"If I could be so lucky," Bill said, and felt those ribbons of grief rise in him again.

Martin wiped his lips with a napkin then wrapped a big-knuckled hand around his paper coffee cup, the wrinkled skin on his fingerbones dripping downward to cover the So-Lo logo Diana designed when she was still pregnant with Maria.

"You read about the funeral?" Martin asked at last. When Bill nodded, Martin said, "They would have buried that poor kid in a cardboard box if it weren't for an anonymous donor stepping in to cover the costs. The world's gone to filth, I tell you." Martin's thin upper lip vanished in distaste.

Bill shrugged and rested his chin in his cupped hand. The bristles of his perpetual five o'clock shadow felt like sandpaper even against his calloused fingers. "No consolation for the family, but he's probably in a better place."

"Damn right he is," Martin grumbled. His face compressed with the violent memories of Kosovo, Kuwait, and Rwanda, and Bill knew that if he didn't change the subject soon, Martin's memories would become table-pounding reminders.

"I hear Ethel's been asking about you," Bill said of one of the So-Lo's regulars.

Martin blushed and swiped the air over his coffee cup. "Nah."

"She's a sweet lady."

"You mind your business, Bill Asket. There's nothing exciting about an old man's love life. What are we going to do? Play *swap the dentures*? That part of my life's long gone, I'm afraid." He looked through the window to watch Jasper Lindauer shuffling by.

"Don't sell yourself short, Martin. It's not good to be alone at your age."

"At *any* age, Bill. Yours too." Martin shook his cup at him.

"Touché," Bill said and rose to greet Jasper, whose painfully slow gait made the overhead bell tinkle again, again, again. At last, Bill pulled the door open for the old man.

"Getting slow in your old age." Jasper pointed a finger between Bill's eyes, then he winked and made his way to his usual seat at Martin's table. "Has she been in yet?" he asked without preamble, looking from Bill to Martin. His few remaining brow hairs went up, down, up, and a sly grin spread across his age-puckered lips.

Widowed a decade earlier, after Eugene Panks had suffered the wrath of an undiscovered tumor on his prostate gland, Barbara Panks bloomed into her seventies like a teenage girl in the upslide of puberty when cute finally becomes pretty. With sideswept silver hair, a slender neck, and the upright shoulders of a much younger woman, Barbara Panks presented a refined beauty verging on regal, and there was not a man over forty who didn't look her way whenever she ventured into the So-Lo to collect Maria or to enjoy a coffee with Bill. Barbara herself often joked with Bill that he'd need to start selling electrified dog collars if he couldn't keep Jasper, specifically, out of the store. Looking now at his overeager face and the way he was licking his lips, Bill considered a straitjacket more appropriate. In truth, Jasper wasn't a terrible person. If no women were around, he was even all right. But put a skirt or breasts or perfume anywhere near him, and reason abandoned the old man, something both Bill and Martin were constantly policing.

To Jasper, Bill said, "You know I won't tell you that, Lindy. You creep the woman out."

"I thought we were friends." Jasper snorted and pushed the brim of his weather-beaten hat further up his forehead when Bill set a creamy cup of coffee in front of him.

"They call people like you *perverts*, Jasper," Martin said.

"Just appreciatin' the finer sex. Nothing wrong with that." Jasper blew at the steam rising from his cup. "You two hear about that kid?"

Bill said, "I can't imagine what his family is going through."

"Money, that's what they're going through," Jasper grunted. "They got one of those electronic fundraisers going on. Stan told me it was already over three bills this morning."

"Thousand?" Martin asked.

"Hundred thousand," Jasper corrected with a glint in his eye. "Not a bad way to turn the tables of fortune, hey? Shit, I wish that technology was around when Irene kicked the bucket. I'd be at Starbucks watching girls in their short shorts get their ten-dollar fruity drinks instead of here drinking cheap coffee with you ugly schmucks."

Bill scratched his chin. "If my free coffee isn't good enough for you, Jasper, you can start paying any time."

"Ungrateful bastard," Martin mumbled into his empty cup and rolled his eyes at Bill.

"Money or not, I'll bet my store they'd rather have their son back. Being poor doesn't mean you love your kids any less. And if a little money comes their way, then good for them. Anything that would make it easier to cope. I say, all the power to them."

Crossing his arms, Bill leaned next to the window reflecting that the loss of a young son might be similar to the loss of a mother to her five-year-old daughter. There was no rationalizing either devastation, of course; when the rug of the world gets whipped out from under your feet, you fall, no matter how sturdy your shoes seem to be.

Martin shot Jasper a superior look, and both men turned to the sound of the bell. A group of teenagers were scuttling in, popping gum and tugging headphones from their ears. Jasper's eyes fell upon the rear of the girl, whose long legs might come level to his chest, should he get close enough to measure.

"Pervert," Martin whispered under his breath, and kicked one of Jasper's orthotic shoes beneath the table.

Bill snagged two fresh copies of the *Garrett Gazette* from the newsstand and tossed them on their table. He said to Jasper, "Keep yourself occupied for a few moments, will you?" When Jasper leaned sideways to peek past Bill at the young brunette heading to the drink fridges in the back, Bill rolled up a *Gazette* and whacked him with it. "Last warning, Jasper. You start behaving yourself or I'll make a few calls and get you in Southbridge. They take losing your marbles seriously these days, and I'm sure Martin here will back me up."

Martin's concave chest inflated with importance. "Damn right I will."

"I'll look until I'm dead, *Ass-ket*," Jasper said defiantly, snorting through his fat nose.

"Not here, you won't."

With an indignant murmur of acquiescence from Jasper, Bill left the table and returned to the counter where he waited for the three teens to make their purchases. The girl had slid the cooler door open to survey the cold beverage selection. Every second the cold air escaped into the store, Bill calculated the rise in the So-Lo's energy costs. That drink, if she actually chose one from unit she was holding open, would tick up his monthly expenses with all the others, but nothing could be done about it. The all-glass fronts of the beverage coolers were apparently not clear enough, for at least half of the So-Lo's customers preferred to *warm* the coolers before selecting their beverages of choice.

The girl was no different, alternately opening one door for a minute, then the next, then another, until at last returning to the first door to take the same bottle of root beer she'd put back a few moments before.

Her boyfriend, or the acne-scarred kid who Bill *thought* was her boyfriend, meanwhile, non-discriminately sauntered between the So-Lo's three aisles and gathered an impressive armful of potato chips, chocolate, and bags of sour candies. Bill didn't have to guess if the pair were going to get high because he could smell the skunk-scent of marijuana on the girl long before she set her drink on the counter. Her evasive, glassy-red eyes confirmed this, but she was quiet and polite during their transaction, so Bill held his tongue. It was not his manner to educate customers on the hazards of drugs, especially now that marijuana was legal in Canada. Sure, she was underage, but who was he to judge? He and Diana had done their fair share when they were the same age as the girl and her acne-scarred boyfriend, and had Diana still been here, she'd remind him of those days with not a hint of remorse.

"Have a good day," Bill said to the departing couple. "And stay safe." He winked at them as only a father could. The girl blushed.

"Right on, man," the boy vocalized from lethargic lips and gave Bill a sideways one-eyed grin of respect.

The door was not quite closed when the third teenager, a lanky boy in a hooded sweatshirt, made to exit after them. Between his cupped hands, Jasper called, "Hot pockets! Hot pockets! Check him out before he runs, Bill!"

The kid froze. In front of him, the door closed and seemed to trap him there. The fabric of his bulky hood pulled low over his brows made the kid's face almost impossible to see, so Bill approached cautiously, hoping the kid's immobility was borne of fear rather than preparation for fight.

With his open palms spread in front of him in a gesture of peace, Bill said, "Mind showing me what you got in your sweater, son?" He pointed to the bulge in the pocket of the boy's sweater. One of the kid's hands went to his stomach, and he slipped his hand into the pocket. "I don't want any trouble," Bill quickly cautioned, in case the kid was carrying a weapon.

Wordlessly, the kid's elbow drew outward. Too slowly the hand at the end of the elbow revealed the beginning of a taut fist. There was something in that fist, something dangerous or even deadly. The way the kid's veins bloomed blue on the back of his hand warned Bill that the So-Lo's quiet morning was over and that, perhaps, it wasn't *all* that was over. Droplets of sweat beaded on Bill's forehead and he stepped back to show to the kid he meant no harm.

"It's okay, son," Bill said before the kid's hand was fully revealed. "Whatever it is, just take it. I won't give you any trouble. Please, just—" From his pocket, the boy produced an apple. He turned his fist around and opened his thin fingers so that the apple sat in the palm of his hand. "That it?" Bill asked, more than a little relieved. The boy's hood shook as he nodded.

"String him up, Bill!" Jasper called out. There was a murmuring at the table as Martin poked his cane at Jasper's ribs, but this Bill ignored.

The overhead fluorescents gleamed off the apple's waxy surface, glittering in that small divot around the stem while the kid trembled.

"Take off that hood, will you?" Bill asked. The kid obliged quickly and braced himself as if for a strike. His eyes clamped shut and his thin nose wrinkled upward with the pull of his anxious cheeks. "I'm not going to hit you, son. I just want to talk. I promise. Just a quick chat and you can be on your way. After picking my pocket, I think that's the least you can do for me. Sound fair?" The kid nodded and creaked open his eyes to look at the floor. "Good. Now put your hand down before it stays like that. Mind telling me your name?" His question was answered with silence, but the boy's hand did go down as Bill had instructed.

"Call the cops!" Jasper shouted.

"Tell them to arrest the pervert!" Martin hollered and threw his napkin at Jasper.

"Please d-don't," the kid mumbled, and Bill realized for the first time the kid was barely older than Maria, maybe only by about four or five years, which would make him twelve or thirteen.

Looking at the sharp angles of the kid's cheekbones and the hollows where no kid should have hollows, Bill realized the kid was skinny almost to the point of starvation. The kid's lips tightened as Bill studied him, but his clear blue eyes were still in the deep end of innocent.

"Someone hurt you, son?" Bill asked, gesturing to the faded bruise on the kid's jaw, near his ear.

The kid slicked his shaggy hair down over the bruise. "No sir."

"Don't let him con you, Bill. He's a criminal!"

"Only thing criminal is your breath, you smelly bastard."

The boy's jaw flickered as he tried not to laugh. "That's better," Bill said as though to a terrified animal that might take flight at any time. He spoke as soothingly as he would to Maria, lowering his tone, slowing the speed of his delivery so that it was almost sleepy. He could feel himself relaxing and hoped the boy was, too. "Now, no one's going to call the police, I give you my word, but I would like to talk to you. Can you do that for me?"

"Yes sir."

"Bill. Call me Bill."

Silence.

"If we're going to have a conversation, son, I'd sure like to know your name, otherwise there's going to be a hell of a lot of guesswork on my end and I haven't had quite enough coffee to figure out what I'm supposed to call you. *Son* seems kind of old-fashioned, doesn't it?"

Those apprehensive blue eyes swept from the floor to Bill's face. "Luke," the boy said softly.

"Luke what?"

"Luke Vorlicky, sir, I mean, Bill." His voice cracked as he spoke, the pubescent dip coming, going, even in those few short words.

"Luke, huh? Well, Luke, you got anywhere to be right now? Serving those handfuls over there worked me up a bit of an appetite and I'd like to make a sandwich. If you'll stay for a few minutes, you can join me and we'll talk and eat, then you can go; no harm, no foul. Any allergies?"

Without giving Luke time to decline, Bill abruptly turned his back and strode to the deli counter, giving the old men a peremptory death-stare to behave themselves while Luke followed silently, averting his eyes.

"I stole a bra once," Jasper offered with an air of experience, loudly enough so Bill scowled at him as he rounded the back of the deli counter. "Didn't wear a bra, didn't need a bra. Up to that point—I was just a whippersnapper myself, mind you—I didn't ever see the things that go *in* a bra. But even then I knew they were the key to the world." He drummed his knotted fingers against the table, longing with memory.

"You still have that apple, boy?" Martin asked Luke. Luke looked at Bill, who winked encouragingly as he placed the apple in Martin's outstretched hand.

A wail of pain filled the So-Lo when the apple connected with the crown of Jasper's hat. Martin sat back, grinning so wide the side lip of his denture plate showed through the opening in his mouth. Jasper's red face steamed with indignation, but an outburst was prevented when Bill looked at his watch and said to the two men, "You two heading to the Legion? If you are, you better get on it. Bingo starts in twenty."

"He wants us out, Martin," Jasper sniffed.

"He wants *you* out, but I might as well get along, too. I got money to lose and time to lose it. I appreciate the hospitality, Bill," Martin said, pushing back his chair and leveraging his cane to stand. He aimed a finger at Luke. "Bill's a straight shooter, kiddo. You're lucky you got him. The old owner would have skinned you alive. You would have been bloody from your toenails to your teeth."

The nascent bump of Luke's Adam's apple jerked upward as he gulped. Biting his lip and unable to look at the men, Luke waited until the bell signaled Martin and Jasper's departure before he spoke in a tone so quiet Bill almost hadn't heard him. "I'm sorry."

"I'm sure you are," Bill said, plating their sandwiches. "But I have to ask, why steal an apple? Kids like you aren't coming in for anything healthy, almost ever. I don't mean any offense by that, it's just that all anyone your age ever wants is filled with either sugar or salt. Nothing that grows on a tree or comes from the ground. If it's made in a factory with ingredients no one on earth can pronounce, I can barely keep it on the shelves, it goes so fast. Legally and by other means, mind you." He carried their plates to the table vacated by Martin and Jasper. "Can you grab that rag on the counter and give this a wipe?"

Luke scrubbed the table probably longer than was necessary but that was okay with Bill. It showed that the kid was trying to make amends and Bill respected him for it. He set the plates down and then pulled two bottles of water from one of the coolers. Luke was waiting with his hands in his lap when Bill returned.

"Dig in," Bill said. "Don't wait for me. I get interrupted so much it might take me the entire day to eat this. Please."

Luke's sandwich vanished before Bill swallowed his third bite. A customer came in and Bill excused himself, sure that at any moment, fed and forgiven, Luke would bolt. But he didn't. Instead, the kid took his paper plate to the trash can and retrieved the rag and wiped the table again, then he sat back down.

When Bill finally returned almost ten minutes later, Luke said, "Thank you for the sandwich and the water. I know I don't deserve it, but I would like to pay you back."

"You have a job?" Luke shook his head. "Money?" Another shake. Bill leaned his elbows on the table and considered the sorry sight in front of him. He said, "I'm not in the business of taking money from people who don't have it. And maybe I'm wrong, but I get the feeling that accepting your proposal would put you in a tricky situation. Am I right?" A shrug. They regarded each other for some time. Luke's knees jittered under the table. "Why the apple? Tell me about that and I think that'd make us even. I'm dying to know."

"Between us?" Luke asked.

"I won't tell a soul," Bill said.

"I didn't want to forget what they taste like."

Bill frowned. "Come again?"

"Fruit's expensive. Why buy an apple when you can buy five packs of ramen noodles for the same price? My mom's been telling me that since I was six, so that's what we eat."

"That all?"

Luke's small shoulders went up. "Mostly. Sometimes we get spaghetti, no meat though, unless it's on sale."

Suddenly the chunky smoothie Maria had made for him didn't seem so bad. "What about milk? Eggs? Vegetables?" Luke's half-hearted answers made Bill's few bites of sandwich turn over in is stomach. The boy hadn't even swiped a good apple, as Bill had noted bruises on the fruit's skin before it met with Jasper's head. "Is this your first time stealing anything?"

"Is it that obvious?"

"It's a good thing you're not a pro, Luke." Bill scratched the stubble on his chin. "That apple shouldn't have been on the shelf in the first place, and my guess is that's exactly why you took it. You didn't want to put me out any more than you had to, am I right?"

"Yes sir."

Now late morning, the store was picking up a steady stream of customers and Bill excused himself several times. He had expected Luke to take his leave but was increasingly happy that he hadn't. By the time the customer traffic slowed down, Bill had been away from the table for three-quarters of an hour. Meanwhile, he watched Luke picking up discarded receipts and deli trash, working quietly to keep the deli and coffee stations clean. Bill also noted the boy doing so almost secretly, as if he didn't want to be caught.

"How old are you, Luke?" Bill asked when he sat back down.

"Thirteen. Well, almost thirteen. My birthday's in two weeks."

Shit, Bill thought. *Too young to hire by Canadian standards.* In fact, even the suggestion of hiring Luke could land the So-Lo in hot water, but by the holes in the kid's sneakers and the nutrient-deficient flatness to his skin, Bill suspected there weren't many people looking out for him. Luke mentioned his mother, but nothing of his father; a situation unfortunately all too common in the tenements around the So-Lo.

Bill said, "If you were a year older, I would have offered you a job today because I don't believe you've ventured onto the path of no return, and I'd sure as hell like to help keep you off it. You're a good kid, Luke." Luke's pale cheeks went pink, and it was that slip of innocence that convinced Bill to flush out what he said next. "I'm not going to offer you a job, Luke, but if, say, every Saturday you happened to visit, I'm sure there'd be a sandwich here waiting for you. Maybe other things, too."

Bill hoped the lack of reference to the word *money* would allow him to deny ever offering Luke a job. He also hoped Luke understood what he actually meant, but this apprehension was short-lived, for a gleam passed over the kid's blue eyes that told Bill his cryptic message had been received.

"Can I visit Sunday, too?" Luke asked.

"Of course," Bill agreed. "I'm busiest from eleven to two."

He could see the kid imprinting the time in his memory and knew then that Luke wouldn't disappoint the So-Lo like so many other stoned-out hires. He stood and Luke followed suit, but when Bill reached to shake the kid's hand, the boy hesitated as though he was unfamiliar with the gesture. Finally, his slim fingers wrapped around Bill's for a timid handshake. Bill wished Luke a good day, fully expecting the kid to take his leave, but he quietly stayed until two o'clock as he tidied up the store.

3

Through the dusty window blinds in Elanor Clyde's small home, the afternoon sun made patterns on the furniture so that everything was lined. The sofa, her reading chair, the piles of junk mail long since useful, were intermittently light and dark, light and dark, and this is what Elanor stared at as she stirred her tea. Tinker rested lazily on her lap, and as she shifted her body so that she wouldn't be drinking directly above him, the cat snorted and dug one of his hind legs into the folds of her belly. "I can't win," she said to herself.

Suffering from a spoiled stomach, she had had a terrible sleep. The runs caught her before midnight, squeezed her again at two, and then every thirty minutes until her alarm went off at seven, when she had to go to work. In her late seventies, Elanor again brooded at Harry's stubbornness. Had he not canceled his life insurance policy a year before he passed, she might have been able to stop working when she turned sixty-five. But she'd married a bastard. She'd known it when she was younger, begrudged it as she grew older, and her willingness to put up with a lifetime of crap had led her to where she was now:

working forty hours a week, greeting indifferent customers at the Bargain-Mart. Elanor sighed and patted Tinker off her lap, unfastened the top button on her slacks, and let the weight of her body slide the zipper all the way down. Much better.

Her stomach growled and she briefly thought of making a sandwich, but even the *idea* of food brought the taste of bile to her mouth. It wasn't just the sickness that turned her stomach, however. Delivering fresh laundry to Cody's basement bedroom that morning had a lot to do with it.

She'd knocked on his door to present that neatly folded pile without any idea of the horrors behind it. But when the door opened and she saw her grandson sprawled on the bed, covered in his own vomit, the smell had constricted her already tender insides and Elanor began to retch.

He hadn't overdosed, as she'd first suspected, but he both looked *and* smelled like death. Cody's habits weren't a secret. It was his addiction that had deposited him on her doorstep those seven months ago, after his parents kicked him from their house, so she knew the demons that lurked beneath his skin. Addiction. Laziness. Narcissism. The nerve-stabbing trifecta she'd borne simply because no one else would. In truth, those first days had been easier. Cody had wandered toward her like a puppy and, ever the fool, Elanor had scooped him (and all his mess) right up. What grandmother could turn a grandchild away? Definitely not Elanor. So she'd taken Cody in and given him the basement and a fridge full of food and left him alone to heal.

Her first mistake was thinking that Cody was going to recover, as though addiction were something your skin could cover and grow over, like earth on a coffin or the settling of dirt over a garbage dump. Her second mistake was thinking that her presence would be enough to warn him away from trouble. His few days of good behavior had almost made Elanor believe they could make it work. But her jurisdiction in her own home was short-lived. Cody's turmoil had spread from the basement bedroom, overtaking the bottom level like floodwater, rising up the stairs and into the living room, the kitchen, until Elanor's only asylum was the confine of her bedroom. And *that* only with the door closed.

First, there were the mood swings. Nasty things that made the house shake. Then there were the larcenies. A five plucked from her purse. A twenty pulled from under the fridge magnet that held the money for the water bill, which Elanor always paid in cash. Small offenses to begin with, and she mostly ignored them because she felt that progress didn't happen with an empty wallet. Had she been on him from the beginning, she supposed she might not have caught him in her jewelry box with his fingers on her wedding ring. Thankfully, she'd caught that one, but when she'd opened Cody's door this morning and seen into his room for the first time in many weeks, she was struck dumb by the obscenities she *hadn't* caught.

She'd seen the bucket of chicken first. The red and white stripes were by far the cleanest things in the room, showing bright and bold against a backdrop of filth. The bucket was overturned on the carpet and several pieces of chicken had tumbled out. It couldn't have been there long, but Elanor wrinkled her nose and began breathing through her mouth. She would have dropped the stack of laundry in her hands if she didn't have the good sense to keep it away from the contamination. Instead, she clutched it tighter as she surveyed the stains that covered the walls like vines. Bits of food were stuck here and there all the way to the windows, the ceiling, as though his food had exploded, and his bedsheets were fouled with what Elanor suspected was *never* edible. Takeout containers were piled on every available space, open and half-eaten, rotting so long they presented many colors of mold. Ants were crawling over the heaps, not to mention a number of bugs Elanor didn't care to identify. The desk she ridiculously thought Cody might use for studying, should he return to university, was upended and pushed on its side in front of the closet. She did not want to know what Cody had barricaded inside.

Worst of all were the piss jugs. One, two, ten, *dozens* of old pop bottles were filled to the caps with yellow-brown urine. She didn't need to open them to know what they were because her own daughter and son-in-law, Regan and Matt, had tossed him out for the very same thing.

Taking that all in, Elanor backed away and put Cody's laundry on the arm of the basement couch and ran to the bathroom, where Cody at least had had the decency to flush. Up came the rest of whatever was inside her stomach; then, using the tips of her fingers to turn on the filthy taps, she washed her hands and patted her cheeks with water. The shock of cold brought her simmering anger to a boil, and Elanor strode back to the bedroom to give Cody a piece of her mind.

She went in yelling, her rage charging out of her so that her temples pulsed, her nostrils flared and her throat abraded with the force of her shrieks. When the good-for-nothing squatter didn't move, she even threw a box of tissue at him. Cody brushed his cheek with sluggish fingers and rolled over. He was so buried in junk that she barely saw the outline of his small chest until he turned over and the filthy blanket rolled off him. That's when she saw the vomit.

What followed was the biggest fight they'd ever had. She threatened to kick him out of the house if he didn't have the mess cleaned up before she returned from work. When she slammed the door and left him, her heart was racing so fast Elanor was sure she'd blink and end up six feet underground beside Harry, when a different kind of hell would begin. Now, with her tender stomach free and the chamomile tea coating her nerves, Elanor dared not go to the basement. She wanted to believe she wasn't hosting a platoon of insects down there, but it was never wise to face your problems while your blood was over-boiled. In time she would go, but not now, not yet.

Tinker mewled for his dinner. Elanor said to the cat, "At least *one* of us can think of food," and wrinkled her nose at him. Another dinner cry from the cat and Elanor began lifting her tired bones from the comfort of her chair, when she heard the telltale pop of a can being opened. The cat ran toward the kitchen.

Elanor listened to the scooping of food into the metal bowl, the rinsing of the can, and the bounce of aluminum off drywall as Cody tossed the can into the recycling bin. He mumbled something to the cat, then he was in the small living room with a plate of her favorite honey biscuits. Cody pushed aside the papers on the coffee table and put the tray down.

"More water for your tea?" he asked.

Elanor didn't answer him. She bit down on her time-brittled teeth and looked away at the television, which she had yet to turn on. She tugged the bottom hem of her cardigan over her belly to spare Cody the vision of her underwear, then took a peppermint from the candy dish and chewed it to nothing while he looked on.

At length, he said, "I'm a fuckup, Grandma."

She wasn't one for unnecessary vulgarity, but Elanor felt his admission wasn't too far off. "Go on," she told the image in her periphery, as she still couldn't bring herself to look upon his face.

He took her cross-stitch hoop off the couch and sat across from her, tracing with his fingers the floral outlines of her orange and pink stitches on the taut linen. "Have you ever felt worthless, Grandma? I mean, like *really* worthless?"

"All life has value," Elanor said. "Even the maggots."

"I deserve that."

"You do."

What came out of Cody was a half-groan, half-sob. He threw his head back onto a couch cushion and tossed an arm over his eyes, still able to see the flames on Kade's face. "Why is life so *hard*?" Cody moaned. "Was it this hard when you were growing up?"

"You have it easy," Elanor said, swinging to face him for the first time since they'd argued this morning. She didn't like the insinuation that his challenges were external, as though his problems had little to do with his own choices. She hushed his coming objection with a hand. "You say this like you had nothing to do with it, but it's all you, Cody; it's all you. Life is hard because you've *made* it hard. Is it always easy? No. But the way you go playing around like nothing matters, well, *this* is what happens." She waved a hand down the length of him. "Look at you. The world's at your doorstep and you go rolling in the weeds. You could do anything you want, go places people only *dream* of seeing, but you're so busy feeling sorry for yourself, you're throwing your future away like it hasn't already been *worked* for. How many times have you flunked out of university, Cody? Tell me that." She caught and held his hazel eyes until he fidgeted with a scab on his shoulder.

"Four," he said, and swept a thin smear of blood across his arm.

"Four," Elanor repeated. "And did you pay a single red cent for any of it? Of course you didn't. You let your parents do that for you because they have a money tree in the vegetable garden." The force of her anger rushed out of her and Elanor stood, open pants and all, and thrust a finger at him. "They worked their backs to bruises to give you every opportunity in the world and you act like it's some kind of penance on you. You should be ashamed."

The palms of Cody's hands went to his eyes, but she knew this trick; trying to make her pity him, getting all teary-eyed so that she would let him be. But after seeing the damage he'd done to the basement, nothing was going to make her go easy on him. Her steam was out, and she was letting it whistle.

"Thirty years old and you look like a weasel, Cody. If you did even an *ounce* of work on anything but getting high and *avoiding* work, your arms wouldn't look like they'd snap in the wind. That poison is killing you, and you don't even know it." The downturn of her lips showed her distaste in full force. He'd become disgusting to her, and they both knew it.

"It's not like that, Grandma."

"It's *exactly* like that. Have you seen yourself in a mirror lately? You're a stick, Cody. Look at you. I can count your ribs.

And what are those marks?" She pointed to a cluster of sores, red and bubbled, under his left nipple.

His hand instinctively covered the area he'd picked and picked and picked after a meth-cocaine twister two days before. It was the same spot Kade had unsuccessfully reached for before he went into the fire. Cody grunted his anguish out. "I need a little time, Grandma. I'm not right. I know I'm not right, but my friend died, for fuck's sake. You don't just get over something like that."

Elanor took in his bleach-crisped hair and wondered if the chemical had soaked into his brains. "Language, Cody. What do we say about bad language?"

"Swearing is for people who aren't smart enough to articulate themselves," he said robotically. "Sorry, Grandma, but you know what I mean."

Shaking a finger at him, she said, "Those sores have nothing to do with Kade Hart's death. You've had them before, so don't make excuses. Your habits and your sadness are two separate things, no matter how much you use one to soften the other, especially since you've been at *this* since high school. You didn't start using *after* he died, Cody Clyde, so let's not pretend you did."

The chill from her words acted upon him like ice, and he felt the tingling of gooseflesh on his bare back. He shivered, wishing he hadn't dirtied every last shirt, or at least had the foresight to give his clothes to his grandmother to wash much earlier than he had. In this moment, seeing her tremble with anger, Cody knew his options were limited. No. Not *limited*. His options were spent, burned so far down the bottom of the wick that the guiding light might forever snuff out if he so much as *breathed*.

He could feel her on the verge of sweeping him from the house like ashes, itching with the long bristles of righteousness to expel him onto the street.

"I don't *want* to be like this, Grandma. I don't want to be a fuckup. I know you hate it when I say it like that, but I am, and I don't know how to change that."

"Rehab," Elanor said, fastening the buttons on her pants so that he would stop looking at the bulge below her bellybutton that she'd grown in sync with Harry's alcoholism.

Cody bridled at the suggestion. "I can't do that."

"You can and you will," Elanor said.

His memories of the Henley Recovery Center were foggy at best. A decade ago, at the tender age of twenty, his own father had dragged him to that grey box building on a morning so cold Garrett's schools and buses were shut down. The weeks leading to his scheduled six-week admission, Cody put up no fuss against the treatment, more to appease his father than for any actual desire to get clean. But on that day, suffering from an awful cocaine crash after his father found his stash and wouldn't leave him alone until his admission, Cody was sick with exhaustion. His father lifted him into the car but even that little effort was too much for his racing heart. Pain ripped his chest and clamped his lungs, and it was only by a miracle that they reached the clinic in time to understand that Cody was having a heart attack. He survived, but his admission lasted only eight days, when he discharged himself.

To Elanor, he said, "It doesn't work for me, Grandma. I'm not like the people they put in those places. They're so messed up; they *need* to go there, but I'm not as bad as them. I know you think I am, but you don't see the things they do. There was a guy shooting his own *blood*, Grandma. I would never do that." He added the second-hand information from Terry's failed stint at Henley, but she wasn't fooled.

"Here's how I see it," Elanor said, taking a cookie. "You don't have any other option. Either you commit to a program or you're out of my house. I don't care if they say they want to keep you there until you collect pension, Cody; you're doing it or you're out. And don't give me the bull that it isn't for you. I don't know half of what you do, but I know it's a sewer life that you're living, and the only way to fix it is to flush it out."

"Grandma—"

Elanor's hands went to her hips. She'd made up her mind. "There will be absolutely no debate on this. You're better on the street than here with me if you're going to be a sewer rat. My stomach can't take your nonsense anymore. You get on that list tomorrow or you're done here, Cody. It's for your own good."

That line again. Everyone and that goddamned line. *It's for your own good.* Told so much by so many people, it meant nothing anymore. His parents used it. His Aunt Lucy used it. Every single one of his former friends used it. Nobody understood what it was like to be him. Parents with unrealistic expectations. Family who reminded him—day in, day out—of the depth of his advantages. No one understood the pressure on Cody to be smarter, bigger, better. It was like walking around with a truck on your shoulders. Who could stand it, let alone carry that weight? Not Cody.

Across from him, his grandmother sniffed, waiting for an answer. "I'll try," he finally said.

The biscuit flew from Elanor's hand to the sores on Cody's chest. She straightened authoritatively when he winced. "And

I'll *try* not to change the locks," she said.

4

A thin flow of fog drifted over the aged roof of the So-Lo on a quiet Sunday morning, keeping the residents of the neighboring tenements in their homes a little longer, lazy in the warmth of their beds. So it was that April Taylor, loyal part-timer and mother of two long-since-graduated women, finished a third game of Sudoku on her cell phone and went to the beverage station to make herself a hot chocolate.

She had just torn the top of the powder packet when Bill snuck in from the back hallway, conveniently attached to the apartment building housing the So-Lo.

"What did I tell you about coming in on your day off, Mr. Asket?" April said in her best motherly tone.

Bill held up his palms. "I'm here on unofficial but especially important business, April. We're out of marshmallows." He went to the nearby aisle and pulled a bag from the shelf.

April stirred the chocolate into a cup of hot water until the powder was dissolved and the water was foamy. Her glasses fogged as she blew over the top of her cup, so she only saw the top half of Bill's head when she narrowed her eyes at him. "That all?"

It took a great amount of effort for Bill not to swivel his eyes like a searchlight over his business. Instead, he reached sideways and grabbed the nearest item on the shelf. "This too."

"Baby formula?" April's eyebrows rose above the high rim of her glasses. "Either you're running errands for the Macies in 2B or you're not as lonely as everyone suspects."

A glance at the can in his hand told Bill that someone had moved the chocolate chips. "Busted," he said, and returned the can to its improper place. "You know I can't help it."

"Try harder." April wagged a finger at him. "There isn't a thing needing done that can't wait until tomorrow, like every single Sunday I've worked for the last eight years. Unless I'm not doing a good enough job for you?" She put a hand on her hip and gave him a look that said Bill *better* not have a problem with her work.

"Couldn't ask for better, April, and I'm lucky to have you. It's just a tough habit to break."

"You know there's a cure for that, don't you? It's called a vacation, Bill. Va-ca-tion. As in go anywhere that is not *here*, put your feet up, drink a little tequila, and pass out under the sun. People do that."

"Maria's too young for tequila," he said. When April's face puckered, Bill added, "But you're right, as always. I'll make you a deal. If you cover for me, say, for maybe two or three days, I'll give you the mini fridge and that neon sign, plus your hours, of course." These were gifts from the local Pepsi representative. Bill had tried hanging the vintage sign on the wall above the beverage coolers, but the additional power draw was too much for the old breaker and kept shorting out the refrigerators. And the mini fridge was such an attraction to local thieves that Bill all but had to bolt it down. The sign and the fridge had been sitting in his office for months, so the solution would help them both.

The thin cord of April's braid swung against her back as she shook her head. "Not doing it for less than five, Bill. Two days isn't a vacation. And I think a week would kill you. You go for five and you've got yourself a deal."

"Four?"

"Don't try me," April growled, and swallowed her hot chocolate.

The overhead bell chimed. Wearing shorts and a light sweater, Luke came in, his shoulders up and neck hunched against the cold. "Morning, April. Hi Bill," he said, and put his backpack in the empty cupboard under the hot dog roller at the end of the counter.

The third week into his tenure at the So-Lo, Luke had become comfortable with Bill and April. The edge that had previously tensed him and seemed to keep him watchful and suspicious of everything had somewhat abated, and Bill increasingly saw the boy Luke was meant to be. There was still little mention of his parents, however, for the more Bill inquired, the more Luke tucked the subject away. He wasn't sure if Luke's parents knew of their little arrangement, but he didn't prod because he felt it might push Luke away. The information would come in time, when the kid was ready.

Bill slipped the marshmallows under his arm and plucked a paper cup from the dispenser. He held it up to Luke. "April's got me craving a cup. Join us for some hot chocolate?"

"Yes, please," Luke said, and then water was poured, powder was stirred, and the bag of marshmallows was torn open.

"You're spoiled," April said to Luke. "He's never given *me* marshmallows before."

"I'll remember you said that the next time you take a bag of chips," Bill responded.

The sideways pout of April's lips made them all laugh. "Forget I said that," she said, and went to the counter to help a young family that had just walked in.

Alone with Bill, Luke quietly drank his hot chocolate, spooning the many marshmallows Bill gave him into his mouth while he looked around the store. In the short time since he'd started working at the So-Lo, Luke's color went from the malnourished grey-white of three weeks ago to a dull pearl that —while not quite screaming health and vitality—looked much better on him.

After a time, Bill said, "Can I ask you something? You can tell me to go wherever it is kids tell adults to go nowadays if you want, but I can't help but wonder what your parents think about this."

Luke knew he couldn't evade Bill's inquiries forever, but he also had questions of his own. He set his spoon in his empty cup and put it in the waste basket, then took Bill's cup and did the same. "Before I answer, can I ask you some questions, too? You don't have to answer them if you don't want..."

"Shoot," Bill said instantly.

"Why did you name it the So-Lo?"

Bill smiled. "That's your question?"

"I have more," Luke said, "but that's the easiest."

"An ice breaker," Bill said. "I like it. Okay, well, that's an easy one. I didn't name it. I got the So-Lo from a man named Willie Flinder. It was 1995, and I was just a squirt myself. In my twenties and didn't have two nickels to rub together. Willie was old. Really *old*. He had eight fingers, and six of *those* on his left. The extra one came out just below the bottom knuckle of his thumb like a little stub." He pointed to his own thumb to show where Willie's bump had been. The way Luke's eyes widened, Bill knew he was imagining Willie's hands, and he smiled. "You'd think an extra finger would make him faster at everything, more dexterous, I suppose, but it gave Willie awful pain."

"What about the other hand?" Luke asked. "How'd he get only two fingers there?"

"Meat grinder," Bill said and watched Luke cringe. "Just kidding. Nothing as spectacular as that. He was born that way. Nicest guy you'd ever meet, he'd give you the shirt off his back if he thought you were cold. Even saw him do it once for a boy a few years older than you. Anyway, the point is, Willie named it the So-Lo because he knew that the people in the area didn't have a lot of money. He wanted them to know they could come to him for their convenience items for a fair price."

Luke's eyes turned upward as he thought about what Bill was telling him. "Did Willie give you the So-Lo? How did you afford to pay for it if you didn't have any money?"

"My turn," Bill said, scratching the bristles on his chin. "I'll answer that, but you got to give me one first. Tell me, do your parents know you're here?"

The sideways twist of Luke's lips answered Bill's question, but the boy sighed deeply and spoke with resignation, as though his answer would signal his termination at the So-Lo. "My mom thinks I'm at Nate's house."

"Who's Nate?"

"I don't actually *know* a Nate." Luke shrugged. "But it was better to tell my mom I was at a friend's than helping out so I could get better food." April finished up at the counter but, seeing Bill and Luke in what looked like a private conversation, she sank back onto the barstool behind the lottery kiosk and began her fourth game of Sudoku.

"I'll send you home with food if you'd like," Bill said. "You can say you won it or found it, if you think that would go over better with your mom. There's no shame in accepting help, Luke. None at all."

Luke shook his head so quickly, the top of his hair flapped up. "She wouldn't like that."

Bill splayed out his fingers in a gesture of acquiescence. "I understand, but the offer's never leaving the table. You want it, you got it, Luke." Uneasy, the boy bit down on his lip. The unconscious action was so innocent, Bill was tempted to open his wallet and give the kid every penny inside it. Anything to make his situation better. Instead, he said, "I'd like to know more about your family, Luke."

"Did Willie give you the So-Lo?" Luke countered.

"Fair," Bill said. "He *did* give it to me, but I worked hard to get it. Willie wasn't ever about handouts for the sake of freebies, if you understand me. He felt that it didn't make people feel good to accept something for free, but that if they worked for it in some way or another, they'd have something to be proud of and *that* was more important than anything." The creases of his eyes flared out as Bill's face warmed with memories. "I was fifteen when I started working for Willie. Stocking shelves. Cleaning the bathroom. Lifting things he couldn't. He didn't pay much, but he made me a deal. He told me that if I didn't miss a day of work until he died, and that if I was never late for even a minute, that he would give the So-Lo to me in his will. I worked four days a week for eight years, graduated high school and college, helped Willie with his paperwork while he taught me how to run a business, and then he said goodbye to the world with a cat on his lap and half of a McCain chocolate cake inside his belly. He was in his eighties by then and had no family to mourn him. And, no, as much as I like you, I'm not in the place to make an arrangement like that with you. Maria will get it if she wants it when she's older. It won't make her rich, by any means, but with a little hard work she'll have a comfortable living."

"Wow," Luke said.

"Wow is right," Bill said. "Now it's your turn."

A brief break in the clouds gave the So-Lo an inviting glow that coaxed a confession from Luke. Without meeting Bill's eyes, he said, "My dad's in prison in London and my mom cleans rooms at the Dirty. And when she's not cleaning, she's drinking." The last word fell out of him bitterly, as though it was sour in his mouth.

The Dartree Motel, locally known as the *Dirty* Motel because of the burned-out *A*, second *R,* and second *E,* languished on a northeastern limb of the city frequented by long-haul truckers, opportunistic drug peddlers, and prudent virgins seeking private spaces for their first encounters. Even a few escorts were known to extend their services inside the Dirty, and the area was widely known for its nightly chorus of breaking bottles, cross-street insults, and sirens of all varieties.

Like all other Garretters, Bill knew the Dirty was no place to make a living, and he wondered if Luke's mother had become an alcoholic before or after she started working at the Dirty. As for his father, well, Bill figured he'd let Luke offer that information up when the time was right. There was no sense in stirring up a brushfire when the wind was blowing.

Bill said, "One of those situations, huh? I'm sorry, Luke."

Luke shrugged. And because he'd grown quiet, Bill asked, "You live near there?"

"We're on Mitton, in those apartments behind the car wash," Luke said.

Marginally better, Bill thought, but only barely. Homes along Mitton were the kinds with flags and velvet blankets in the windows instead of curtains. The siding of every fourth or fifth house deteriorated like an old rash, but there was a recent push to gentrify the area. In the last year alone, the face lifts of seven homes made the area almost tolerable to passersby, though what existed *behind* those thin veneers, few could say.

The visit now taking longer than expected, Bill knew that Maria was waiting for him up in their apartment. He thought to invite Luke to join them for lunch, but he knew that there were boundaries that couldn't be breached unless he had Luke's parents' permission. Bill himself would never allow Maria into the home of a stranger, and though Luke and Bill were no longer strangers at this point, neither was their association known broadly enough for Bill's comfort.

"I'm going to bring Maria down here for lunch. Keep an eye on April for a few minutes while I'm gone, will you? She's got a salty tooth and the pretzels keep going missing." He winked and left Luke to tend to the store.

In their modest apartment three floors up, Bill fetched Maria, who was eager to spend the late morning in the store with her new friend. The preceding weekend, during Luke's fourth shift, the air seal on a bag of gummy bears had broken open when a very pregnant and very clumsy customer bumped into an aisle-end candy rack. Most packages were still in saleable condition, but Luke had used the one pack that wasn't to set up an easy game of tic-tac-toe with Maria, greens versus reds. He'd let her win every time. Since then, she had been enamored with him, and Bill couldn't blame her. As far as he could tell, Luke was a good kid. He came in early, conversed comfortably with the So-Lo's regular customers, and never had to be instructed twice. Because the So-Lo had no official uniform and staff wore whatever they felt comfortable in, it was easy to pass off the boy simply as a helpful kid. The hourly minimum wage Luke received at the end of each shift was always exchanged in an empty beverage cup so that it looked like Luke had only come in for a frozen drink, like most kids his age. Perhaps it was paranoia to keep these exchanges away from the So-Lo's security camera's range, but Bill was not willing to risk lasting evidence for any employment official who might pull the So-Lo's license. It was obvious that Luke had little working in his favor, and although Bill was determined that the So-Lo, at least, *would* be there for him, it would be done so cautiously, until Luke was of legal working age a year from now.

Maria bolted through the interior door ahead of Bill. She saw the top of Luke's head near the window and ran to him. "Dad said we get pizza, Luke! What kind do you like? I like cheese. Do you like cheese pizza, too? Wanna play a game? I got carrots and cucumbers this time because Dad says we need vegetables. I'll be carrots. You be cucumbers, okay?"

She shook a plastic bag full of vegetables at him. Her blond hair held back in a pink headband, Maria had the playful dark eyes of her father, wideset, with little crescents beneath her lower eyelids when her cheeks came up in an unrestrained smile.

Luke hailed Maria over to one of the two deli tables, where he had already laid sheets of plastic wrap on the table and sketched a tic-tac-toe lattice on top. "Cucumbers it is. But be prepared to lose ... bad."

He cracked his knuckles for effect, causing Maria to turn her headband around and squint at him. Then carrots and cumbers were unbagged and placed in neat little piles in front of each opponent. While they waited for the pizza to arrive, Luke let Maria win the first few games; partially because he loved seeing her little face squish up in eight-year-old superiority, but also because he hadn't had a cucumber since before Christmas. The taste was almost foreign to him now. Crisp and still cold, the cucumber tasted of luxury and of health, and of all the things unavailable to him for so long. He had the urge to lose every game as quickly as he could, just to have the fresh taste on his tongue while it was still cool.

After a time, Maria crossed her arms, bored with winning. "You're not trying, Luke." She pouted. "It's not fun if you don't try." When Luke won the next four games, Maria slumped her chin onto the table and said, "You don't need to try *that* hard."

The overhead bell rang, and the aroma of pizza filled the So-Lo. Bill opened the boxes at the end of the counter, where April sat playing Sudoku, and then the four of them were enjoying hot slices of pepperoni or cheese pizza. Customers entered, April rang in their purchases, and Luke tidied the beverage area, frequently returning to his pizza, amazed food could taste so good.

When traffic slowed, April regaled Luke with a story about a customer who wanted to buy the So-Lo's expired products, intended for sale in a competitor's store. Bill explained that he declined this request, as he declined a woman who came in with sixty-two coupons and tried to buy his entire rack of single-serving nuts, and the old man who wanted Bill to accept the six bags of garbage in the back of his truck since the So-Lo had more *responsive sanitation* than his apartment complex, as the man had put it. Luke laughed so hard he spit pizza out of his mouth, and this made Maria laugh until her apple juice spurted from her nose. It was the best day Luke had had since he won a box of popsicles in his school's Spring Read-A-Thon almost four years ago, when he was nine. So it was like this, with Luke fed and happy in an unguarded moment, that the exterior door opened and Ben Rigby walked in.

The profile of the stranger drew no attention from April, Bill, or Maria, but Luke dropped behind the counter as if he'd been shot. Bill set down his pizza and glanced down at Luke. The boy's color had drained, and he was sitting on the floor with his knees tucked tight to his chest. Luke was so still, Bill had to look twice to make sure he was still breathing. Then Bill understood.

Luke was afraid.

Oblivious to Luke's fear, Maria poked his shoulder. "What's wrong, Luke? Are you playing hide and seek?"

Bill waited for Ben Rigby's tall frame to wander further away from the counter before he put a finger to his lips and silently mouthed *shhhh* to her. Sensing that their fun time had come to an end, Maria nodded as April pulled her close.

"Why don't you two go grab one of those games you've been trying to get me to play, huh?" Bill said, holding April's eyes. To April he said, "They're in the apartment. No need to hurry. I'll keep the pizza warm."

Clutching Maria's hand, April turned to leave, but Ben Rigby was coming down the pantry aisle with a four-pack of toilet paper, right in front of them. Maria must have made a face because the man bent, flipped the toothpick he was chewing to the other side of his mouth, and whistled in Maria's face. "Looks like you've got a mouthful of sours, little girl. Either that or a mouthful of turds. What's a pretty little thing like you making a face like that for?" His mouth split wide open to reveal two uneven rows of stained teeth.

"Don't mind her," April said, pulling Maria away from him. "Kids, you know?"

"I get it," the man drew back and stood tall over April. "That's why I don't want 'em. They're only good when they're someone else's, know what I mean?" He winked and slid his fingers over the brim of his cheap straw cowboy hat and hooked a finger through a loop in his belt, where the soft roll of his belly bunched up against the buckle. April smiled politely.

Behind the counter now, Bill said to the man, "Can I ring you up?" hoping to expedite the man's departure.

"You sure as hell can," the man said, and set the toilet paper on the counter. He dug in his back pocket for his wallet and spied the open pizza boxes. Before Bill could stop him, the man tugged two pieces of pepperoni pizza from the closest box, folded them in half like a sandwich and began eating them.

April and Maria, who should have left by now, cringed in the periphery. "I need a pack of rolling papers to go with the ass wipe," he said, chewing their pizza.

It took all of Bill's strength not to toss the man out. In his long experience with customer service, Bill knew that negative interactions were all but guaranteed. It came with the territory. Of course, most customers were good people. They were polite, if not friendly; some had even become his closest friends. But men like this stranger in front of him, with his stained white shirt that showed more dark chest hair than Bill cared to see, and a meanness to his booze-worn face so sharp and disturbing that the fuzz on the back of Bill's neck stood on end, were the kind who wanted trouble. They liked to see Bill's employees squirm. They enjoyed it. And they would push and push and assert their power until they got the reaction they wanted. But since he'd taken over the So-Lo, Bill had never squirmed. Willie had taught him that reactions escalated like cats under water, and that it was best not dump on them if you didn't want them to scratch and howl. Bill's tolerance for bullies like this had intensified over the years, and in most cases he was able to pre-emptively diffuse their abuse, but he was also aware that some bullies carried weapons. Bill himself had been held up eleven times over the years, eight with knives and on three occasions with guns, so he knew that quick reactions would not favor him. He said, "Wish I could help you on that one, but we stopped selling rolling papers a few years ago. If you head out and make a right, go four blocks down, the 7-11 has them."

"Shit," the man grumbled and pulled money from his wallet to pay for the toilet paper. He took another bite of his pizza sandwich while Bill counted his change, but a quarter fell out of his outstretched hand and rolled off the counter under which Luke huddled. When the expectant ping of the coin banking off the floor did not happen, the man leaned over and watched Bill pick the coin from the top of Luke's head.

"Is that *you*, Fuckface?" the man exclaimed. "Well, I'll be a dragon's ass. What the hell are you doing down there? Aren't you supposed to be in school or something?" He slid his toothpick to the other side of his mouth again and leaned so far that his belly pushed the boxes of pizza over the edge of the counter.

Outed by a stray quarter, Luke stood and pushed the pizza back. "It's Sunday, Ben," Luke said, averting his eyes.

Ben slapped the counter. "Respect, Fuckface. What's my name?"

"Sorry, Uncle," Luke said so quietly, Ben had him repeat it.

"That's better," Ben said. "Now what are you doing on this side of town, hiding like that? You stealing from this man? You better not be stealing, or your dad will tan your ass when he gets out." He thrust a dirty finger in Luke's face.

Bill cut in. "Luke's not stealing—Ben, is it? He's come to see me about a job. We've been looking for a sitter for my daughter and Luke's friend said he might be interested. I figured we'd get to know him over pizza." The lie was so quick on his tongue that April gave him a thumb's up from behind Ben's back.

"Oh, yeah?" Ben asked.

Staring at the floor, Luke nodded.

"Why's he hiding then?" Ben asked.

Maria broke free from April, ran up behind the counter, and linked her arm with Luke's. "We were playing hide and seek, but you just told on him. Now I know where he is. Got you, Luke." She tagged him.

Bill hooked a hand around Maria's small shoulders and pulled her close to him. He gave her a squeeze, then looked at Ben. "As you can tell, he's pretty good with Maria. And I think she likes him too."

"I do!" Maria agreed.

Ben stuffed his change into his wallet and tossed the receipt Bill gave him onto the pizza. He took the package of toilet paper and propped it onto his shoulder, holding it there like a decades-old boombox and raised his chin to Bill. "You paying him?"

"Of course. We haven't discussed the details yet, but I'm sure we'll get to that," Bill said.

Ben sniffed, chewed his toothpick some more, then spit it out. It was a clumsy spit, not enough force to really go anywhere but land below his chin in the middle of his shirt. The wet gob bloomed grey and gross, and they were all looking at the wood that had shredded and splintered where he had chewed on it when Ben finally stepped back from the counter. "All right, then. Can't blame a guy for trying to make money. You be straight with the little shit, you hear?" He pointed his thumb and index finger at Bill, the angle of dirty, rough skin as sure and as condemning as a real gun. The message was clear.

"It's the only way to do business," Bill said. "We'll take care of Luke, I promise."

The heavy *thunk* of Ben's boots taking him out of the store was a relief to all of them. When the door closed behind him, they watched as Ben headed in the direction of the 7-11.

As his hat finally cleared the corner of the So-Lo, it was Maria who spoke. "Who's *that*, Luke?"

Luke's hands went to the back of his neck. He interlaced his fingers and craned his head toward the ceiling. "That's my dad's friend. They make me call him uncle even though we're not related. He'll tell my parents he saw me here." The nascent color previously blooming on Luke's face seemed to have evaporated with Ben's visit; he was almost green with worry.

Bill said, "Maria, show April where the games are, huh?"

"But Daddy—"

"And maybe order us some Chinese or something while you're up there," Bill said over Maria's protests. "I think our pizza has spoiled."

April nodded, gave Luke a commiserating smile and tugged Maria out the interior door toward the apartment foyer. The door closed behind them, and Bill turned to Luke. He was zipping up his sweater.

"You going somewhere?" Bill asked.

Luke shrugged, his bony shoulders deflating with grief like a chastised puppy.

"I'm going to tell you something, Luke. I want you to listen to every word I say because I'm not sure that you've ever heard what I'm about to tell you, and it's important." Bill leaned against the counter, crossing his arms and legs, and held Luke's eyes with his own. "What other people do is no reflection on you. None whatsoever. How they choose to live their lives has no bearing on you. A lot of times, especially when we're younger, we have no choice but to allow them into our lives, but that doesn't change your worth; understand?"

"You're not going to fire me?" Luke asked, fidgeting his fingers inside his pockets.

Imagining Maria in the same luckless situation, Bill wanted to hug the boy. Instead, he lowered his chin and again lifted his eyes to the despondent kid. "No reason to. We're going to do the opposite, in fact. I think we should make your employment official, Luke. You're old enough to babysit, no law against that. You can help me with Maria, and if you happen to be in the store when someone you know comes in, she's so close you'll have an excuse. The only thing I ask is that you tell your mother. I don't like fooling anyone and I'd prefer it if she knew. You can tell her you're babysitting, that's fine, but at least she'll know where you're spending your time." Bill didn't think it was possible for Luke to look even more aggrieved, but the shavings of his hard life floated to his surface like scratches on a mirror. He looked like he was going to cry. "You want to keep working here, don't you, Luke? Am I wrong about that?"

"I *never* want to stop working here," Luke said. "But once I tell my mom, she's going to make me give her the money I make."

"Ahh," Bill said. "One of those situations, huh?"

Without looking at Bill, Luke nodded.

Bill thought for a moment. He drew on his experience with the neighborhood kids, some of whom came from families similar to Luke's. Faced with eviction or the prospect of going hungry, some mothers and fathers ashamedly accepted their children's support. Others demanded it regardless of the situation, depending on their teenager's income from after-school work to support drug, alcohol, or gambling addictions, or bridge lengthy periods of financial insecurity. No matter what parents told their children, kids talked, and the stories made their way to the So-Lo, where they embedded deep in Bill's heart. He couldn't save every kid, but he vowed to do his best by them, often giving them discounts or free food, and offering his soon-to-be expired products at up to a ninety percent discount for the families he privately identified as most in need. An unexpected outcome of his generosity was a wide perimeter of neighbors and customers who were fiercely loyal to the So-Lo, with many former local residents traveling great distances just to support his business. Eventually, sellouts and bankruptcies were the plight of many, if not most, convenience stores in Canada, but the So-Lo was comfortably holding its own, due in large part, Bill thought, to the tenets of empathy.

He cleared his throat. "I'm happy to hold on to some of that money for you, Luke. It's your call, but if you'd like, I'll keep it safe with me until you ask for it. You can take every penny you've earned at any time, I won't hold anything back. Whatever you decide to tell your mom you're making, that's none of my business. You get fifteen an hour from me, and whatever you want to hold for safe keeping in Bill's Bank won't be broadcasted anywhere but between us."

A chuff of laughter erupted from Luke. "Bill's Bank?"

"I thought it had a nice ring to it."

Luke unzipped his sweater and dropped it on the back of April's chair. Then he told Bill that the name sounded great to him.

5

The slow shuffle of feet filled the sterilized halls of the Henley Recovery Center on a rainy June morning. From the first level, the second, the third, fifty-eight men trudged to the common area meeting room on the main level, where Program Director Dr. Alice Gutman waited with Henley's full cohort of Recovery Facilitators to discuss the previous evening's unfortunately public suicide of Jim Drumlin, days before his scheduled release.

Fronting the second-floor group, Cody Dean Clyde led the men to a row of seats behind the first-floor group, where they twitched uncomfortably and exchanged condolences and expressions of stunned surprise. When the third-floor group arrived, Dr. Gutman silenced their conversation with a two-fingered peace sign held high. The men hushed.

"Thank you," she said. "I would like us to open with our daily reminder that control begins with ourselves. Shall we?" She extended an open palm to the men, who promptly recited tennis player Arthur Ashe's decades-old advice.

"*Start where you are. Use what you have. Do what you can,*" they chanted.

"Good," Dr. Gutman said. "Let's be mindful that no matter what situation we are faced with, we can only control our own reactions. It's okay to be upset. It's okay to cry, but always, always be kind to yourselves." A few addicts wiped their eyes. A handful of newer admissions huffed indignantly at Dr. Gutman's suggestion. She went on. "We've gathered today to discuss Mr. Drumlin's unfortunate passing. I know that many of you not only witnessed Mr. Drumlin's passing but worked fervently to prevent it, and for this we express our gratitude. Your courage and ongoing resistance to the disease of addiction will serve you, your families, and those you love well." She tucked a strand of her silver-black hair behind her ear and looked over the rim of her red-framed glasses, encouraging them to share their memories of Jim Drumlin as an exercise in healing.

The long-termers knew the drill, knew that they wouldn't be excused unless they made an effort, so they were the first ones to share, even if they had had little to no interaction with forty-seven-year-old Jim Drumlin. Tony Zenling, a recovering heroin addict, told the group he'd only seen Jim in passing, but that he believed Jim had the strength in him, as they all did. This was met with a round of nods and murmurs of agreement. Armando Consta, a third-time patient at Henley, said that Jim was so good with a basketball, he could have "kicked all their asses on the court." A trio of men hooted at this.

For the next hour, Dr. Gutman and her seven facilitators let the men speak, admit their pain, confess their worry of dying like Jim Drumlin. Those who saw Jim barricade himself in his room, shoving not one but both beds and both night tables against the door, unanimously revealed their remissions and begged to have their admissions extended. They could not so easily get over Jim's cries as he tore through Henley's hallways, shouting that he was going to cut himself. Nor could they ignore the haunting memory of Jim's blood splashing against the window as they frantically worked the door handle below. Jim cleverly waited until Henley's staff were on a shift change and when they were so occupied, he leapt from the recreation room and declared his intention. The commotion was witnessed by almost half of the inpatients, who quickly apprised the others of the tragedy. Staff were at the door within thirty seconds, but their arrival was no use. By the time they managed to open the door and push the furniture away, Jim Drumlin was beyond rescue.

Cody wasn't very familiar with the man, only that he had been hot-tempered. On one occasion, Drumlin had asked Cody if he knew anyone willing to sneak their urine in for him so he could pass his drug test. Cody laughed at the suggestion because he didn't know anyone who was clean, except his grandmother. Eventually, Cody heard that Armando Consta's girlfriend had managed to smuggle three bladders of pee into the facility, which Armando then traded to Cory Miller, Nelson Simpson, and Jim Drumlin for Oxy and a baggie of heroin. That had been just over a week ago. Now, as his counterparts took turns reflecting on Jim, pretending to miss him, Cody wanted the whole production to end so he could return to his room and take a nap. He yawned.

"You said something, Cody?" Dr. Gutman pointed him out. Sixty-five heads turned to him.

Five weeks into his stay, Cody knew better than to keep quiet when called upon. It would just prolong the inevitable. They would wait until the silence compressed him, pinched his mouth open, and squeezed out whatever he had in him, in all its ugliness, for all to see. He said, "I guess I'm still in shock, Doctor." The men beside him nodded.

"Shock is a very natural reaction," Dr. Gutman reported. She blinked, expecting Cody to continue.

He scratched the hair at the back of his neck. "I mean, I'm sad, I am. I thought Jim could have done it, you know? He could've beat his demons. I really thought so." He paused so he could appear hesitant to say what he was going to say next, but this was only for effect. In Henley, all conversations and experiences were boomeranged back to the men. Cody said, "But it makes me wonder; if it can happen to a guy like that, it can happen to any of us, can't it? What's stopping *us* from going off the deep end like he did?"

"You think Mr. Drumlin went off the deep end?" Dr. Gutman removed her glasses and wiped the lenses with the hem of her tunic.

Cody shrugged and called upon his small reserve of aptitude. "He wasn't on *shore* like the rest of us. It just makes me wonder what happens when we get out. What if we get pushed into the deep end and we can't swim, Doctor?" The guy beside him nudged Cody's shoulder and Tony Zenling actually clapped him on the shoulder. He sat back, smug with his performance.

Seizing Cody's comments as a matter of interest to the whole group, the men were subjected to a roundtable discussion on self-control. Cody didn't care. He'd performed perfectly. His apparent openness would serve him well when it came time for them to consider his release. He let the next thirty minutes wash over him until they were released. Eyes glazed, Cody returned to his room.

His roommate, Samuel—nicknamed *Smack-ule* by the men scoring from him—was in a scheduled counseling session with his brother and sister, so Cody had the room to himself. Cody flicked off his shoes and fell on his bed. His daily therapy sessions, both private and in group, weren't until the afternoon, so he had hours before he'd be forced to expel the contents of his brain. He wished for his cellphone, but that had been relinquished to the admissions staff on his first day. Times like this, when the weather was crap and he had nothing to do, usually led him to drink or use, but the ultimatum given to him by his grandmother left him no choice but strict sobriety. She'd know if he used. She'd know it if he even *thought* of using; therefore here he was, bored out of his mind, admittedly looking better than he had in years.

He hadn't thought he'd survive those first days. His stomach had knotted. His skin had been as tender as if he had a body-length case of road rash. His eyes had burned and his head thundered with pain. Cody had been certain he was going to die. Absolutely sure of it.

But he hadn't.

Against all odds, against Cody's own belief in himself, he began to get better. Those early pains that had made him feel like a stabbing victim were gone. The pressure in his head went away. The shakes that had made it impossible to eat or drink had subsided. He'd stopped shitting himself. The hallucinations of Kade dancing on a bed of coals he could even almost forget.

He flipped onto his stomach to watch the rain fall outside. The apparition in the window, half there, half gone, looked almost respectable. He wasn't the terrible sight he'd once been, but once he opened his mouth and saw the reflection of his teeth on the glass, it put him in a sour mood.

Fuck Jim Drumlin. Fuck Henley. Fuck Terry and Edwin and Billy and Charity. Cody brooded. A few more weeks and he would be out. A few more weeks and his new life would begin.

Three hours later, feeling especially shitty about himself, Cody lumbered to the second-floor office of his therapist, Dr. Brenda Reed. She greeted him with a slight bow that allowed him a view inside her low-cut shirt. He supposed she did it on purpose; something to anesthetize the men, shock them into divulging their secrets. She had a small pink mole on her left tit that Cody couldn't help but stare at, and he had to put a pillow over his lap for the first ten minutes of every session to hide his erection. He played with the corners and squeezed it against his stomach to make her think it made him feel more comfortable while sharing his thoughts, but really he just didn't want her to see his small cock expanding inside his jeans.

"Let me begin by telling you how proud I am of you today, Cody," she said. "It takes a strong person to speak up the way you did in front of all those people. Death isn't an easy subject and your willingness to welcome the topic at a time when you're hurting shows just how far you've come. Well done." She leaned forward and touched his arm.

He looked at the mole until she swept her waist-length hair over the front of her shoulder and covered it.

"I found your metaphor about swimming interesting, Cody. I think we should unpack that a little."

Unpack. One of her catch words. He hated when she said it. Like there was a compressed treasure-trove of his thoughts just waiting to be unwound. Like Cody was some fucking puppet, squeezed tight on mental coils that needed oiling, turning, *space*, to release.

"Would you care to expand on that, Cody?"

He hugged the pillow.

"Are you concerned about returning home? You have another," she flipped a page in her book, "three and a half weeks. Tell me how you're feeling about this."

This was their game. Her pretending to care about him, him pretending he had nothing to say. His eyes swept to the curve of her hip.

"Okay. Let's try it this way, Cody. Are you still having those dreams?"

There was a feather poking out of the pillow. Cody pulled it, rehearsing his story in his head.

Everyone in Henley knew about Kade. The kid's good-looking face had made the local paper more times than the daily horoscopes since he'd died. *Tragic Accident Claims Teen's Life*, the *Garrett Gazette* published the morning after. There was a picture of Kade with his school's soccer team and another of him playing street hockey with a bunch of second graders. On the second page there was a collage of teens consoling each other: hormone-crazed girls in short skirts and shirts, crying over the boy they would never get the chance to use to make their friends jealous.

Charity's trailer made the paper too. Journalists drew to the eyesore like bugs to a zapper, salivating at the junk piles and the toilet cooler not as an opportunity for reform but for shaming the destitute. The day before his admission, when he visited, Charity had tacked sheets over all her windows to keep people from looking in. He felt sorry for her, but she was tougher than she looked. Beneath her pocked skin and brittle bones, Charity was diamond-tough. She could handle the reporters just like she could handle the police. She was the reason Cody was in Henley and not in handcuffs.

Buzzing on that Oxy high, Cody had been having an okay time that night. He'd been in that place in his head where things went his way, a secret space where people respected him and Terry didn't exist. Then Kade screamed. It was a death yell that made Cody's toes curl. And when he opened his eyes, Kade was on fire, reaching for him.

Terror-mad, the four of them—Cody, Charity, Edwin, Billy—tried pulling Kade out when the fire caught the jacket he'd tied around his neck. It swept over him like wildfire and singed their hands and their heads. Edwin joined Billy in yanking Kade's feet, but Kade's belt got caught on some metal rods Terry had thrown in a few hours before. He was stuck hard. Cody, as high as the rest of them, tried to put the flames out with his beer, but the few drops that came out evaporated in a smoky fizzle. By then, the sounds coming from Kade were inhuman.

Then Kade threw himself out of the firepit and hit Terry square in the stomach.

"Pat him down! Get his head! Put it out!" Charity yelled.

Terry scrambled out from under Kade, patted the hot spots on his shirt, and ran.

Billy tore off his jacket and smothered his cousin. Smack. Pat. Rub. Again. Again. On Kade's shoulders. Around his neck. All over his chest. "Call 911!" he shrieked. "Stay with me Kadester! Stay with me! I've got you! I've—fuck!" No one moved.

"What?" Edwin cried.

"He's—I don't think he's breathing! No. No. No! Oh God. Oh God!"

Cody stumbled to the kid and put his head to Kade's chest. The heat of him burnt Cody's ear. Besides the crackling of Kade's skin, there was no movement there. None of them knew CPR, but still Cody pushed his chest like he saw in the movies. Part of Kade's jacket broke away under his hands. It had melted to Kade's skin and torn the flesh over his heart right off. Cody vomited.

Billy howled. "Oh fuck! Oh fuck! Wha—no, man, no. No, Kaddie, no." He shook Kade's shoulders. Kade's head flopped around like a balloon filled with sand.

"Give him air! You've got to breathe into him," Edwin ordered, pointing at Billy. "It doesn't work if you don't breathe into him." He looked at Kade's blackened face and pointed to where he thought Kade's lips might be.

"I c-can't. You do it. You didn't t-take the p-pills."

Edwin knew that Billy had turned chicken because a stream of piss darkened the front of his jeans. Blubbering through his own snot, Cody was no better. And Charity was holding back the dogs, who were lunging at them. "If I'm breathing, you're fucking pushing, Billy."

"Just do it! He's going to die!" Charity cried.

Billy pushed Kade's skin back in place, then he pumped, retching and sobbing, until Edwin pinched Kade's nose. When his charred nostrils disintegrated, Billy stopped pumping.

"No, man. No!" Edwin patted Kade's cheeks. It was like touching a burnt marshmallow.

Charity dragged the dogs into the house and slammed the door. She leapt off the deck. "Keep trying! Don't stop. You gotta keep going for it to work."

On his knees, crying so hard his throat sounded like it was on the verge of tearing open, Billy threw his head back. "No. Kaddie. No. No. No. Noooo. Please, no. No Kaddieeee."

Charity's neighbors always kept to themselves unless someone had money. The ruckus outside wasn't enough for them to open their doors but the rustling of curtains fifty feet away made Cody lower his head. "Someone's going to see us. Someone's going to come. What the fuck do we say?"

"*That's* your fucking concern?" Charity snapped and pointed at the blackened heap that used to be Kade Hart. "He needs help. He—"

"He's dead, Charity," Edwin said. "I think he was dead before he fell on Terry."

"B-but he jumped. He was still moving."

"He didn't jump, Char. His body couldn't take it and he died. He wasn't breathing. Did you feel anything, Billy?"

Billy wailed into his hands.

Lights were beginning to come on in the nearest trailer a hundred feet away. "What do we do?" Cody asked again.

"I'm on proby, man. They catch me anywhere near a scene line this and they'll lock me up," Edwin said. He pinched the bridge of his nose to stem the headache forming behind his eyes.

"Me too." The way Billy looked at them made their hearts hurt.

"I got nothing to do with this," Cody said, wishing he wasn't so high, thinking if Whitney hadn't left him, maybe none of this would have happened.

When she looked at the three of them, a kind of hate began to infect Charity. She had always known they were rough around the edges, but they were the kind of guys that didn't take shit, and she'd initially liked that about them. Now she saw them for what they were: as weak as the cheap rubbers Edwin always broke. "Go," she said.

Edwin reached for her, but she recoiled from the hand that only moments before had been on her ass. "I'm sorry, Char—"

"Get the fuck out of here before I tell the cops you did it," she spat.

"Char—"

"Now!" She marched to the door and let the dogs back out. Mongrels though they were, one word from Charity and they would attack. "Get the fuck away from here or I'll let them chew your yellow fucking cocks off!" She put her teeth to her lower lip and whistled. The dogs snarled off the deck.

Cody, Billy, and Edwin ran just as Charity's elderly neighbor, Beverly, called from behind a window screen. "Chari-tee! What you have happening out there? What's that noise about? You better not be doing those drugs! I don't want no needles on my porch again!" The old woman began scratching the screen as though they were cats that could be scared away.

In the distance, the dogs barked.

The rest Cody heard from Charity.

"I asked about your dreams, Cody." Dr. Reed tapped her pen against her notepad.

He pulled another feather from the pillow. "I wish I would have been there. I keep thinking if I was there, maybe I could've saved him, you know? Like, keep him away from the fire or kicked his ass back anywhere but there." He'd told Dr. Reed that he and Kade hadn't been close, so it saved him a lot of questions, but still she liked to zero in on the guilt he told her he felt.

"Regret is not a companion you want to carry around, Cody. We all need to feel it sometimes, yes, but it's important that when it occurs that we do not get attached to it. Remember the jacket with all the pockets? The good items are light so we can carry lots of them. We can fill our pockets with gratitude, forgiveness, acceptance, patience, courage, resilience, and so much more. They don't weigh us down. But all the thoughts and feelings that cloud our judgment of ourselves are heavy. They weigh us down; they burden our minds. They fill our pockets with things we don't need, feelings that are unhelpful and most often untrue. If we don't empty those pockets from time to time, things build up, and then what happens? You can't progress because your coat is too heavy, or your pockets break and spill out and you trip on the stones." She sat back and put her finger to her lips. "If Kade were alive today, what would you say to him?"

He'd tell him to stay the fuck away from Terry, *that's* what he'd say, but to Dr. Reed he said, "I'd tell him I wish I could've done more."

She nodded as he spoke. "I want you to write Kade a letter, Cody. I want you to pretend he's alive, and I want you to tell him all the things you want to say. You don't have to show me the letter. In fact, I don't *want* you to show me the letter, so you can really let all your feelings out. Say everything. Bring it to our next session and we'll go for a walk outside where you can burn it and free yourself of those feelings that are weighing you down. What do you say?"

Ahh. The burning of the letters. There was a steady stream of them, sparking and puffing near the reconciliation benches in the back field. Smackule bragged about the letter he burned was actually a picture he'd drawn of Dr. Reed's tits. Armando's letter was nothing more than a list of all the people who owed him. Cory Miller's letter was just a blank paper splattered with jizz. But every time those papers caught fire, Dr. Reed reported on their personal growth and they were one step closer to freedom.

Cody said, "I'd like to. The guys all tell me how they feel better after they do it."

She reached forward and touched his hand. "I'm so proud of you, Cody. You're making real progress." He pretended not to look down her shirt.

6

Fifteen blocks away from the Dartree Motel where Ruby Vorlicky scrubbed the residue of someone's shit off the cracked linoleum in room 8, Bill and Maria Asket began their walk. The humid June evening wetted their shirts to their backs, but they enjoyed the chirping of crickets and the scuttle of families out for exercise as they sipped their Slurpees. Maria insisted on carrying one for Luke, and though it was melted by the time Maria gave it to him when they met up at the Novadale Bridge, Luke chugged it like it was the best thing he'd ever had.

"Thanks, cheater," he winked at Maria.

"You just gotta get better at wining, Luke."

"And you got to get better at being a *gracious* winner, honey." Bill nudged Maria. She stuck her tongue out at Luke, like she did every time she whooped his butt in tic-tac-toe.

They walked on, over the calm water of the Callingwood River and six sets of train tracks at the City's switchyard, then down an apartment district whose tenements deteriorated the closer they got the motel. Bill pointed at buildings whose histories he knew, and they played a game at guessing the stories of the ones he didn't.

"Drugs," Maria said of all of them.

"Dropouts," Luke said. "At least that's what my mom said."

Bill looked at the boarded-up windows of a bottom-floor low rise. "Willie told me that you shouldn't use one color to paint a whole canvas because you'll never get a clear picture. I think you're both right, but only partially. Look at that one up there, the one with those purple flowers on the balcony. You think they do drugs?" Maria shook her head. "You think they finished high school?" Luke shrugged. "The point is," Bill told them, "you *don't* know. Maybe the people with purple flowers are running a meth lab in their apartment and they put flowers out to make people *think* they're decent people. Or maybe they really are. The ones with the boarded windows might be trying to protect their kids from whatever goes on in the street at night. Or maybe they closed them off so people can't see the illegal things happening *inside*."

Maria said, "Or maybe they can't afford windows."

"That too. What I'm trying to tell you is that this might not be my favorite area of the city, but that doesn't mean the people here are worth any less than the ones living in those mansions on Simon Avenue. I know plenty of rich folks who should be in prison for the things they do, and a ton of poor folks who would rather starve before even *thinking* of stealing from someone. But I could just as easily flip that to be the opposite. We never really know, do we? The only way is to look past where people *are* and watch what they *do*."

"Like that guy?" Luke gestured to a man on the other side of the street urinating on a mailbox.

"When you gotta go, you gotta go," Bill sighed and hurried Luke and Maria along. After a time, he said, "You worried about introducing us to your mom, Luke?"

"She won't like you," Luke said. "But don't take it personally. She doesn't like anyone with money."

"I'm not rich," Bill said.

"Have you lived in the same place for your whole life?"

"Two, actually. My childhood home, where my parents still live near the baseball diamonds, and you know where my apartment is."

Maria tugged the hem of Luke's t-shirt. "How many places did you live?"

"Seventeen, if you don't count my aunty's. We go there sometimes when we have nowhere else to go. It's better now that my mom's at the motel. They let us stay there sometimes. It's not as bad as everyone thinks it is."

Bill understood. From what he'd learned about Luke's family so far, he knew they were the type that never got a break, that were always struggling and maybe would *always* struggle. A few of those kinds of families frequented the So-Lo and Bill did what he could to help when he could, but it was never enough to change their fortune. Often, it *was* drugs or alcohol that kept them from stability, but many times, unfortunately, it was the obscenities of violence against mothers unable to escape their partners. He saw it in their flinches and sunglasses and bruise-branded bodies.

He saw the same thing in Luke.

"That's got to be tough," Bill said.

Luke shrugged.

The rest of the walk was quiet but for the shouts of Maria squealing at butterflies or screaming at bees. By the time they got to *Glazed*, an artisan donut shop relegated to a space between a defunct dry cleaning business and a rundown liquor store, Bill had to give Maria a piggy-back ride because her legs were sore. Once she saw the pale blue building, however, she leapt off Bill's back and ran into the store.

"My mom thinks we just met," Luke said quietly while Bill caught the door.

"We did," Bill agreed.

Inside, the building was cool. Plumes of sugar-coated air engaged their stomachs but while Maria drooled at the display counter, Bill followed Luke to a table in the corner where a woman sat with her back to them. From this angle, Ruby Vorlicky looked almost as small as Maria. Bill could count the bumps in the woman's spine. If her collared shirt wasn't so loose, he was sure her ribs would be visible, too. Though it was illegal indoors, she was smoking a cigarette and tapping the ashes in an empty coffee cup from another store.

"Mrs. Vorlicky?" Bill said as he approached the table.

She did not take his hand, but instead glared at Luke. "I've been here for twenty minutes."

"Completely my fault," Bill said. "It's so nice outside, I figured we'd walk. Can I apologize with a donut?"

Ruby's green eyes ran down the length of Bill. She snorted. "That'd be all right, I guess. Anything chocolate and coffee, if it's hot. Luke likes the ones with nuts on top, and get him a water, too. That walk's got him flushed red." Ruby put her hand to Luke's cheek and touched the hair at the back of his neck.

While Luke sat with his mom, Bill placed their orders and waited at the counter with Maria. When they returned with their tray, Maria's donut was already gone.

"Lukey used to be like that," Ruby smiled and exposed a missing tooth on the side of her mouth.

"She didn't try real sugar until she was almost three. My wife gave her one of those chocolate puffy things, and after one taste that's all Maria ever wanted."

The side of Ruby's upper lip went up. "Married, are you? And your wife sent you to meet me? Is she strange or something that she couldn't come herself? We get enough weirdos around here. I don't want Luke running around with those kinds of people." She pointed her cigarette at Bill and they all watched the smoke curl toward his face. Under the table, Luke nudged her foot. "What?" Ruby snapped at him. He sagged in his seat and covered his face with his hands.

"It's okay. I'd probably be wondering the same thing if I were in your position," Bill said. "Truth is, Mrs. Vorlicky—"

"Call me Ruby."

"Well, the truth is, Ruby, that my wife Diana had a rare form of cancer, so it's just been me and Maria for the last two years." He put another donut in front of Maria to pre-empt her tears. A moment later, her mouth was filled and her attention was on the wall of televisions where three different cartoons were playing.

Ruby put her cigarette down. "He tell you about his father?"

Luke shook his head, saving Bill from sputtering out an answer.

"Prison." Ruby said matter-of-factly. "Between you and me, a funeral would have been easier. Coming, going. Gone so long sometimes you forget you're even married. Then you come home from work and he's got his feet up on the table wantin' sex and supper." Bill pretended not to notice Luke pulling his shirt over his face. Ruby gestured to him. "He don't like it much, but a father's a father. You got to take what you can get, or you'll end up getting nothing with him. Your girl is lucky."

"Lucky" wasn't a word Bill would use to describe their lives since Diana passed. Maria was doing all right, but he felt himself languishing between hopelessness and grief too often to consider himself anything but broken. The store helped, as did Maria's optimism, for which he was now especially thankful.

"Will Luke's father be out soon?" Bill asked.

"Don't know."

Ruby lit another cigarette. By now, the traffic at the counter had subsided and the women behind it were glaring in their direction, seeming to debate whether or not to approach their table. Ruby blew a perfect smoke ring at them, then looked at Bill.

"Joe does whatever the hell he wants. Sometimes he's good and they let him out early, but sometimes he stirs 'em up and stays longer. He's got a mean temper if you're not careful." Her eyes swung to Maria and then back at Bill. "You don't seem the temper type, if I may say so."

"Not unless the Habs are losing to the Leafs." Bill smiled.

Ruby didn't smile back. "If I let Luke watch your girl, are you going to treat him right?"

"Of course."

"How much are you paying him?"

"I paid my old sitter ten an hour before she and her family moved away. Does that sound fair?" Bill had come upon this figure during his walk with Luke. The fifteen an hour he would actually pay him would be their secret. They agreed that Bill would keep the extra five dollars an hour and give it to Luke whenever he asked for it. Earlier, Luke had warned Bill that his mother would take most, if not all, the money he earned at the So-Lo and though he hoped it wasn't true, Bill couldn't shake the truth he felt, having met Ruby.

"Ten's all right," she said. The Dartree logo on her blue and yellow uniform puffed out as she slid her cigarettes into her pocket. Ruby stood, kissed the top of Luke's head and told him not to wait up for her. She twirled a bulging, grey fingertip in front of Maria's nose. "Lucky girl," she oozed at the child with a mouthful of donut. Then she left.

7

There was no celebration when Cody returned. Late July and the perfect weather for a barbeque on the back deck, he somehow expected *something* to come home to. But there was nothing and no one, not even his grandmother, who was in the middle of her shift greeting fellow penny-pinchers at the Bargain-Mart. Not a single person was willing to pick him up, so she'd arranged and pre-paid for a taxi to bring him home. The sound of the empty house after so many weeks with too many addicts came at him like an uppercut. The jolt of it nearly knocked him back outside.

Cody dropped his bag at the door, humming the quiet out.

Dr. Reed had told him it would be like this. Again and again she'd reminded him, but all he could pay attention to was that mole on her boob. Like a lighthouse that demanded consideration. Blink. Still there. Blink. Still there. He should have been prepared for the loud quiet, but he was too battle-broken to defend himself. Old feelings began to creep inside, began to scratch at his newly closed injuries. He'd been standing in the same place for maybe a minute, maybe an hour, he didn't know; all he knew was that he couldn't move.

Then the cat brushed against his legs and released all of Cody's bad air.

"Hey buddy." Cody picked Tinker up and carried him to his bedroom. The cat purred, patiently nestled in stiff arms outside the bedroom door. "Should we go in?" he asked the cat, hoping at least one of them would take charge. Tinker blinked, and Cody took it as a sign. He steadied the cat against his chest with one hand and with the other he opened the door.

The containers of food were gone. The bugs, mostly. His grandmother had cleaned, scrubbed, replaced or covered the damage he'd done. It no longer looked like a junkie's toilet. It smelled of blankness, like the room was waiting to see what would be made of it.

He put the cat on the bed. But what happens when you try to get someone to do something they don't want to do? They don't do it, of course. Cats never listen. Addicts less than cats. Tinker jumped off the bed and left the room. Cody went to his desk and took the phone he wasn't supposed to be using from his drawer. Then he scrolled through names he should've deleted. Edwin. Charity. Billy. Terry. All sewer rats, just like Cody. Or, more appropriately, like Cody *used* to be. Or maybe like Cody was still learning *not* to be. Maybe Cody was a sewer *mouse*. And mice weren't so bad, were they? Some people kept them as pets.

"Squeak," he said to the lonely room.

The room answered with a cricket-chirp of silence that hurt his ears.

He spent the next three hours staring at the ceiling, trying not to call anyone and let them know he was out. The worst thing about the silence, about the nothingness, was that it made him wonder why none of them texted him. Not one. Not a hello. Not an invitation to hang. Not even a buttered-up stab at a score. Even *that* would have made him feel better. Fuck them. He hoped they rotted in hell.

Angry now, Cody scrolled through his contact list and, one by one, deleted the insignificant names. And the crazy thing was that Cody did feel a little better, a little lighter, when he rid their weight from his life. By the time he reached Terry's name, goddamn it if he didn't feel almost giddy. "See ya, scrotum face!" He punched the delete button with the small bulge in his jeans and welcomed the pain. It meant that Terry was out of his life for good.

He was sleeping when his grandmother finally came home. The telltale heavy-heeled wobble of her walking to the kitchen woke him so he dusted the chip crumbs off his neck and went upstairs.

"Look at you. Almost makes me believe I didn't see a rotting skeleton on my couch those weeks ago." She came at him with open arms and squeezed her bulk to him. "How the hell are you feeling my dear boy? You look like a thousand bucks."

"It's a million, Grandma. The expression is a million bucks."

Elanor pursed her lips and held him out at arms' length. "I know that, Cody Clyde, but you're not quite there yet. Did you have dinner?" She picked a crumb out of the hollow of his neck and inspected it.

He shook his head. "I just woke up."

"I suppose that's all right. You had a big change today, didn't you? A little rest never hurt anyone. What do you say we celebrate with a bucket of chicken? We'll eat and you can tell me everything I missed while you were away. Sound good?" She patted his chest and then sent him out the door with fifty bucks and instructions to get a bag of red licorice with the change.

She didn't trust him yet with her car, so he walked the seven blocks to the KFC. Usually, the walk winded him and he'd have to rest halfway there, halfway back, but his legs were strong and his muscles weren't all chemed up with shit that cramped him. For once, the chicken would still be hot when he got home. *How 'bout that?* he thought.

With his new legs, the Novadale bridge sped by. The Callingwood River breezed behind him. The KFC grew farther, farther, until at last Cody entered the So-Lo to get his grandmother's licorice. When he came out, Terry was leaning against the brick, lighting a cigarette.

"I heard you were in Henley, shithead," he said.

Cody lowered his head and marched past him. "Go away, Terry."

"Awww. Don't be like that, now. I've been trying to call you. I had to find out from Tucker where you were. His brother was released a week after you got there. Said you looked like a can of smashed assholes." A sneer skidded across his face. When Cody didn't answer, Terry leapt away from the store and followed him.

Cody squeezed the bag of licorice like a stress ball. In out. In out. He quickened his pace.

Terry's stratospheric temper began rolling, churning, spitting. His boots struck the sidewalk so heavily Cody could feel it three paces ahead. The chuff of Terry's breath slapped his back. The reek of it burned his eyes. The asshole probably hadn't showered since he'd seen him last, Cody thought.

From behind, Terry pounded the small space between Cody's shoulder blades. Cody wheeled forward and dropped the chicken. He spun around. "What the fuck do you want, Terry?"

"That's better. Was that so hard?" Terry yanked his spit-stained tank to his face and wiped his leaking nose. His shirt came back wet. "I just want to talk."

"I don't want anything from you, Terry. I'll get kicked out if I start anything again." The bucket of chicken had opened inside the bag, so Cody knelt and used the side of the bag to put them back in and closed the cardboard lid. "Just leave me alone, Terry."

Terry lorded over him, huffing and grinding his teeth the whole time. Then he reared back his big black boot and punted the bag out of Cody's hands before he could pick it up. The bucket splattered on the side of a passing Toyota and the chicken went skittering across the road. A trio of dogs yanked their helpless owner onto the street, and it wasn't until each one had a piece of chicken in its mouth before they allowed themselves to be led back to the sidewalk.

Respect myself enough to walk away, Cody intoned inside his head. *Respect myself enough to walk away. Respect—* Terry spat on him. Right between the eyes. It slid down his nose, crept toward his lips but he took his own shirt and scrubbed it off before it reached his mouth. He obliterated the bag of licorice, squished it tight until his nails dug into his skin. The pain helped him concentrate, helped him remember the things they'd tried teaching him at Henley. *I am in control. Only I can decide who*

I am. He thought of Dr. Reed's mole. Right there in front of him, taunting him like Terry's fucking beard. Speaking his name. Looking for a reaction. "I'm done with you, Terry," Cody heard himself saying. His voice hobbled out of him, but still it was there. It limped to where Terry stood and infuriated him more than if Cody had actually slapped him.

"Oh yeah?"

Cody stood, looked at the lost chicken, and turned toward home.

Terry swore. He threw his cigarette at Cody's neck. He kicked up such a fuss that customers coming out of the So-Lo stopped to look at them. Cody walked. Against all odds, he walked.

Then Terry unleashed a move that made Cody's blood curdle. "Murderer," he said.

Dr. Reeds affirmations flaked away. Henley's stop gap sutures unraveled. His grandmother's expectations for him were swept out in the current of his rage. Cody pinwheeled his fists like a small, pale fighter plane diving down, down, on Terry's chest, stomach, thighs.

His effort surprised Terry but didn't hurt him. Terry stumbled back, laughing, crying now at the little man's featherlight strikes. He bent over, choking on his laughter, until Cody, winded, embarrassed, dropped his arms. "What do you want Terry?" he panted.

"Don't like the truth, do you?"

"Don't say that, Terry. You know that's not what happened." Cody spun around to see if anyone was listening.

To save their asses, Charity had told the police that she was alone when Kade showed up at her trailer in the middle of the night, stumbling drunk. She said she sat with him for a while and went to fix him some food to help him sober up when Kade fell into the fire pit. Vendors of disaster, the local and national papers homed in not only on the teen's premature death but also on the dereliction of Garrett's lesser-kept trailer park and the inescapable plight of its inhabitants. Only the local *Garrett Gazette* suggested the hardships were cause for examination of inadequate government support for families with lower socio-economic status. The few public statements that Charity gave were so convincing that locals created two fundraisers: for Kade's family and for Charity herself. The fundraiser for Charity closed at almost a hundred thousand dollars. The one for Kade's family raised over three.

She had convinced them all, telling no one the truth, not even Cody, whose recollection was spotty at best. Passed out in an Oxy-booze oblivion that day, his only memory was Kade's scream. Everything before that was painted black. Everything after, stained grey. All Cody knew for certain, however, was that Kade's death had been an accident.

Terry rolled his tongue against his cheeks, then his face widened with the understanding that he had the upper hand. "You don't remember, do you?"

Cody blinked at him.

"You don't," Terry said with finality. "Fuck, man. Here I was thinking you split because you didn't want to get arrested, but that's not it. Can't fucking believe it." He paced the sidewalk back and forth, back and forth, dragging his stained fingers through his hair, through his beard. Palms out and with his sharp little teeth exposed like an uneven row of needles, Terry said, "I know you're sober and I don't want to mess with that, man, but you need to hear the truth. One drink at the Dory and I'll tell you everything. No bullshit. I told you I got your back."

Cody looked at the chicken being flattened by cars, at the growing crowd outside the So-Lo a short distance over, and finally at Terry, who would find a way to tell him what he wanted to tell him, whether Cody wanted to hear it or not. "It has to be quick," he finally said, relenting.

Of course, it wasn't quick.

Absorbed in the withering underbelly of Garrett's northside, they settled into their old habit of Terry irritating Cody and Cody drinking just to handle the abuse. By the time they were three ryes in, the bar was sufficiently noisy for Terry to tell Cody what he had to say without being overheard. Swoops of overloud laughter and classic rock forced Cody's ear to within three inches of Terry's rotten breath, so it was both his brain and his stomach that churned when Terry told him the truth.

That he, Cody Clyde, had tripped Kade.

And that when Kade had reached for him, Cody had knocked Kade into the fire.

That Cody had done it.

That Cody was a murderer.

Two bumps of cocaine did not make Cody feel better. A hit of Oxy did not make him feel better. More of this. More of that. A chunk. A dot. A dip. A nip. A shot. The Dory slipped away. Terry evaporated. Dr. Reed's mole fell off. His grandmother . . . who is she? Who is *he*? What—

8

Martin Gimbel stood at the So-Lo's counter for the better part of five minutes, trying to get Zeke Engel's attention. A twice-a-week part-timer like Luke, eighteen-year-old Zeke had been employed at the So-Lo going on four years, and though he worked hard when necessary, he just as often got distracted with his phone, watching skating videos, trying to figure out the tricks he'd yet to master. Zeke's earphones were so loud that Martin's own ears hurt hearing the punk coming out of them.

"Poke him already," Jasper ordered from his seat beside the deli.

"I don't want to scare the boy," Martin said.

"Scare him?" Jasper scoffed. "He's got his goddamned cheek pierced. You poke him because if I have to get my ass up there with my knees the way they are, I'll rip that blasted thing off his face."

Martin's cane came up slowly and crossed the lottery display. The rubber tip appeared just over Zeke's phone.

Zeke flinched and his phone went sliding across the counter. He plucked his earphones out. "Sorry Marty! Were you waiting long?"

"About bloody time!" Jasper called.

"Is it a good video at least?" Martin winked at Zeke and leaned an elbow on the counter.

"Nothing I can't do," Zeke shrugged. "What can I help you with, Marty? More coffee?" He rounded the counter and followed Martin's slow walk back toward the deli.

"Crapper needs paper," Jasper answered for Martin. "If you weren't glued to your phone you'dve known that." The shake of his head was shared by other Jaspers in other stores about other teens, grouching over work ethic that wasn't just lost, it hadn't been taught at all.

"I'm on it," Zeke said immediately, and headed toward the washroom as Martin gave him a commiserating grimace.

Bill emerged between the pantry aisle and the magazine stand. "You talk to my employees like that and you can shit at home, Jasper."

"They're not employees if they're not working."

"All the same, Jasper. We had this talk, remember? Nice gets you places. Mean gets you a table somewhere else. *If* they'll put up with you."

"Hmmph!" That was Jasper's last word before the overhead bell rang and Luke arrived to relieve Zeke from his shift.

Luke's hair was tussled high from his windy walk. Since their arrangement had become official with his mother, he routinely walked from the Dirty to the So-Lo for his shifts so he could save on bus fare. By now, Bill and his regulars were used to the healthy flush of Luke's cheeks from the pre-work exercise, but today Luke looked almost grey. A layer of sweat took hold of his face, and his pupils were dilated so wide his blue eyes were nearly black.

Bill rushed to catch him in case he fainted. "You all right there, Lukey?"

"Uhhh..."

"Luke?" Bill now patted his cheeks, squeezed his shoulders, rubbed his arms. "Come on, Luke. Tell me what's going on. Stay with me, kiddo." He gestured to Zeke, who was standing in the periphery. A chair appeared a moment later. Bill guided the shaking boy onto the seat.

Faster than any of them could have imagined, Jasper shot up and whipped his coffee right into Luke's face.

Martin stabbed his cane at Jasper's toe. "Why'd you do that for? You coulda burned 'im!"

"Worked in Nam." Jasper huffed then pointed at Zeke. "If *he* was doing his job, it would have been *hot*. Lucky you were lazy today. Look!"

Luke sputtered. He blinked. He wrinkled his nose. Then his mind finally caught up to where his body had taken him. "Bill?" The boy smelled the coffee and wretched. To everyone's relief, nothing came out.

It was Martin who rushed to the beverage counter and yanked a handful of napkins from the dispenser. He patted Luke down while Zeke got Luke a bottle of water, which Bill made Luke sip while he recovered.

"How you feeling, bud?" Bill asked. "You okay?"

They gathered around, choking him with their worry. He wasn't used to so many people looking out for him. A streak of red flushed his cheeks.

"He's going down!" Martin pushed Bill closer to Luke, but then Luke held his hands up.

"I'm not going to faint," he said. "At least I think I'm not. I just need a sec. Give me a moment."

The circle around him widened. Zeke zipped away and returned with an armful of chocolate and candies. "Little man's got to get his sugar up. My older sister gets like that sometimes. A snack'll make him feel better. What'll it be, Lukester? I got Whoppers and those Space Ninja Gummies you like. Some sour strips, Coke bottles, Kit Kat..."

The Space Ninjas were snatched and opened before Zeke could finish. Luke put a handful in his mouth and they watched while he chewed. "Thanks Zeke," he said at last. Color came back to his eyes.. His skin gasped at the sugar and revived.

Bill bent over in front of him. "Are you sick, Luke?"

The boy's hair rustled.

"What is it then? Your mom okay? Is your dad—" Bill didn't finish. Luke's father's incarceration wouldn't be shared, at least by him.

"No. Everything's the same, but—" Luke bit his lip. Four faces closed in, waiting. Then his lips began to tremble and up his throat came a rush of alarm. "I think I saw a dead body. I think I saw a dead body, Bill," he repeated and fell into Bill's open arms. He held on, then his fear finally breeched his tear ducts and he was blubbering wetly onto Bill's shirt.

Bill held him. "Easy now, Luke. Easy. You're safe here. You're with us. We got you. Tell me what you saw and let's see if I can help. Can you do that, Luke?"

Luke sniffed.

"Give him some room," Zeke ordered. Martin and Jasper fell back a few steps but stayed near, watching, listening.

"Breathe. In. Slow. Out. Slow. Just like that. Do you think you can tell me what you saw, Luke?" Bill's eyes darted to the apprehensive old men leaning so far over to hear that Martin was balanced directly over his cane and Jasper was practically on top of him. "Maybe some privacy will help?" he suggested. Jasper grunted.

"It's okay." Luke wiped his eyes. "They can hear." He inhaled, held it in, pushed his breath out, slow, slow. "You know that donut place we went to? He was in the building beside that. The window was broken, so I looked in."

"That closed up dry cleaning business?" Bill asked.

"Uh-huh. I know it's not the best part of town, but no one's ever touched that place before. You saw it, Bill. It was fine when we passed it, wasn't it?"

"It was. Closed down but looked okay from the outside from what I remember."

"That's what *I* thought. There's a lot of boarded up places near there and lots with broken windows, too, but not that place. Maybe that's why it stood out to me. I don't know what made me do it, but I saw the glass all busted up and it made me look. I wish I hadn't."

"What was inside, Luke?"

Luke wrapped his arms around himself, shivering with memory. "It was a *boy*. He was lying face down in the middle of a bunch of broken glass and stuff."

"Maybe he was sleeping," Jasper put in.

"Uh-uh."

Bill crouched so that his eyes were level with Luke's. Even on that first day when he'd caught Luke stealing, he'd never looked so anxious, and Bill couldn't discount the feeling that Luke was telling the truth. Or at least that Luke *thought* he was telling the truth. "What makes you think he wasn't sleeping, Luke?"

"His eyes were open."

Martin gasped. Zeke's hands went to the back of his neck, where he tugged and twisted his shaggy hair.

"You should have stuck your finger in one," Jasper said. When they all looked at him, he closed one eye and sized each of them up with the other. "Any of you had to belly-crawl over a field of red ants to check your company for signs of life while rockets were fired at you? No? None of you sissies? Let me tell you babies something: you poke a man's eye and he'll tell you if he's alive. Quicker than trying to find his pulse, I tell you. That or shove something up his ass, but a lotta guys shit themselves when they die. Fifty-fifty chance you'll just get your hands dirty for nothing."

Martin buried his face in his hands.

"What?" Jasper said. "That's how it goes sometimes."

Luke couldn't hold back his laugh. It made his color come back, and he stopped shaking. For once, Bill appreciated Jasper's foul mouth.

"Zeke, can you stick around for a while and make sure these two don't get into any trouble? I'm going for a drive with Luke."

Zeke looked at his watch. "I got about an hour and a half."

"Good. If I think we'll be any longer, I'll call April and see if she can come in for a bit or you'll have to close up until I'm back."

"We'll cover for you," Martin offered.

"Can you work a cash register?"

"He can't even button his pants," Jasper shouted, pointing at Martin's open fly.

"Let's hope we don't need you to," Bill said with a wink, then led Luke through the pantry aisle toward the interior door of the apartment lobby. Zeke, Martin, and Jasper watched them leave. They took the stairs to the lower garage where Bill's Volkswagen beeped.

Luke shuffled toward the SUV and stopped. "I'm scared, Bill."

The fear on the boy's face hit Bill's heart then slapped his brain. He realized he hadn't asked Luke what *Luke* wanted to do, and that taking him back to scene—if it even *was* a scene—would terrify him. He wouldn't want that for Maria, were the situation reversed, so it would be wrong to ask it of Luke. Bill locked and armed his vehicle again and put his keys back in his pocket. "I'm sorry, Luke. You have every right to be scared. And I had no right to expect you to go back there. If what you suspect is true, we should call the police. They'll investigate so we don't have to. But I can drive you home if you'd like. I can handle Jasper and Martin on my own."

"But what if it's not true? What if he was just sleeping?" Luke bit his lip. "I don't want to get in trouble."

"You won't get in trouble, bud. If someone is hurt, you'd be helping them. No one's going to fault you for that." Only, Bill recognized that look on Luke's face. It told him that Luke wasn't afraid of the police. No. He was afraid of getting in trouble from *someone else*. "Is your dad home, Luke?"

The mention of his father paled him. "He told my mom he'll be out in a week, but he's almost never out when he says he's going to be."

In this moment, looking at the trembling boy in front of him, it took everything Bill had not to march to that jail and give Luke's father a reason to *want* to stay incarcerated. "All right, kiddo. You tell me what you'd like to do. The ball's in your court. I can call the police and keep you out of it. I can drive there and check it out myself. Or we can go together. Or none of the above. If someone's hurt, I think we need to help them, but we don't want to cause any trouble for you. You want to hang with Zeke while I go for a drive?"

"I'll come."

"You don't have to." Bill unlocked the Volkswagen.

"I'll just show you where he was. I'll try not to look."

"You want me to call your mom?"

A hard no.

"All right. Get in and promise me you'll stay in unless I tell you it's okay to get out."

The boy's hand stretched to Bill and they shook.

In the car, Bill tried making small talk to keep Luke's mind off their mission, but nothing worked. Whether he asked Luke about school or teased him about the girls who flirted with him as he heaped their soft serve into cones every Saturday afternoon, Luke's mind was elsewhere. There were no laughs as they passed the river. There was not a chuckle, a giggle, not even a groan to get Bill to stop ribbing him. Just those worried blue eyes in a small body worrying like an adult.

At the switchyard, they stopped for a passing train. Bill turned. "Once we pass the tracks, I'm driving you home. I can't let you do this, Luke. Not the way it's affecting you. I know where to go. There's no need for you to point something out to me that I can see from the window." He opened the sunroof to let the summer air feather their hair, warm their skin.

"I shouldn't have left him there, Bill." Luke hugged his knees, burying his face. "I should've checked to see if he was okay. What if—" A hitch rose up his young throat. "What if he's dead because of me? Will they put me in *jail*?"

The thought of Luke and his father sharing a cell was as improbable as Jasper employing tact. "Is that your worry? You think you're going to end up like your dad?"

The boy whimpered.

The last few cars skidded past them. The crossing arm rose and slowly the cars ahead coughed and groaned and began crawling forward. "Anyone ever tell you that depravity isn't hereditary, Luke?"

The smaller head lifted. "What's depravity?"

"You know how there are good ways of doing things and treating people and bad ways of doing it, too? Depraved people don't spend too much time trying to be good or treat other people good. They're mean. Sometimes you don't know they're mean because they keep their meanness inside, but they let it out when they think no one's looking. And sometimes they don't care if anyone's watching or not; meanness is their identity. What I mean to say is that just because your dad made some bad choices doesn't mean *you're* going to. My dad might've kept us in the same house growing up, but every now and then he got blistering drunk. Never laid a hand on me —I don't want you to think he did—but he had these words, these nasty words that hurt me worse than any hit ever could have. It would have been easy for me to slip into his same habits, try them on in my own life, but my choice was to keep that kind of hurt away from the people close to me. That's why I don't yell or beat my chest or any of that. I had to choose to be like that, Luke, just like you can choose the type of person you want to be." Behind them, a horn blared. Bill flipped the driver a peace sign with his fingers. "Am I making any sense? Tell me to beat it if you want."

"I want to be like you, Bill."

"I'm driving you to the hospital so they can check your head."

"Don't be funny."

"In that case," Bill scratched his chin, "you'll work until you're a hundred. We better get you some proper shoes now to protect your back."

"Ha. Ha."

A block ahead they would reach the intersection that signaled the beginning of the city's lowest-rental apartment corridor. A left turn would take them to Luke's house. A right would return them to the So-Lo. Neither would lead them to the defunct dry cleaning business. The car slowed. "What do we do, Luke?"

Squinting against the sunlight, Luke sighed. "I'm coming. I saw how you got when April got cut on those cardboard boxes. You can't handle blood."

"You never said anything about blood." Tiny dark hairs rose on Bill's forearm.

A bony thirteen-year-old hand pointed at them. "That's why. You can't even handle the *word* blood."

The steering wheel got hot under Bill's palms. The gas pedal became a brick wall. The windows seemed to cave in on him, compact his body, press the air out of his lungs. His armpits tolerated the afternoon heat but now they were swampy, and their cold heat nauseated him. He turned on the air conditioning, blasting it full in his face. He leaned toward the vent until his nose was almost touching the dash. They were going half the speed-limit, which was all right with the old man drinking from a brown paper bag as he jaywalked in front of them, but not okay with the expletive-tossing woman behind them in the thirty-year-old Pontiac with a taped-up window.

"See what I mean?" Luke said.

An empty parking spot presented itself on the right, so Bill slid in but left the engine running. "I'm fine. I'm fine."

"If you can't handle it . . ." Luke said with that sly catch in his throat only teenagers could muster. His raised eyebrow goaded Bill, needled the fear right out of him.

"Almost cut off my baby toe with the lawnmower when I was your age. Hated the sight of blood ever since, but it's not so bad if it's not mine. Let's do this, huh?" Bill gestured to the faded façade of Can-Do Cleaners on the opposite side of the street; beneath the fascia, the middle window had been recently broken. "Doesn't look so bad," Bill said as they stepped out of the car. The fresh air quieted his stomach, flattened the hair on his arms.

Perhaps it helped that the donut shop next door was bright and dancing with people, or perhaps it was the steady stream of locals staggering out of the adjacent liquor store, fumbling with the caps of their hidden mickeys, but it seemed an ordinary day in an ordinary place to Bill. There were no gawkers or pointers or tragedy magnets. There were no emergency vehicles. No ambulance, police car, or forensics unit. There was no police tape or any evidence the Can-Do had been investigated at all. Still, when they crossed the road and passed the liquor store, Bill couldn't help but notice Luke falling back slightly, biting his thumbnail.

A production of laughter and sugary air filled the space in front of them as a box-laden group left the donut shop. Bill reached into his wallet and pushed a twenty at Luke. "Why don't you get us a couple of those cinnamon things you had last time? I'll meet you in there."

Luke brushed past him. "We'll go together."

"Anyone ever tell you you're stubborn?"

"It's a personal choice." The side of Luke's mouth stretched slyly.

"Try to teach a guy a lesson, and this is what I get." Bill threw up his hands and skipped ahead of Luke.

In its former glory, Can-Do Cleaners could have been a completely respectable seventies era hangout. The hole through which Bill peered showed him a small storefront with interlocking panels that created a Chevron pattern behind the neon logo on the far wall. The logo was missing the first half of the name so that *Can-Do* was only a series of bent pins, while *Cleaners* was in good, albeit inoperable, condition. No doubt some local needed inspiration so badly the missing neon had emigrated to a living room wall or basement athletic studio some time ago. The lobby housed an old vending machine that someone had failed to push through the entrance to the abutting self-service laundromat with a wider outer door. Whatever could be stolen or redirected had been, and everything that remained was bent and covered in dust.

There was no blood. There was no body. Just the visible coating of abandonment.

Relief seeped through Bill's pores. He turned to Luke. "Someone must have been playing a trick on you, kiddo. There's no one here. See?"

Luke looked away. He bit his lip. He shuffled his feet. His hands went into his pockets.

"You didn't just look through the window," Bill said, studying the fidgeting teen. "You went in, didn't you?"

A couple carrying a toddler passed them. The little girl blew raspberries from chocolate-smeared lips. Tiny plump fingers tried to catch Luke's hair, but the father caught her hand in time and with an apologetic smile, the family walked on.

"I just wanted to see inside. I didn't break the window. Honest, I didn't. It was already like that when I got here."

Bill lowered his head. Through still lips, he whispered, "Where is it?"

"In the back. Under that spinny thing."

"The conveyor?"

Luke nodded.

A quick glance around told Bill that no one was watching them. Crouching under the busted glass, he stepped into the building. "If anyone asks what we're doing, say my wallet was stolen and we saw a bunch of punks throw it in here."

"No one says *punks* anymore. They'll know I'm lying."

"Say *shitheads*, then."

"I'll say assholes."

Bill frowned. "I didn't say that word until I was almost an adult."

"You didn't grow up around here. It's our next word after *Mommy*."

"Got me there."

The floor was littered with cans and take-out trash. A spray of busted glass spread from the sides of the Chevron partition over the counter, where dozens of couples etched their loyalty into the orange laminate. Above, several of the ceiling tiles had been either ripped away or splattered with nothing either of them wanted to inspect. The window might have only recently been broken, but somehow people had gotten in and made their destructive marks. It wasn't the worst Bill could have imagined, but neither did it speak highly for the area. A number of needles, blackened spoons, and empty beer bottles were strewn behind the counter.

"You saw all this?" Bill asked.

"Uh-huh." The boy was unfazed.

"You do this often?"

"Uh-huh."

Bill stopped his slow trek. Luke almost knocked them both over by bumping into him. He looked at the boy as he recovered his balance. Wire-thin legs poking from black shorts. Kneecaps like tennis balls. Arms that might one day fill a shirt but were now as narrow as clappers in bells. All belied his experience.

"Ever get caught?" Bill asked.

"No, but I saw a naked woman once. She was playing with needles and ran at me when she saw me. She had this big scar across her stomach that was oozing. I threw my backpack at her. Told my mom I lost it, but she didn't believe me." He rounded the partition toward the back area while Bill followed, sidestepping a pair of headless mannequins positioned erotically. "She wouldn't give me dinner until I found it. Oh my God, it was dark. I could barely see anything. There was this little wall in the room, like a half wall or something, that I thought she was hiding behind. I thought she was going to jump out at me."

"Was she gone when you got there?"

"Uh-huh," Luke grunted. "But I saw her on the way back at the 7-11. She was with a girl I go to school with. I think she's her mom, but I didn't say anything about it."

"You're a good kid, Luke."

The compliment went unacknowledged, partly because Luke wasn't used to receiving them but mostly because seconds after they passed the mannequins, a battlefield bloomed into view. The disemboweled ceiling, half-clinging, half-severed from its core, was pierced by sunlight stabbing through a moldy skylight. Cabinet doors limped off hinges. Wallpaper was scalped. Amputated worktables were slumped in the act of disintegrating. The overhead conveyor, crippled on the far end, bore the flags of victors on the nearest: grimy bras, filthy underwear of many sizes, a number of diapers, and the crusty tubing of an intravenous line. Everything—ceiling, floor, walls —was speckled with blood.

Something akin to the mewl of a kitten escaped Bill's lips. The hair on his arms marched into place. His skin grew cold. His blood retreated from his brain. He staggered.

"Bill?"

Slowly, slowly, Bill slumped to the floor, working to stay conscious. He put his head between his knees, breathing, unable to shake the knowledge he'd have to throw away everything that touched the diseased ground.

Luke knelt beside him. "I told you it was bad. Are you going to be okay?"

Were it not for his responsibility as the adult amongst them, and had he not been afraid of catching something, Bill would have already fainted, no doubt kissing the ground. At the moment, he counted himself lucky that his disgust overrode his phobia.

"Yeah." He swallowed the bile rising in his throat. "I'm good. Just need a sec. I believed you, Luke, honest I did, but . . . but I didn't think it was going to be like *this*."

Purposefully, Bill focused on a newspaper stained with what only could be urine near his shoe. The paper was torn down the middle, but the date was visible: October 20, 2017. Four years ago. Someone had drawn a patch over the one visible eye of New Zealand's newly elected prime minister. Another had sketched Superwoman's costume on her torso. Even here, there was conflict. The kind face behind the pen marks, which reminded him so much of Diana, kneaded his nerves. Color came back to his face. With a long push of air through his cheeks, Bill finally raised his head.

"Where was the guy lying?"

Luke had been standing in front, so Bill had been spared the vision of what was under the conveyor. But now Luke stepped aside and pointed to the person-sized spill of blood, still wet on the scarred linoleum. "There," he said.

9

It had been a long time since Elanor visited a graveyard. Sure, she was at the age where people commonly pushed up those gaudy plastic flowers deposited by offspring uninterested in visiting more often than necessary. But so far, only one person she was close with had shoved away from the functions of life. And he had been a bastard. Elanor *despised* bastards. She didn't visit them after they were gone, in any capacity, so graveyards were still foreign to her.

She'd brought fresh flowers, something she thought the boy might've liked. Blue and purple. The sky opened and fell once her feet touched the gravel, as if it had been waiting for Elanor to arrive. *Let's really set the scene*, it seemed to say, and brought a chill that crept up the sleeves of her jacket and slid down the collar of her shirt. Her shoulders tugged up to fend it off. A moment later, the umbrella above was shuffled as Cody removed his jacket and draped it on her shoulders. She tried pushing it back to him. "You need it for yourself."

"I'm good, Grandma," he said, and wrapped an arm around her while they looked down at Kade Hart's paltry grave marker.

The slim metal plate, etched with the boy's name and birthdate, shone in the dark grass. Almost nothing of the six-figure amount raised for the family to cover funeral expenses revealed itself above ground. Not only was the burial site at the end of the cemetery where unidentified bodies were interred, but he didn't even have a headstone. Elanor plucked the few rotten flowers off the thin plate and laid the new ones down.

"You better be buried in gold," she said to the marker.

Behind her, Cody pinched the bridge of his nose to stem off the feelings he didn't want to feel. He closed his eyes, wrestling with tears and a much different graveyard experience. When he'd last visited the cemetery, he'd done so as a bereaved friend. Today he did it as a murderer. A cry ruptured his lips. It broke free, fell out of him and collapsed on the grass above Kade's body. It screamed his guilt, confessed to everything, begged for the release of pressure on his soul. None of this was intelligible, of course. All Elanor heard was an ache emptying. A terrible sound. A sour sound. But in the turbulent upchuck of emotion, she felt healing on the periphery. Real healing. The kind she knew Cody hadn't yet encountered. The kind she knew he had to experience if he was ever going to recover and resemble a decent human being.

His cries fell like ashes from a cigarette. Choking inhalations. Staccato weeps that tapped from his tongue, drifting down until they were joined with the earth. They tore at her heart, but this was better than altogether stopping the outpour like he'd almost done those few days ago. She much preferred his sobs to an explosion of blood from his face to his stomach like he was as injured as the boy underground.

That night when she'd sent him to get dinner, he hadn't come home. Knowing Cody, she was convinced he'd slipped back into that sewer life. She expected him to return high. She expected him to have excuses. He *always* had excuses. But not this time. This time he came back looking like roadkill and told her he'd tried taking his life. What could she say to *that*? She couldn't kick him out, couldn't reprimand a person teetering on his last strand of life. It would push him over, and Elanor did not want him to die. She only wanted him out of the sewer, and was that too much to ask? Of course she forgave him. Who wouldn't?

He was sober when she cleaned him up the next morning. She inspected him for drugs—eyes, mouth, veins—and found not a trace of anything. He'd tried cutting himself, but poorly. The slits were shallow, but they bled, oh how they bled! And while she took his clothes and waited outside the shower in case he fainted, begging him to let her drive him to the hospital, muffled revelation spat out of him.

He felt responsible for Kade's death. He should have been there, should have warned him that bad things happened in their circle.

She'd waited until Cody had a towel around his waist, then she'd cradled him like a baby. A big, damaged baby.

And yet, the day now seemed like a miracle, as though the bloodletting had somehow cleansed him. The whites of his eyes were whiter. The congested routes of blood vessels around his irises, no longer traveled by opiates or depressants or stimulants, had been decommissioned. The fat he'd snorted away, which had not fully returned during his stay at Henley, puffed back a little here, more there, like his face had been puttied and put back *on*. He could almost pass for a decent human being, Elanor thought. A little jittery, but who wouldn't be after something like that? She understood that whatever happened to him that night was transformative and that, even more, whatever it was . . . was *good*.

Overhead, a cloud passed, and their shadows spilled onto Kade's pathetic excuse for a tombstone. Elanor stood and stepped back so that Cody could have a moment.

"Say your piece, Cody. This is your chance. He's not going anywhere. Tell him what you want to say." She nudged Cody forward. He leapt sideways so as not to stand on top of Kade's body.

A moment later, with his grandmother huddling under a tree and the rain beginning to soak into his sneakers, Cody knelt and stumbled through a quiet prayer for a boy he barely knew but would go hell for. Rain soaked through the knees of his jeans. Thunder rumbled somewhere nearby, but still he knelt, imbuing his grief on the boy who couldn't hear, couldn't forgive.

A flicker of lightning brightened the cloud-packed sky. Cody rose and joined his grandmother.

Though she prepared his favorite—fried chicken and mashed potatoes—he took no dinner. With reassurances that he was okay, she watched him descend to the basement.

Inside his room, Cody pulled his computer chair to the door and pushed it under the knob. He thought she probably wouldn't open it anyway, but just to be sure he pushed his desk half a foot over, in front of the jam. Part of their arrangement for his continued tenancy was the removal of his lock, and she had had the knob replaced while he was in Henley. She had yet to barge in on him, but the threat was there, even more so since he'd come home looking like a shit pile that morning.

He gave it a minute, listened for footsteps down the stairs in case of a surprise inspection, but then he heard her chair scrape against the linoleum as she pushed back from the kitchen table and limped with her sciatic-inflamed legs toward the sink to wash dishes. Overhead, the stopper was plugged into the drain and the unmistakable sound of water filling the sink made him relax.

Cody yanked his shirt off and stood sideways in front of the mirror.

There it was.

Maybe three inches. Long and dark like a leech, but fuzzy like old mold on expired yogurt.

Pulsating.

He poked it. The fuzz stiffened and stung him.

Cody bit his lip to keep from crying out. He did not want his grandmother to come running. Somehow, he knew the thing on his side also didn't want his grandmother to come running because the sting abated. A ridiculous thought, but everything about it was ridiculous.

As if they were a reel inside his head, Cody unwound the last eighty or so hours, when the nightmare had begun. It didn't start with the bucket of chicken being punted across the street or with the suffocating awareness that his grandmother would be disappointed in him.

Those were toddlers' dreams in comparison.

The terror unfolded like a snake and rattled out of Terry's mouth, spitting Cody's sin. The poison ruptured his eardrums and whittled its way to his brain while they drank in the bar. In another life, perhaps Cody would have woken in a heap of fear-sweated sheets and gone on to forget what scared him while he slept. Instead, Cody pried his drug-puffed eyes wide enough to never want to open them again.

He thought he'd murdered someone, there was so much blood.

But when his head pivoted around, around, like an in-ground sprinkler, he saw that he was alone and that the blood was his. His arms were sliced. His hip. And there was a split around his neck, from ear to ear at the nape, too shallow to be serious but that had bled like a motherfucker, like he had tried to stop hearing what Terry had told him.

Cans rolled off his stomach as he sat up. A barely touched bottle of Silent Sam fell between his legs. Something pinched his palm. A needle from the night before. It skittered across some piss-stained newspapers when he flicked it away.

The skylight, grimy like a fish tank weeks past cleaning day, told him it was daytime. Maybe the day after he saw Terry. Maybe a month after that. He couldn't tell. The only thing he was reasonably sure of was that he was alive but looking like death.

Something in the filth-littered corner moved. Cody squinted, but the dark held its secrets.

"Hello?"

The room responded with the sound of a paper bag being dragged across the floor. Then it crinkled.

"Terry? Stop fucking around, man. I can't deal with your shit right now." He put his hands on the cleanish place under his body and pushed himself to his feet.

Fingers crawled over his shoulder.

Cody vaulted away. His shriek bounced off the walls, filled the dirty room like bacteria in a petri dish. He did not want to look back, couldn't look back, sure that whoever had cut him had come to finish the job, but the sound of something clanging above him brought his head around. An IV tube dangled where he'd bumped it. He laughed uneasily, wiped the back of his head, and kicked a soda can to the dark corner. A mouse scurried out of the bag toward a sliver of light under the exit at the far end of the room.

"Fucker," Cody said to the mouse.

With his fear retiring to its waiting area, he was finally able to take in his surroundings without his heart palpitating like it was going to explode. Not the worst place he'd ever found himself but definitely close. Needle trash and feces were almost always part of his awakenings. Blood, not uncommon. He scratched a nagging itch on his side and felt the edges of a dime indented into his skin. *Figures*, he thought, and tried to pick it away.

It didn't budge.

He began to lift his shirt to inspect the coin that had somehow been glued to him when he heard footsteps in the other room. Cody tiptoed over the trash, away from the blood. Then he sank into the shadows and edged toward the rear doors. A chain was holding the two handles together, but he was able to push the right door open enough to squeeze himself out.

Cody ran.

Away from his blood and the IV tube and those footsteps, he zipped down the back alley, one side street, two. A mother pushing a stroller did an abrupt about-face when she saw him, dashing away with terror-clotted cries as though Cody were an unsatisfied murderer. Without breaking his stride, he shucked his bloody shirt and tossed it into a bush. Better. Not much, but good enough that if he was fast and people didn't get a good look at him, he might pass for someone with a terrible sunburn or torso-size birthmark.

But his grandmother wasn't fooled.

Running and skirting open areas, his throat dry as if he'd swallowed a bucket of sand while he was unconscious, he knew she'd be waiting for him, and that no excuse would keep her from tossing his ass into the street. He correctly guessed that his bag would be packed and ready for him at the door, and he braced himself in case she threw it at him. But one look at his blood and the cuts and she threw up such a fuss, you'd have thought he died. It gave Cody an idea.

His confession wasn't so far off from the truth. He *had* thought of flipping off the topside of the earth, giving it the big one-fingered salute in a haze of dust. There was no outright attempt, no premeditation, but it *could* have happened. After what Terry told him, it wasn't as if he shouldn't have ended up down beside Kade anyway. Living. Dead. He was in hell no matter where he was.

Fat grandmotherly tears welled up under the soft hoods of her eyelids, the kind that tells you the weight of the world is on their sturdy shoulders and you just added one stone more than they can carry. They were the kind of tears that make grown men cry. He couldn't help it. He blubbered like a child, and when her tears fell, they hit him like a burst dam and almost drowned him right there in the living room. Even the cat scrambled out of the deluge, darting for the kitchen with a look over its shoulder that said it was on to him.

However, since then she had been intensely agreeable to the point that Cody regretted not using the excuse sooner. Only when her outbursts of affection threatened to suffocate him did he feel guilty, but their partnership had never been more amicable, so he felt he'd done them both a favor. A little exaggeration had never killed anyone, right? It often made them prime ministers and presidents, and that wasn't so bad. The thought brought him back to the creature from leech lagoon suctioned to his ribs. Only, it wasn't really a leech. He knew that like he knew Terry grew his neck beard to cover a sideshow-worthy weak chin. The thing on his side looked like a leech, at least today it did. Yesterday it had looked like a small dark caterpillar. The day before, when he'd first noticed it, it had looked like a black dot or a circular scab. The one thing he did know was that it was growing, and that he couldn't get it off. Also, and he couldn't be sure of this, he thought that it was in some way, somehow, *communicating* with him.

If he was still high, he might have welcomed the thing, likely would have struck up a conversation with it. He'd done it before with lamp posts and remote controls and fridge magnets; some he thought *did* actually talk back a time or two. The philosophical part of him that contemplated the Earth's makeup whenever he was high tended to remind him that everything on the planet *came* from the planet, just arranged differently, so wouldn't it be possible for one of those arrangements to strike gold like Frankenstein did? Out of trillions and quadrillions and, well, possibly infinite combinations? Narcotics convinced him of it so strongly that even sober he found himself wondering if it were true, that a chair *had* talked to him, that a *blanke*t had said his name. He felt a bit silly for not dismissing the idea, but he couldn't help it.

The thing on his side was different, though. The fact that it was alive and suctioned to him put the potential for some futuristic physics shit way closer to reality. So strange, even to his fried brain, that he started documenting it once he realized that he couldn't take it off because it didn't *want* to come off. He'd gone old school and sharpened a pencil and got out a fresh sheet of paper because his grandmother had confiscated his phone. It made him feel like a kid and hurt his fingers, but seeing his observations helped alleviate the fear that he was on the back side of crazy. Proof was on the paper.

5:17 p.m. — quarter size. Still can't get it off. Things that don't work: picking it, scraping it, salt. Reacts to peroxide (stings). Lighter (stings). Lemon juice (stings). Slap (big sting). ~~*Vibr viber*~~ *shakes when touched. Gets bigger when I try to kill it.*

7:39 p.m. — size of a Loonie. Happy when left alone. No sting. Warm feeling when I pet it. Wonder if it's peeing on me.

8:11 p.m. — blew on it. Went flat.

8:34 p.m. — likes Coke.

This entry came about purely by accident when he swallowed the wrong way and ended up coughing a swallow of soda out of his wind hole. He'd had his shirt off to watch the thing. A dozen drops of ice-cold Coca-Cola splashed on his bare skin. They washed over his visitor, and wouldn't he be damned if the thing didn't *absorb* the drink? Not unusual, Cody thought. Given the chance, who wouldn't sneak a sip? He couldn't blame it. But what struck Cody was that when the sweet liquid was drawn into the creature, Cody *himself* felt a tine of pleasure spread from his side, inward through his stomach, his lungs, the underdeveloped muscles in his arms and legs. *What's this?* he wondered. Curiously, he put the mouth of his Coke can to the skin below his armpit and splashed a little more on the thing.

Euphoria mushroomed from his ears to his ankles. His skin tingled. His vision sharpened so that he could read the label on his pencil even when he held it out as far as he could. *HB #2*. He slipped the pencil back in the plastic cup, shut his eyes, and withdrew a pen, closing his fingers around the label in the middle. Then he strode to the other side of the room and put the pen on the windowsill.

BIC medium, he read without hesitation from ten feet away.

He tested the thing for hours that night. What was clear was that it would punish Cody for bad behavior but reward him for good. A smear of peanut butter nearly gave him an orgasm, but when he pinched it, Cody felt fire in his balls and ice in his heart. A drop of his grandmother's cheap wine seemed to confuse it because one moment it singed him but the next it warmed his belly like he'd had a bowl of chicken soup. This should have alarmed him, should have made him dash to the hospital and demand they cut it off, even if they had to take a rib or two with it. People who weren't Cody could afford to do that, but it wasn't so simple for him. First, he'd have to figure out how to get there. That would require his grandmother's car or his grandmother's money for a taxi or bus ride to the other end of the city and she wasn't about to let either of those go without an explanation from him. Either way, she would insist on driving him so she could tell the doctors how he'd harmed himself. They'd tie him to a bed in a soft room until he forgot what sharp things could be used for. Then they'd ship his ass back to Henley to talk to the mole on Dr. Reed's boob and burn another one of his fake letters while she praised him for his progress.

No fucking way.

He'd rather have the thing policing his every movement then let the purveyors of morality lock him up. He might deserve to be incarcerated for what he'd done to Kade, but that didn't mean he actually *wanted* it to happen. He was fully capable of creating his own prison. Isolation: check. Curfew: check. Someone watching him and waiting for him to fuck up: all the fucking time. While his grandmother hadn't actually locked anything up, she now kept a sharp eye on whatever he could use to harm himself. She moved the kitchen knives to her bedroom and brought them out only when she was cooking, after which they were promptly washed and returned. Then there were the night terrors and the bland food and the constant roll calls to make sure he was still present and breathing. The only thing he hadn't developed was a fear of bathing, but he was sure that if the thing grew he might not enjoy the sight of it taking over his body.

That night, as he lay in bed stroking the creature with the pad of his pinky finger and wishing he had his phone so he could search the internet to figure out what it was, it lent its peace to him. He slept solidly for ten hours. By morning, feeling better than he had in years, Cody decided to keep his new pet.

10

A world with friends was a world he was thankful to be in, Bill thought as he flipped his last pancake. He turned off the stove and took the maple syrup from the cupboard. Maria squealed when he put the stack in front of her, giggling at the topmost flapjack that he'd fashioned into the shape of a cat. The whistle-high pitch always made him smile, always made him wince, and he wrinkled his nose and poked her belly until she fell into a pile of eight-year-old laughter as warming as midday sun.

Maria's small fingers gently worked the cat pancake from the top of the stack and put it on Bill's plate. He raised his eyebrows.

"I promise you it doesn't *taste* like cat," he said.

"I'm saving it for Luke," Maria told him, and set another two aside before pouring a healthy dose of amber over her remaining pancakes.

He kissed the top of her head. "I love you for it, kiddo, but that one's yours. Luke's a dog man, remember?" Bill peeled back the lid of a container he'd already filled. On top was a palm-sized fluffy dachshund with a golden body and bronze ears. Whatever spaces weren't full of pancake were filled with blueberries all the way to the lid.

"He's got more than me."

"He's got exactly the same. Besides, you can get a million of 'em any time you want. Breakfast, lunch, dinner, snack; I'll make you so much you can use them for a pillow if you want." He saw the wheels turning in her head and before he could warn her against it, her ear was in the syrup.

"Seems I've been eating my breakfast the wrong way," Barbara called out as she entered the apartment. She put her purse on the side table, slipped off her sandals, and shuffled barefoot to the kitchen to give Maria a kiss on the side of her face that wasn't mashed in Bill's hard work.

Bill sighed. "She takes me too literally sometimes. Have you eaten breakfast? I have food that *hasn't* been up her nose if you'd like?" He dragged the plate from under Maria and gave her a wet towel to wipe her face.

"Wait a minute, Bill Asket!" Barbara's silver hair flagged behind her while she ran to prevent him from scraping Maria's pancakes into the trash bin. She picked a small piece from the plate and put it in her mouth, moaning extravagantly. "I've always wanted to try pancakes and earwax. It's delicious, my dear!" She ruffled Maria's hair and winked at Bill, then proceeded to the sink to wash her hands. "Baby, why don't you take your breakfast in front of the TV so I can tell your dad about my hot date last night. He was an *amazing* kisser." She grinned naughtily.

The kitchen was vacated immediately.

"You know," Bill said, "in a few years she's going to want to stick around for a story like that."

Barbara took a cup from the cupboard and filled both their mugs with coffee. "Well, she's certainly not going to hear it from *you*."

"Kids don't like hearing about their parents' love life."

"You have to *have* a love life to actually talk about one. Speaking of which, have you called Susan yet?" Barbara's blue eyes, dark and deep and full of mischief, bore into him. "I'll take that as a no. Any particular reason this time? Maybe she's got a third leg? Doesn't brush her teeth? God forbid she's a Republican..."

"She's Canadian, you know that."

"Doesn't mean she can't be nasty."

Bill craned his neck and peeked over Barbara's slim shoulder to see if Maria was listening. He lowered his voice. "We're going for coffee on Friday," he said.

"Stop the presses."

"It's a start, and it's all I got in me, maybe *all* I'll ever have in me again. Sometimes I think it would be easier to swear off dating for the rest of my life. Ugh. Even the word *dating* sounds cheesy to me. I don't remember it being this hard when I started seeing Diana."

Barbara clasped his fingers. "That's because your heart did the work for you. Now you've got *her*, your head has to do the heavy-lifting." They watched Maria mimic the program she was watching, something with zombie princesses that she knew line for line, and their conversation grew quiet until Maria asked for a glass of orange juice with precisely thirty-seven ice cubes.

That sounded good to Bill. He got them each a glass, taking care to crush Maria's ice in case she decided to count. He drank his down then added sparkling water to the cubes in his glass and held it to the side of his neck. He sighed. Not yet noon and the day was becoming a scorcher. Already, heat baked through the inner walls of the old apartment. Even with the blinds drawn to keep out the sun and the windows open to let in the breeze, they were sweating and the butter he put out had melted a river over the side of the dish and onto the table.

Barbara rolled up her sleeves and fanned her face. "Tell me why we live in a building without air conditioning?"

Bill took the towel off his shoulder and wiped his forehead with it. "It's home."

"Ah. That. While we're on the subject, I think the boy's *living* in that god-awful motel. Maybe I'm wrong, but I've offered to take him to the apartment he *swears* he lives in, but there's always an excuse to drop him where his mother works, even when she's not working. Before you ask, *yes*, I did a little digging myself. I more or less know her schedule, so I know when I've been put on. That's no place for a child. Prostitutes and pimps crawling all over. You know I had someone offer to sell me whatever I wanted? He was quite a persistent fellow. I told him that if I wanted screw a pudgy bum with a receding hairline, I'd go to one of the Johnson's swinger parties and swap keys with someone's husband."

Water sprayed from Bill's mouth. "You didn't."

She slapped the table. "Of course I did. And then he offered me a little of this, a little of that, all the highest grade, naturally. *Definitely* not mixed by some trafficked children sweating at gunpoint in a shack in Columbia. You bet I told him what he could do with *that*." She swatted the air as if sweeping away a mosquito, and though her skin was dampened with sweat, she shuddered. "It's no place for an *adult*, let alone a child. I'm wondering if a call to Child Services might be in order? I don't want to poke my nose in their business, but that's no place for him. I can't help but worry if my offer to see him home safely is going to be short-lived because he just won't *be* there one day."

Her eyes stretched with concern, and they shared the terrible understanding that Luke wasn't experiencing a cartoon childhood but one of the unfortunate infomercial-types where the kids went to school without breakfast after a night without dinner and returned home to police cars and whispering neighbors.

He went to the sink and splashed water on his face, on the back of his neck, wishing that he could scoop Luke from that corrosive environment. The longer he knew the boy, the stronger his paternal current leaned toward him. His tidal concern, rising, rising, flooded his good sense so that when Luke wasn't at the So-Lo, all Bill could think about was whether he was eating enough, where he was sleeping, if his father had been released from prison—but mostly Bill wondered if he was safe. It kept him up at night. It ate at him during the day. It muddled his work.

Their crime-scene discovery had only made things worse.

Unaccustomed to Bill fainting, Luke hadn't understood that he was still alive. Apparently, the boy beat his chest trying to revive him, but Bill didn't remember any of that. The moment he had seen the blood beneath the conveyor, spread wide and wet, Bill's body did what it always did during times of stress: it shut down. He was out before he hit the ground, and it was the sickening *thunk* of his shoulder hitting the floor that made Luke turn to see what had happened. He'd seen Bill's face mashed up against the piss-stained linoleum, right next to a wad of gum and the sharp end of a hypodermic needle. Luke rolled him over, checked his vitals as best as a panicked thirteen-year-old boy could, and banged Bill around to restart the heart that hadn't stopped. Then he dug his thin fingers into Bill's pocket and drew out his phone.

The police arrived in minutes.

As it turned out, there was no crime. Or if there had been, both the victim and the perpetrator had fled. Less likely, the police contended, was the possibility that the perpetrator carried his or her victim away, since there were no drag marks and no drops of fresh blood beyond what was under the conveyor. Even the most vigilant criminals tended to leave evidence, they told him, but the evidence simply was not there.

After Bill fended off the paramedic's attempts to examine him, he gave his statement to the police, who waited for Ruby to arrive before taking Luke's. She sat quiet with her jaw clenched while Luke answered the constable's questions, occasionally twirling the tuft of hair at the back of his neck whenever his answers garnered an appreciative nod. When it was over, they were dismissed with Constable Brander's pledge to keep them informed on the outcome of the investigation. It wasn't long before Brander made good on his promise, sounding just as perplexed as Luke and Bill had been.

"I checked the Garrett General and all the clinics in the city, but there were no reports of injury that couldn't be explained; none that would have done what we saw, anyway," Brander had said on the phone. "There are a few folks that like to stick around that area, looking for cures where there aren't any, if you know what I mean. We checked in on them and not a single one is missing a limb. No backroom births either. Unless someone comes forward with more information, I'm afraid we don't have anything to investigate. My guess is some animal got caught in the wrong place at the wrong time."

But Bill hadn't believed that. There were no signs of anything but from beasts of the human variety. The kind that got high, got revenge, got into trouble because life wasn't already trouble enough. The only kind of animal that willfully wrecked their bodies *and* their minds. He'd thought to ask Brander how they could tell the difference between human and animal blood.

"That's the forensics team's department," Brander had said. "Something to do with coagulation when they mix it with something. I can't explain the science behind it, Bill; there are far more capable people than myself who can tell you how it works, but this isn't our first rodeo. We may be a small department, but we share resources across the province, sometimes the country. If there's something to find, we'll do our best to find it." There was a pause on the line and Bill thought Brander had gotten disconnected, but then Brander said, "I'm sure it's not an animal, Bill, but doesn't it sound better to think it is? Don't go calling PETA on me, I've got three dogs, two cats, and whatever my boys've caught and hidden in their rooms. Wouldn't have it any other way. I'm just saying that sometimes it's better to believe a lesser evil so you can sleep at night. In my line of work, I don't get that option very often because I have to follow facts, but before science tells me where to go, I still like to think things aren't as bad as they seem. Understand what I'm trying to say?"

"I do," Bill told him.

"If we find anything, we'll let you know. In the meantime, I'd advise you and Luke to stay away from the area. There's more danger and dirt than anything else down that block and I wouldn't enjoy attending a *real* crime scene on your behalf, if you get me."

Bill did. Brander's advice was solid enough as far as Bill was concerned, but not for a boy who had little choice but to traverse the neighborhood. Luke simply did not have another option. Ruby worked and lived at the Dirty, which meant that Luke was stuck with bedbugs and pushers and prostitutes. Worse, the peddlers would close in on him the older he got, if they hadn't succeeded already. As for Ruby, it was obvious she had the same concerns for her son but was in no position to remedy the situation, and likely never would be.

Had it been Maria to discover the blood, Bill's decision would have been swift. He would have forbidden her to go anywhere near the neighborhood. Of course, neither he nor Maria needed money badly enough to jeopardize her safety, and Bill would die before he would ever let it come to that. Ruby, however, had little choice. The events of her life had led her to where she was. Whether it was lack of opportunity, degenerate partners, or perhaps she had been borne into the whirlwind of destitution and it refused to spit her out—whatever the case, she was desperate. Desperate enough that she wouldn't hear of Luke and Bill terminating their arrangement so Luke wouldn't be forced to pass the area by himself.

The suggestion was half-hearted, conveyed with no more conviction than a couch potato has for running a marathon, but it had to be offered for Bill to be at peace with himself. As sole proprietor of the So-Lo, it would next to impossible for him to commit to driving Luke to and from the building on a regular basis. Most days he was already slammed with paperwork, not to mention supply issues that never seemed to go away. On top of that, he ran a lean schedule with little overlap. As much as he liked the boy, he knew that any promises he made to see him safely to work would amount to a burden that could see the So-Lo's delicate bottom line turn red.

The woman loved her son—that much Bill couldn't deny—but it bothered him that she seemed much less concerned with Luke's safety than *he* was. Sure, she could forbid him to enter any more boarded-up buildings, but what of the dangers outside these spaces? For a neighborhood rife with "danger and dirt," as Brander had so aptly described it, the safety zone was eyelash-narrow.

Once the police had dismissed them, Bill walked Ruby and Luke back to the Dirty, where Ruby returned to her shift under the slimy eye of the paunchy manager. "Food ain't providing itself," Ruby said, and left the two of them without another word.

When a cockroach crawled over Bill's shoe, he asked Luke if the boy still wanted to work at the So-Lo. Luke's teary-eyed affirmation brought them back to the store that afternoon, where Bill leaned on his support network to help him through another bind. It took him all of three minutes before Barbara insisted on accompanying Luke to and from the motel.

"I carry bear spray and a rape whistle in my purse," she said. "Thankfully, I haven't had use for them yet, but I've been dying to try them out."

That was weeks ago. So far, the arrangement had gone off without any trouble. Barbara carried herself as woman who would take not an ounce of sass so that despite her small stature, locals near the Dirty were increasingly giving her space.

Presently, she said, "I'm not trying to get the boy taken from his mother, but I don't see how any good can come from him living in that filthy motel."

"We're not his parents."

"Sadly, no."

"But we can keep him employed and fed as best we can, and if he ever needs somewhere to go my hope is that he'll know we'll always have room for him." Bill put the container of pancakes in a plastic bag and added another of cut cucumbers and carrots on top, knotting the bag before handing it to Barbara.

"You're a good man, Bill Asket. Don't let it go to waste. Take Susan for *dinner* on Friday. A man's got to eat and a woman hates doing dishes. You both win that way." Barbara stood and stretched her spine. She took the bag from Bill and gave Maria a kiss on the top of her head. "Hey, munchkin. There's a new Disney movie coming out on Friday. Want to be my date?"

Maria's squeal practically shredded their eardrums.

"Looks like you're free on Friday. If you don't make a reservation somewhere half-decent, you bet I'll let Maria decide how much butter to put on our popcorn and we'll put handprints all over your couch when we come back."

Even though she winked, Bill knew she would make good on her warning.

11

Today was the day. In the pre-dawn hours of a soon-to-be scorching morning, Cody woke alert and ready. He glided off the mattress, lifted his fingers to the sky, rose on the tips of his toes, and thanked his new friend for another glorious sleep. It didn't answer, of course, but it vibrated to let Cody know he was welcome.

The last few weeks had been incredible for Cody. After making peace with his new appendage, his life had turned around exponentially. Slick—the name he'd given to his little friend after testing dozens of monikers on it only to have it pull him toward the TV when a cheesy infomercial for an automated home control system, *Slick Click*, came on—was nothing short of a marvel. Sure, it was getting a little large, almost the size of Cody's own hand, and if it kept growing at the same rate, it would soon be impossible to conceal. But the short time Slick had been with Cody made him increasingly feel it was better than winning the lottery. Exponentially better. The lottery didn't make you stronger. The lottery didn't make you smarter. It didn't make your pocked skin turn smooth or your deserted-island ribs fill to muscle in the span of a vacation. No. The lottery did none of those things. Was it, too, that he'd grown *longer*? *Bigger*, even? The lottery certainly the fuck did not do that. No sir. The bigger bulge in his shorts was no happy hard-on that went away after a yank. It stayed. There it was now, down the leg of his boxer shorts, a better version of himself than he'd ever been. All because of Slick.

He smiled and looked in the mirror. Even *that* was better. The drug-crumbled gums, almost impossible to ignore, were now a very healthy pink. The rusted enamel that made women squirm and sidestep away had faded. His teeth hadn't been this nice in years, yet now they were shining back at him in the mirror. Borderline bright. And the same even could be said for his brain. He *got* things that used to be beyond his understanding and caused him to withdraw so others didn't see his eyes glaze over with dumbness. Things were also starting to make sense. Like politics. Before, he'd avoided political discussion as much as Terry avoided hygiene, not because it didn't matter to him but simply because Cody had had a hard time keeping everything straight. Liberals, Conservatives, atheists, they had been all the same to him, and perhaps still were, but the lines were becoming clearer as Slick sharpened his perception. Now, for instance, Cody grasped the concepts of immigration reform, egalitarianism, the issues with Canada's technically multiparty (but actually two-party) system that held the country in an expensive pendulous state wherein change almost always *changed back* with each election.

It was like Cody had learned a new language. Ideas once foreign to him had become part of his own language, and he could thank Slick for it. More—and this was something of which he was certain—people now took to him like they hadn't since he was a buck-eyed child. He was asked for directions instead of avoided like the drifters that sometimes lurked outside the liquor stores until far past closing. Women way beyond his level sought him out, asking him for help with really not-so-heavy items at the store, then slipped their phone numbers into his hand with a wink and sometimes, tits be to shit, puckered and blew him a kiss. Even Whitney had shown up at the house one afternoon with regret on her face and nothing on under her skirt.

In his past life, Cody might have taken her right there and then just to remind her what she'd lost when she left him for Jimmy, but he didn't for two reasons. First, he'd heard that she'd been not only with Jimmy but with at least three other guys since they'd broken up, one who was rumored to be spreading the clap to half of the city, and another who, word had it, had something much worse. Secondly, even if Whitney had turned celibate, there was the predicament of how to hide Slick. You could only fuck with your shirt on so many times before your partner wondered if you were hiding a rash or not interested enough to spend the extra few seconds to remove your clothes. Once or twice it might work, but eventually suspicion would outgrow the relationship. The last few weeks had gone so well for Cody, there was nothing he wouldn't do to protect his new friend and keep him hidden. Not that Cody himself was celibate. *Whitney* might pose a problem, but new women certainly did not. The way women threw themselves at him lately made hasty relations easy, even *expected*. All he had to do was unzip. Nothing had to come off.

Slick quivered against his skin. Cody took the jar of honey off his desk and slathered Slick with it. The amber liquid became the consistency of water and, as quick as a snap, was sucked into Slick's soft body. Instantly Cody felt as though he'd drunk a coffee. Energy rushed through his veins, torrented through his blood.

"Good morning to you, too," he said down to Slick, and while Slick didn't talk, it pushed its acknowledgement to Cody's brain.

That was another thing about Slick. The bigger it got, the more Cody came to understand it. He—Cody believed Slick was a *he* for no other reason than because Cody was a *he*—made known his wishes not only by tugging, pulling, pinching, and kneading but by, well . . . Cody thought there was some sort of thought osmosis there, if that were such a thing. Easy questions —if Slick liked a particular program or wanted banana cream pie, for instance—were almost always answered physically with discomfort or pleasure, but the deeper questions, like where Slick had come from, were either avoided entirely or shoved into Cody's psyche. This was how Cody discovered that Slick was, in varying parts: cocaine, heroin, meth, Oxy, watered-down beer, tequila, tears, whatever viruses and bacteria Can-Do's floors were scabbed with, and fuckloads of his own blood. All smashed together like a peanut butter and jelly sandwich, with a few crawly things on top. That Slick was his own creation, as though Cody had somehow *fathered* the creature, should have put him off, but instead it made Cody feel as intelligent as Dr. Frankenstein, and as powerful as the spark that gave his monster life.

Dressing now in the bathroom, Cody removed the bandage he'd taped over Slick and watched him come alive. Tiny manus (a word that had come to him in his sleep), stretched outward with fingers that undulated in the humid air. One, two, sixteen strings uncoiled and *breathed* the scent of Cody's body spray, swaying this way and that like weeds at the bottom of a lake. Warmth spread from his side.

"Like that one, huh? I thought so. Got to be on my game today. No shenanigans if she says no, you hear? She doesn't like it when you change me like that. It scares her. I've put her through enough without making her feel like she's going crazy." He cocked an eye at Slick in the mirror. The manus crisscrossed like an indignant teenager. "I mean it. Just her, okay? Be nice. If she kicks us out, we have nowhere else to go. She's the reason we get to eat. You like to eat, don't you?"

Slick rose and fell, rose and fell; a ripple of thick jelly with the personality of a class clown when it was happy, a tyrant when it was not. Right now, it was somewhere in between.

Cody dressed in a smart pair of slacks (his *power pants*, his grandmother called them) and a clean white shirt. Slick didn't mind the shirt as long as it was thin and there was space to peek between the buttons. Together they left the bathroom and went upstairs to make breakfast.

In his former life Cody could barely figure out the toaster, but now he was whisking eggs, chopping spinach and chives, and squeezing oranges while the coffee brewed. He added a layer of the strawberry jam he'd made a few days before to his grandmother's toast, then brought it to her spot at the table. She shuffled in a moment later, tying the belt on her robe.

"Holy smackers, you spoil me. You make me wish I'd been a widow much earlier, Cody. If I'da known you could do this when Grandpa was alive, I might be a divorcee instead. Save *all* of us a world of trouble."

"That's not nice, Grandma." Cody poured her coffee. "He wasn't so bad."

"I'll tell your father you said that." She filled her mouth with omelet and pointed her fork at him. "And speaking of the *vanished*, have you spoken to him lately?"

Even with Cody's new health, his father was still a touchy subject and Slick knew it. He started to feel the thing Slick did whenever he was irritated on Cody's behalf. Darkening Cody's irises. Reddening the whites around them. Sallowing his skin. Veining out the skin on his neck. If he let Slick go on, Cody would look like a poisoning victim, minutes from death. Internally he'd be fine, but externally he'd look like a fresh bolt of hell. It was Slick's way of letting others know that his host was untouchable, though it'd really only happened to his grandmother a few times before. She eyed him curiously and shook her head as though to clear away an apparition.

He turned his back to his grandmother and pressed his forearm to his side. The reflection in the window above the sink would have made him piss himself if it weren't his own, and he turned on the tap forcefully as a warning to the creature on his side. His color normalized. "Mom says he's been busy with work. No, don't say it, Grandma. I know we should talk, but I can't make him do it if he doesn't want to. I messed up too many times—"

"You're his son, for feather's sake." She banged the table with the end of her fork. Spinach omelet dropped onto her knuckle.

Elanor leaned over her plate and sucked the omelet up. "I don't need to see your face to know you're mocking me, Cody Clyde. Take that smile off your face, boy."

"Sometimes you need to swear, Grandma. Feathers just doesn't have the punch you want it to." Elanor swatted the air with her hand. "Oh! You know what I mean without me having to say it. I'm angry, Cody, is that what you want to hear? That son of mine had his own chances when he was younger, and did I disown his high and mighty rear end when he stepped off the straight and narrow? You bet I did nothing of the sort. He might not've had substance issues, but he got himself in a world of trouble borrowing money he couldn't pay back without our help."

Cody's eyes went wide.

"You don't think I wanted a bigger house? A nicer neighborhood? I'm not saying he's the whole reason we're not living like the Penners or the Botchers, but he's part of it. He'd hang himself before he ever let *you* know that, of course. You know what I think? I think it's not *you* he's avoiding, but the ghost of his own mistakes. He doesn't want to be reminded what a devil he was." She slurped her coffee, wiping her mouth with the back of a hand. "I raised him better than that. Sorry, Cody."

"It's not your fault, Grandma. Besides, why would I want to talk to him when I've got you to bother?" He returned to the table and sat, then nudged her slippered foot with his toe.

"Every man needs a father, Cody. Even a shitty one." Elanor gasped at herself. She pressed a fist to her mouth. "See? He's not even here and look what he does to me."

"Don't get yourself all worked up," he said, and snatched her empty plate when she made to rise.

Her grey eyes speared him. "You've outdone yourself with breakfast, and the house is so clean it's almost sterile. Consider me appropriately buttered, Cody. What do you want?" She saw the answer on his tongue, stuck there as though she'd fastened it with her observation. "You're dressed for a high-rise and behaving like I'm the Queen of England. Out with it before I say no."

The tingling down his spine told Cody it was only a matter of time before Slick disinterred that darkness again. As long as he remained calm, Slick would remain calm. He let a breath out, took another one in and said, "I want to go to school."

Elanor's mouth dropped open.

Cody raised his hands. "I know I'm supposed to be paying rent, but I thought about it and I think—I *know*—it's time for me to get serious about my future. My grades weren't the best in high school, but they weren't bad either. I wasn't, as you like to say, *in the sewer* yet."

"You've looked into this?"

He nodded. "It's not law or medicine or anything like that—"

"Don't sell yourself short." She wagged a finger at him.

"I don't deserve you, Grandma."

"I've been telling you that for years."

"Anyway," Cody said. "There's a program in London I'm interested in. In Social Work. I figure I have enough experience not getting things right that I know how to keep them from going wrong for other people. Give back a little and get a degree while I'm at it. There's still room for me if I wanted to go in September. And it's close enough that I could drive in every day, as long as you let me stay here. But I'd have to apply now. The counselor I talked to says she'd take my application if I got it in this week." Speaking, Cody liked how Slick polished his words, elevated them from the gunk a sewer rat would spew to something at least moderately intelligent—convincing, even.

Elanor rubbed her chin, considering. "They give you a scholarship for passing the pee test at Henley?" They both knew she was stalling to make him squirm, though the wait was only uncomfortable for Cody. "This conversation giving you cramps?" she asked, gesturing to the hand on his side.

"Dehydrated," he told her, straightening despite the pain.

At that very moment, Tinker came into the kitchen and rubbed against Elanor's leg. She went to the cupboard under the sink, fetched the bag of treats, and scattered a few across the floor. Tinker scrambled after them, but when the cat neared Cody's foot, it sprang backward and hissed. Cody's eyes flashed dark, only for a second, but Tinker growled and bolted out of the room.

"You'd think you stepped on his tail, running like that . . ." Elanor looked over the serving hatch and spied the cat huddling under the couch.

"He's just mad I didn't give him bacon today."

"How much do you need, Cody? Besides free room and board. Let's hear it while the breakfast is still calming me." Her hands went to her hips.

He faced her again, saw her tapping foot, her chin thrust forward, and couldn't help cowering a little. "It's too late to apply for a student loan for this semester, otherwise I would . . ."

"How much?"

"Ten thousand," he said and was surprised when she didn't flinch. Instead, Elanor sighed through her nose and folded her arms across her belly. Cody knew to wait while she turned the request over in her head. But Slick wasn't so patient. Cody's new cheeks sucked inward. His smooth skin withered like an apple. His lower eyelids collapsed into a curtain of sagging skin, black with rot.

Air whooshed into Elanor's lungs.

"Grandma?" Cody said, knowing with certainty what Slick had done to him, but hoping to pass it off as an early morning, *your-coffee-hasn't-kicked-in-yet* hallucination.

Elanor turned her head, sure she wasn't seeing quite right. Then she reached toward the table and threw her orange juice at him. Suddenly, Cody was just Cody again. His carcass filled with health and life. His disemboweled face gathered the way it should, the way it had been, right before Elanor's seventy-six-year-old eyes. Her fingers went to her mouth.

"What happened to your face? You . . . I saw . . . but . . . oh, God, oh, God, I'm sorry. What've I done to you? What was I thinking? Lord, what's *happening* to me?" Her old hands reached for him, trying to take back her reaction, her *fear* of losing her mind like some of her friends. Then she did something much worse than throwing juice at him. Then and there, in their kitchen in the middle of the morning after a beautiful breakfast, Elanor cried.

If Slick wasn't attached to him like a barnacle on a boat, Cody would have removed his wet shirt and dried off with a dish towel. Rather, he slipped out of his grandmother's grip, retrieved the roll of paper towel and began blotting himself, dabbing extra hard where Slick was. "I knew it was a lot of money," he chuckled ineffectually, "but I didn't think I'd get this reaction."

"It's not the money!" Elanor howled at him. "Of course it's not the money, Cody. I don't have much, but whatever I have is yours. You know that. You're all I've got. But of course now that you're all fixed up, *I'm* the one to lose my marbles. Like *I'm* doing those drugs or something." Her face paled and when she spoke again, her words were a low boil, simmering with alarm. "Is that it? Have you slipped me drugs, Cody? Is that why you've been doing all the cooking lately? I won't be mad, just tell me . . . was there something in my food? Did you do this to me?"

The way her bottom lip trembled, the way her fear played out from the shaking of her stomach to the twitching of her eyes, Cody wished he could tell her there *was* something in the eggs. That there wasn't a creature playing Pictionary with his skin every time it was trying to get its own way. "I wouldn't do that to you, Grandma. Never. And I'm clean, remember? I swore I would never do it again, and I haven't. Not a drop of anything. I swear."

Elanor clamped a hand over her mouth, squeezing her chin until loose folds of skin seeped between her fingers like overrisen dough. Her eyes popped open. "Oh God! Listen to me! I'm going crazy. I must be. Of *course* you're sober. Of course you are. I didn't mean to say that you weren't, after all the work you've done. I don't know what's come over me lately. Don't listen to a word I say. None of it." She took the roll from him and dabbed until he gently swatted her away.

While it did play in Cody's favor for her to believe her mind was malfunctioning, especially while Slick was part of the household, he didn't like the pain it caused the only person who'd been there for him. He tried to soothe her. "When's the last time you had a check-up, Grandma?"

Elanor flinched. "I *am* going crazy, aren't I?"

"No," he said. "I don't think that at all. But when I was in Henley, they taught us that chemical imbalances can make us feel that way and that *drugs* weren't going to make us feel better but proper nutrition, rest, and vitamins. Maybe you're low in something. There was a guy on my floor who thought he was seeing things, but it turned out he was just low in vitamin D. He was better after they figured it out." It wasn't true, but when Slick pushed the story into his head, Cody knew it was the right thing to say.

"Maybe I should see a doctor. You think I should, Cody?"

"I'd suggest starting with vitamins, first. Get some sleep, too." Wet shirt and all, he gave her a one-armed hug, careful to keep his other elbow between Slick and her body, but the swell of her belly folded around him. For a moment, he thought she'd sensed Slick, but when she pulled back there was no curiosity on her face.

She sat again, this time with her elbows on the table and her lips against her steepled fingers. She said feebly, "I'll try anything you tell me to." A glint passed over her faraway eyes, her remembering face. "I don't mean to sound condescending, so please don't take it that way, but you were so low, Cody. Probably the lowest a human can get, that I've seen anyway. I didn't ever know how *dead* a person could be while still alive, but there you were, in the living room, your whole body bleeding like a head wound. And you know what? It wasn't the blood that scared me. It should have, but it didn't. It was your eyes, because there was nothing in them. All that blood, but it's your eyes that I'll never forget. They were *empty*. So empty. And the stranger thing is that now they're all filled up again. I don't think Henley did that to you. Addicts don't just roll out like summer peaches. They fall out of those kinds of places with bruises and hurt that sometimes never goes away. Even with all the sunshine in the world pointed at them, they have a hard time outgrowing the rot inside them. I saw a counselor of my own when you were in there and I figured out a few things for myself. I know there's more to why you changed so much."

"Oh?" Cody said, for Slick's ready reply had not reached his tongue. He wondered for a moment if the orange juice had killed Slick, but the thought was immediately countered with movement against his side.

Elanor said, "I think you did it yourself. You got *yourself* out of that sewer. You crawled out of those pipes and you closed the lid on that life. That's what I think you did."

Cody relaxed. "I'm trying, Grandma."

"Don't say it like that. You're not trying, Cody, you've *done* it. Look at you. Filled out like an athlete, spit-shiny new from morning until night. You even talk different. You think about things now, Cody. Real things. Important things. And people are talking about you. I ran into Catherine Beecher the other day and she said you carried her groceries to her car without her even having to ask you. In all these years, I don't think I've ever seen you do that. And Dr. Huxley said he saw you coming out of the pharmacy when you picked up my prescriptions, and he was so impressed with your improvement he told me you must've found some miracle cure for life and that whatever regimen you're on should be prescribed to all his patients."

I'm no saint," he said.

"I'm not saying you are. I'm saying that I want *you* to tell me what to do so I can have a little of what you have. I don't want to wake up tired anymore. I don't want to see things that aren't there. I don't have the option of quitting my job, but I also don't want to feel needles in my knees when the day's done. I think you can help me with that. I really do. Anything has got to be better than the way my bones and my brain have been feeling lately. I'll take the vitamins and eat kale until the toilet's green if that's what it takes. But I can't do it by myself. I wouldn't know how to begin if I tried. And if after you're done with me and I'm no better, poison me and bury me out back with the cats."

The muscles in her face tightened and Cody saw that she was serious. He went to the coffee pot and filled her cup. "I'm no miracle worker, Grandma."

"Yet there's a miracle pouring my coffee."

He sighed. "I can't promise anything."

"I'm not expecting you to."

For a time, they drank in silence. Tinker, still under the couch, let out an occasional hiss to let them know he was still there. When Elanor excused herself to take a shower, Cody did the dishes and returned to the basement, where he removed his wet shirt.

Slick had grown.

The mound on his side, that morning about the size of his hand, now stretched from his navel in the front to his spine in the back, like a flattened reptilian football suctioned to him. Ligaments of fear tensed throughout his body, as if to squeeze away the invader, but Slick either took no notice or couldn't be bothered to reprimand Cody. He knew Cody needed him. He knew if Cody somehow managed to purge him from his home that, like a peach from a tree, Cody would rot. His skin would wilt. His body would deflate. His allure would take an about-face and he would once again be the corroded, loathsome maggot everyone knew him to be.

"You're nothing but trouble," Cody said down to him. "You couldn't be nice just for one minute? Just one? She didn't do anything wrong. But you go and freak her out because she's not bowing down quick enough. Honestly. What the fuck good are you if you act out like that, huh? I could have had you cut off me, you know that? The doctors would have put you in one of those jars and studied you for science. How'd you like to have them poke around and slice you up? I can still do it, you know. I don't care what you've done for me. She's off limits. I told you that."

The manus on his side ruffled, but no thoughts were pushed into his head, which Cody thought was good. It was important to make sure Slick knew who the boss was. "If you want to stay with me, you have to listen to me. My rules, or I don't care what happens to either of us."

There was silence on his mind. No pain or pleasure driven about his body.

"Tell me you understand," Cody ordered.

Accents of understanding came at him then. Lifted and lilted with a gentle massage to his torso, a hug to his heart. A peaceful melody unrolled within him.

"Okay, then. I'm glad we agree." Because Slick seemed sulky, if that were possible for such a creature, Cody added, "I don't want you to think I don't appreciate what you've done for me, it's been great, but we've got to think about the long term. If this is going to work, we can't mess with people. I know you're learning, though, so I can't be too hard on you. We good?"

Slick's hide came up and went down in agreement.

That night, with his grandmother mollified and the house once again in order, a ripple of discomfort in Cody's side woke him. He thought he'd accidentally rolled over on top of Slick, as had happened before, but when he felt around he found he was on his free side and that Slick wasn't against the mattress. Sleep overtook him a few minutes later, but he was soon awakened again with that same ripple of pain.

He sat up and turned on his bedside light. Cody gasped.

In the few hours since he'd gone to bed, Slick had become engorged. From end to end, Slick's body was swollen, his hide ballooned out to the half-dome of a soccer ball. Stretched so tight Cody was sure it was going to burst. Squinting, he spied a heaving network of arteries through the overtaxed membrane that beat to the same rhythm of his own heart. He gulped. "What's going on?" he whispered, afraid to wake his grandmother. "Are you okay? What's happening?"

No response.

The dull ache that woke him was growing sharper now. Cody's entire abdomen began to tremble, and he sucked in a breath and clenched his teeth until the pain subsided. "Are you dying? Is this what happens to me if you die?" he moaned.

No response.

The fear that he'd irrevocably angered the creature sprang to his mind. "Look. I'm sorry, okay? Is that what you want to hear? I get it. I was too hard on you. I won't do it again. Just—"

The membrane pulsated. In, out, in, out, like a panting dog.

Cody howled into his pillow, again, again, sure he was being *severed*. Skin from muscles. Muscles from bone. Filleted like a fish. But then, as quickly as it had come, the pain subsided. The pillow came away wet from his face. "You *are* mad at me," he illogically cried down to the parasite.

Then the panting grew quicker. The arteries beat faster. A sudden clap of pressure squeezed him. He let out the air he'd been holding. It crackled back in. Out once more. In . . . but the pain was too severe for Cody to open his throat and fill his lungs. Pricks of light took over his vision, exploding stars drawing him toward oblivion. In his periphery, gloom descended, syphoning all color, all light. He was on the verge of passing out when the pressure let up and the darkness receded.

His first words once he was able to catch his breath were a cacophony of expletives. He wiped his eyes, understanding in this moment of agony how foolish he had been to let Slick stay. The weight of his blanket, now heavy as a sack of bricks, hurt his legs, and he shucked the blanket off. The sheet went too. Fully undressed but for his underwear, Cody yelped at the sight of himself. His veins were the darkest blue. His creamy skin was now mottled red.

"Don't be like that," he pleaded. "I didn't do anything wrong. I—"

Cody was stabbed. From the inside. From the outside. Everywhere, he felt the blade. He cried out. Above him, the sound of his grandmother stirring in her bed brought even greater terror. If Slick could hurt him like this, he could hurt his grandmother too. Cody fought against the pain. He bore down, gritting his teeth, tensing his entire body, quiet but for the howls he now trapped inside his mouth. Freely crying, sure he was dying, Cody trembled. With his last vestiges of strength, he pointed his finger at the engorged bubble on his side. Then he pressed.

An extraordinary burst of pain tore through his body. It curled his toes. It bent his fingers. It stopped all other functions required for life.

Then it was over.

By some miracle, Cody was still alive. He relaxed his taut body onto the sweaty sheets and looked down.

The bubble had deflated.

But now there was a tiny red-brown speck next to Slick, just above Cody's navel. A replica of Slick when Cody had first discovered him.

Then Cody understood. To make peace with Cody and to help his grandmother, Slick had produced another like him—or *her*—self.

Slick had given Cody a baby.

12

Every August for the last twenty-two years, the Cruising Conway Carnival spread its temptation along the fairgrounds on the northeastern edge of the city. The roadshow, anticipated by young and old alike, fanned midway sounds and midway smells for four quick days, until teeth and stomachs were adequately rotted and wallets were more than adequately emptied. Only those who'd battled the lighting-quick hands and time-sure deceptions of the game-dealers had any reason to frown during this sugar-coated period, but Barbara, Martin, and Jasper plodded into the So-Lo with Luke that Saturday afternoon with faces as gloomy as mourners at a funeral.

On his knees restocking his regular customers' favorite varieties of Chunky Soup, Bill saw the melancholy on the adults and stood. He was about to point out their long faces but held the observation when Barbara gave him a look and darted her eyes toward the boy.

Bill jerked a thumb at Martin and Jasper and said to Luke, "How were our boys on their maiden voyage? They give you any trouble? You manage to get Jasper to shut up for once?"

Already trudging to the table by the window, Jasper didn't respond to the quip, which told Bill that something had happened.

Luke put his knapsack in his cubby behind the counter, laughing. "He's embarrassed because he farted."

At this, Barbara couldn't help but grin as she joined the men at the table. "It wasn't *really* a fart, though, was it Luke? More of a squeak." She winked at Jasper, whose attention was out the window on the other side of the street, anywhere but at the table. "Anyway, we don't really know it was Jasper, do we? Maybe it was *me* that greeted us like that. I did meet your father, and men do that to me sometimes. They rattle my stomach. Can't help it." Barbara held Bill's curious stare.

That Barbara, of all people, seemed to be defending Jasper— the man whose eyes were permanently fixed on her chest, whose hands more than once stole squeezes of her rear, and whose mouth uttered the most sexualized and profane overtures— suggested to Bill that hell had frozen over.

Martin rested his cane against his thigh. "I'd like to make an offer," he said loudly. "But I'm not going to do it in front of Eager Ears over there. Bill, how 'bout you send Luke to collect Maria so we adults can plan ways to annoy and bore them for the rest of the day?" He accepted a cup of coffee from Bill, wrapping his big hands around the paper until the cup all but disappeared.

"Sounds good to me," Bill told him, and turned toward the counter. "Luke, while you're up there, grab the snack tray from the fridge and bring it down. And make sure Maria brushes her hair. She seems to be allergic to it lately, but maybe you can convince her she won't die without all the knots near her ears."

Luke sped away.

They watched the interior door slowly close, not a single word spoken among them until the click of the plunger whiplashed their attention back to Bill. "Someone tell me what's going on before they get back. You met his father, I take it? Everything all right?"

Jasper grunted. "Some father. Man's a criminal. They shouldn't let him around that boy."

"Or that woman," Barbara added of Luke's mother, Ruby, recalling the finger-shaped bruises on the other woman's collarbone.

A customer came in then. Bill acknowledged Mrs. Grimly with a wave and vaguely kept an eye on the counter while Barbara, Martin, and Jasper recounted their story to him.

It went like this:

An hour before, Jasper and Martin had surprised Barbara when they showed up at her apartment to escort her to what they called "the shit side of the city." By now her routine was common knowledge among the So-Lo's patrons, as was the fact that until the previous weekend Barbara's trips to the Dirty were mostly uneventful. All that changed, however, when last Sunday morning Barbara came upon two men and a woman collapsed on top of each other near the motel's dilapidated office, four doors away from Luke and his mother's room. The reek of sweat, vomit, and alcohol would be enough to warn anyone away, but Luke needed an escort and Barbara knew better than to go around the back of the motel to approach Luke's room from the opposite direction. The front, at least, was on a busy street where there could be *witnesses,* should anything happen. She gave the tangled trio a wide berth, a good fifty feet or so, keeping an eye on them the whole time.

It was a mistake.

With her eyes entirely on the drunk pile, Barbara didn't see the shirtless and shoeless man lurking in the shadow of the stairwell at the opposite end of the building until it was too late. He snatched the back of her shirt, managing to untuck her blouse from the waistband of her pants. She spun around so fast the momentum of her body yanked him against her. She came inches away from the angry red sores blistering his face, his dark matted hair, his wild, surprised eyes. Barbara screamed. On a shiny Sunday morning. In the middle of a parking lot on a street already lively with activity, Barbara Panks screamed for her life. Then she hit him, ineffectually clipping the top of his left shoulder with the diamond ring she had bought herself on a whim last February. Either too high or too drunk, the stunned man did not let go but stood there, blinking, swaying as though using Barbara's blouse to hold himself up. She did not want to touch his horrible face, sure she'd break through his paper-mâché skin and plunge her hand into the diseased pulp of his brain. But Barbara Panks was also not ready to forfeit her golden years to the grimy hands of this shell of a human, either. She reared her hand back, readied her fingers, and thrust the manicured index and middle fingers of her right hand into the man's eyes.

That did it.

He let go of her shirt with a yowl then stumbled backward, catching the back of his ankle on a parking barrier. Unable to recover his balance, he fell against a motel room window already webbed with cracks and broke right through. The sound woke the drunks and they began moving too, not yet at their feet but waking when they didn't want to be waked, groggy and growling. While the shirtless man thrashed in the windowpane, pawing at his eyes and the cuts to his spine, Barbara dashed to Luke's room and banged on the door.

As usual, he was ready and opened it on the second knock. The sounds outside the room would have terrified almost any child she knew, especially her own when they were younger, but not Luke. He took one look at Barbara's panicked face, glanced down the paint-chipped walkway toward the action, exited the room, and closed the door behind him. Like witnesses to a traffic accident, their heads had swiveled to the commotion in the broken window as they passed, where a startled old man and much younger woman hurried sheets over their naked bodies. Barbara refused to think of these two as a couple, for they surely weren't that, though they almost definitely had been *coupling* when the shirtless man crashed in on their arrangement.

Of course, it wasn't Barbara's heroic thrashing of the shirtless man or the pyramid of drunks or the broken window that Luke had related to Bill the second he entered the So-Lo the previous weekend, but the scene inside the bedroom, in youthful detail, with a smattering of overdramatic heaves and shudders as only a kid revolted by the things recently learned in health class could do.

Right then and there, Bill insisted that the travel arrangement be called off and that *he* would start escorting Luke, at whatever the cost. He would rearrange his longstanding schedule. He would have Luke in later or earlier. Or—if it came right down to it—he would close the store long enough to speed to the Dirty and back. Anything to help a good kid like Luke have at least a smidgeon of decency in his life, and of course anything to also keep Barbara away from that place.

But cranky old gentlemen have that time-hardened veneer that sometimes softens like bread in water. Upon hearing Barbara's account, purpose inflated Martin and Jasper's sunken chests, strengthened their tired muscles, and brought forth tucked-away energy that envigored them as if they were teenagers again. Come hemorrhoids or arthritis, indigestion or constipation, they would join Barbara from now on. And fresh from fear, she did not reject their chivalry, but now, six days later, it became clear that their first outing might be their last.

Reluctant to walk the distance, the trio took the elevator to the apartment's garage, where Jasper pulled a dusty tarp off a 1984 Jetta, as blue and as shiny as Barbara's eyes, Jasper had noted, at which she rolled them with a sigh. This began a battle between the retired commander, Martin Gimbel, and the retired muffler repairman yet hard-working perve, Jasper Lindauer, for the passenger door. The struggle suggested their masculinity was at stake, but Barbara had beat them both to it. She opened the door herself and took the front passenger seat, then locked the doors until they shouted through the windows that they would behave.

She waited until Jasper's telltale sway told her he was good and tired, then she let them in. They not so much sat as *dropped* onto their seats, and the force of their rears hitting the seat covers squeezed out little squeals of air that sounded much too much like farts in Barbara's opinion. Both men blamed the sounds on each other, then Jasper fired up the Jetta, sitting a little straighter than Martin, for at least he still had his license. The whole time Barbara suffered their nattering, she wished she had insisted on taking her car instead, but she knew those two old fools would have been helpless in her rear bucket seats, and she would have had to save them. The only bright spot of the ten-minute drive was when they passed Can-Do Cleaners, where all three of them forgot the unpleasantries long enough to appreciate the bustle of workmen in front of the building. Two men were outside replacing the broken window while another was working a pressure-washer outside. Inside, silhouettes of more people in the acts of cleaning or repairing caused Martin to suggest that maybe Bill and Luke's bloody discovery was a turning point for the area, and that some good might actually come of the mystery.

But no sooner had the words come out of Martin's mouth that a hypodermic needle hit Jasper's windshield. They had followed its track to a woman splayed half on the sidewalk, half on the road, with the heavy ball of her head hanging low on her chest. She had just enough energy to throw the needle before her muscles went slack and she became another obstacle to step over on the way to a fix, a score, or back-alley rendezvous. The Jetta sped up and they were quiet for the rest of the ride, and when Jasper finally rolled the Jetta into the Dirty's parking lot a few minutes later, all three were scanning for trouble.

On the second level the doors of two rooms were open, with people leaning against the railing and smoking cigarettes outside, enjoying the sunshine. Jasper ordered Barbara to stay in the car while he collected Luke, but when she looked at him in a way that scared him more than the woman with hypodermic needle had, he mumbled an offhanded apology and told her that he and Martin would stay in the car.

Outside, meanwhile, Barbara knocked on Luke's door. She'd purposefully left her purse on the floor in the car but today she'd worn a panic alarm bracelet on her wrist. She fidgeted with the bauble her eldest had given to her after reading an article about a rise in assaults on seniors, and Barbara thought it was a good thing that she'd never felt the need to wear it until now. It was at least four, maybe five years old and when she'd tested it this morning to see if the battery still worked it screeched so loud it nearly pierced her eardrums, and she had to slap it off.

To her left, footsteps were dragging from the stairwell, and Barbara felt a tinge of fear travel down her spine. She looked up. One group of smokers had already departed and the second was just finishing. Then the dragging sound was joined by a clunking sound, like someone was attempting to break a bottle against the wall. Barbara turned to the Jetta, saw Martin already dozing with his mouth open in the back seat and Jasper picking his teeth with his keys in the rear-view mirror and realized that her guardians were no more looking out for her than puppies for traffic across a highway.

Again she looked at the second level. The man was grinding his cigarette butt with the toe of his shoe while the woman in a pink bra beside him took one last puff and tossed her cigarette over the railing and onto the hood of a Pontiac with a taped-up window below. Then she was alone. There were no smokers or strollers or even a single window with the curtains open, just Jasper and Martin and the dragging, clunking sound.

Barbara gritted her teeth and knocked once more, now aware that she'd been in front of the door for much longer than usual. The thought occurred to her that perhaps Luke was sick, that maybe he'd caught a tummy bug or that runny nose that always seemed to be going around. Those steps again. And then someone—a man, she was sure—belched. Thank God it was daylight and, yes, thank God for the two old fools sweating their arses off in the Jetta behind her, she thought, and stiffened a little, keeping her eyes on the stairwell at the end of the walkway but making sure to also look around. Not like last time. Last time Barbara had made a mistake. This time she would be ready. Last time she'd gone for the eyes. This time Barbara Panks would go for the balls.

She knocked again. There was some rumbling behind the door that told her Luke was on his way. It made her soften a little, but then the clunking sound grew nearer. From the periphery, a pair of thick ankles appeared. Then a man floundered into view, as wide as he was tall. The greasy casings of his t-shirt and shorts collected around his midriff so tightly he seemed almost *severed* below his navel. He had a tangle of hair that reached past the sweat stains on his armpits, and even though he was still far away, Barbara held her breath.

The man wobbled toward Luke's room. He raised his arm to drink from the paper bag he was clutching, but his aim was bad and the bottle ricocheted off the side of the hotel. *Clunk, drag step, clunk.* He went the pace of a toddler just learning to walk, but still Barbara felt that tide of fear, rising, rising, rising, with every step he took. She knocked again. Harder this time.

"Luke?" she said, almost pleading. "Are you there, Luke?"

The curtains in Luke's window moved. For a moment, she thought she saw someone peek out as though to check who was at the door. It gave Barbara the strange feeling that something was wrong. Jasper must have thought so too because he honked the horn. Barbara sprang forward with a yelp. The blast startled the clunking man and he wheeled backward and caught himself against the wall, holding his head like he'd been struck. Barbara was about to march to the Jetta and tell Jasper where he could stick his horn when Luke's door swung open.

But it wasn't Luke.

"The fuck you want?" said the man in the doorway.

He had a wide mouth and ear-to-ear teeth like the Cheshire cat, but a litterbox shade of brown. Under the stubble of his shaved hair were a number of tattoos inked by either an amateur or a stoned and farsighted tattooist without glasses. But those blue eyes were undoubtedly Luke's, and Barbara understood as she trembled before him that Luke's father had been released from prison.

"Ah," Barbara said in her best don't-mess-with-the-convict voice. "I'm here to collect Luke. Is he here?"

Luke's father—Barbara was still unsure of his name—grunted. He rolled his tongue under his bottom lip and opened the door a little. In the space between the man's torso and the crook of his elbow, Luke's mother Ruby was visible, sitting at a small table near the bathroom. Barbara had met Ruby many times, either at the room or in passing as Ruby pushed a wobbly housekeeping cart from one room to the next. Though Ruby often fidgeted during their encounters, there was never a time that she didn't eventually smile and thank Barbara for taking care of Luke. But she didn't smile then. Nor did she get up to greet Barbara, as she sometimes did when they met at the room. Ruby stared down at the fingers in her lap and did not acknowledge Barbara at all.

"You know my boy?" the man said.

Barbara glanced at Ruby for any hint of what she was supposed to say, but Ruby was as occupied as the hourly-rental rooms on Friday and Saturday nights. There was no getting through to her. Barbara said, "I'm sorry. Please forgive me. You must be Luke's father? I'm Barbara. Luke babysits for a friend of mine and I'm just here to pick him up." She didn't offer her hand but a time-pressed smile she hoped would expedite the exchange.

"I don't know anything 'bout that. Rube?" He turned his face to speak to his wife, keeping his eyes forward. "Rube, you got him working now? What's this all about?" Ruby seemed to shrink as he spoke. She drew her feet off the floor and hugged her knees to her chest. The new angle of her body exposed the back of her slim neck, marked with finger-shaped bruises.

Further down the walkway, the stumbling man murmured something incomprehensible then chucked his paper bag at the Jetta. It bounced off the top of Jasper's door frame and shattered when it hit the asphalt. Unfazed, Luke's father pulled a cigarette from his breast pocket and lit it. Barbara turned away from the smoke to see Jasper's door fling open. The old man was out of the car quicker than Barbara thought possible. Not even when he'd spilled hot coffee on his lap at the So-Lo had she seen him move so fast. He threw his hands up and shouted at the tosser, but when he finally sighted the culprit, Jasper dove back into the Jetta and locked the doors. Martin, meanwhile, continued to doze in the back seat.

"That your ride?" Luke's father gestured with his chin toward Jasper's car. "You expect Luke to ride with those two? Can he even keep the car between the lines? Looks a bit old to be driving."

"We made it here all right. I'm terribly sorry, Mr. . . . ?"

"Joe."

"Joe," she repeated. "I'm terribly sorry, but I do have some things to do. I'd like to grab Luke from you, if you don't mind." When Joe remained unresponsive, she added, "We have an arrangement. For babysitting." She paused. "Unless you'd prefer driving him?" Barbara gestured to the parking lot and Joe's nonexistent vehicle.

The corner of that wide mouth hitched up. His lips puckered and he rubbed his jaw as though she'd given him a riddle he couldn't figure out. Behind him, Ruby collected herself. Her jaw pulled back in its socket. Her skull jittered upward. The forgotten connections of her bones gathered and pulled taut with their puppeteer back at their handle. Ruby pushed back from her chair and stood, holding her belly, still not acknowledging Barbara. Addressing only Joe.

"He's sitting for that girl; I told you," she said. "He likes it. And they treat him right. Lukey? Lukey, come on out, honey. She's here. You've got to go." Ruby tapped on the bathroom door with feather-light fingers as though a knock would be too much. Too brave. The whole room might implode if she knocked.

They watched the turning of the handle. Ruby. Joe. Barbara. Slowly, slowly, the handle went round, squeaking until the plunger retracted enough for the scuffed and stained door to be drawn open.

"You want me to come yank your ass out? You heard your mother. Make her wait one more goddamned second and I'll tan your hide until *you* need a bloody sitter. Get out here." Joe puffed his cigarette angrily.

The boy who exited the washroom was not the boy Barbara had returned five days earlier. Except for the sideways part in his hair, very little had changed. But his eyes, made shiny with the So-Lo's care and community, had dulled. And the eagerness which Barbara, Bill and the others so much enjoyed appeared to have escaped him. The boy who ventured out was smaller, hunched; *on guard*, Barbara thought.

Joe slid his cigarette to the other side of his mouth. "That's better."

From the doorway, Barbara waved. Luke brightened.

"Be good, Lukey." Ruby kissed the top of the boy's head, inhaling his scent for some time before gently nudging him. A look between them, exchanged too quickly for Joe to pick up, hinted that Luke did not want to leave his mother alone. She kissed him again and guided him away. "I'll see you when you get back. The motel was full last night, so I've got lots to keep me busy." And away from *him*, her eyes added.

Luke crossed the room and tried to pass his father, but Joe caught him by the arm. What was meant to look like a fatherly hug appeared to Barbara as a headbutt. One of Joe's tattoos—a misshapen skeleton above his ear—struck Luke's forehead. The boy didn't wince, but neither did he seem too appreciative of his father's display.

"You too good for me now, shitface?" Joe ruffled Luke's hair.

Luke quickly patted his hair back down, gave his father a one-armed hug, and stepped out of the room before he could be pulled back.

"We'll have him back in a few hours. It was nice meeting you, Joe." Barbara waved past Joe at Ruby and gave the man a tight-lipped smile. Then she turned on her heels and thanked the lucky sky she had managed to hold her tongue.

Luke was quiet in the car. Even when Barbara asked about his week. Even when Martin told him how Jasper mistook a tube of hemorrhoid ointment for toothpaste and was green in the face until Bill poured him a fourth cup of coffee. Even when Jasper offered to let Luke drive and teach him if he didn't know how. His quiet was so heavy on all of them that their own bones sank deeper into the seats, their own minds were compressed and dense with concern. Their fifth passenger, Silence, hung hard and unwelcome until Jasper could take it no more. He spied Luke in the rear-view mirror, wrung the steering wheel, and did what had to be done.

Jasper squeezed.

The resulting squeak was the length of ten choruses.

Three noses were instantly sealed. Barbara gasped. Heroic effort was made by all to trap laughter in their mouths, but then Luke's dam burst and gales of laughter blasted out of him. More, more, more, filling the back seat with chuckles and giggles and great belly laughs from the floor mats to the roof. The crack spread to Martin and Barbara's ready walls. Torrents of amusement whirled from open spigots. Spittle sprayed from lips. Tears streamed from eyes. Pent up glee poured forth from three throats. And everything was intensified by Jasper's indifference. Ten and two, hands on the wheel, straight-faced, Jasper never once cracked a smile, which made them laugh harder and cross their legs in hopes of delaying an altogether different kind of torrent.

Now in the So-Lo and with Luke upstairs collecting Maria, Bill heard the story to the very end, including the reason Luke had rushed to put his hair back into place.

"He's been hit," Barbara said, keeping her eyes on the So-Lo's interior door for Luke. "I'm sure of it. He's got a nasty mark under that hair. You see the way he's parting it? He's covering a bruise. And I don't believe for one red second he walked into a cupboard. That criminal hit him, Bill, mark my words."

Bill pulled the bristles on his chin. "It's tough to prove something like that."

"That good-for-nothing father of his almost knocked him out as he was leaving. Smacked him right in the head. I saw it with my own eyes." Barbara's nostrils flared.

"I saw it from the car," Jasper seconded, taking a handkerchief from his pocket and wiping his forehead. "He hurt him, Bill, and what's worse is that I think he *meant* to. He tried making it look like a hug to us, of course; any fool would do that if he has an audience. I don't think we can prove anything unless we ask Luke directly. But a conversation like that might drive him away." He sighed then kicked Martin under the table. "You should take care of him, Marty. Make that devil think twice about hurting our boy."

"Why me?"

"You got nothing to live for."

The end of Martin's cane found the middle of Jasper's stomach. "I should have *taken care* of you the day I met you, smartass." Jasper grunted and shoved the cane away.

Bill had never condoned violence, but the solutions grinding through his head were neither legal nor practical. Luke was a good kid, and even if he hadn't been, no alternate world existed where hurting him would be acceptable. The thought of confronting Luke's father crossed Bill's mind, but that would do no good. A man who had spent more time in prison than out of it wasn't likely to discuss Bill's concerns calmly. No. Bill would get hurt. Luke might get it even worse. And Ruby was definitely not immune to Joe's assault, either. The rare heat of anger flared through him.

"Stop!" Martin cried.

"Bill!" Barbara shouted. "Bill! You're going to break it."

Like a ship sighting a lighthouse, Barbara's voice broke through Bill's blackness. His sense returned and he directed his attention to the back of Martin's chair. His grip had bent the top rail. Bill jerked his hand away. "Sorry Marty," he said.

Barbara grinned appreciatively. "Now go to room 107 and do that again, and our problem is solved."

"He hasn't made a move in almost three years, he's not going to make one now."

"Are we talking about Luke's father or my love life, Marty?"

"Either works," Martin said. "Both are useless."

Just when Bill readied himself for another lecture on his personal life, the interior door swung open and Maria bounded toward them, followed by Luke, who was carrying a tray. Already, Luke seemed to have forgotten the encounter at the motel. His sunny smile was bright and eased their worry enough to loosen their frowns.

"Ah! The spring brigade. Come give this general a hug." Barbara's wide arms scooped Maria in, but the girl was quick to extricate herself and pounce on Martin. She sidled onto his knee and threw her hands round his neck.

"Honey, you're going to hurt him," Bill warned.

"Let's hope so," Jasper said.

Maria's dark eyes were little specks of mischief. She laid her freshly brushed blond head on Martin's shoulder and blinked up at him.

"Luke told you somethin', didn't he?"

"I told her it was a secret," Luke said. "Because you didn't tell me." He shrugged.

"Not a secret. An *offer*," Martin tapped the tip of Maria's nose. "But you beat me to it before I could talk it over with the boss. Bill, will the building implode if these two aren't here for a few hours?" Martin's not-so-subtle wink was caught by all of them.

The family he'd curated since he met Willie Flinder those many years ago tugged at Bill's heart as they waited for his answer. He said, "I was hoping to have some taste-testers for a shipment of rotten broccoli coming in, and the toilets needed a good wash today—that's definitely a two-person job—but I suppose it could wait for a bit. What'd you have in mind, Marty?"

Martin told them.

Maria squealed so loudly that Martin's ear rang. Luke leapt around the store like he was stepping on fire. Both kids were delirious with excitement. The three shoppers in the store were powerless not to be infected with their joy. Graham Tolley, who lived on the top floor of the apartment building, tucked the loaf of bread he'd been holding under an arm and raised the other wildly above his head to join the celebration.

"What are we celebrating?" Graham asked.

"We're going to the carnival!" two voices squealed. Graham laughed.

Rising now at the command of the kids yanking his arms, Martin eyed them squarely. "This is a trial. You two have to keep up with us three," he waved a finger at Jasper and Barbara. "Jasper don't look like much, but he's mean on an electric scooter. You got to watch your heels when his thumbs are hot."

"And play all the games you want. Marty's buying." Jasper smiled slyly.

The current of their fun swept Barbara up and out of her seat. Though she had known the men for years, she had never spent time with either Martin or Jasper (God forbid) outside of the So-Lo but wouldn't miss Luke or Maria's cheer for the all the dinner dates in the world. The motherless girl was like a daughter to her, and Luke might as well have been fatherless with the way Joe was. She picked up her phone and canceled her plans with Charles.

After a quick stop at their apartments for comfortable shoes and sweaters in case the evening cooled, the cyclone of enthusiasm departed. In the wake of their flight, the So-Lo became quiet. Bill wiped the tables, rearranged a shelf of scattered candy, and attended to customers, all the while working a plan of how to help Luke.

13

Elanor felt glorious. She hadn't enjoyed being on her knees this long since she and Harry were young and Harry hadn't yet become a bastard. But it had been hours—not minutes—now, and she could go for hours more. There were no pillows under her kneecaps, nothing at all to soften the friction of cartilage against linoleum, yet she hadn't needed a single break all day. It was Cody who had to convince her to stop cleaning long enough to eat and drink. The way she felt, Cody could tell her to tie rocks to her ankles and jump into the sea and Elanor would listen to him. He was the reason for her newfound health, and she vowed to keep it all costs.

She dipped the rag into the bucket and watched the suds eat up the grime the way she supposed Slick was doing to her. Eating the grime. It was a funny thought, but lots had been funny to Elanor since Cody had sat her on the back deck and revealed his secret late one night, when the temperature was too hot to sleep. The shade of the black cherry trees had always kept the small square of wood a little cooler and pleasantly shielded Elanor from the vision of her neighbors. Cody must have been hot, too, because she wasn't there long before he joined her that evening.

Even in the moonlight, Cody's health had been striking. He was not just filled out but muscular. Looking at him, she wondered if he were taking steroids, but back when Cody had dabbled in everything, Elanor had done enough research to know that the drug eventually poisoned the skin. Except for the recent shading of a vein on his temple, her grandson's skin was newborn-perfect, and his muscles were not overdone like a twined-up marshmallow. They were smooth and bumped like the Olympic swimmers she saw on TV, only shorter. Over the last month, Cody had also let the natural color of his hair return, dark and gold. The way it caught the moonlight, it was as if Cody had his own personal spotlight to brighten him. He had grown so beautiful that the men in Elanor's favorite soap operas looked almost ugly in comparison. It tickled Elanor that she might eventually make the soap opera women look ugly too, and she giggled.

She scrubbed the baseboard of their new business and beamed at her reflection. Her moldy exterior had been shedding since that night on the deck so she didn't need to see a clear echo of herself on the board to know her wrinkles had filled or that her skin had tightened. Elanor hadn't looked fifty even when she *was* fifty, but now she was turning heads of the workmen around them, most not a day over forty.

In this unflattering position, Elanor would have worried about her stomach swaying like a cow's udder, but a quick peek down reassured her that her stomach was flat and tight. Another miracle. She thanked her lucky stars for Slick, and as if Slick could read her mind, her new friend rewarded her with the spread of warmth across her shoulders.

It hadn't started this way, though.

They had been sharing a pitcher of pink lemonade when she innocently pressed upon Cody the importance of attention and diligence if he wanted decent marks at university. Elanor had expected ready agreement not only because she was the sole benefactor to his new venture but also because Cody had seemed sincere when he approached her in the kitchen for the loan. Instead, Cody faltered. His slow response prompted not a lashing, really, but a reprimand. It was all the money she had, she'd said, and she wouldn't waste a penny of it on him if he wasn't going to be serious about his education. She'd rather join Harry in hell than be bled dry by her own grandson, in her own house. With the stress Cody had put on her, she couldn't help it.

Had it been dark, she wouldn't have seen him change.

But it wasn't dark.

The moon was out and over them, lighting this and that, making shadows of the flowerpots and of the furniture and of the candles on the table. Across from her on the small sofa, Cody's shadow was unaltered, but the moonshine magnified the instant deterioration of his face. Health succumbed to rot. His nose shriveled. The smooth crescents under his eyes darkened, more and more, then were soot-black and humming with the movement of insects. His cheeks drew inward with the decay of time, though to Elanor it had all happened at the speed of a blink.

A scream had bubbled up her throat, but it was too large, too loud, and caught there until it choked her. Elanor clutched her throat, her chest, wild-eyed and fending off the devil's advances. That rotten face came closer, and though she couldn't breathe, Elanor could smell the stink of him. Something like old fish in an expired carton of chunky milk.

"Grandma!" Cody shook her.

The fact that her grandson's voice was coming from the corpse shaking her shoulders brought an eruption of bile to the back of her mouth. Elanor turned her head and vomited on her good cushion, the one that Cody hadn't ruined with his cigarettes.

Then the lemonade hit her face.

Elanor blinked.

His pure face was close to hers, once again angelic, once again enchanting. "Sorry, Grandma, but it worked for you in the kitchen, so I figured it might work for me."

"C-Cody?" she blubbered weakly.

He'd asked if she was all right but the shock of what she'd seen stuffed her ears with revulsion. Nothing she saw, smelled, or heard could be trusted and Elanor had tried to tell him that, but what came out was the jabbering of a schizophrenic in a canyon.

"I need to tell you something, Grandma."

Elanor's bottom lip trembled so badly her lower denture was beginning to loosen and clack against her gums. "Kill me, Cody. Put me out of my misery. I can't live like this anymore. I saw the devil in you. I saw it! Oh! My brain is gone!" She squeezed the sides of her head as though she could rid the visions from it like puss from a pimple.

He reached for her.

She flapped him away. "Don't come near me, Cody! Who knows what I might do! If the devil comes back I'm going to give it to him and I don't want to hurt you. I don't but I will, oh if I see that face again I will, so help me God."

"Grandma," Cody said slowly, carefully. "You have lemonade on your face. I'm going to give you my shirt so you can wipe it off. I'm telling you this because when I do, you're going to see something that's not an illusion. It's going to look strange; it might even scare you, but I promise you that it's real and that I'm all right and that it won't hurt you. Do you understand what I'm saying?" His whisper fluttered to her in the still air.

"Did you put something in the lemonade, Cody?" she asked almost hopefully.

Cody shook his head. "No, Grandma, I didn't. But something's been put in me. *On* me, actually. Do you remember the day after I saw Terry? When I came home looking like . . . well . . . like whatever looks *worse* than roadkill?" Elanor's sharp intake of breath acknowledged the memory. He went on. "I didn't realize it at the time, but it wasn't just *me* that came home that morning. I guess the best way to put it is I picked up a hitchhiker, but she was so little that I didn't notice she was there until she got bigger."

"She?" Elanor squinted, trying to make sense of his nonsense.

"Uh-huh. She, at least I think it's a she but she could also be one of those species that is both a he and a she. Or unisex, or whatever they call them. I'm not sure. The point is that somehow, with all the booze and everything else I did that night, I *made* something, Grandma. I know it sounds strange, but I woke up and she was there. Right under my rib. Believe me that at first I tried everything I could think of to get her off me, but then I realized she was healing me." He rubbed his cheeks then flexed his biceps. "*She* did this, Grandma. She did everything. I had nothing to do with any of it. My body, my brain, my teeth—"

"I thought you went to a dentist," Elanor interrupted, touching her own teeth with a shaky finger.

His eyebrows went up. "With what money? I was broke, remember? And the kind of work I needed would have taken a lot longer than a few days."

Elanor was silent. In no rational world could she believe him.

He stood and stepped toward her. "I think you need to see her, Grandma. She's the reason my life changed. I know I haven't always been honest with you, but that was before. I'm different now. She made me different."

"Don't show me, Cody. I don't know if I can handle it." She shielded her eyes.

Somewhere, tires squealed and a muffler backfired. Normal sounds, Elanor thought, not the nonsense Cody was spewing.

He took her hand and knelt in front of her. "Do you honestly believe I could have done all this by myself, Grandma? Change my body like this? Change my behavior like I have? Tell me. It's okay. You won't hurt my feelings. You were right that I was a sewer rat and that I had a sewer life. I did. I was the biggest rat of them all. But not anymore. You can't believe I did this on my own, do you?"

A tear rolled down Elanor's closed eyes. Then she slowly shook her head. When she opened them, she said, "I'm sorry, Cody."

"Can I show you Slick now?"

"Slick?"

"She seems to like the name."

Elanor hesitated.

"I promise she won't hurt you."

She gave him the smallest nod.

Cody's smooth fingers gripped the hem of his t-shirt, then he peeled the fabric up and over his head.

Her gasp filled the night sky.

On her grandson's otherwise flawless side was the biggest leech Elanor had ever seen. In her estimation, the thing took up half of his torso, maybe more. It undulated like a slow-moving tide. Up, down, in, out, cresting on one side, then the other. Left. Right. Hovering. Shifting. The dark mysteries of its swells overtook his body, millimeter by millimeter, right before her eyes. It was horribly dark, the color of dried blood, and when Elanor pulled back, it reached *forward*.

She scrambled backward, lifting her bottom to the top edge of the chair and pulled herself onto the railing of the deck. "Get that thing away from me!"

"Slick won't hurt you—"

"You heard me! You've brought home the devil, Cody! Get it away!"

He sat back on his heels. "I know it's hard to understand."

"Cody Dean Clyde, you get that thing away or you're out for good!" Elanor pulled her feet up in case the thing scurried her way, but her stomach was too big for her to hug her knees. She dropped her feet to the other side of the railing, away from Cody. If she had to jump, she would, even if she broke both her ankles doing it.

He put his shirt back on. "Is that better? Can we talk now?"

"What the *hell* is that, Cody? Is that what those drugs did to you? Either I've lost my mind or that sewer's taken you again." Never had Elanor thought she'd *want* to lose her mind, but the alternative before her eyes was so much worse.

"Come down off the railing and I'll tell you, Grandma. Nothing's going to happen."

"Says the devil himself."

Cody sighed, got to his feet, and took a step back. "I'll pack my bags tomorrow if anything happens. Can you come down now?"

Clots of fear jellied her muscles and Elanor found that she couldn't bring her feet back around without falling. But Cody looked so sincere, so desperate to make things right, that she extended an arm to him. "Help me down, Cody."

He made a point of keeping the side of his body with the monster away from her while he lifted her off the railing. She'd been wearing her sleeveless nightgown, the one that tented out to let her body breathe, so she keenly felt the slight pinch under her armpit before he let go. If it had been earlier, Elanor might have thought she had been stung by a bee, but the only insects out now were the mosquitos and the moths. A gurgle of surprise passed from her to the grandson, who gave her a conspiratorial wink. Elanor pawed the skin under her right armpit and felt a tiny bump where she had been stung. "What have you done to me? My God, what have you done!" She jumped around ineffectually, trying to get the thing off.

"I'm helping you to become the best version of yourself. Just like me, Grandma. I love y—"

Elanor screamed.

"If you just give it a minute, you'll see what I'm talking about."

"I want you out! Get out of my house. You won't spend another second under my roof, you evil-dealing—"

There were more words on her tongue, but a strange feeling came over Elanor and they dissolved before she could speak them. Peace pervaded her nerves and she at once began to feel calm, like she had when her doctor prescribed her Xanax while she supported Cody during his earlier bouts of addiction and sobriety. The glass in her joints melted. The acid in her muscles evaporated. Her blood pressure came down, down, trickling like a brook instead of the Niagara rush her pills tried to tame. Open-mouthed, she dropped into her seat, then swung her stunned face to his.

"See? I told you Slick was awesome. You feel it, don't you?" Cody asked.

"Wha...I...how?"

"That's Slick, Grandma. That's how I got like this. How *you're* going to get like this. You told me you wanted my help, so you have my help and Slick's help. How do you feel?"

Elanor felt like a fucking queen, that's how she felt. In this case, vulgarity was necessary because there was no other way Elanor could put her new wellness into words. She felt decades younger, possibly even better than that. She rolled her wrists to test out her new body. No stiffness. She extended her legs to try out her new knees. No pain. She stretched her neck, curled her toes, arched her spine. A cartwheel crossed her mind. Her smile was wide. "Like an Olympian," she had said.

Now, hauling her tenth bucket to the sink, and the gallons of sloshing water seeming the weight of a butterfly wing, Elanor only wished she'd known Slick earlier. Maybe she'd still be married, but to someone worthwhile who didn't pick his ass when he thought she wasn't looking. Maybe someone handsome. And rich. Definitely that.

Music came from the speakers, one of Cody's soothing selections to set the mood they were all trying to attain at the new Can-Do. A pianist's fingers held peaceful notes, made even the workmen in their dirty overalls relax. "How's this?" Cody called out from behind the counter, painted a fresh coat of white.

Elanor gave him a thumbs-up as she passed. She put her hands on her hips and surveyed their new space. They'd done a fine job of converting the old building into a place people would actually want to visit. Gone were the gaudy panels behind the counter. Gone were all traces of neon. All the dust, grime, graffiti, drug paraphernalia, and bodily fluids had been scraped, tossed, scrubbed, swept, mopped, sanitized, and washed away. The walls were white. The new laminate floor was light grey. Everything old had been either replaced or covered. The only remnant they decided to keep was the name: Can-Do. Locals were already familiar with it, plus it saved Elanor and Cody the extra cost of changing the fascia outside. Most importantly, however, it declared limitless opportunity for all who wanted it. *YOU* Can-Do was their motto and Slick would make it happen. For them. For everyone. And it would make Elanor and Cody rich.

Once they began planning, it didn't take long. The building was already vacant and neither of them were occupied with anything important. Even Slick seemed pleased with the idea, stroking their brain stems, strengthening their tender parts, encouraging them along. She had as much to give as they wanted, as anyone wanted, as long as she was happy.

Elanor thought it would be the best wellness business in the whole city, perhaps the whole world. Sure, they could have situated it elsewhere, in the trendy downtown core where everything was overpriced and overstuffed, but the Can-Do was what they (she) could afford, and it was Cody who'd insisted on the location. He had been born again in the Can-Do, so the Can-Do it would be. $11,643 of Elanor's savings, temporarily earmarked for Cody's education, was quickly redirected for the venture—but even with the empty bank account, Elanor had never been happier. That sewer life was over for both of them.

"Well," Cody said, taking her shoulders and guiding her to the front door, where he spun her around. "What do you think?"

The mark on his temple had grown darker since he'd revealed his secret, the result of several spawns. Elanor would not let Cody call the process *birth*, though it had definitely felt that way. The tearing of the insides. The soul-splitting pain. A helpless little being squirmed to life. But Slick was not a baby, nor was Slick—at any stage of growth—helpless. The miracle of birth was celebrated around the world, yet a little part of Elanor was uneasy about the creation—not uncomfortable enough to put an end to the whole thing, of course—but enough that it sat like a beacon on a shelf in her head. She couldn't exactly shout it to the world. She couldn't send out post-partum photos of the squiggly creature. No one would want to hold it or feed it or nurture it. But once a tether was made, they would love it more than their own babies. Need it more than air or water.

Although they could not stop others from spawning Slick, their advantage was that of time: they were the first. Over the last few weeks, both Elanor and Cody had spawned almost every night to ensure they had enough supply to start their business. Slick not only acquiesced but was eager to help them. It made the house smell of sweat and dirtied the sheets with their tears and saliva and the fluids of creation. Goo, mostly. A red-brown gelatin that propelled fledgling Slicks out of their parents onto Cody and Elanor. The little ones wouldn't grow until tethered with parents, so for the time being they looked like peppercorns stored in a jar.

"What do you think, Grandma?" Cody asked again. "Does it make you want to start a new life?"

"I already have." She squeezed him.

A toolbox clanged closed and the foreman waddled over to them, hitching up his sagging pants. He removed his hard hat and wiped his forehead with the back of a hairy arm. "Gotta say, I wasn't sure how it was going to work, but you had a vision. I'll give you that. Looks real good, if I say so myself. Mind telling me how it all works? What you're selling, I mean?"

"We're not selling anything," Cody said immediately. "We're lending *potential.*"

The foreman's face puckered in confusion. Cody wrapped an arm around the foreman's neck and drew him to the mural behind the front counter that they had commissioned from a local street artist desperate for quick cash. "See what that says? It says Can-Do. But look around it, broaden your vison, expand the boundaries. What else do you see?"

The foreman scratched his head, squinting at the wall. "I'll be damned. There's a face—no—a lot of faces around it, mixed in like a hologram. That's pretty neat."

"What are the faces made of?"

"How'd I miss that?" The foreman slapped his knee. "All the faces are made up of letters. Y. O. U. As in *You Can-Do*?" he asked Cody.

"You got it."

"Well, you're too smart for my blood."

"Never underestimate yourself," Elanor said behind them. "That's what we're going to do. Show people their full potential. Starting tomorrow."

A quick head-to-toe scan of the two—mother and son, he thought—was all the foreman needed to believe what she'd said was true. Poorly concealed twin bruises marred their temples, but otherwise they were the kind of people other people would be drawn to, like movie stars. He figured that maybe they were just thinking too much, and that their brains couldn't handle the intellectual overload. He'd read things like that could happen. The *Social Storyteller*, his favorite tabloid, was filled with similar truths the government didn't want Canadians to know.

He said, "You know, I think this is something my wife might be interested in. Mind if I send her your way? Do you have a brochure or anything?"

Cody flipped him a card from the box they'd picked up just this morning. "Tell her to bring a friend. We're giving a group discount."

The foreman thanked him, rallied the rest of his crew, and departed.

"Tomorrow," Elanor said to Cody when they were alone.

"Tomorrow," he said.

Slick trembled.

14

The wipers couldn't keep up with the rain. Only a few times a year did Garrett get weather like this, but with the luck Bill was having lately it seemed only natural for the sky to open right over him the moment he put his key into the ignition. It got worse as he drove. Each raindrop on the roof of the car was a hammer stroke to his already pounding headache. But he couldn't put the trip off any longer. Not if he wanted to sleep. Not if he wanted to save Luke.

He reminded himself that he had absolutely zero authority over the boy. He wasn't Luke's father. He wasn't even legally Luke's employer. So there was little recourse to him except attempting to get through to Ruby. And if that didn't work, Bill would call the police, even if it meant never seeing Luke again. Anything to protect him.

Back at the So-Lo, April and Zeke had tried to make him smile with all the possibilities for the unreturnable pallet of boiled eggs Bill had accidentally ordered during one of his more distracted moments, but even Zeke's suggestion of egging Jasper's car hadn't cheered him. Instead, Bill told them to put what they could in the dairy refrigerator and divide the rest amongst the apartment's tenants.

More than once, Bill had to wipe the inside of the windshield with his arm, but the car quickly fogged up again. His mood soured. Diana would have laughed at him hunched over the steering wheel like this, grumpy and cursing his luck and trying to see the road, but she would also have been proud of him. It kept him going. Even gone, she always would.

He was proceeding at a crawl when the whip of raindrops eased. Bill looked at the sky, hoping the worst of it was over, when a figure appeared on the road. He slammed his brakes inches away from a jaywalker. The thudding of his heart overtook the swishing of the wipers and he sighed as he put his forehead to the steering wheel, reflecting that if he kept going like this, he'd have a heart attack by noon. As if to let him know she was still there, the jaywalker slapped the Volkswagen's hood. But the silent apology he mouthed died on his lips the moment he saw the woman's face.

Past the wipers and through the rain, under the dark hood of her sweater, her rotten face smoldered with fury. She had clots of skin hanging off her cheekbones, shriveling like the burning ends of a rope. Her nose decayed. Her forehead disintegrated. Her chin decomposed. The wipers went left. She still had eyebrows. The wipers went right. They were gone. Within five swipes of the blades, everything that could decay did. Bill blinked, but the apparition didn't change. Her skull gleamed. He stared at her absent eyes and rubbed his own. Behind him, a horn blared. The sound seemed to gather the components of the woman's face again and then she was whole, smiling as though the near accident was no one's fault, no one's at all. She shrugged and walked away.

Drivers sounded their horns and gestured angrily at him as he pulled the Volkswagen into an empty space in front of the donut shop where he was meeting Ruby again. For a time he sat behind the wheel, unsure if he'd just suffered a panic attack or if the stress of the last few weeks had shorted the circuitry in his brain. By the time his heart and breathing slowed, the rain had stopped, and Ruby was standing outside his door, her missing tooth almost pressed up against the glass.

"Something wrong?" she asked when Bill exited the car. "I must've been here five minutes, but you didn't see me. You didn't hear me knock?"

Bill shook his head. "I guess I blanked out there for a second. A woman ran in front of my car. I almost hit her. She gave me quite the shock. You didn't see someone in front of my car, did you?"

Ruby frowned. "No, but whoever it was deserves to be hit. She wouldn't get my sympathy, crossing the road like that." She scowled and lit a cigarette, turning her head to exhale over her shoulder.

He changed the subject. "Sorry to keep you waiting. Is Luke inside?"

"He'll be a few minutes late. Joe's got him cleaning his new car."

This was the best news Bill could have hoped for. He would have Ruby alone long enough to talk about his concerns, should his rattled nerves allow him to articulate his thoughts. "Congratulations."

She turned and led him toward the donut shop. "It's nothing fancy, but Joe says it will go for a few years if we take care of it. Luke's already had his first ride, and he loves it."

Stopping to put his keys in his coat pocket, Bill realized that in the fog of leaving the car, he'd forgotten his wallet in the console. He told Ruby he would meet her inside, at which she puckered her lips sideways and blew out a thick cloud of smoke.

"I'm not buying," she said as she opened the door.

"My mother would roll over in her grave if you did." Bill smiled at her eyeroll and returned to the Volkswagen.

His head was still spinning from the phantom in the road when he depressed the lock button on his key ring. *Glazed* was only twenty feet away, but what drew Bill's attention as he stepped away from the car was the building to the left. What had appeared to Luke and Bill a murder scene barely two months ago was now a brilliant production of whites and greys, from walls to furniture. The new owners had kept the name, centered in a mural of aspiring faces on the wall above the counter. New glass had been installed, and waist-high planters of purple flowers stood on both sides of what used to be the main entrance to the laundry. The area where the self-service laundromat entrance had been was walled off and painted over. Nothing spoke of crime or addiction or vandalism. Everything implied opportunity and health and growth.

It was a new bird in an old nest. Bill had never been opposed to gentrification. Sometimes neighborhoods needed a facelift, and sometimes they needed a transplant such as his own neighborhood had recently undergone with a condominium development nearby. But the situation of this gleaming gem in the middle of Garrett's most drug-inhabited, crime-riddled, dilapidated neighborhood appeared as intelligent as shorts in a snowstorm. He didn't see any scenario in which a business of this caliber would survive here.

Stranger still was the clientele.

On a street where fashion was timeworn, donated, or stolen, and where dental care and dignity were forfeited for the basic necessities, the people inside Can-Do were unusually fit and attractive. The woman on the phone behind the counter was ageless, for Bill couldn't figure if she was thirty, fifty, or somewhere in between. The man in a matching white shirt had such a beguiling smile when he spoke to the group in front of him that Bill could swear a younger woman asked for—and received—either an autograph or perhaps even a phone number. Her awkward blush was ignored by the man. He just went on talking, pointing to the mural, himself and the woman behind the counter, then to another man and woman standing off to the side, also in crisp white shirts and pressed black pants. They, too, looked like models.

The door to the donut shop swung open. "Are you coming or what?" Ruby called from inside, drumming her finger on her hip.

Bill apologized for the third time in as many minutes and joined Ruby inside. He'd been so stupefied by the phantom jaywalker and again by the transformation of the dry cleaning business that he'd wasted his time. Luke would be here any minute.

He took Ruby's order and brought it to the table, observing for the first time that she wasn't in her work uniform. "You've got the day off, I take it?" Bill started awkwardly.

"I work tonight," she said. "We're always busy on the weekends. Tuesday's usually my day off, but the manager switches that whenever his girlfriend's in town because he knows I'm the only one that won't tell his wife. It's none of my business." Ruby drank her coffee and picked her muffin while they watched for Luke. The silence between them grew.

Finally, Bill said, "Ruby, I've been meaning to talk to you about Luke."

"Is he in trouble?"

"Of course not. At least not with me." He hoped these few words were enough, but Ruby didn't catch on. Bill continued, rubbing his palms against his jeans. "It's not easy for me to say this, Ruby, but I've got some concerns about Luke. He's been with us for a few months now, and I think I've gotten to know him pretty well. He's a good kid. There's not a mean bone in his body. Maria loves spending time with him and so do I. You raised him right and you should be proud of that. But ... I guess what I'm trying to say is that I'm worried about him. Since Joe's been back—"

"That's got nothing to do with Luke."

"I think it does," Bill disagreed. "He's not the same kid he was before Joe came home. And I didn't want to mention this until I was sure about it, but I can't deny what's in front of my own eyes. He's been hurt. Those bruises on him aren't accidental, Ruby, and I think you and I both know that. They're shaped like fingers, and when they're not shaped like fingers they're the size of fists. Please tell me I'm wrong about this."

Ruby didn't speak, but she'd gotten fidgety and started picking the paper sleeve around her cup.

"They're the same bruises you have on your wrist, Ruby."

She tugged the sleeve of her jacket down. When she spoke, she stared at her cup, her words coming out as an admission not only to Bill, but also to herself. "Joe tries. I know it doesn't look like it, but he does. He's not a fancy guy like you or those people in the window next door," she thumbed toward Can-Do. "But when he's got his head on straight, he's a hard worker and he can be kinder than anyone else I know. It's his temper that gets us."

"Have you ever spoken to anyone about this?"

"No one listens to me," Ruby said. "They see my uniform and the way I talk—I'm no businesswoman, understand—and they look the other way. Like I deserve it. And maybe I do."

"No one deserves this, Ruby. Especially not you." As he had with many customers who'd confided sad stories or tragic events, Bill reached across the table and took her hand. The movement was automatic, something ingrained in him, but he realized his mistake when Ruby flinched. He pulled his hand away. "I didn't mean to startle you. I'm sorry, I shouldn't have done that."

She changed the subject, now comfortable enough to look at him. "Luke's special, ain't he?"

"He is," Bill agreed. "And I don't want to see him hurt any more than you do. Luke doesn't deserve it. No kid does. And even though I'm not his father, I have a responsibility to help keep him safe.

"Do you understand what I'm trying to say?" He could feel his face growing hot with unease, so he took a long drink of his iced tea.

"They'll take him away from me." A film of tears lined Ruby's eyes.

"They won't if you do the right thing. I know it's not easy, but you can't let Joe hurt him anymore." He didn't tell Ruby that if he saw another bruise on Luke, he would call the police himself because she would perceive it as a threat. She was already cornered, shivering like a mouse at every hiccup, and Bill knew that one step too far and she might take Luke and run, with no one to help him. He added, "And you can't let him hurt you either, Ruby. You say no one listens to you, but I'm here right now listening to you. If you need me to talk to Joe for you—"

She cringed. "He wouldn't like that."

"Okay, then. If you need me at any time—if you're scared or he's getting mean with either of you, even a little, you have my number. Call or text me any time. I'll answer it. Can you do that for me?"

"Boo!" From the open door, Luke called to them. He was soaking wet, and Bill realized that he'd probably been walking during the worst of the rainstorm.

"He didn't drive you?" Ruby asked of Joe, puckering her face at the sight of her son.

Luke shook his head, splashing them until their hands were up and the napkins on the table were dripping. "I wanted to walk. Sorry I'm late, Bill."

"I didn't wait long. If anything, it's your mom who's been waiting on us slowpokes, but we were just finishing up. Can I get you something to go, Ruby? A snack for later? Whenever I'm here, I can't help but bring some home. Must be the sugar. They sure know how to make addicts of us, don't they?"

Ruby declined his offer. She gave him curt smile and kissed her wet son on the cheek. Then she was gone.

Luke ordered a donut that was decorated to look like a monster for himself and one that looked like a cat for Maria. To this, Bill added a box of assorted donuts for Zeke, April, and whichever customers joined them in the So-Lo today.

Outside, Bill was once again struck by the transformation of the business. He said to Luke, "Of all the things I'd expect to see around here, that isn't one of them. Have you seen this, Luke?"

The boy nodded. "They covered the front after a bunch of people cleaned it out, but they took them down a few weeks ago, or maybe longer than that. It doesn't look the same at all."

Bill slowed. "You been inside yet? Feel like making a quick detour?" He gestured to the new Can-Do, wondering if Constable Brander was aware of the crime-scene makeover, then supposed he was. The cop was no idiot. He was well aware of the area, and Bill was sure that even with a fragment of the vicinity capped like a rotten tooth, Brander would remain close, should its neighbors need excising or the cap crack.

"I tried," Luke said, "but they kicked me out. They said it was for adults only. But maybe they'll let me in with you." He pulled the polished handle and held the door open for Bill.

Perfumed air whooshed at them. It was more unexpected than unpleasant, with no hint of the sweat or liquor common to the area. This, too, struck Bill as odd, like the company was trying too hard. Bill's experience with the So-Lo had taught him that customers wanted honest transactions in a comfortable environment, but more importantly that a little care and concern created an army of loyalists. The perfume might work in Yorkville or Montreal, but not in an area where perfume of any sort was a luxury. It spoke of ego or poor judgement, but he was not yet sure which.

"Ah!" said the woman, rising from a chair behind the desk where just months ago there had been feces and drugs. "You've brought us a snack, I see." She gestured to the boxes in their hands.

"There's plenty, if you'd like one," Bill said, opening his box for the woman.

She smiled politely. "Ask and you shall receive, our motto. Jesus might have said it first, but we *deliver* on our promise."

Bill closed the lid of the donut box before the woman's eager fingers could reach for one, pretending he hadn't seen her advance. Ten seconds in the building and he'd realized all the paint and the newness were just thick coats of ego. The woman's smile did not leave her face. If anything, it split wider.

She folded her hands together. "How can I help you?"

Bill tipped his chin towards Luke. "My friend and I were in this very spot not too long ago. It looks nothing like it did then and we were in the area, so we figured we'd come see it for ourselves. I can't believe what you've done with the place. It's incredible, actually."

The woman nodded at his praise, although a bit disinterestedly, as if she'd heard similar reactions before and had grown bored of them. "We perform miracles," she said.

"What exactly is your business, if I may ask? Are you a church?" The way the woman talked and the way the group had been enamored by the man made Bill figure he might not be too far off. But it wouldn't be a church, exactly. Possibly one of those new-age, *Sam's-the-prophet-of-crazy-town* schemes, but definitely not a church.

"Oh, you flatter!" said the woman whom Bill now knew as *Elanor* by the gleam of the nametag over her shirt pocket. "We are liberators, Mr. . . . ?"

"Just Bill," he said, wondering how long she would try to hold him here and finagle some sort of commitment from him.

Elanor stepped out from behind the desk. Closer up, she was older than he'd originally thought, but trim and obviously well-preserved. There was a thick smear of makeup on her left temple at least as big as a deck of cards, covering a darker patch of skin, either a birthmark or a bruise, he thought.

"Bill," she said, purring his name. "We are liberators of self. Motivators of capability. We are full of incredible potential—each and every one of us—and we're here to *mine* that potential. Polish what you already have until it shines."

Luke stifled a laugh.

Elanor's brows knitted, exposing even more of the mark near her hairline. "Would you like a tour of the facility?"

Again, the pretention. How a few layers of paint and the removal of garbage in the same space constituted a *facility*, Bill didn't know. He supposed the act, from the metamorphosis-promising woman to the white-washed walls, was such a diversion from destitution that it might attract customers like lambs to spurge. The analogy was something Bill's grandfather liked to use whenever something didn't sit right with him, even if it *looked* right, because disturbing the weed spread its trouble to other areas where you didn't want it to be. Though a building of Can-Do's caliber *should* be a totem of restoration in the impoverished neighborhood, Bill couldn't shake the feeling that the shiny new building was the *spurge*.

Just then, the man Bill had seen speaking to the group earlier emerged from behind the mural, where the former Can-Do's dry cleaning operation used to be.

"We have guests," Elanor said to the man, who had an even bigger mark on the side of his face that he'd made a poorer attempt to cover.

"Welcome," he said. "Has my grandmother offered you a tour? We don't usually allow kids, but since you're armed with donuts, we'll make an exception in this case." He winked at Luke.

Bill took Luke's box and put both boxes on the counter. "Don't want to ruin your hard work," he said to the man, then he and Luke followed the man around the counter and behind the partition.

The entire back space had been subdivided into six smaller rooms, three on each side, with a hallway down the middle leading to the double doors that had been chained together when Bill and Luke had investigated. Except for the carpet, everything was white. There was no dirt or blood or intravenous tubes, no fast-food bags, no diapers or mold. Although the previous condition had made him nauseous, Bill almost preferred it to what he saw because now it was more unsettling. Without good reason, Bill had the claustrophobic feeling of being trapped. People could have fled the old Can-Do, but the new one . . . well, it seemed as sticky as a web.

The man spun around as smoothly as a dancer. He was no taller than Luke, but was built solid and strong, with lean muscle filling out his clothes. A bulge under his shirt suggested a colostomy bag or massive hernia. The man's hands instinctively concealed it from Bill's curious eyes.

He said, "Since we're getting to know each other, I should introduce myself. I'm Cody." He offered his hand to Luke, then to Bill, who gave Cody both their names. Pleasantries exchanged, Cody opened his arms (like Jesus on the cross, Bill thought). "This is your canvas. Blank. New. Full of potential. And available to those who want to elevate themselves."

Luke scrunched up his face.

"You lost me," Bill said. "*Is* this a church?"

Cody addressed Luke. "Do you paint, Luke? Or draw?"

"I draw comics," Luke said.

"Great. I want you to think of drawing your comics, Luke. When you have a blank page in front of you and all that creativity inside your head is just waiting to burst out. Do you always draw what you see up there? Does it turn out *exactly* as you imagine it to be?"

"Sometimes."

"And sometimes it doesn't?"

"Not always," the boy admitted. "Sometimes it looks nothing like what's in my head."

Cody wiggled a finger in front of him. "*That's* what we do. We make what's in your head a reality, but with health, social, and financial success. Doesn't that sound pretty great?"

"You make what's in people's heads become real?" Luke frowned when Cody nodded. "But what if what's in their heads isn't good? People don't always think good things. Sometimes their thoughts are bad." Luke had enough experience with bullshit to know how to cut through it, so Bill was proud of Luke for asking the question.

"That's the beauty of what we do, Luke. Transformation starts with the inside out. If what's inside is bad, then we change it to good." Cody had bent down to say this to Luke as though he were a toddler and not a teenager of his own height.

Bill put an arm around Luke's shoulders, snugging the boy close. "How does it all work?"

Rising to face Bill again, Cody said, "It starts much like this. A tour and a conversation. Then our transformation team consults with our clients in our pods," he gestured to the rooms on both sides of the hallway. "There's—"

Abruptly, Cody stopped talking.

They turned around to see if they'd been interrupted by someone—a member of the transformation team Cody mentioned, or a client—but no one was there. Gone, too, was the animation of his face and body, as though a switch had been disconnected. Bill had seen epileptics freeze like that. Two of the So-Lo's regulars had epilepsy, but it was only one—Joanna Fowler—who stopped mid-sentence at the onset of a seizure. It never lasted long, and Bill thought it was a good thing she froze because it signaled to others that she needed help. On more than one occasion, he had helped Jane to the floor and put a blanket under her head to soften her tremors until they passed, and he began removing his jacket to do the same for Cody now.

"Sir? Cody? Are you all ri—" Bill started, but then Cody began speaking again.

"—a thirty-day free trial, so there's no risk to you. You came on a good day. If you want, Elanor can watch your son up front while we chat further in one of the pods."

Luke gave Bill a sidelong glance and looked back at Cody, who smiled at them as though nothing had happened.

Bill didn't correct Cody but gave Luke's shoulder a squeeze. "Thank you for the offer, but my life is pretty much how I want it to be."

"*Nothing* could get better?" Cody pressed and delivered a lightning-fast once-over that implied Bill was a lesser man, but that he could be a better man like Cody if he wanted to be.

Diana came to his mind. Their motherless daughter came to his mind. The abused boy next to him consumed the rest of it. But these weren't things the Can-Do Crooks could fix, nor would Bill ever let their tricky fingers try. "My life's just about perfect," he said.

It seemed that Cody was going to insist, but then he didn't, maybe because Bill didn't give him puppy dog eyes or feed on the crap he was selling. Cody led them back to the front counter where they collected their boxes. Elanor was busy with a couple at the far end of the counter, giving the man and woman the same spiel she'd given Bill and Luke only minutes before. Luke sucked his lips inside his mouth and bit down to keep from laughing, but the knobby knees below the hem of his shorts were shaking with amusement.

Bill thanked Cody for the tour and was about to leave when it occurred to him to ask about the crime scene he and Luke had seen in the back room. He turned his body so that his back was to the man and woman to keep them from overhearing.

"Oh, one more thing, Cody," he said in a voice so low that Cody leaned toward him and cocked his ear next to Bill's face. Up close, Bill saw that Cody had actually done a good job of covering the mark on his temple but that it was much worse than Elanor's. Black veins spidered behind the coating of makeup, worming under his skin—*pulsing*, Bill thought. He looked away from the man's face. "I'm hoping you can put our minds to rest on something. The last time we were here, it looked like someone had been hurt back there. Right where those rooms—"

"Pods," Cody corrected without moving his head away.

"Right where those *pods* are. There was blood, a lot of blood, like someone had been murdered."

"Murdered?"

Bill nodded. "We filed a police report and everything. I was just wondering if you knew what happened back there."

"I wasn't aware of that," Cody said, but Bill sensed that Cody was lying, as he stiffened and shot a look at Elanor. The veins on his temple seemed to multiply. Then Cody pulled his face back and Bill was saved from seeing them squiggle again.

Now it was *his* turn to pressure Cody. He palmed the bristles on his cheek, thinking out loud. "I'm surprised. Something as big as that would be hard to miss, unless they cleaned it all up before you moved in. They would've had to do a hell of a job to make it habitable, especially for a business like this."

Cody looked at his watch. "I guess the faster they cleaned it up, the faster they could lease it. Money talks, right?"

"You know, I think I'll circle back with Constable Brander. I'm sure he'd be happy to hear what you've done to this place. Who knows? He might even be interested in becoming a client." Brander buying into Can-Do's drivel was as likely as Jasper averting his eyes from any of the So-Lo's female customers, but he let Cody think him sincere.

As if the visit couldn't get any stranger, Cody's small fingers curled into tight fists—not to fight, it seemed, but to restrain himself. The tendons in his neck flexed, his teeth gritted, his body trembled, and it looked for a moment like Cody was going to shoot off like fireworks and end up neck-deep in the ceiling.

By now, the couple at the front had been collected by one of the Can-Do's transformation team members and were heading toward the pods in the back room. Cody, meanwhile, had grown so flustered by whatever Bill had said that his eyes began to water and the veins on his temple palpitated so fast and so hard it looked like they were about to burst.

"Have a g-great day, y-you two," he said through clenched teeth. Then he disappeared behind the mural.

"And be careful out there," Elanor said, now sitting in her chair. "The storm's not over yet."

Outside, Bill unlocked the Volkswagen for Luke. He glanced one more time at the sanitarium passing as a personal development business.

Elanor had the phantom's face.

15

September dusk lingered like a bad dream. The intervening light, not dark enough for the streetlights to blink on yet not bright enough for Cody to risk a walk, intensified his sour mood. Remembering the guy and his kid made it worse. He went to the front door and turned the deadbolt. Salvation Station was closed.

Elanor turned off the overhead lights and they retreated to Cody's office in the back, where Charity and Edwin were already waiting for them.

Even in his terrible mood, Cody couldn't help but appreciate her transformation. Of all the people Slick had revitalized, Charity had had the most dramatic change. He'd only known her with rashy skin, pitted with acne scars and meth itch, and with those eyebrows plucked so thin Cody had to squint to see them. Worse, she'd had a habit of over-spraying her hair so that it was always crusty and stiff as a board, and when the wind gusted near her trailer park and made it rise like wings, he thought her hundred-pound frame might one day fly away.

But Slick had obliviated that woman.

What leaned against the filing cabinet inspecting her nails was a smooth-skinned, silky-haired starlet, delicately curved in form-fitting black dress pants and a silk white blouse. Perhaps the most beautiful woman in the city. The added benefit of seeing her eyebrows without having to squint was that it was easier to tell that she was happy. And happy meant money.

"How'd we do today?" Cody asked as he dropped into his chair and faced his team.

"I got twenty-two," Charity said proudly, now twirling the glossy dark hair at the back of Edwin's neck.

"Seventeen," Edwin said, leaning into Charity's fingers.

Looking at a paper in her lap, Elanor raised her hand. "And I have thirteen already scheduled for consultations tomorrow."

The news was not just good but great. It meant almost twenty thousand today—at five hundred bucks a pop—for the recruits Edwin and Charity tethered, with the promise of more tomorrow. If it kept up like this, they would all be rich and none of them would have to work another dead-end job again. And it was such a contrast to when they'd first opened three weeks earlier that Cody still had a hard time believing it.

As his grandmother doled out Edwin and Charity's take—two grand a piece—Cody recorded the transaction in a spreadsheet on his laptop, relieved they hadn't sunk. Sure, every penny of the investment was his grandmother's, but it would have stung Cody just as bad if they'd lost it.

Their first Monday morning, he'd flung open the door certain they'd have to beat back customers, but there had not been even a trickle. By noon, they hadn't had a sniff. By two, the only person who'd entered the new Can-Do was a man who'd chased his dog inside, but he quickly leashed the terrier and dashed back outside with an apologetic wave.

Slick had pushed the image of a magnifying glass into Cody's head, suggesting reconnaissance, so Cody had swapped his dress pants and shirt for jeans and a t-shirt, then gone door-to-door down the block. He walked to the donut shop first, then Paw Paradise, the nameless shoe repair store, Bob's Barbershop, two pawn shops, an adult video store, a check-cashing business, Skinz Tattoo, Mounds Gentlemen's Club, Harlan's Grocery and finally the liquor store. When Cody asked what they thought of the new Can-Do, half hadn't even known the dry cleaning business was gone and the other half said the new Can-Do didn't belong on the block. When Cody asked why, their answers always came down to the price: it was too expensive.

That struck Cody as odd because none of them knew the price. It wasn't on a brochure or printed on the wall, and it certainly wasn't painted on the window the way many nearby businesses did on their own storefronts. But it *looked* expensive, they told him. And down Hobson Street, expensive had no place. Secondary to the first complaint, the new Can-Do seemed . . . well, *just plain weird*, as Tom (not Bob) from Bob's Barbershop put it. Even the piss-stained brown-baggers that loitered in front of the liquor store two doors away could not be convinced to peek inside.

For three days there was nothing, then at the end of the fourth day a scream on the street took Cody outside. A woman and a man were playing tug-of-war with the woman's purse. She'd been crossing the street toward the corner grocery when a man twice her size snagged the strap and tried to take off. But the woman wouldn't let go. The man's chest-length hair and matted beard curtained the woman as he struggled to pry her fingers off the strap, but then he began yanking and tossed her off her feet. She still wouldn't let go.

"Hey!" Cody called, but then the thief whirled around with the strength of his bulk and heaved the little woman aside. A moment later, he and the woman's purse were already at the end of the block.

Cody was mere steps away when he finally recognized Charity. He liked to believe it took him a while because it was dark and because the man's hair had covered her face, but it hadn't been that. In the months since Kade Hart had died in her fire pit, Charity had withered into the skin of a haggard old woman. She was rutted with decay, from the deeper scars on her cheeks to the eviscerated enamel on her teeth to the corroded sockets of her bloodshot eyes. If she had been thin before, she was positively emaciated that day, her matchstick bones struggling to bear the feather weight of her wizened organs.

He had scooped her off the street with no more effort than picking up a Saturday newspaper, and brought her to his office while his grandmother stayed at the reception desk fretting over her investment.

It wasn't for many minutes until Charity recognized him. She'd been recalling the description of the man who'd stolen her purse when she stopped talking and gasped. "Cody?"

"Hi Charity," he said, because he was too shocked to say anything else. If Slick hadn't come along when she had, Cody would've turned out just like Charity, maybe worse, and it dawned on him as he looked at her how depraved his life used to be.

Her hand cupped her mouth. "But how? What ... no ... is that *really* you, Cody? How the fuck'd you get like this? You win the lottery or something?"

Cody told her that it was something like that. He'd been blessed while his friends had been condemned, and it made him think of Edwin and Terry and Kade. Especially Kade. The tall boy with the baby face. The boy with so much promise. The boy who had been better than any of them. Henley had attempted to arm Cody with a bunch of bullshit coping mechanisms, but those kinds of things didn't work when you'd killed an innocent kid. Nothing took away the soul-piercing guilt or the mind-shattering shame.

Nothing except Slick.

This gave him an idea.

While Charity had never been refined, languishing instead in disorder and destitution, her decline hinted that Kade had pierced *her* soul and shattered *her* mind, and that both were on the verge of total collapse. And his clean white office only made her look worse, like a bug under a microscope.

They spoke a little more, small talk of Edwin mostly. Then, because he didn't want to be attending Charity's funeral before Christmas, Cody forged ahead.

His pitch was smooth.

He told her that Can-Do could transform her life, her mind, her body, and her bank account. Then he unlocked the safe at the bottom of his desk and removed the jar of what he told her were *motivation patches*. They were the reason for everything she saw, and if she wanted to change her life like Cody had, the patch was the key. He waved a mole on his elbow past her face to prove he wore his own patch proudly.

To her credit, Charity listened to his testimony with the attention of a juror, but when he removed one of the round little progenies and offered it to her in the palm of his hand, she squished up her nose, doubtful. "That tiny thing did all that for you?" she asked.

"That tiny thing is called Slick, and it's the most important part of our program." Under Cody's shirt, Slick quivered at the compliment.

Of course, he hadn't told Charity *all* about Slick. Not that Slick was a living creature and *definitely* not that Charity would be inseparable from it once tethered. Not then, anyway. God save his soul, when she reached to take it from his hand—he hesitated. Slick had fixed his ugly skin and his ugly mind, but Slick's help didn't come free. There was the way Slick controlled him, for one. He'd learned to navigate her temper, but it wasn't always easy. She was increasingly temperamental, showing her phantom face freely now whenever she felt slighted or didn't get her way. The times he felt her rage boiling to his surface, he'd had to hide like a child. And he was hiding a lot lately. Stranger still was that he'd begun to feel his grandmother's experience as though it were his own, as though *her* tether was also his. Her euphoria became his euphoria, her indignation became his indignation, but less potent, like expired medication. It made him tired.

Then there was Slick's bulk. She had grown over his entire stomach and back and was starting to branch further. That morning, she'd overtaken his right ass cheek, and by that afternoon she'd begun creeping down the back of the same leg, and he knew it was only a matter of time before she literally consumed his cock. The sex he'd enjoyed when she'd first empowered him had now become impossible unless the woman was drunk or high enough to forget the pillow-sized leech on his body, but he felt like a rapist when he tried it, so he'd stopped altogether. And the way she was growing, Cody might not be able to piss, let alone rape, by the end of the month. For all the advantages she'd given him, discretion wasn't one.

It would be easy for anyone who hadn't experienced Slick to let her go. But it wasn't easy for Cody. Despite her dominance, she made him a better person, made him right and helped him cope with Kade, and he wouldn't give that up for anything in the world, even his cock. So his hesitation in giving Slick to Charity was a deliberation over the lesser evil, but not for long. One would kill her fast and the other would at least make her happy on the way.

He'd given it to her.

Now the evidence of his good decision put the two grand in her new Louis Vuitton purse and reminded him that one of tomorrow's consultations was a freebie.

The promotion had been Charity's idea. Within minutes of tethering, a dam-burst of ideas flooded her brain. People won't buy into what they don't believe, she'd said, then rationalized that the best way to get them to believe was to show them. The more locals elevated by Slick, the more others would be willing to attend consultation sessions. She was right. The next morning they gave twenty patches away and watched the skeptical recipients bloom with surprise. Their walking advertisements generated so much interest that by the end of the second day every session had been booked and Cody had asked Charity if Edwin would consider switching careers.

He thanked Charity for the reminder and wished them a good night, then poured himself a glass of wine, compliments of the newly tethered liquor-store manager next door.

"Oh, you read my mind," Elanor cooed, removing her stilettos. She rubbed her toes while Cody decanted a full glass. "I might be able to walk in theses puppies now but even Slick can't make them comfortable." They clinked their glasses, the growing mound under her armpit evident in the width of her reach. Slick hadn't yet deformed her the way Cody knew she was going to. "Something's on your mind, Cody Clyde. Tell me what it is so I can fix it for you."

"Do you think we're doing the right thing, Grandma?"

She didn't answer for some time. Then she said, "I think we're doing what we're doing, no more or less than anyone else is. When I ask myself if what we're doing is *wrong*—because that's really the question, now—I imagine where these people would be without our help. Lonely. Broke. Pushed so deep in the gutter they can't fight their way out. We're changing them, Cody. We're giving them a fighting chance. Sure, there's some nasty bits that go with it, but I'd take that over my old life any day." She raised her glass to him in victory.

But Cody knew Slick wasn't victory. Slick was penance. His grandmother had yet to see it that way because Slick hadn't engulfed her the way it had engulfed him. She could still cover the bruise on her temple, and she didn't blank out like he sometimes did now. Her memories were still fresh. She didn't have to work for them as he had to. She could still remember the names of her pets and the name of his grandfather and all the friends she hadn't seen in years but wanted to impress. Cody couldn't remember the name of the cat that shot off like a bullet any time he walked by. He used to know it. At least he thought so. Something with a T and a K. Or maybe not.

He could put these things out of his mind because he couldn't stop thinking about what Slick was doing to *her* mind. Her sweetness had soured like a pickle, and she was progressively less like Red Riding Hood's grandmother than the wolf. Sly. Like an addict.

She bumped him with her toe. "And don't you go worrying about me. I see the way you look at me. Never play poker. You'd lose your shirt."

"Grandma—"

"I'm good, Cody. You gave me life, you know that? It only took seventy-six years. I know the consequences, don't think I'm stupid. Could I live another ten years? Twenty? Maybe I could, but for what? To sit in one of those homes, playing bridge and drinking prune juice all day? That's not what I want. It never was. So I get a little fuzzy headed; dementia does the same thing. And as for this"—she touched the mound under her armpit—"big deal. I say let her take whatever she wants from me. Just let me have some fun before it's all gone. The circle of life, isn't it?"

"I'm sorry."

"Don't you dare be sorry. For everything you've ever done, don't you dare be sorry about this. I won't allow it."

He sighed. "I guess we're both going down together." They took up their glasses and cheered.

"Do you think that donut guy is going to give us any problems?" Elanor said as they drove home. "I heard him say something about talking to a constable. Was that right?"

"It's nothing," Cody said. "He's sending us a new client, that's all. I'm not worried about it. If he starts asking questions, we'll just give him a free sample."

"The donut guy or the cop?"

"Both."

16

Bill was tired. Since Diana had passed, he'd only gone to bed at dawn when he couldn't sleep and his mind finally gave out. Sometimes he'd gone weeks that way, crying until his eyes stung and his face hurt, sad like his world had ended again at that moment, and the next, and the one after that. Mornings like those, after his soul disgorged, he'd still give Maria his reassuring face, even if he felt nauseous with misery.

But today's tired was a different kind of tired. Last night, he had called Susan, more for the distraction of his stress over Luke, and found himself talking and laughing until well past midnight, after the restaurant had closed. It had been their third date but the first over dinner, and she had giggled when he got tomato sauce on his chin. She dabbed it off with her napkin, but it was no use. By the end of the meal, the stubble under Bill's mouth was red. She smudged some sauce under her own mouth to make him feel better, and that made them laugh even more. The times he sensed Diana with him, he felt she was on *Susan's* side of the table, laughing alongside her, giving Susan her approval. It pained and pleased him.

After the restaurant closed, neither of them wanted the night to end, but Bill was not ready to progress the way it looked like Susan wanted it to progress. When he hesitated, she instantly suggested one of Garrett's several all-night coffee bars. After two espressos and another glass of wine, it was four a.m. and he'd driven her home, giving her a peck on the cheek. It was soft.

He was at the counter still thinking of that soft cheek as he tapped his clipboard and scanned the inventory sheet. "Either of you see Ricky since we eighty-sixed him?"

"Not me," April shook her head. "Razors go missing again?"

"Five packs," Bill told her.

"He was in last week. I forgot to tell you. I didn't think he got anything because I caught him before he reached the counter. He must've snagged them before I kicked him out. Sorry, Bill." Zeke's voice drifted up from the lower shelf of canned soup in the panty aisle, where he was sitting cross-legged on the floor, counting.

"He didn't see it because it wasn't on his *phone*," Jasper called from his seat near the window. "I watched the whole thing. Ricky could've pocketed the whole rack, for all *he* was watching."

Bill looked up from his clipboard. "You saw it and you didn't say anything?"

"Not my business."

"All right." Bill rounded the counter and went to the coffee station. He pulled all the cups from the dispenser. "Since it's my business and I have to *pay* for those razors, you'll have to start paying for your coffee. Same price as everyone else. You can purchase your cup on the way in to save you a trip. Got to balance the books somehow." He stood beside Jasper with an armful of cups.

Martin sat back in his chair and folded his hands over his belly. "You kicked the gift horse, Jasper. And he just kicked you back." His raspy laugh made Zeke and April snicker.

Jasper lifted his rear and dug his wallet out of his pocket. He tossed two twenties on the table and scowled at Bill. "Buy yourself some razors that work, scruffy."

Getting money from Jasper was like squeezing blood from a stone, so Bill swiped the twenties before Jasper could take them back. "I think we'll let Luke and Maria split this for cleaning your car. But the price will double if you keep your lips zipped next time you see someone taking something they didn't pay for. Understood?" He flicked the bills against his fingers.

"They wanted to clean it," Jasper grumbled.

"You told them they'd get a surprise." Martin smacked Jasper's shoulder.

"Your shit stain on the back seat wasn't enough of a surprise?"

"Bill Asket, since when did you open a daycare? I think we need to teach the children how to talk nice," Barbara said behind them. She was holding a plate of scrambled eggs, bacon, and toast, which she gave to Bill with a sly smile. "I figured after spending all your energy last night, you needed to replenish your stores." She winked at him, knowing full well that he hadn't spent his energy the way she was suggesting.

Bill ignored the innuendo and the two men who were now gawking at him and stuffed a forkful of eggs into his mouth before they could storm him with questions.

Barbara rolled her eyes at Jasper and Martin. "Speaking of the circus, those two are bouncing off the walls up there. It might be another late night for you. They've made *plans*."

Tired as he was, Bill was looking forward to having Luke spend the night. It would give Maria something to look forward to while Luke helped with the inventory during the afternoon, and it would give the kid a break from Joe. Since his conversation with Ruby at the donut shop, he hadn't seen any fresh bruises on Luke, but the way the boy had winced when Bill tapped him on the shoulder the other day implied that Joe had maybe not changed his ways, just changed his *locations*.

Bill had been debating whether to ask Luke about his father, figuring that if all went well today, he would. He knew that Luke saw him as a pseudo father, a kinder stand-in, and might be willing to share out loud what they both held in their heads as long as it didn't get back to Joe. Bill couldn't promise that, but he *would* promise Luke that he would do everything in his power to keep him safe, no matter what he confided.

The overhead bell chimed and Ethel Bon Hoeffer, a garrulous widower with an eye for Martin, entered tugging a small girl. "Pick anything you want, Dee Dee," she said, then spotted Martin at the table. "And take all the time you need." Ethel released her hand and Dee Dee flew to the candy section.

Ethel's perfume reached them far before her body did, and Martin began to cough.

Jasper kicked him under the table. "I heard her husband died of suffocation."

"Be nice, boys," Barbara chided before Ethel approached.

A regular customer since his apprenticeship under Willie Flinder, Bill had known Ethel for decades and affectionately called her *Bonnie*, as in Bonnie and Clyde, because she'd once confided that her name made her feel like a boring old maid. She'd loved the moniker so much, she had it embroidered on a scarf she wore every fall. The same red scarf was tucked into the collar of her jacket now.

"How's my girl today?" Bill asked, accepting her hug.

The simple question prompted a ten-minute recapitulation of Ethel's issues with her doctor, neighbors, and the contractor undertaking her kitchen renovation. By the time she was finished, Bill's breakfast had grown cold, and Jasper had more than once flinched awake when his chin dropped off his hand.

"Sounds like you could use a coffee, Bonnie." Bill poured a cup and put it on the table.

She took the empty seat next to Martin, sidling closer to him than to the vacant space in the other direction. "Thank you, dear. I'm all right. It's just so hard being single at my age. All that money Raymond left me doesn't make it easier." Her eyes twinkled at Martin, but it was Jasper who sat a little straighter, his interest piqued. Ethel sipped her coffee. "But look at me prattling like a bird. You must think I'm a Patty Pouter, the way I talk, but I've got some great news too. Charlotte and Mike are getting back together."

Barbara shot a look at Bill. The last they'd heard, Ethel's daughter, Charlotte, had been attempting a trial separation while her husband Mike worked out his gambling issues after re-mortgaging their home and cleaning out their bank account without Charlotte's knowledge. It was only when her debit card was declined during a grocery shop that Charlotte discovered Mike's addiction. That had been six months ago, so the news that they were getting back together was a surprise.

Ethel held up a palm. "You don't have to say it. I know what you're thinking, and I thought the exact same thing. I mean, how in the world can she trust him, right? If that were me, I said, I wouldn't take him back. No way. I'd change the locks and bar the windows. But apparently he's on one of those new age programs, like one of those empowerment seminar kind of things, and he's taken a liking to it. Charlotte says he's a new person. Nothing like he used to be. If he keeps it up, I think it just might work."

Jasper, Martin, and Barbara were indifferent to the news, but it made Bill think. "It's not that new place down Hobson, is it? The old dry cleaners?"

"That's the one. You know it?"

"I'm familiar," Bill said.

Ethel frowned. "You're giving me that look you give *him* when he's blowing smoke up your arse," Ethel gestured to Jasper. "What's the problem?"

"I'm not sure there *is* a problem," Bill said. "But Luke and I took a tour there when I was picking him up the other day, and something didn't sit right with me. I don't know how to put it, but I think if something feels too good to be true, it usually is."

"Charlotte was skeptical too, so Mike's taking her for a consultation on Monday so she can see it for herself. If I've got nothing to do, I might just tag along." Ethel's eyelashes fluttered at Martin.

A knot tightened in Bill's stomach. The suspicion that the consultation wouldn't be good for Ethel made him look from her to Martin and back again. Martin seemed to know what Bill was thinking because he shook his head. The movement was so subtle it was imperceptible to Ethel, but it was clear as glass to

Bill. He elbowed Martin on the shoulder as if an idea had just occurred to him and said, "Hey Marty! You were looking for someone to go to the Antiques Show. If Bonnie is free on Monday, maybe she'll go with you."

Ethel immediately forgot about the consultation. She was free and already planning her outfit. Martin, on the other hand, grew green under Jasper's silent heckling. Martin said, "Jasper'll drive us. He's got a clock that needs cleaning. An *old* one. Some might call it decrepit, but those antique people might see some value in it. I'll bet they'll have to look really hard past the dirt." Vengeance spread across his face.

"Well, I haven't been chaperoned by *two* men since my twenties," Ethel said with a blush. "Let's make a date of it. You can pick me up early so we can have lunch. Or do you want breakfast? We can do *both*! First we'll go to . . ."

She prattled until even Barbara's eyes glazed over. Dee Dee, meanwhile, had already made multiple selections and put them on the counter, going back for another armful when she saw that her grandmother wasn't ready to leave yet.

As Jasper and Martin bickered against Ethel's growing plans, Bill excused himself to continue the inventory while Barbara went to collect Luke from *Glazed*, where the street was still busy and the light still shone. Alone with his thoughts in the storeroom, Bill thought of Susan and Luke and now Bonnie. That Can-Do had gotten to her son-in-law was no surprise because Bill had heard of at least three others who'd sought— and received—new leases on life: Vanessa Penner, Perry Searles, and Brandy Fogel, Police Chief Dan Fogel's ex-wife. Across the small city, news of Brandy and Vanessa's fresh skin and tight bodies had women green with envy and battling for their own consultations. But it was Perry Searles—the fifty-eight-year-old pasty accountant who'd recently suffered the deaths of two grandchildren on a swing set—that had Garretters from eleven to eighty-seven rumoring that the new Can-Do was not just transcendental but possibly even *magic*.

Bill had known Perry since grade school, with Perry ten years ahead. Perry had given Bill good advice when he'd first taken over the So-Lo, counseling him for free during the early years then accepting only nominal fees whenever the So-Lo's taxes were due or Bill had a problem requiring Perry's experience. The accountant had been a smoker since his teens, and his yellow-brown teeth and sallow skin had long given him the appearance of sick old man. But when Bill met with Perry for advice on how to incorporate Luke's wages into his books—or if he even should—he was too shocked by Perry's appearance to remember any of what he had said. He had a baby's pink skin. A movie star smile. And the sagging depression that had wilted his shoulders and stooped his spine was gone. He was cheerful and assertive, and offered ingenious solutions to Bill's secretive business arrangement with Luke.

Part of him was happy for Perry, but the other part—a more insistent part—was concerned not about Perry's transformation itself, but about the *speed* of his transformation. His Can-Do consultation had taken place barely a week ago. If Perry were the weather, the stock market, or even death, Bill could accept the clip, but it was too fast for a human, and definitely too fast to be natural.

Later that afternoon, with April gone and Luke and Zeke completing the confectionary counts, Bill closed the door on his small office and called Constable Brander.

"I didn't forget about you," Brander said when Bill stated his name. "I just didn't have anything to report yet. As far as we know, no one died because there's no *body* to prove it. And the only missing person's report filed since you and"—he shuffled some papers— "*Luke* took your detour was a dementia patient that's since been found. I'm afraid we may never have the answers you're looking for. I'm sorry that doesn't help."

"That helps plenty," Bill said. "But I guess the reason I'm calling . . . I'm not sure how to put this, but I was wondering if you have any information on the people that took over the old business."

"Information?" Brander asked.

"Have you seen what they've done to the place?"

"I haven't, but you're making me think I should; why is that?"

He appreciated the constable's no-nonsense approach, but it made him feel awkward about calling. He fell silent, unsure of how to begin, then he recalled what Brander had said the last time they'd spoken. "Remember when you said it's better to believe a lesser evil so you can sleep at night?"

"Uh-huh," Brander said vaguely.

"I think it was good advice, but since that new place opened up I haven't been able to sleep. Something's weird there. I can't explain it, but I can't shake the feeling that maybe your crime scene *was* the lesser evil than the spacey setup that replaced it. It looks sharp, like something in Toronto or Vancouver—and that's fine, honest—but the people going into that place are coming out different. As quick as pennies shined on a conveyor belt." He was sweating by the end of his clumsy explanation, so he opened a bottle of water and turned on the time-yellowed box fan that had come with the building.

"Different how?"

Bill explained about Perry and about the residents he'd seen when he'd last collected Luke.

Every fifth or sixth person as stunning as a newly hatched butterfly.

"That doesn't seem so bad to me."

"It doesn't *sound* bad," Bill agreed, "but the two that run the place—they've got bruises on their faces, like someone's hit them in the same spot. And when I went for a tour, they were acting as though they didn't want me to ask questions. I couldn't get any details from them, and when they *did* talk, they were vague. Maybe even a little angry."

"Nothing you've told me suggests they're breaking any laws, but I could pay them a visit and look into their hokeypokey for you. I'm always up for an old fashioned next door, if nothing comes of it. Stereotype be damned."

"I'll buy," Bill said gratefully.

"This one's on me. I've got a budget to use and a belly that knows it."

Afterward, with a gust of relief easing his nerves, Bill returned to the apartment where Luke and Maria had constructed a fort spreading over the entirety of the living room, with only the front open for TV viewing. Blankets were slung over the backs of kitchen chairs then pinioned with books to the seats so their roof didn't sag. A string of white Christmas lights had been scavenged from the storage room and clothes-pinned around the top. Through the back slit of their castle, Bill spied the two portable mattresses Maria used for sleepovers bookending a tray filled with snacks: chocolate chip cookies, pretzels, strawberries, cucumbers, sour rainbow candy, and a big bowl of popcorn. Winds of childhood rustled the blanket walls. Breezes of laughter escaped from the castle and filled the apartment.

Barbara passed him a glass of wine. "There's more action in this house than I've seen all year. First you and your marathon date and now these two and their conquest of the apartment. I'm thinking I should make plans to build a fort of my own tonight." She winked.

"Charles?" Bill raised an eyebrow.

"Uh-huh. I think I'm going to keep him for a while, but if he can't build me a castle like *that*, he's outta here."

They clinked glasses, watching Maria and Luke scurry about in last preparations before the movie. The *Goosebumps* logo was frozen on the screen. The toilet flushed, two cans of cream soda were snuck from the fridge, then the lights were dimmed and the movie began. Bill opened the door to the balcony, where Barbara joined him. The moon was clear and full in the auburn sky, the thrum of chatter from neighboring balconies sounding like crickets in corn fields.

"That thing with Bonnie, about her son-in-law, I don't think you're wrong," Barbara said after they settled.

"Oh?"

"I know what you're talking about. It's like the neighborhood had, I don't know, not a face lift but a *people* lift." She snapped her fingers. "Just like that. It's the strangest thing. I know people can change, but so many that quickly? If I didn't see it for myself, I would have thought it impossible. It makes me wonder what they're doing in that building, you know? If it's a bunch of bullshit, or if I've turned skeptical in my old age and that's how the world is *actually* working these days."

Bill sighed, "Things *have* gotten quicker. Or maybe we've gotten slower."

Music swept over them from the pub in the adjacent apartment building. Barbara patted her thigh to the familiar riff, both of them thinking, considering.

"When you went there," she said, "did you happen to notice anything on the sides of their faces? You're going to think I'm paranoid for saying this, but the people I saw had marks right here." Her dancing hand went to her temple. "Bruises. Like they'd all taken a good punch. The building is so... *new*... you know, so I peeked inside while I waited for Luke. Just through the glass as I passed—not like I cupped my hands like a stalker or anything. It just struck me as odd. Two people like that, then more on the street with the same mark. People like *us*. It's weird, isn't it?"

He told her about his phone call to Constable Brander.

"And I thought I was the paranoid one."

"Nothing wrong with being a concerned citizen."

They finished their wine. Barbara hugged the king and queen of Candyland Fortress goodbye, and Bill put water to boil for pasta. He was washing their wine glasses and listening to the roar of monsters from the TV when his cell phone rang. He wiped his hands on a dish towel and answered.

The calm voice on the other end of the line said, "Is this Bill Asket?"

"It is."

"Mr. Asket, my name is Jane Finch. I'm a patient coordinator at Garrett General. I was given your name by Isabelle Ruby

Vorlicky. You know Mrs. Vorlicky, sir?"

Bill didn't know an Isabelle, so it took him a moment to understand that the woman was talking about Ruby, Luke's mother. Alarm swept through him. He glanced at the tent, then went down the hallway to his bedroom and closed his door. "Has something happened to her?" he asked when he sat down.

"It would be best if we talked in person, Mr. Asket. How soon can you be at the hospital?"

17

Swells of nausea churned Bill's stomach. He stood in front of the building where he had become a widower. Where Maria had become motherless. Where Diana had taken her last breath. The memory paralyzed him. Waves of time spent and of time lost buckled his knees and snagged his breath, and he felt the building looming over him like an executioner, knowing his haste had been wasted. The institution seized him and he was powerless against it until the wail of an ambulance loosened its grip.

Swallowing the lump in his throat, he put the keys he'd been clutching in his pocket and went inside.

He hadn't been in the hospital since his heart had been torn out of him, but he could see it hadn't changed its wicked ways. It was filled with moans and sobs and so much pain it seemed to bleed misery, dropping onto this head and that soul and those cheeks. The atrium and its five tortured floors amplified its meanness. He hurried to the elevator, inside which the pressing of the walls crushed his lungs. Darkness mashed up against him so heavy that the woman with the bundle of flowers riding to his same floor asked if he were okay and the little boy holding her hand hid behind her legs, afraid. His response limped out. "I'm ... f-fine."

Slowly, too slowly, the elevator rose, and by the time the doors opened, Bill's heart was thundering and he was drenched in sweat. He brushed past the little boy and keeled over, panting for air.

The woman touched his shoulder. "If I could take your pain, I would. I don't know you, but I want you to know that. I'm sorry for whatever you're going through. Are you alone? If you need someone to come with you ..."

Bill raised a palm to reassure her. "Thank you. That's very kind. I'm sorry. I'm just ... remembering, I guess."

"Don't forget to remember the good stuff too." She smiled down at the boy and back up at Bill. "There's *strength* in the good stuff. Take care, now." Tugging the boy behind her, she walked away.

As though the stranger had *pushed* Diana inside his head—in the yellow dress when they first took Maria home from the hospital, with windswept hair in front of the campfire after a day at the beach, on a barstool beside the coffeepot, waiting for it to fill—Bill instantly felt better. Proceeding to the nursing station, he smoothed the front of his shirt and wiped his hands on the back of his jeans.

"I'm here to see Ruby Vorlicky," he said unsteadily to the lone nurse sitting at the desk. "Isabelle, I mean."

The nurse clicked some keys and looked at him through the big round spectacles anchored on her wide nose. "Jane will be right with you. It'll just be a moment." She gave him a tight smile, as though to keep her lips zipped lest disclosure spill out.

"Mr. Asket?" said a woman arriving from a neighboring hallway. There was a thin file folder in her hand, which she held to her chest as she led him to a consultation room at the end of the hall. She was a good foot taller than Bill and he had to take two steps for every one of hers. By the time he sat in the small dim space, his heart was again beating fast.

Jane shut the door. "Can I get you something to drink? A water or coffee, perhaps?"

He declined. "Ms. Finch—"

"Jane," she said politely.

"Jane," he echoed. "I think you called the wrong person. I barely know Ruby. Are you sure I'm supposed to be here?"

She nodded. "She asked for you by name. She says you're a family friend?"

"I am."

"Then you're the person I need to speak to. Since Isabelle—Ruby—has no living relatives we can trace and we can't find her husband, I have authority to discuss her medical and domestic situation only with you."

"She said this?"

"She did," Jane said. "She was very clear that we speak only with you." There was a pause as she opened the thin folder and began turning pages. "Earlier this afternoon, Ruby was involved in a domestic assault. I can't speak to who assaulted her because she won't say, but for the time being, Ruby is safe. That said, she has been severely injured. She's suffered multiple rib fractures, internal bleeding, a broken nose and an orbital fracture. A few of her teeth have been knocked out as well. This brings me to why you're here. Until she recovers, she won't be able to care for her son. Child Services prefers Luke to be removed from the home while the police investigate. They've spoken to Ruby and she suggested that Luke remain with you, if you'll agree to it. My professional concern is Ruby's care, but we know that her recovery will go much more smoothly if she knows her son is in a safe environment."

"Of course," Bill said at once. "He's welcome as long as he likes."

Jane pushed her shirtsleeves to her elbows, folded her arms on the table and leaned forward. "Good. You can expect a call from the caseworker at Child Services to go over the specifics and formalize the arrangement. I believe it's Admara Rahmbit. She's good. In the meantime, I'm here to answer any questions you have. From my end, I would also strongly recommend against Luke visiting, at least until the swelling in Ruby's face goes down. It can be extremely traumatic for a child to see a parent suffer, and I don't think it would be good for him to see her right now."

The lump Bill had swallowed earlier rose in his throat again. "Can I see her?"

She gave him a sympathetic smile. "I think Ruby would like that."

Out the door and down the corridor they went, passing one room, the next, another, serenaded by a chorus of beeps and groans and the haunted minor keys of raspy exhalations and mechanical inhalations. Bill bit the inside of his cheek to keep his anguish at bay and to remind himself that Ruby needed him more than he needed to escape his memories. Jane walked confidently, purposefully forward, but Bill couldn't help but see a man in one room cross himself at an older woman's bedside and a teenage girl in the next room read quietly from her phone to a middle-aged man with a series of wires stretching from the collar of his hospital gown. He didn't guess at their ailments.

Finally, they passed the nursing station and Jane stopped at the only room with a partially closed door. She tipped her chin toward it. "She's in a private room for the time being. Go on in."

A million pounds of fear nearly toppled him. He dragged it, inch by inch, into Ruby's room.

There were no flowers, no balloons, no get-well-soon cards, and Bill suspected there never would be. There was just Ruby and her swollen purple-black face. She stared at him.

"Hi Ruby," he whispered from four feet away.

She grunted a response, and it made her wince. Her left eye—still white, still green—shut out the pain but her right eye—dark as a fresh coat of blood—just stared straight ahead, too broken to do anything else.

"If you want me to go..."

"Sh-ay," she breathed, and Bill saw in that terrible moment that her teeth had been sawn like boards, cut to the roots, and that her tongue, so used to working sounds at the roof of her mouth, slid in and out without a barrier to hold it back.

A blast of nausea soured his stomach, but he took one of the bedside chairs near the window and pushed it so that it was next to the bed. It was too low. If he sat, Ruby would be a foot above his shoulders. During Diana's last days, she had preferred her bed low so it would be easier for her to hug Maria, and he proceeded to the buttons he remembered, forcing back the tears that were threatening his eyes.

When he faced her again, he said, "You don't deserve this, Ruby."

Her left eye blinked.

"You don't have to tell me what happened, Ruby, but seeing as you asked for me, I think you want to tell me. Am I right?"

She nodded.

He tried to focus on her whole face, to reassure her that it wasn't so bad, but the right side of her head drew him toward her like a traffic accident. Angry pink scalp glowed where there should have been hair. On her forehead, her cheek, her jaw, bumps swelled like eggs under the thin carpet of her pummeled skin. Finger strokes wound around her neck, cigarette burns stippled her earlobe, and in between the tape strips on Ruby's nose, there were *teeth marks,* put there by Joe.

"Tell me what happened, Ruby," Bill said gently.

With her crippled mouth and her mutilated face, Ruby explained. "He wanted my last cigarette, but I didn't give it to him."

He waited for more. "Is that it? He did all of this to you because he wanted a smoke?"

Ruby's words were tired words. She picked up her trampled tongue and spoke. "His car broke down and he wanted me to go get him a pack, but I'd just come off work and I was tired. I didn't want to walk, so I said I'd borrow some from the manager. He gives me smokes sometimes." She swallowed. "Joe's got this thing with people making him look bad. He said it didn't look right for his wife to go bumming things from people, even my manager. I told him he didn't care, but *Joe* cared." Her good eye looked away. "He wasn't always like this. You probably don't believe me, but he wasn't."

The last thing he wanted was to make her feel bad, so he said, "I believe you."

She settled a little. Her tightly wound shoulders uncoiled their tension and sank against the pillow. "Joe used to be smart. He used to work, too. Warehouse, mostly, but he was at that muffler repair shop on Mitton for a while. You know it?"

Bill nodded.

"They said he was the hardest worker they'd ever seen, but that only lasted a little while. He got fired for stealing. He swore he didn't do it, but now that I think about it, he probably did. *I* can't borrow anything without making him look bad, but he can take whatever he wants. He doesn't think it makes him look like an asshole." Her lips pressed together.

"What are you going to do now?"

She shrugged. "Same as I always do. Cops don't help me. And any friends I ever had were scared off by Joe. I'll get out and go to work. Joe will get arrested—if not for this, then for something else—and then it will be just me and Luke until Joe gets out again. I used to think that maybe his fight would leave him, but he's like those dogs that get meaner the older they get. He might not see me for months or even a year, but he'll *remember*. He never forgets what his teeth are for." The hand with the intravenous line touched her nose.

It occurred to him to offer a space for Ruby at the apartment, but the idea was overridden by the fear that Joe would find it. Maria already lost a mother, she did not need to lose her security too. "That's a terrible way to live. I'm sorry." He stared at his feet, thinking. After a time, he said, "Ruby, if I found a place for you, would you consider it? It wouldn't be much. If it weren't for Maria, I'd invite you to stay with us, but I think I have a solution that could work better for you, if you'll consider it."

"I can't pay you."

"I'm not asking for your money. I'm trying to help you."

She didn't answer, but her lip trembled. "I know that Luke and I . . . we don't look like much. I know our situation shows, but I'm working on it. I swear to God I'm working on it. Every time I put that damn apron on and scrub another man's toilet and clean another woman's sheets, and every time I get cussed at because I can't make those cheap rooms look like the Ritz fucking Carlton, I swear I'm working on it. Just the other day I thought, *Ruby, we're getting somewhere. We are.* All those nicer people in the area, even the junkies cleaning themselves up, the prostitutes wearing suits, I figured things were turning around for us."

The allusion to Can-Do was not lost on Bill. He was glad Ruby's neighborhood was getting a *people lift*, as Barbara put it, and if it meant there was less trouble for them, that was a good thing. Looking at Ruby, broken but hopeful because of some mystery Bill could not explain, he decided that if Brander's visit to Can-Do yielded nothing, he would accept the mystery for the miracle it seemed to be.

Just then, a yawn shuddered her swollen face. He pushed back from his chair and stood. "Things will turn around for you. This is just a pothole on your way to a smooth road. Luke's safe with me, and Joe's not going to get him, I promise you that. You take your time and recover the way you need to recover. If you need anything at all, don't call *him*, okay? Let me help you."

She snorted. "That's why he likes you better than his own dad."

Bill reddened, knowing that if Joe knew that, or even suspected it, Luke might end up in the hospital, too.

Before he turned to leave, Ruby said, "Don't bring him here yet, and don't tell him it was Joe."

"He'll know," Bill said.

"Don't bring him here. If you do anything for me, do that. Not until I'm ready, okay?" A tear rolled down the cheek of her good eye.

"Not until you're ready," he agreed.

Back in the parking lot, he hurried to the Volkswagen, the events of the last few hours disorienting him like a fog. He got inside, buckled his seatbelt, and started the engine. Then Bill Asket began to cry.

18

Cody shut his eyes. His office was too bright. The lobby was too bright. Everything gleamed like a spotlight. Even the dark. Sights and smells and sounds drilled into his head and serrated the pulp inside. A thunderclap of pain seared him. Then another. Ten times more the pain thrust at him, to the rhythm of his own heart. He swallowed three Advils dry, spread his arms to the edges of his desk, and tried to *will* Slick to heal him.

The sponge on his side quivered.

"Come on," he said, spitting it out because the pain had caught his voice, "I've given everything to you. Everything. You're going to die if *I* do. Don't you see that?"

It had to be true, Cody told himself. If he died, where would Slick go? Who would take a fifty-pound, life-sucking leech? Who would want the slithering thing suctioned to their body so that they couldn't piss, couldn't fuck, couldn't *be*?"

Puppies don't stay puppies forever, his grandmother had said when he was little and trying to bargain all the money in his piggybank for a mutt. She didn't tell him that some puppies eat your fucking cock and you end up pissing out of a hole you didn't know existed. Or that once you got a mutt, it controlled you until one of you died.

His head throbbed. His eyes burned. He wished he could have gone back to that day when he'd first spotted Slick and cut her off. Back then he'd had a chance, but there was no chance now. All his strength was hers. All his energy was hers. Nothing was his anymore. And he understood that it never had been, not even then. He pulled himself up, lumbered to the door, and locked it. If his grandmother were to come in when Slick finished him, she would want to be dead too, and he couldn't have that. At her insistence, there was a full-length mirror on the back of his door so she could check her makeup and hair. He had avoided it, but now he stood across from himself, half the man he used to be at his lowest. Cody Clyde. A small man made large. His parasite belly, his parasite ass, his parasite chest bulged and challenged the seams of his extra-large shirt. Sure, his skin was still Hollywood, but the bruise on his temple was Salem, and the gelatinous mess around him was Vlad's Sighișoara—only, Cody was impaled from *within*.

"Do it already," he implored his reflection. The mound under Cody's shirt shifted to the left. He steeled himself for pain, for the end to the pain that never went away, for his reunion with Kade until the devil shucked him below. "P—" The circuits in his brain misfired, then started up like an old engine. "P-p-please. I can't take t-this any m-more." The mound under his shirt moved to the right. Cody hit it. With the hands that were his and not his and with the might that was his and not his, he fought, he raged, he scratched and tore and twisted and struck, quietly, so his grandmother wouldn't hear. "Fucking do it already! Just d-do it! Please!" Crying, his voice spitting out of him and dripping down his chin, Cody begged to be free.

Slick's phantom face appeared in the mirror and Cody knew in that ugly instant . . . the phantom had always been himself. Unveiled, his dark self was the most vile, most selfish, most hideous creature he'd ever seen. More twisted and depraved than even Slick. The thing had made him a god, but oh Lord, it had brought out the devil in him too.

Cody fell to his knees, bracing himself against the ugliness in the mirror. Then he bit his lip until it bled, croaking his shame, when a great tide of movement made him look where he did not want to look.

His shirt ruffled like laundry on a clothesline.

His pants puffed out, in, out, as Slick stretched and twisted and released.

Carefully, like a slowly peeled sticker, Slick began to detach. First Cody's calves, then his thighs, then his cock—his cock! — were free. His hips, his back, and finally his stomach. Out the bottom of his right pantleg she came, worming forward, more and more until she was fully out and lumped in the corner near the door.

New tears sparkled in his eyes, but they were good tears, tears Cody hadn't cried since he was a child. His headache disappeared. The bruise on his temple vanished. But so, too, did the smoothness of his skin and the blockade between himself and the memory of Kade. The fire came back to him. His guilt clobbered him. And when Cody Clyde looked in the mirror, he saw that the shirt was draped over his body like a parachute over a twig. There, in his office while his grandmother and Charity and Edwin worked the front, Cody peeled off his shirt to inspect the damage.

Slick had emaciated him.

His collar bone was the meeting of two candle sticks. His ribs, two trays of pencils. His skin was thin as smoke and the color of ash. The veins that somehow sustained this body were fine as webs spun long ago. Everything that was not bone caved inward, deep inside, as though drawn in by a black hole, a locus of erasure inside his own body. He gulped. A tiny pea traveled up and down his throat. It was his Adam's apple. "W-what t-the f-f-f," he stuttered, but could not finish, because the vision of his needle teeth stole his breath.

Then all the memories he did not want to remember breached his feeble refusals and barreled back. Kade's baby boy skin. Kade's baby boy dimples. The fifteen-year-old-boy Cody had murdered. "Ahh. Ahh." He hid his face in his hands, moaning, hurt more by his own sin than by the horror of what he'd become.

Slick undulated against the floor as if to say, "Take a good look. You need me. You always did. You're a *murderer* without me. A child killer. You want to be a child killer, Cody? Go ahead."

Unable to stop himself, he dove back at her.

She accepted him at once, folding around him like paperclips to a magnet.

Kade faded, faded, and then he was gone. Cody lifted himself off the floor and got dressed, his shirt once again snug. He stood there for some time, understanding that with or without Slick, he would soon be dead, or that maybe whatever had been salvageable had already died, and this was his hell.

"Cody?" Charity knocked. "Do you have a minute, Cody?"

"One second," Cody called. He rushed back to his desk, drank a heavy gulp of whisky from the tin in his drawer, smoothed his hair and patted water on his cheeks. He glanced at the corner where Slick had been, then he opened the door.

"Shit Cody, you don't look so good." Charity sucked in air through her teeth. He told her he was fine, but her face twisted with doubt. "Are you sure? If this is a bad time, we can talk later."

Cody knew he might not have a *later*, hell, he might not have a *next minute*, so he smiled and said, "Whatever time I have is yours."

Her stilettos clicked against the floor, and she lowered herself into the chair on the opposite side of his desk. The way her jaw was set and the way she fidgeted with the ring Edwin had slid on her finger over the weekend hinted that Cody wasn't going to like whatever had brought her in.

She said, "Before you freak, you need to hear me out. All the way to the end. I know you're not going to be happy about it, but if you really, I mean *really*, think about it, it won't seem as bad as it sounds."

That drilling in his head again.

"Say you're going to l—" She paused. Her eyes stared blankly ahead.

Cody flapped a hand in front of her face, but she didn't blink, nor did she immediately continue. The disconnections—his, hers, Edwin's, his grandmother's—were more frequent now, but Cody sensed them all, like a control switch on a motherboard. They were all secondary devices to his primary, their signals crisscrossing the overloaded highway in his brain.

He looked at his watch and counted down to the time when Charity's circuits would connect again. His eyes swung back to her.

"—isten to me. Promise?"

"Promise," he said, figuring it couldn't be that bad.

But it was worse than bad. The moment she spoke Terry's name, Cody knew it was terrible. "You know how Eddie and I got that new apartment? Well, I went to the trailer to pick up a few things and Terry was there, said he'd been sitting there all morning. I told him he should have called if he wanted to talk to me, but of course I didn't tell him I changed my number. He didn't look good, Cody. He looked *awful*, just awful."

Cody groaned. "Tell me you didn't—"

"What else was I supposed to do? He saw me and knew something was up. I couldn't exactly hide it now, could I? Look, I know he deserves to be in jail for what he did to Kade, but I couldn't just leave him like that, Cody. He's hurting, too, probably more than any of us."

His mouth fell open and he tilted his head as if he hadn't heard quite right. "What do you mean, *for what he did to Kade*?"

She hesitated and glanced at the open door to see if anyone was listening. "You know..."

"Maybe I don't," Cody said.

"You don't remember?"

Cody remembered getting out of Henley and he remembered Terry knocking the bucket of chicken out of his hands and he remembered Terry telling him that he, *Cody*, had tripped Kade into the fire. But Cody had never remembered actually *doing* it. The shock of Terry's story convinced him it was true, but seeing the look on Charity's face made him wonder if the last few months of torture had been directed at the wrong person.

He relayed Terry's account of the night. As he spoke, her eyes widened, her lips parted, and she shook her head, back and forth, back and forth, like a metronome timed to the beat of lies.

"All this time you thought . . . ?"

Grief whistled into him. Relief whimpered out. He nodded.

Charity reached across the table and took his hand. "Oh, Codes. No, no, no. It wasn't *you*. Oh God, no. I swear it on my life."

She leaned close and whispered the true account of that dreadful night, little hiccups of anguish accenting the worst of it. Then she rushed around the table and hugged him. Her small arms barely reached around, but she held tight and pressed her sympathy into what was left of his body and what had become of Slick's.

Cody sniffed and hugged her back. The over-tensed strings of his nerves relaxed. As he held her, the last few months swept over him, almost overwhelmed him. Until now, the ebbing of his guilt was an unburdening only Slick had been able to achieve. Had Terry not painted him with the murderer brush, Cody might have had a smooth recovery under Henley's guidance, might never have needed Slick. But Terry's soul-crushing lie had caused him to accept the parasite and all its trouble as easily as taking a breath.

He stiffened and drew away. "You knew that . . . what he . . . and you want to help him? What the fuck for?"

She flinched. "I know he's not good, Cody, but we can make him *better*, don't you see? Think of it that way. If we don't do something, Terry's going to keep on being Terry and all that goes with him. He's going to keep on fighting and stealing and basically being the world's biggest asshole. There are other people to consider. They put up with his shit just as much as any of us, but it doesn't have to be like that. We can help them. We'd be doing *them* a favor, not Terry."

There was nothing Cody wanted to do less than help Terry, but Charity wasn't wrong. In the ranking of the world's most contemptible people, Terry was somewhere between a Ponzi scheme magnate and whoever had invented baby cages. Cody had no illusions that he was any better, not with their burgeoning business of life-sucking leeches, but neither did he feel he was any worse. The only difference between them was that Terry had more time left. This made Cody think: he was beyond salvation, but maybe, maybe, if he took care of Terry, he could redeem at least a sliver of his soul, feel *right* about something. Still, the thought of having to see Terry's pubic-hair face and broken-bottle teeth repulsed him. He was about to say that Terry didn't deserve their help, but then he realized that it was *exactly* what Terry deserved.

"Talk to me, Cody. Don't be like that. If we don't help him, he's going to rat, you know he will. He'll blow this whole thing up and he'll *tell*." She stressed the last word so he knew what she was insinuating. "But it won't be the truth, Cody. He'll tell it like he told you."

"Set up an appointment—"

Charity cringed. "He's already *here*. Eddie's got him in pod three. Don't be mad, okay? He followed me here. I didn't know what else to do."

"You should have led with that." He was about to say more when his grandmother's head appeared in the doorway.

"Your two o'clock is in pod one," she said. With an apologetic glance at Cody, Charity dashed out of the room. Elanor frowned. "Am I going to have to throw you in the shower again, or do we need a hose this time? We've signed two firemen who could give you a good dousing if you need it."

He looked at the woman whose fate he'd sealed and felt the broken pieces of his heart rattle against his rib cage. The mound under her arm had grown so large, she couldn't put it down. Just last week she had still been able to fit the tailored blouses she'd bought, but now she was relegated to oversized sweaters. Even then, she appeared to have a third breast the size of a watermelon tucked below her armpit. It was the same width as the bruise on her face.

She stepped inside and closed the door. "Don't look at me like that. I know what you see. You're looking at my *gift* like I've got cancer. Wipe it off this instant or I'll have the scumbag Charity brought in do it for me."

"I'm sorry, Grandma."

"I don't want your pity. You brought me *life*, Cody. Better than I could've ever hoped for. You won't want to hear this, but I have a better love life now than I did when I was with your grandfather."

As if he couldn't feel worse, the taste of vomit erupted at the back of his throat. He choked it down.

"You should be happy for me. No one has sex at my age. Either we're too afraid we'll shit ourselves or we fall asleep before we get undressed. It's true, Cody. Norm doesn't care about *this*." With her other hand, she pointed to the growth where Slick was. "He likes it. His is almost just as big as mine."

Her cheeks flushed. "We use them as foreplay. It's quite freeing, actually."

Now the vomit did come. It hit the floor and splattered on his shoes.

"Stop being an infant," Elanor chided. She went to the cabinet on the far wall and retrieved her purse, then put a roll of antacids in front of him while he wiped his mouth with a tissue. "You know what I've learned? I've learned that life's too short. Worry just speeds it up. *Zoom*. And it's gone. Just like that. I've got no time to waste bothering over being proper anymore, so I'm going to cuss and—"

Don't say it, he thought, but he knew what she was going to say when her circuits connected again in precisely seven seconds.

"—fuck until I can't. And that's a perfectly fine way to go. There's a lot of people who don't get to be my age, Cody. A hell of a lot of them. Don't think for a solid second I'm not thankful I've got what I've got. Hear me?"

Against his will, against everything in him that was still *proper*, he nodded. She clicked her tongue at him and left without another word.

"Just kill me now," he muttered to the empty room.

In answer, Slick eased his headache. A peace offering, he figured, but it had hurt so bad the relief made him resent Slick a little less. Sitting there, wiping the puke off his shoe and trying to forget about his grandmother's sex life and the lie of all lies Terry had told him, Cody couldn't hate Slick, not really. The choices he'd made were all his own. He had no one to blame but himself. It was his grandmother who'd taught him that. Henley had only reinforced it. Were it not for Cody's Can-Do overdose,

Slick wouldn't even be here. So all the trouble and all the deformities and all the impending death were his own doing. He sighed through his nose, wishing he had died that day.

He took another sip of whisky, smoothed the wrinkles on his shirt, and spritzed himself with cologne. He didn't feel like a million bucks, but he sure as hell would smell like it when he saw Terry. A moment later, he left his office and strode toward pod three, the farthest room away.

The door was closed. Outside, Cody hesitated and then Slick did a strange thing. She wound toward the back of his body so as not to show Terry she was there. Like an animal rearing for ambush.

"Well fuck me if I ain't seen Jesus," Terry said before Cody shut the door.

Cody held his tongue.

Terry leaned back, targeting Cody with one narrowed eye. He whistled. "Looky, looky what a cookie! Haven't seen your face in so long, I almost forgot what you looked like, but it sure as hell wasn't this." His pubic-hair face and his pinhole eyes cut high then low, as though scraping away the shell he'd known.

"What do you want, Terry?"

Terry's dirty hands flew up in a wide V. "I want what anyone wants, what we all want. Nothing wrong with that. I just figured since you're a big businessman now, you might have something I might like. Word is you're a hotshot, a magic man, crackerjack fixing the stack. Don't act like it's not true, you smell like money."

Cody's fists curled. Rage boiled up inside him and he felt Slick's phantom face simmering under his skin, but it was Slick, not Cody, who tempered his fury, soothing him as she had when she was first with him. He counted as his chest expanded with air. "We do all right." *Murderer*, he thought. He pulled the chair opposite Terry's further back and sat down.

"Well? What do you want me to do, Cody, beg? I'm not fucking begging. No reason to. You and I both know what'll happen if you don't hook me up." The corner of his mouth split into a smirk, the hair below his chin curtained sideways, and Cody saw there were white specks in it—cracker or breadcrumbs, maybe, but more likely meth that Terry had been careless with.

Mists of excitement came to him then. Slick's eagerness to get at Terry moistened his back, layering it with a sheen of what could be sweat or whatever came of a parasitic orgasm. Slick *wanted* Terry, actually wanted him, more than any other recruit they'd since enlisted. Not for the first time it occurred to Cody that Slick preferred degenerates, as though the challenge of fixing them—and subsequently destroying them—was her purpose, her *modus operandi*.

Cody could relate. There was no one on earth he wanted Slick to *fix* more than Terry. And Cody was determined to stay alive long enough to watch him fall. He sat back and stretched his legs, slinging an arm over the back of the chair. Slick spread out around him in the thinnest layer possible.

"I'll help you out, Terry." He thought of the pitch they gave recruits. *Do you want to elevate yourself? Your new life starts with Can-Do. Can-Do can make you.* Terry wouldn't believe that bullshit, and Cody didn't want to shovel it to him. Instead, he drew from his pocket the little bottle of peppercorns and held it up.

Terry squinted. "That it? You're telling me those turds did all this"—he waggled a finger at Cody— "to you?"

Slick tightened at the word *turds*, and for an instant Cody felt as if he were wearing a hardened clay mask.

Cody said, "That's our secret. We call it Slick. Just stick one anywhere on your body and Slick will do the rest."

"You're shitting me."

Cody brought out the mole on his elbow, flashed it to Terry's bloodshot eyes, then rolled down his sleeve again. "That's it."

"Is this some kind of trick? You fucking with me?" Terry scowled. "I'm supposed to believe that did *that* to you? To Charity? All those fuckers out there? No way, man. No way. I'm not buying it." He huffed, and his noxious breath hit Cody like a slap.

"Try it." Cody pried the lid off the jar and with two fingers plucked one of Slick's progeny out. He held it out to Terry and smiled with his Hollywood teeth. "Put it anywhere you like. Most people like it somewhere discrete that you can cover, but anywhere is fine. Even your face."

Disbelief wrinkled Terry's blistered lips. "You don't swallow it?"

"Just put it on your skin," Cody said.

"Like China White? Fenty?"

Cody nodded, as though the comparison made it safe. *Just like fentanyl, you pube-faced fuck.*

Terry tucked his hands under his armpits and thought. It was a slow process—him trying to figure out Cody's trick, Cody knowing Terry never would. He hummed, he rolled his tongue under his cheeks, then under his bottom lip where a cluster of sores were scabbed over. "I don't know, man. Sounds too easy."

"What's it hurt to try?" Cody's arm stretched further. The white room and the white walls and the white lights made that tiny little speck of Slick that much more innocuous. "No one has to see it."

Terry picked the little ball out of Cody's hands, sniffed it, brought it within an inch of his eye, then spread the hairs under his chin and stuck Slick behind the curtain of hair on the soft underside of his throat. On Cody's back, Slick practically thronged with joy. A moment passed, then another. The overhead ventilation grew loud with their silence. The whistling of Terry's deviated septum was practically the siren of a tea kettle.

"If you're fucking with me . . ." Terry warned.

"Give it a second," Cody said, aware that Slick was already tethering.

"I thought you'd end up like Billy," Terry said when nothing happened. He fixed Cody with a look that made Cody want to rip his face off.

"Billy?"

"Shit, I figured out of all of us, *you'd* be the first to fry your mind meat. Billy's sizzled, man, *sizzled*. A burnt pancake. Black bacon. Went silent like his tongue got torn out and banged his head against the wall till it cracked. The wall *and* his head. I hear he's talking now, but he doesn't make much sense. Something about chicken fries or black marble or shit like that. He's in the looney unit in London. Or maybe Barrie. Can't remember. He's fucked either way." Terry shrugged, and with a sigh, he squeezed his bottom lip. "I'm starting to think you're playing me, Versace."

The moniker almost made Cody laugh, especially because Terry had mispronounced the fashion brand and it came out as *Ver-say-chi* instead. But he didn't laugh. He was too busy watching Terry's beard untwist and shine before his very eyes. The hair that had made Cody's own intestines knot now smoothed and neatly straightened. Terry's testicle neck, all wiggly turkey wattle as long as Cody had known him, unwrinkled and filled like a deflated balloon gone back the other way. Terry must have felt it because his eyes widened and his mouth opened and he let out a little *glut glut glut* sound as though he was gulping water.

I hope he drowns, Cody thought, knowing that in time Terry would. Slick was tethered to his goddamn neck, after all. With any luck, Slick would suffocate the son of a bitch before the month was done. Suddenly the loss of his own cock didn't seem so bad. Cody smiled and flashed his phantom face. Terry was done for, anyway. "You okay, Terry?" his skeleton mouthed.

Terry sprang out of his seat, patting his jerking body, gaping at Cody's absent eyes and decrepit skin. "What the fuck'd you do to me? Why is— What are y—" Terry's hands flew to his neck, then to his mouth, his ears, the top of his head. "Hawwwwww..." he moaned.

Placidly, Cody observed Terry flail and knock about the room. He had learned that each transformation went faster than the last, as though with each new spawn Slick was learning how to get it right. Like the progression of a writer on his tenth book or a painter on his twentieth portrait. Where Cody's own elevation had taken weeks from start to the beginning of the end, his grandmother's had taken half of that, and Charity's a fraction of his grandmother's. With over three hundred recruits and counting, Terry was converting before Cody's eyes at the speed of a toilet flush. *Big shits go bye-bye*, Cody thought, and grinned.

Bent over in a spasm of confusion, Terry overturned his chair. A glaze of anger reddened his cheeks and puffed his veins. He *glut-glut-glutted* again, took up the chair and hoisted it above his head. Cody flinched at the swing coming at him, but then—midair—the chair froze. Terry's eyes swung to his sleeveless arms, where his matchstick bones swelled and where his boil ridden skin swallowed up the track marks and the infections. Slowly, slowly, his new arms lowered the chair. A squeak rose in his throat as his nailbeds pinkened and his pale-addict hands tanned to a light golden beige. "Cody?" he said, all rasp out of his voice.

"How do you feel? She's pretty great, isn't she?" Cody said.

"She? How?" Terry said.

All rooms were fitted with full length mirrors for moments like this, and Cody pointed to the one on the back of the door now. "Check it out," he said.

The chair went back to the floor. Terry took one step, two, testing his new feet and his new legs. He stumbled. He wobbled. Another step. His spine aligned. His shoulders drew back as if pulled by a wire. It was the progression from hand-walking ape to runway-strutting model.

Terry gasped at his reflection. Gone were his pinhead pupils and his drug-sagged lids. The eyes that hadn't been white for so long now looked bleached, his irises the color of sea blue urinal pucks masking the piss. His rutted skin, tracked by dependence since the day Cody had met him at the Dorion, gathered and packed and smoothed. And when Terry opened his mouth to cry out, twenty-eight brilliant white teeth imitated the movement. By the time Slick was finished, Terry was not just pleasant to look at but *handsome.*

"You've got to be fucking kidding me!" Terry blurted. "No way. No fucking way. Are you serious? Holy shit, Cody!" He marveled at his biceps and triceps and glutes and abs as Cody looked on. "Am I dreaming?"

Cody stuffed his hands in his pockets and leaned against the wall. "Feels like it, doesn't it? I felt the same way, but you get used to it after a while."

"What *is* this?" Terry said, inspecting Slick's nesting place on his throat.

He gave Terry the fabricated story that had become the core of their sales pitch. Slick was the perfect mix of vitamins, minerals, and amino acids, with a little psychological affirmation thrown in, discovered the morning after a hangover. It was his gift to the world, a way to right his wrong, to atone for Kade's death. He struggled not to tear Terry's eyes out after the last part, and he felt Slick doing the same. They were still on the same team, it seemed.

Still, Terry didn't confess. Didn't take the miracle of his transformation to retrieve the lie he'd thrown at Cody. Instead, he drove it deeper, like a thumb on a tack. "Maybe if you'd got this sooner, he'd still be alive, huh?" Focused on the mirror, Terry picked his new teeth.

An explosion of hate charged Cody's face, his fists, and he was about to bring all his fury and all his anger and all his grief down on Terry's perfect little head when someone knocked on the door.

"Cody?" Edwin called from the other side. "The police are here."

19

Maria woke squealing. Off the bed and down the hall and to the kitchen she flew, jumping and galloping until Mr. Turner in the apartment below them banged on the roof with his cane and shouted that it was only six a.m., and could they keep that racket down? For a minute, it worked. Then her excitement grew, grew more, until it whistled out and hammered Bill behind the eyes.

He put down his coffee and sighed. "Deal's off if I go deaf."

Luke removed the fingers plugging his ears. "Is it safe now?" he said, wincing in case Maria started again.

"Uh-uh-uh," Bill shushed her before her puffed out cheeks could blow again. "If we wake Mrs. T, she's going to come and we'll never get her to leave. You want to go today or tomorrow?" Maria's eyes grew as wide as Oreos. Vera Tallington, a rose-haired, bifocaled woman affectionately known as *Mrs. T* by her neighbors, was as old as she was inquisitive and had a habit of inserting herself wherever there was news in the building. The obligation Bill evoked instantly quieted her.

"Today," she whispered.

"Okay then," Bill whispered Back. "Now you two eat while I shower." He went down the hall to the sounds of bowls being drawn from the cupboard and Maria asking Luke which he preferred, Sugar Corns or Sweet-O's.

The water ran hot and he took his time, feeling rested after another night's peaceful sleep. Though Ruby was still in the hospital, she was recovering, and Bill took comfort in the fact that for the time being both she and Luke were safe. After the weekend, if the bandages on Ruby's nose were removed and the bruises had healed enough to camouflage with Barbara's makeup, he and Ruby had agreed that it might even be time for a visit from Luke. It pained Bill to keep Luke away almost as much as it pained Luke to *stay* away, and though he hadn't relayed the specifics of her injuries to him, Bill felt that deep down Luke knew his mother's condition and who was responsible for it. Meanwhile, Bill did everything he could to make life normal for the boy, from helping him with homework after school to treating Luke and Maria to movies and dinners and more than a few games of bowling, to suggesting he help Maria choose a kitten for her upcoming birthday, which they were doing today.

Diana had wanted Maria to grow up with an animal, believing that pets helped nurture responsibility and empathy, but the day they planned to adopt a kitten, she had felt unwell. By that evening, she couldn't get out of bed. The next morning, she had needed his help to walk to the bathroom. Come afternoon, she had been admitted to the hospital, where she had stayed until her last breath three weeks later.

Since then neither he nor Maria had wanted a cat, nor anything that would remind them of the love they'd lost or the life that could have been. But that sneaky magician, Time, had wound its way through them, marking with its sundial the increments of company, of Barbara, of April, of Zeke, Martin, Jasper, Susan, and now Luke. Especially Luke. New purpose eased them into better days. Concern for Luke had begun to mend their crippled hearts. And though they would be making their selection without Diana, Bill knew the time was right.

Back in the kitchen, the carnage of breakfast spread from the sink to the television. Maria had insisted on serving Luke, as evidenced by the trail of milk leading to two bowls on the coffee table, full to the brim. They ate with their faces over their bowls, debating which cartoon character was the spy.

He gave Luke instructions to keep Maria out of his bedroom, should she go looking for presents, and told Maria that if the kitchen wasn't cleaned by the time he returned from the store, they would be buying a lizard instead. By the time his shoes were on, the TV was off and the faucet was already running.

Down one flight of stairs, two, all the way to the So-Lo he went, eschewing the elevator for exercise, confinement for freedom. He pulled the knob on the interior door and felt the familiar prick of pride for his business.

From the deli counter, April waved. "I'm starting to think a day off will kill you."

"If we could be so lucky," Jasper grumbled, but winked to let Bill know he was only half-serious.

"Just checking in," Bill said.

"He doesn't trust you," Jasper told April.

Martin elbowed him in the ribs. "Your ass has been parked there so long he's probably making sure you haven't *died*."

Jasper smacked him with his hat.

The microwave dinged. April took the eggs she'd cooked and topped an English muffin with them, added a thick slice of cheddar cheese and carried the plate to Martin. "Maria must be bouncing off the walls," April said, knowing a kitten would carry the Asket name by the end of the day. "Is it still Fluffball Marshmallow Asket or Cuddlebear Angel Bee Asket?"

"I've got another a-word for you," Jasper laughed.

Bill ignored him. "We're going to let the cat decide, apparently. Maria's got a few names she's going to run by the kitten and see what happens."

"I like it," April said.

"We'll be a few hours, maybe more, but if you need anything, I'll have my cell."

"And call you so you can rush over and make sure the shelves are straight? I'm sure we'll be fine without you. See all the cats in the world, and don't come back until you do." April took Bill by the shoulders, spun him around, and gave him a gentle push toward the door.

Pausing in the doorway, Bill said, "Boston cream or cruller?"

"Tim's or the good stuff?"

"The good stuff."

April topped Martin and Jasper's coffees then excused herself to talk to Bill. She lowered her voice. "Why all the way over there? Luke need something from the apartment? Is Ruby *home*?" Her eyebrows knit up.

Luke's stay was well known, and though Bill had been vague on the extent of Ruby's hospital admission, everyone at the So-Lo had been rooting for her recovery. "Not yet. They say she's going to need another week, maybe a few days more. I'm meeting that officer I told you about while Barbara takes the kids for donuts. There's a pet shop across the street."

"Cops like cats. Proven fact," April said. "Get one for him and you'll never get a ticket again."

"Or," Bill said, "just don't break the law, huh?"

"That, too." She shrugged.

An hour later, with Barbara in the passenger seat and Maria and Luke in the back trying to persuade Bill to adopt *two* kittens, they set off. Early October, but the old Volkswagen warmed at the pace of a traffic jam, and their breath fogged the car until they crossed the Novadale Bridge and turned onto Hobson. Bill hadn't been to the area since his visit to Creepy Cleaners, so he hadn't seen the renewal Barbara raved about whenever she collected Luke.

There were no boards on windows, no addicts collapsed in alleys, and no backseat transactions. Sidewalks were swept, graffiti had been removed, and new lights illuminated the tidy street from storefronts to apartments. Music played from speakers not stolen and perfume wafted from flowers not trampled. Smells of bread and slow-cooked meat for the evening's supper were as new as the people, now reading books, now walking dogs, now meeting each other without suspicion.

"Wow," Bill said, pulling the Volkswagen into a stall in front of the corner grocery. "You weren't kidding. If I live a thousand more years, I don't think I'll ever see anything as incredible as this."

Barbara unbuckled her seatbelt. "I told you. It's been getting better every day. I hear they're getting their own YMCA just over there." She reached across Bill and pointed out his window to an empty parking lot near the abandoned rail station. A chain-link fence had been erected since Bill had last visited, with an excavator, loader, bulldozer, and several forklifts locked inside. A sign zip-tied to the fence stated that it was the *future home of the Hobson YMCA*.

Bill leaned over the steering wheel to get a better look and shook his head.

Barbara frowned. "What? This is a *good* thing. They should have built one here a long time ago. I'll bet half their problems would have been solved."

"It's good for the area, absolutely," Bill said, "but how the hell does a YMCA spring up overnight?"

"It's not up yet," Barbara said.

"Yes, but they're starting construction on it. Those things take months, *years*, even. There's permitting and approvals and usually one heck of a bidding process, not to mention community information and feedback sessions. Tell me, how does a neighborhood like this was just a month ago get to that stage that quickly? I haven't heard of any consultations. Either someone is greasing some pockets or there's something strange going on."

"*Greasing pockets.*" Barbara laughed as they got out of the car. "It's a YMCA, not a casino. April's right, you *do* need a vacation."

He locked the car. They gathered on the sidewalk outside Harlan's Grocery, then Maria and Luke skipped ahead while Bill and Barbara walked a slower pace. The passersby were cleaner than he remembered. Clothing was spotless, hair was combed, and not a single person didn't smile and wave, smile and wave, at them or at no one in particular, like happy, empty drones. Bill was thinking that maybe he did need a vacation, that it had been so long since he'd truly relaxed that his mind had forgotten how to rest, when a woman with a bruise from her eyebrow to her chin caught his attention. She'd had the same bruise he saw on the Can-Do Creeps, in the same place on the left side of her temple.

Barbara noticed it too, because she turned to look at the woman as she passed, then a man, then two teenagers, then a very attractive delivery driver. Her hand reached for her own temple. "Maybe we both need a vacation," she murmured.

As if lured by Barbara's recognition, the woman, the man, the teenagers, and the delivery driver all turned toward her. The teens stopped walking. The woman pivoted on her heels. The man's coffee, which had been near his face, went down to his side, where he held it still as ice at night. The delivery driver pressed his breaks until the van stopped in the middle of the street, letting it idle as he looked at her.

A chill ran down Barbara's spine and up Bill's. Ahead, Maria and Luke were still skipping, engrossed in childhood, oblivious to the three women walking elbow-to-elbow toward them, with three identical dark marks on the left side of their beautiful, laughing faces.

"Slow down!" Bill called.

Their enchantment popped by Bill's caution, Maria and Luke began to swing toward his voice when Maria set her eyes on the trio of laughing women. Not on their red-stained lips or their magazine-worthy cheeks or their glossy mannequin hair, but on their bruises, only their bruises, as a child is wont to do. She politely pretended she hadn't seen, but it was too late. The three women stopped in their stride right in front of Maria and Luke and *glared* at them with all the meanness of a junior-high principal at the beginning of detention. And when Maria and Luke backpedaled and ran to Bill's side, three phantom faces flickered just once, and then were beautiful, yet bruised, again. They were the same faces as the phantom pedestrian that had smacked the hood of Bill's Volkswagen not long ago. The one he'd convinced himself he hadn't seen.

Bill clamped Maria's hand and Barbara clamped Luke's. Though he was too old for handholding, Luke squeezed Barbara's fingers until they had passed the women and were safely inside the donut shop.

"Well, I think we all need a spot of sugar, don't we?" Barbara said brightly once they had joined the long line near the counter. Over Luke and Maria's heads, she gave Bill a look that suggested they be quick about it.

Bill looked for Brander but didn't see him. He casually scanned the café, noted another bruise, another, yet another, and though it was ridiculous, a trepidation scratched at him. "You two stay close, you hear?" Maria and Luke nodded at once.

Luke said, "Did you see it, Bill? The—" he made a face and pointed to his temple, then stuck his tongue out and pretended to choke himself. Barbara gestured for him to quit it, which he promptly did.

"I saw it, all right. I'm not sure what the hell that was, but I saw it. You okay, kiddo?"

Maria nodded up at him, but she'd gone pale and her bottom lip quivered. "They looked like monsters, Daddy."

"They looked like Mrs. T without her makeup," Bill said to make her giggle.

Just then a blast of cold air swept into the café, followed by Constable Brander, holding on to a hat that threated to fly off his head. Bill raised an arm to greet him.

Brander stomped his feet on the mat, strode to the end of the line, and stretched out a gloved hand. "Getting windy out there. Gotta love fall in Canada; if it's not snowing, it's blowing. Eeesh! Nice to see you, Bill. Sorry for the wait. There's some work going on at the switchyard, and I got caught up on the wrong side of it. Must've been a hundred of us waiting on that damn train by the time they lifted that arm up." He noticed the others and tipped his hat to them, smiling with twenty-eight perfectly white teeth.

The line moved forward. Barbara nudged the kids toward the counter, pointing out the Boston creams and the vanilla sprinkles and the monster cookies, having them guess the ingredients to keep their attention away from the other patrons. A few minutes later, she and Bill parted to opposite sides of the café so Bill could talk privately with Brander.

The presence of a police officer should have comforted him, but Bill couldn't help looking over his shoulder to peek at Barbara, Maria, and Luke. No one in the café had reacted the way the trio of glaring women or delivery driver had, but a growing sense of unease made his coffee taste bitter.

He added a packet of sugar and said to Brander, "Thanks for meeting me. I'm sure you have more important things to do, but I appreciate your time."

Brander waved Bill's worry away. "It's nothing. I'm in the area anyway." He removed the lid from his coffee and blew the top of the liquid to cool it. Bill noticed that in the time since he'd last seen Brander, the man had lost a significant amount of weight, maybe forty or fifty pounds, and that the long-night pouches under the man's eyes had seen a good amount of rest.

Brander must have caught Bill's observation because he said, "I was barely older than Luke when I started at the department. I didn't know what I was getting into—none of us ever do—so I've seen a lot of shit in my time. Most of it in this area. Right here. It takes a toll, seeing the things I have, and I'd be lying if I told you nothing surprised me anymore. That might have been true the first time I met you and Luke, but I got to say, a complete rejuvenation of thug and drug street wasn't on my list of expectations. Used to be I couldn't leave the neighborhood. I'd finish one call and just go on to the next. Sometimes I could spit to it, it would be so close. There's no peace with that kind of life. Try to leave it at work and it just follows you home like a hungry dog, whining all night so you can't close your eyes without hearing it." He snorted through his nose. "I had the worst beat for years. Drew the short straw, you could say. But now I've got the best in the city. Nothing going on here but people looking out for each other."

"You found nothing, then," Bill asked, understanding what Brander was telling him.

"It's a case of no news is good news. I met with the owners and they seem like fine people. Maybe a little new-agey for me, but nothing I saw raised any alarms. They're just committed to helping people, *elevating*, they call it. As for the bruises you mentioned—now, I did see those, on quite a few people actually. It's basically a high-tech hickey. They have a machine with this hose on it and they sit you in a chair and make you release all your negative energy, and the machine sucks it up. It's a low-grade suction, nothing that will suck your brains out or anything. And people around here seem to think it works. And maybe it does. Maybe it explains why I'm getting eight hours every night instead of two. I'm not complaining."

Bill pinched the bridge of his nose and sighed. "I'm getting old. I remember when everyone went keto, then there was that charcoal thing, and a few people in my building were crazy about colonics for a while there. Now it's Can-Do contusions. I can't keep up."

With no new patrons since Brander had entered, the café faced a lull in traffic and began to grow warm. He unzipped his jacket. "I'm with you. But if you want my opinion, I think this one's here to stay. And I kind of hope it does. My wife and kids would be happy, and it sure would make for easy times between now and retirement." He smiled with those bleached white teeth of his and did something that made Bill's stomach turn. A trickle of sweat had beaded down the side of the officer's face and, without thinking, Brander removed his hat to wipe it away with the back of his wrist. His hat had been covering a bruise on his left temple.

Bill immediately averted his eyes. He reached into his pocket and pretended to check his cellphone for a message he hadn't received. And while Brander's hat retreated from his periphery, he typed a message to Barbara, telling her that the weather in New Brunswick was the same as the weather in Vancouver, and hoped she understood what he was trying to say. He said to Brander, "Can't get a day off. Everyone wants to own their own business, until they realize that the business owns *you*." He groaned, perhaps a touch too dramatically. "Just lost power to our refrigeration units. I appreciate the update, but if I don't get there soon, our regulars are going to revolt."

Brander laughed. "Remind me to never own a business. I'm free for the first time and, unless the neighborhood implodes, I'm never going back to that life." He stood and shook Bill's hand again. "If you need anything, you know where to find me."

They parted, but even after Bill returned to Barbara, Maria, and Luke, he could feel Brander's eyes on his back.

Outside, they hurried to the Volkswagen and locked the doors. Bill draped an arm over the back of his seat to face Maria and Luke. He pointed to Paw Paradise. "You know these pet stores actually borrow their animals from the Humane Society? They loan them to the stores, hoping people will adopt them. I'll bet if we go to the source, there'll be fifty cats instead of a few. You'll have more to choose from if we go there. What do you think?"

After conferring with Luke, Maria agreed it *was* a better idea. She fastened her seatbelt. "Are there monsters there, Daddy?" she asked.

"Let's hope not," Barbara answered for him.

Bill started the car, relieved to put space between them and the Can-Do Crazies, wondering how they had gotten to Brander. Wondering if he would ever feel right sending Luke home.

20

There were few days Cody had luck. It had been the case since he'd bulleted into adolescence, and stayed the same after he crashed into adulthood, so he'd learned not to expect much. But near the river, the sun was shining, the air was warm, and the sands of Terry's life had begun to drain more swiftly. He could almost hear Terry's time running out; the degenerate drops crumbling off the block of life, falling to the shit heap below. Sure, Slick had overtaken Cody's entire torso and both his legs, but she was creeping up Terry's *face*. Cody might not be able to fuck or fight, but soon Terry wouldn't be able to *breathe*, and that made every day a good day indeed. Behind his sunglasses, his eyes swept aside to where Terry was talking to a representative from the city, reviewing their options for a memorial bench in Kade's memory.

"Uh-huh, uh-huh," Terry's lips puckered. "This sounds great and all, but what do you have in the low hundreds. Got anything between one and two?"

"You can run an ad in the *Gazette*," the woman said, closing her folder and hugging it to her chest. The look she gave him suggested Terry might as well tape a poster to a streetlight in the rain.

Cody said, "We'll go with the platinum package."

"Your money," Terry grumbled under his breath.

"I'll send the contract over this afternoon," the woman said to Cody, then gave them both a tight smile and left them on the riverbank.

When they were alone, Terry shook his head and grunted. "Guilt's expensive. If you don't feel it, you don't pay for it." He knelt, picked up a flat stone and threw it into the river, where it sank.

"It's the right thing to do."

"Only if you're guilty." Terry threw another rock.

Cody scanned the empty riverbank and the deserted walking path beside it. A quick push would send Terry into the water. The asshole couldn't swim, so it wouldn't take long. But there would be no fun in that. He wanted to see Slick worm up Terry's chin and snake into his mouth. He wanted to see Terry yowl in pain the way Kade had. He wanted Terry to know he was going to die in the worst possible way. Not fast like Kade, but slow, the shroud of death drawing over him like an unhurried, suffocating hand. "We should go," he said. "Busy day today."

Terry cleared his throat and spat, then turned toward Elanor's car. He made a face when he dropped into the worn passenger seat. "I don't know why you're still driving this piece of shit. We've got buckets of money rolling in and you're in a granny wagon. Your face and your car don't jibe, man. Might as well be Johnny Depp driving a Yugo."

Cody wasn't flattered. He knew Terry was trying to butter him up with the comparison. Since his elevation, Terry had sidled his way into Can-Do's business like a vulture to roadkill. Or swindler to money. Somebody had to take over for Cody when he was gone, Terry had reasoned. As his own death was not far behind, Terry argued that he and Slick would find a way to coexist and that the reason Cody hadn't figured out how to do so yet was that Cody wasn't as sharp as him. He didn't *get* things the way Terry got things. Only, Cody knew that wasn't true. Terry thought he could negotiate with Slick, as though there was something he had that Slick couldn't already take if she wanted. Once Cody had thought so, too, but when the spawns started feeding back their messages and the *energy* they'd siphoned from their hosts to the growth on his body, Cody learned that Slick needed no one. She had an army to feed her. She didn't need Cody or Terry. She could purge Cody's living body *or* corpse—it didn't matter—and roost in trees or bunk in the sewer or nest with the clams in the bottom of the river. As long as her children were gathering, their hosts would wither like sunflowers in November, and Slick would continue to thrive. He put the car in drive and unrolled the window, feeling the breeze between his fingers, wishing he were strong enough to resist her.

Two minutes hadn't passed before they stopped at a red light. A car full of women stopped beside them. There was a ruckus of movement between the front seat and the back, and the brunette behind the wheel honked the horn. Terry and Cody looked and saw five women batting their eyelashes and fluttering the tips of their fingers. *Come hither*, the blonde nearest them in the back seat seemed to say with her eyes. By the look of them, they were university students, oversexed and under-attended, itching for a story to tell in their dorms.

Terry gave it to them. He leaned his head out the window and gestured to the women to lower their glass. Four windows went down and four heads poked out. Only the driver remained inside, hands on the wheel but with a flirty posture that outdid the rest. Sparks of estrogen threatened to ignite both fuel tanks as the women tittered and cooed and inflated lips, eyes, and breasts.

"Pretty ladies got the time?" He growled testosterone. And before the women could respond, he flung open the door and tipped his chin to his chest. "I got the time if you want it." Five sets of fluttering eyes cast downward where Terry's cock impersonated a wristwatch.

In their former lives, with their former bodies and all the allure of warthogs, the women would have revolted. Police would have been called. Terry would have been arrested. Maybe Cody too. And though the flash of a stranger's dirty cock was no one's idea of a good time, the women gasped and giggled and eventually drove off. In the rear window, three sets of middle fingers told Terry what they thought of his watch.

Cody hit him and pressed the gas pedal.

"What? Just having a little fun. You need to lighten up, man. What good's all this if you can't have any fun with it?"

"It's not exactly fucking legal," Cody hissed. "We don't need any attention."

"Psssh. No one's going to touch us with the cop around. Chill, man."

"He's only one guy, Terry. It's not like he's got the whole fucking force in his pocket. You want to keep making money, stay low, okay?"

Terry zippered his fly. He reclined the seat as far as it would go, then stuck his booted heels on the dashboard, sitting frog-legged the way Cody had the night of the fire. Above the glove compartment, a smear of mud appeared between Terry's feet. "You haven't changed a bit. Still the weak-ass snowflake you've always been, hanging off your grandmommy's titty like a stuck vacuum."

"You want all this to go away? Don't think it can't, Terry. It doesn't matter how many people we've got under us. We don't need to give anyone a reason to poke around. Just cool it, that's all I'm asking."

"What?" Terry pointed at his temple. "This won't get their attention? C'mon, man. The *sucking the bad energy out* story is only going to last so long. The whole fucking neighborhood's going to have to start wearing sheets over their goddamn heads. And don't get me started on the whole *Children of the Corn* creepy shit they do when someone looks at them the wrong way. She's got to cool her jets." He reached over and flipped the sun visor down. He thrust a finger at the pulsating sack behind his beard. "Hear that? Cool your jets, bitch." The last part was unnecessary, but he felt it got his point across.

In a flash, the cilia on the sack became strands became ribbons became cords, whipping around Terry's neck and squeezing until a wet gurgle came out of his mouth. His arms shot to the noose Slick had fixed on him and tried to pry her fingers off. She squeezed tighter. Terry's eyes bulged. His skin grew red. Purple. Then finally when the stars in his vision threatened to become crossbones, she gave him one more tug and released the hold on his neck. Because, just like Cody, Slick was in no rush.

"I-I'm-m s-sorry," Terry coughed. "Sorry. I didn't mean it. I just... if you... if they..."

"Leave it—

"—Terry," Cody said, unaware of the pause.

Terry went on. "I mean to say that the longer she goes incognito, the longer this will all work out, for all of us." He flinched as if Slick was going to choke him again, but she didn't.

He still thinks he can fix it, Cody thought, noting that Terry didn't mention the impending deaths. *He thinks he can drain the poison, salt the leech, negotiate with the terrorist.* But Cody knew better. He had no illusion of a cure. He knew that anyone who'd ever experienced Slick and had her depart would dive back in and let Slick take whatever was left of them, just like he had. Their recruits were addicts and adulterers, thieves. They were the poor of circumstance, of mind and of body and while they might not have chosen this particular demise, they were all like his grandmother, Charity, Edwin, and even Terry: take them to paradise and they never wanted to leave, even if it gave them cancer.

Of all their recruits—his grandmother excluded— only the cop hadn't accepted Slick willingly. Horace Brander had come in nosing around, asking questions that shouldn't have been asked, antagonizing them with his watchful eye and clever mouth, inciting them until even Cody couldn't suppress his phantom. Brander had pissed himself when they surrounded him in Cody's office. "Oh God! Oh God!" he'd bleated and blubbered. He hadn't known that they weren't mighty and that he could have taken all five of them if he really tried, or that if he ran he'd live another thirty years. Instead, he'd gaped at their terrible faces and tried pulling his gun, shaking too violently to get it out, until Elanor stepped forward and touched his wrist.

The effect had been instant.

Brander's coffee-stained teeth dazzled. His take-out food belly shrank. The decades of sleep he'd lost found him once again. Rest *oozed* from his pores. So began the beginning of Brander's end.

Cody sighed and turned onto Hobson, unable to stifle the melancholy oozing from his own pores. By the time he parked, Terry was scrambling to get away from him, and that was fine with Cody. He didn't want him around, anyway.

For the rest of the morning he was moody, so much so that his grandmother told him to take a walk and Edwin offered to drive him down Mitton where blowjobs were quick and wouldn't give him herpes. Cody declined. He worked disinterestedly another few hours, and when he could no longer handle their advice, he put on his coat and left.

Clouds had rolled in and the sun he enjoyed on the riverbank was now cloaked and dim. Though a breeze began to needle his skin, he needed to be alone where he could think. Months ago, he'd made the walk as a runt gone idol. Now he was trudging it as lord turned pig farmer. He drew up his collar, feeling like a swine. Slick folded around him, understanding but not caring, easing the burden on his right side by spreading her weight to the left. She wasn't completely evil, but neither was she good. The duality made him bitter, and he stewed on it as he passed the tracks at the switchyard and headed toward the red and white building where it had all begun.

He ordered a bucket of chicken—all drumsticks—a large poutine, a small bowl of corn, two biscuits, and an iced tea, and took the bag to a bus stop near an old apartment block. He wasn't taking the bus, but the seat was abandoned, and he did not want to eat at home. Cody opened the bag. Container on top of container, the mound was startling, maybe a foot and a half high. It was an appropriate amount for a last meal, he thought. Some guys go big with steak and lobster, bowls of blue M&Ms, whole fucking turkeys. Cody just wanted his KFC and for Slick to finally do what she was going to do.

He bit into his chicken, crying, knowing he appeared insane, feeling that maybe he *was*, when a squeal caused him to turn. A little girl was running toward him. Cody spun around, thinking that she was running from a bully or the group of boys on bikes that had passed on the street not long before, when sharp pricks began spidering up his left leg.

Cody looked down. There, a tiny black and white kitten was scampering past his knee. Its scalpel-sharp nails cut through Slick's spread-out hide and into Cody's own skin. She shuddered and shrank from the pain, then stretched from the cuff of Cody's pants and went for the furry assailant.

"Sully!" the girl cried, coming upon them fast.

Cody lowered the chicken. Saw the girl. Saw the tendonous cords spiral up his calf. Saw the kitten now on his thigh, now his stomach, now his chest, perforating Slick as it went, homing in on the drumstick in Cody's hand. With a shake of its rear, the kitten sprang at the drumstick just as Slick struck.

Still steps away, eyes wide at the sinews snaking toward her pet, the girl screamed. "No!"

Instinctively, Cody swiped the kitten with his other hand before Slick could catch it. It mewled, paddling its legs in midair. Slick flapped across Cody's body, thrashing like an unmanned end of a fire hose. Cody lifted the kitten and dug his right heel into his left calf. "Hide," he muttered under his breath before the girl came upon them. Slicked sucked back under Cody's clothes, brooding.

A moment later, a teenage boy bounded up beside the little girl, panting. "I told you not to let him out," he wheezed, bent over with his hands on his knees. "He's faster than you think."

The little girl didn't respond, nor did she take the cat Cody held out to her. Mouth open, she stared at him, unblinking.

"Maria?" The boy frowned.

The girl Maria didn't speak.

"Hey."

The boy nudged her, and when she still didn't acknowledge him, he took the wiggling cat and followed the direction of Maria's gaze. There was a flash of recognition. His jaw tightened and he took hold of the girl's hand and thanked Cody for catching the kitten. Then he dragged Maria and the cat along while she watched Cody over her shoulder. They murmured something, looked back, and quickened their pace to the convenience store below the seventies-era apartment building where Cody's grandmother bought her lottery tickets.

Watching the boy's gangly frame hurry the girl away, the memory of the boy and the man came to him. They had come from the café next door, carrying a box of donuts. They had simple names, Mike or Brad or something like that, and the man had asked Cody if Can-Do was a church. The boy—*Lane*, he thought—drew comics, and he and the man were terrible at hiding their suspicion. Cody remembered that part the most. They had seen Cody's blood and thought someone had been murdered, and Cody had thought that they weren't too far off.

He had *succumbed* that night, hadn't he? But it was the man who'd sent Brander poking around, so was it he or Cody who had sealed Brander's fate? Cody considered this as he packed up his chicken and returned it to the bag.

Back on the sidewalk, with Slick already repairing the dozens of pricks the kitten had made, Cody continued toward home. Not twenty steps from the bench, he looked ahead to the So-Lo. The little girl's face was pressed to the door, watching him through the glass. An older teenage boy, maybe even a college student, peered where she pointed.

Directly at Cody.

"Well," he said to Slick, who was still mad at him for saving the furry assailant. "You couldn't stay hidden forever, could you?"

Slick stung him to let him know she didn't care about being seen. Not anymore. Once she was finished with Cody, she'd bury herself somewhere where her children could feed her like hundreds, thousands, even *millions* of mother birds. She would grow and grow, underground if need be, collecting energy, compressing her layers like oil, until she was too big to extract. No one could stop her then. And if a little girl saw her? Slick would take care of that. She had lots of help now.

"Don't even think about it," Cody said when she pressed her plan to him. "No kids. That was the deal." But even as he said the words, he knew they were a lie. There never had been a deal because Slick didn't negotiate. If she wanted a child, she would find a way to get the child. The thought curdled his stomach and he had fight to keep the chicken down.

He was raising a peace sign to Maria and the older boy, two fingers to say that everything was a-okay, when the man who'd sent Brander after him appeared beside the little girl. Cody put on his best salesman smile and waved.

The man waved back.

Cody thought it would be more suspicious to walk on than to meet the guy who'd remembered him, so he strode across the grassy boulevard, into the small parking lot, and went inside.

Maria and the younger boy stepped back as he entered, but the man stepped forward and shook his hand. "Never forget a face, but I'm terrible with names. Cody, is it?"

"You're better than you think," Cody smiled. "Brian, right?"

"Bill."

There was an awkward silence. Cody immediately felt like a fool, so he plucked a bag of Doritos hanging from a wire clip behind Bill. "You live around here?" Cody asked when he realized Bill was still beside him and that Maria and the boy he'd given the kitten to were observing him from a table near the deli. Two old men also sitting there squinted daggers in his direction.

Bill said, "I've been to your business, now you've been to mine. It's not as fancy as the Can-Do, but we do all right. How's it going over there? You still—what'd your grandmother call it? —liberating people?" The corner of his mouth twitched as though he were stifling a grin. Cody couldn't blame him. They *had* laid it on rather thick that day.

"Can't keep up. We're booked solid through January," Cody said, realizing that Bill was glancing at his temple, now at the mound on his side, now at the lumps on his arms, at the bulge on his legs. "To tell the truth, I could use a break already. No time to sleep, and even fast food is too slow these days."

"Not a bad problem to have," Bill said. "Well, I can't do anything about the rest, but how 'bout a cup of coffee? We're not Starbucks, but the regulars seem to like it. Maria said you got our cat back, so it's on me. Least I can do."

His false geniality should have warned Cody away. Instead, he found it refreshing to have someone who wasn't tethered speculate about him. It meant that even once he was gone, there was hope that Slick might be discovered before it was too late. As long as Slick didn't get to Bill first, that is.

"If you don't have time . . ." Bill started, then one of the old men called out from cupped hands.

"Tastes like shit, but it keeps you regular!"

The boy who draws comics tittered, but the girl didn't laugh. She was still staring at Cody.

Whether it was an invitation or interrogation, a tinge of curiosity spurred him forward. He took the vacated seat next to the man with the cane, the one who hadn't said the coffee tasted like shit. Maria sidled away to her father, holding the squirming cat.

The man without the cane crushed Cody with his eyes. He wagged a finger at the side of Cody's face, where his bruise was showing through the concealer Charity had retouched before he left. "You a trouble-maker? Haven't seen that much shit on a face since Trudeau at that party."

"It's a condition," Cody said, without explaining further.

The man grunted and moved his hat to make room for the coffee Bill put down. A small bowl of cream, sugar, and stir sticks was leaning against the wall under the window. He stirred in some cream and watched it swirl in his cup. When he looked up, he saw that the man was looking at his bag of chicken. Cody said, "It's still warm if you want some."

"He's always hungry. Can't bring anything in here without him sticking his nose in it," the man with the cane said.

And this is how it went for the next forty-five minutes. Paper plates were distributed, names were exchanged, and by the time the others were done eating, with them doing most of the talking, Cody felt the most relaxed he'd been in ages. No one told him to take a walk. No one told him how they were going to *fix* things. No one wanted to hurt anyone else. There was no Kade or Slick or dirty wristwatches, just Jasper and Martin insulting each other and explaining how they'd met Bill, while far away at the register Maria and Luke whispered and watched.

Their plates cleared and the coffee drunk, Jasper and Martin departed, both giving hearty thanks to Cody for the meal Jasper said was fresher than anything Bill ever served. Cody saw in the ridicule an affection that pervaded the So-Lo like a friendly coat of paint, from the worn but polished floor to the pot lights that gave the interior a comforting feel, not like the chain stores that practically x-rayed you with fluorescent lights. In the time Cody listened to the old men, several customers came in. All but one knew Bill by name, yet by the time even that one left, she and Bill had become friends. All in all, it suggested a life Cody had only seen on TV. The cradling kind of life that took you in, no matter how much money you had or what you looked like. The kind that swallowed you with cheer, where everyone was worthy, unless, that is, you were a troublemaker, as Jasper had said.

The tinkle of the overhead bell announced a young family entering. Luke and Maria stayed at the register while the family toured the aisles. Bill waved to the man and woman then strode back to the table where Cody was zipping up his jacket.

"Before you go," Bill said, twisting his mouth for the right words. He lowered into the seat across from Cody, glanced back at Maria and Luke, and faced him with a hardness Cody hadn't seen before. "I don't know how to say this properly, so I'm just going to say it. I think there's something strange going on and that you know what it is. I saw that building, Cody, I know what it looked like back there. *Brander* saw what it looked like back there. Tell me, how does a building like that, in an area like that, suddenly get a business like yours? I might not be big business, but I've been around long enough to understand that if it smells strange, there's usually something rotten nearby."

"We wanted to give back—" Cody started, but Bill cut him off.

"I heard you were charging five hundred," Bill said. "Is that what you charged Brander, or did you give him a special discount to *elevate* him, as you say, and get him off your back?"

"We have nothing to hide."

"Then why are you covering that thing on your face? I don't buy the vacuum story, like Brander said, or it wouldn't spread like you've got ink dripping inside your skin. And how do you explain the weight loss? Did you suck it out of his face? Maybe bleach his teeth while he was out?" He was trying to keep his voice down, but the couple lifted their heads to the sound of their argument. Bill winked and smiled, and the couple soon lost interest. He leaned over the table. "One person, two, I could look the other way. Maybe even a dozen if they didn't look hurt, but they don't look right, Cody, and they sure as hell don't act right, and I think you know what's wrong with them."

"If you want to know how it works, I can set you up with an appointment."

Bill pinched the bridge of his nose. "Let me try this another way. I know when someone needs help. I make it part of my job. I don't know you, Cody, but I get the feeling you need help. You've aged thirty years since I met you. You don't look good. I don't do *mean*, Cody. That's not me at all, but you look sick. And I think you know why."

"It's a condition," Cody said weakly.

"Sure looks contagious."

"I appreciate your concern . . ."

Cody made to stand but froze when Bill put a hand on his arm. "I think you're dying. It's a terrible thing to say, but I know what death looks like. I saw it in my wife. It's like your outside is already gone but your inside is too afraid to recognize it. Those people I saw near your business, they all looked like you did when I met you, all shiny like they've just come back from vacation, but I've got the feeling they're going to be exactly like you not long from now. A whole lot of them. Am I wrong?"

Ancient tears rolled from the vaults where Cody stored them. A sting of pain jabbed the corners of his eyes while old channels were lubricated and dust blockages broke apart. The trapdoor hinges opened a little more, a little more, then out squeezed dust-jellied tears that stuck to Cody's eyes. He wanted to tell Bill that he was right, about everything, about the Can-Do, about himself. He wanted to take back everything he'd ever done. Most of all, he wanted to take back Slick.

Inside his clothes, Slick squeezed a warning. Betrayal would cost not just Cody but *Bill*, and possibly everyone else in the So-Lo. The girl. The boy. The family. One lash and she'd tether.

One strike and Bill would be just like Brander or Charity or his grandmother. The man who made friends with everyone would wither and die. He would become an accomplice just like the others, and Cody's hope for a future without Slick would die alongside of him.

Slick advanced to the openings in Cody's cuffs, the hem and collar of his jacket, throbbing against him, waiting for him to speak.

"Do you need help, Cody?" Bill asked. His eyes went to Cody's wrists, his neck, the mark on his temple.

"I can m-make you an appointment," Cody said, drawing the collar of his jacket closed, holding it together in a tight fist.

Bill leaned back in his chair and sighed. "Okay, then. Can't make you talk if you don't want to, but I'm going to ask that you don't come back here until you do. No hard feelings, but I got people that depend on me, and I do what I have to do to protect them. You might be harmless, and I could be crazy for thinking you're not, but something doesn't sit right with me and until I figure it out, I'd prefer you keep your distance. And if you decide you want to talk, I might change my mind." He didn't offer his hand, but instead drew a card from his breast pocket and pushed it across the table with his index finger.

Cody took the card. It had the So-Lo's information on it, with Bill's name printed in bold at the bottom. He cupped it in his hand, knowing he'd never call.

21

Almost three weeks after Ruby's admission, Luke and Bill entered the atrium of the hospital with five bundles of flowers, two helium-filled balloons, six magazines, a small white teddy bear, and a *Get Well Soon* card stuffed with not only dozens of good wishes from the So-Lo's patrons but also a sizeable stack of money—all for a woman most of them had never met.

The gesture, orchestrated on the sly by Barbara, Martin, and Jasper, touched Luke so much that he began to cry, and that made Bill and Maria cry, and as he and Luke waddled toward the elevator with full hands, they determined not to look at each other so as not to bring the tears again. Luke hid behind the flowers and Bill hid behind the balloons and when they finally faced each other in the elevator, they cracked with laughter so hard they forgot to press the number for Ruby's floor and ended up riding the elevator top-to-bottom again until a serious-looking man came in and snorted at them.

"Are you excited, Luke?" Bill asked unnecessarily, if only to keep them both from laughing.

The flowers in front of Luke's face shook. "Uh-huh," he said behind them.

They squeezed out of the elevator, careful not to bump the flowers, then wound through the antiseptic-smelling corridor. His first visit since Diana died had brought him to his knees, but after visiting Ruby every day the mean fingers of memory had begun to soften their hold on Bill's nerves. What he felt in this five-story immersion of suffering was no longer the soul-crippling grief that had once buckled him, but a deep gratitude for the time they'd been given to say goodbye.

Closer to his mother's room, Luke began to break ahead of Bill, quickening his pace as they progressed down the hall. The flowers in his hands rustled, and by the time the galloping boy reached his mother's room there was a trail of petals on the floor. He dashed inside, but Bill slowed his own pace to give them more time for a private reunion.

He tugged the balloons behind him, the unseen gathering tickling his eyes, when a voice from inside the room made him stop. It wasn't a doctor, Bill knew, because the man was apologizing to Luke, calling him *son*, calling him *Lukey*, and telling Luke to come give him a hug. Bill looked at the nurses' desk, at Ruby's room, back at the nurses' desk. One female nurse was typing something into a computer and the other was flipping through a patient's chart, neither alarmed nor wary of the criminal twenty steps away. He gritted his teeth and stepped to the doorway where Ruby and Joe were folded around their sniffling son. The flowers Luke had brought were in a heap on the floor.

Quietly Bill began to retreat, then Ruby's eyes opened and she beckoned him inside. He hesitated, tried to pass it off as though he didn't want to intrude on the sacred family moment, but she saw through his revulsion and waved her thin arms until he relented. Joe, the wife-beating, child-terrorizing degenerate, finally released his hold on Luke and turned to face Bill for the first time.

It was like looking at a before and after photo of a drug addict, only the man in front of him was the *before* version. Joe was nothing like the photos the police had shown him when they were first investigating the assault on Ruby. The man in the picture had had a head full of tattoos and teeth as dark as coffee. The man in the picture had had mean eyes and a wide, crooked scowl that seemed to split his face like the jowls of a ventriloquist's dummy. If *that* man had entered Ruby's room, there was no doubt in Bill's mind that Joe would already be in handcuffs.

But the man in Ruby's room wasn't the man in the picture. The tattoos were covered with glossy bronze hair. Joe's teeth had shed their stains and become whiter than sand. His skin had molted its flakes of dependence and glimmered with wellbeing. Even his eyes had slipped their whisky-yellow casings and shone a blue as clear as a summer sky. The bare-armed man with the oily shirt in the police photos stood before him anew, in a pressed, white button-up, fastened to the collar. Only the drippy, nickel-sized bruise on his temple betrayed his secret.

"Mr. Asket, is it?" Joe stretched out a hand.

"It is," Bill said. He released the balloons next to Ruby's bed and jammed his fists in his pockets.

The unrequited gesture sucked all the air out of the room. Luke and Ruby whipped their heads to the criminal, waiting for the explosion. Luke backed away. Ruby bit her lip with the still broken stubs of her teeth. She snatched Luke's hand, squeezing it until her knuckles were pressure-white.

Joe said, "I understand. You have every right to be angry at the man who did this to Ruby, but you're not looking at that man, Mr. Asket. That man died. Burned up by his own sin. I swept his ashes into the trash myself, and he's not coming back. I promise you that."

Bill's nostrils flared. It was all he could do to keep from giving Joe a taste of what he'd done to Ruby. Inside his pockets, his fists tightened.

Ten smooth fingers spread out before him. "I'm not asking for forgiveness, Mr. Asket. *That* man doesn't deserve it. You and I both know that. But I want you to know that I'm going to earn her trust if it's the last thing I do. Luke's too. I'll do whatever it takes." Joe patted Ruby's blanket-covered ankle and when he looked to his wife and son, Bill would be damned if there weren't tears in his alien eyes. "They deserve the best and I'm going to give it to them. I'm hoping we can be friends, Bill. You've taken good care of my family and I owe you for that. If you ever need anything—"

"I'd like a moment alone with Ruby," Bill said.

"Of course." Joe said immediately. He went to the door, his wide, benevolent smile never leaving his face. His skin flickered, but only Bill caught the phantom behind it. Then he was gone.

Ruby raised a hand. The intravenous line attached to her wrist caught on the teddy bear Luke had brought, and it fell to the floor. "I know what you're going to say."

"I shouldn't have to say it." Heat rose from Bill's collar.

"I know. I know. But you see him, don't you, Bill? You see what he's like now? He wasn't like this. He was *never* like this."

Her eyes swept to the ceiling. A long push of air snorted from her nose. Luke retrieved the bear and the flowers, pretending not to be interested in what she was saying. "When I was a little girl, I used to dream of being married. My parents got me this doll, it was second hand, but there wasn't a scratch on her. I remember brushing her hair and dressing her up in all these outfits, like she was a doctor or a veterinarian or an astronaut. And she'd go on pretend dates with my other toys. I'd pretend they were princes, of course, and they were always handsome and kind. I remember thinking she was me." She watched her son retrieve a plastic bucket off her bed tray and walk to the bathroom to fill it with water. "But the first guy I met was Joe. He made me see that my dream was silly."

"It's not silly."

She screwed up her face, the bloodshot and broken eye now white and healing, and just the faintest green bruise on the right side of her face showing through the makeup the nurses had applied in preparation for Luke's visit. "You don't get that people like me . . . well . . . it's easy to spoil our magic. You get to keep yours longer, so it stays with you even if you think it's gone. You don't have to worry about where you're going to live tomorrow or if there's going to be food today because it's always *there*. And your people are too. It was never like that for me. The first one to stay *was* my prince. It's hard for you to see that, but that's how it is. So, yes, he was a bastard. Luke knows it, and I know it. Don't think we don't know that. But I can't look that man and not know in the bottom of my soul that he's done what he's done for me and Luke. He fixed himself for us. I might not be much to look at, but when I get out of here, he's going to help me, Bill. He's going to elevate me and we're going to get better together, and Luke will have the kind of life your little girl has. He deserves that."

Bill's heart seized. The contents of his stomach liquified into an acid that burned right through him. Luke was arranging the flowers in the plastic container and knew as he looked at Bill that something was wrong. "Don't do it," Bill said, his whole body trembling with fear for Ruby, for Luke. "I know it sounds good, but it's not. You've got to trust me on this one. Please don't do it."

"What? It's not like we're joining a *cult*." She laughed and when Bill didn't share her humor, she fixed him with all the incredulity her recovering face could manage "I've got a right to that kind of life if I want it. I'm tired. I'm hurt and I'm tired of not having the life you and all your *middleclass Mabels* have. You're not rich but you sure as hell aren't poor, either. Joe can fix that for us. Can't you see that? We can have an easy life, too."

He dragged his fingers down his face, pacing the small space alongside the bed. "It's exactly like a cult. They drink the Kool-Aid or whatever shit those people are selling them and *sure* they turn into goddamned butterflies but then they turn into moths, and everything is a fucking flame." He was so worked up he was panting. "Sorry, I don't mean to get like that, but it's not safe. I know what he's doing and I know the people who are doing it to them. It doesn't last. Those people get sick. They think it's a cure, but it's not. Luke saw it for himself. Tell her, Luke."

Luke glanced at his hopeful mother then averted his eyes from Bill, crouching to pick flower petals off the floor. "I think it's okay," he said.

"You really think that?" Bill asked him.

This seemed to unsettle Luke, and for a moment he was the same boy with the tennis-ball knees and pale skin, stealing a bruised apple. In as few words as possible, he told his mother about meeting Cody at the Can-Do and recently seeing him again at the So-Lo. He admitted that Cody *had* looked unwell the last time he'd seen him but excused his appearance with the cold weather and greasy chicken. As he spoke, courage began to seep back into him. He reported Maria's tale about snakes inside Cody's jacket when he caught the kitten, and that maybe Bill had put ideas in her head because he was jealous. The Can-Do was bright and shiny, and the So-Lo, though a different type of business, was not.

Bill wasn't hurt. He saw the boy struggling for approval from the only relatives he had, saw how his mother nodded on encouragingly, and how badly both wanted their family whole. "I'm sorry you feel that way, Luke."

Ruby said, "You've been a big help to us, but now it's time for us to be a family again. Lukey will pack up his things and come home, where he belongs. I appreciate everything you've done, even if you don't approve of what we do. Thank you, Bill. I mean that."

Bill closed his eyes. His sigh was the mournful low of a snared animal. A passerby in the hallway looked his way, offered a sympathetic smile, and carried on. He clasped a hand over his mouth to contain his worry and hoped they felt the rupture of his soul.

"You act as if I'm dying." Ruby frowned.

"Ask him about the bruise before you do anything. Even if he's nice and says all the right things—and he will—ask him about it. Just do me that favor," Bill pleaded.

"Should I ask him about the snakes, too?" Ruby snapped. "Maybe he's hiding a goddamn lizard up his sleeve? You know what I think? I think *you* should be in a hospital bed. I'm sorry for trouble we caused you, but you're not talking straight. Joe will bring Luke home. He'll get his things later."

"But—"

"Goodbye Bill," Ruby said.

In the corner where he had retreated to study the electrical outlet, the baseboard, anything but the squabbling adults, Luke waved limply.

With Ruby glowering and Luke avoiding him, Bill stood in the doorway and tapped his temple. "Ask him about the bruise, Ruby," he said. Then he left.

The hallway swallowed him, and the peristalsis of working equipment and rushing attendants and whimpering patients muscled him forward, out into the parking lot. He drifted to his car and there he sat with his hands on the wheel until his shaking subsided. He considered calling Jane Finch, the patient coordinator who'd discussed Ruby's admission with him, but he knew that Ruby had never actually admitted to the police or to the hospital who had put her in there. Given Joe's history, they'd all *assumed*, of course, but only Ruby could prove their assumption. And she wouldn't do that. Not now. Definitely not now.

Fog had begun to settle on the windshield, so he put the wipers on and turned the climate control to defrost. He thought of Brander and wondered how many other officers had been elevated by Can-Do, then supposed that it had to be many. In a normal world, police would investigate mass injury. They would be suspicious of hundreds, if not thousands, of people with distinctive, drippy bruises who glared at you if you noticed them. Health departments and other people like Bill would take notice. Municipal, provincial, and federal governments would descend. He wondered where they were and why he was the only one concerned about it.

The windshield began to clear. He looked up at the hospital, recalling his father's battle with dementia and the toll Diana's death had taken on his sanity, and wondered if Ruby was right.

22

Somehow, he got back to the apartment. He didn't remember the roads or the lights or if he'd hit anyone or even if the car was still running, but he didn't care. Luke and Ruby were in trouble and Bill couldn't help them. He sagged through the door and dropped his keys on the floor.

"Well, you look like hell ridden over," Barbara said when she saw his face. She was drying a glass with a dish towel. She tilted her neck to look behind him. "Where's Luke?"

"Maria, honey," Bill said to the child on the couch knotting a bracelet on a plastic loom. He sat beside her. "Remember Cody? The man who caught Sully for you?"

"The octopus man," she said, nodding and twisting blue, green, and yellow strings that the kitten swatted from the floor.

Bill dipped his head to get her to look at him. "I want you to tell me what you saw, honey, I'll believe whatever you tell me, no matter how crazy it sounds. You said Cody had a . . . a snake in his jacket. Was it a snake, honey? Really?" The perversion of his words wasn't lost on him, and he hated himself for uttering them. He softened his face so as not to frighten the girl.

The small hands laid down the loom and the small head shook, once, twice, and was still. "No, Daddy."

By now, Barbara had come behind them, intently watching the exchange.

"What was it then?" Bill asked.

Maria's innocent eyes lifted to her father's. "I don't know."

"Could it have been his arm, maybe?"

She shook her head. "It came from here." She pointed to the bottom of her pantleg to show him.

Bill frowned. "So if it wasn't a snake and not his arm, what was it, honey? Do you think you could draw it?"

"Where's Luke?" Maria asked.

"He's with his parents," Bill said. "But he might need our help. I need you to show me exactly what you saw, okay? It might be nothing, and if it is that's *good*, but if not—" He paused. "It might be important."

A small nod.

Barbara rustled paper and markers from the kitchen table. She put them on the coffee table in front of Maria. The girl touched the markers, rolling them off the paper. She drew a rudimentary man on a rudimentary bench. She gave him thin but lumpy legs, an overstuffed middle, and arms with bulging elbows. Bill and Barbara looked on, watching Cody come into focus. He looked like any other cartoon, could be any real-life person, really, but then Maria scanned the markers once more, flicking them with the tips of her fingers, and hurried to her bedroom. She came back with a dark purple marker and set it to the paper. A serpentine limb weaved from the bottom of the cartoon man's pantleg, thick as a soup can at the bottom, thin as an antenna near Cody's chest. The limb wasn't smooth like a snake but instead was coated in hair or spikes or some kind of filament that both the marker and the child couldn't adeptly conjure. What was very clear, however, was that cartoon-Cody was protecting a cat from the reaching limb and that he wasn't surprised there was a creature in his pants. Before she was finished, she added a blotch of purple on the cartoon man's temple in the same color as the spiky limb.

Maria set down the marker and leaned away from the drawing as though the limb might reach through the paper and grab her like it had tried to grab the cat.

Bill pinched the sides of the paper and held it up. "What is it?" he wondered aloud. "A mini Loch Ness monster? A new species of land octopus?" He closed an eye and held the paper at arm's length. "Can't believe I'm saying that," he added with a puff of air that rustled the paper.

"Whatever it is," Barbara cut in. "It's got to be what's making those people act so strangely. That mark"—she pointed to the cartoon bruise on cartoon Cody's temple— "is the same color as that snake-thing. Is there a reason for that, hun? Did you do that on purpose, or did you do that because it was the marker already in your hand?"

"They're the same color," Maria said. "And they're both kind of . . ." she searched for an explanation. "Like Jello."

"What do you mean *like Jello*?" Barbara asked.

"Not like Jello," Maria changed her mind, finding a better comparison. "Stretchy like . . . like cheese pizza when you pick it up from the box. You know how some cheese stays on the pizza and some is still attached to the other pieces? Like that. Maybe a bit harder, but like that."

The adults looked at each other, their eyebrows pressed low over their eyelids while each puzzled and wondered and thought about the eight-year-old's description. Bill said, "I saw the thing on his face, but it didn't look *stretchy* to me. It looked like a bruise or maybe a birthmark. But since so many people seem to have them, I don't think that's what it is. It's . . . I don't know what it is."

Maria pinched the paper from her father's hands and pointed at the snake-thing. "It didn't get stretchy until *that* came out. Then it got gooey."

The nonsense that came from his daughter's mouth, true because she had yet to develop the motives of age, bewildered him. He kissed Maria on the head. She returned to her bracelet-knotting while he and Barbara went to the balcony where they could talk without little ears turning into satellites. It was cool and the breeze sweeping over the city brought a humidity that sank into their bones. Neither of them cared. They peeked through the windows at the girl making a bracelet for her best friend and the unease that befell them made them shudder.

"I'm going to tell you something," Barbara said, now looking over the balcony at the adjacent apartments lighting like fireflies in the afternoon gloom. She stretched her slender neck away, then toward him. "I've spent my fifties trying to be thirty, my sixties trying to be forty, and now my seventies trying to be an age I've never felt I've been. At my age, people expect me to be like those little old ladies you see on TV or read about in books. Too weak to open a jar, quivering like every breath is my last. I never wanted to be like that. Ever. I swore I never would. But the funny thing is that no matter what you do to your body, you can't fool your *mind*, can't make it believe that it hadn't been sitting in its own jar in your head, collecting people, storing places and events. I've seen things, Bill. I've seen sunrises and sunsets just like you, the moon coming and going, heard screams from space and scratches under the earth. I don't believe we are the only beings on Earth, nor do I believe that the stopping of a heart stops anything at all. If I was younger, I wouldn't believe any of it, but that mind of mine, well, it's wise enough to know that I don't know anything at all."

"What do you think it is?" Bill said.

Barbara's breath was beginning to show itself in silver-light vapors puffing from her mouth. She shrugged. "Some lonely sea monster? The baby of Bradbury's not-so-lonely beast? I have no idea, but I don't think anything that comes with its own warning label is good."

"The phantom faces," Bill agreed.

"Uh-huh."

"Joe's one of them now," he said. "Like Cody used to be when Luke and I first met him. A regular prince, if I ever saw one. He had the same mark on his temple. Not as big as Cody's, but you couldn't miss it. When Ruby gets out of the hospital, she says he's going to *elevate* her, too. She figures they're going to be one big happy family."

"My God!" Barbara put her fingers to her lips. "What about Luke? We have to help him. What if they ... he ... ohhh!"

Automatically, they turned to check on Maria. She had finished her bracelet and was dragging a long piece of string around the couch that the kitten was chasing. He leaned his elbows on his thighs and worked the knots in his palms with the pads of his thumbs. "He's with Joe right now. There's no way he's going to let me near him. He was nice in the hospital, but that's their trick."

Barbara snatched his arm. "Talk to Cody. You said he seemed to want to talk to you. Maybe you can convince him to stay away from Ruby and Luke."

"I don't think he'll listen. I told him not to come back. That doesn't exactly invite confidence, now, does it?"

"Try," she insisted.

He nodded, drew his cellphone from his pocket, and searched for Can-Do's phone number. It was unlisted. Thinking the café next door might be able to send him a message, Bill found the number and dialed it. An automated message cheerily intoned that they were either busy with customers or on the other line, and to call back another time. He hung up, waited a minute, called back, and got the same message. After five minutes, ten, nothing had changed. He paced the balcony, called again after another five. Same response. He checked his watch. After five.

"Maybe they're closed," he said.

"What about the other businesses?" Barbara asked, but when she looked at him and he at her, they knew that no one down Hobson would help them. They wouldn't help because they'd all been condemned by the same beast that had condemned Cody.

"I have to go there," Bill said quietly.

"If I wasn't a pacifist, I'd have given you a gun."

He laughed, but it was an uneasy laugh. "If you weren't a pacifist, I wouldn't have taken it."

"You can't go alone."

"I can't ask anyone to come. You know what it was like. If I bring people, it would only make it worse, especially since you and I are the only ones who've seen what they're really like. Besides Maria and Luke," he added. Across the divide, a woman came out to her balcony and adjusted her satellite dish. Two floors below, a man was shaking out a rug. Bill stood, went to the railing and looked down at the busy street below.

"Maria's been wanting to try those cookies April makes. Maybe we can call her and they can make them together," Barbara suggested, not looking at him.

"I can't let you come. We need someone here who knows what's going on. And if something happened to me—"

She smacked him. Hard enough to make him step back. When he turned, her pale cheeks were red and angry. "Don't you do that to me, Bill Asket. Don't you go talking like that. I love that boy just as much as you do, but I won't have you risking God knows what for something we can't control. There's got to be a better way."

"Which is?"

"I don't know," she grumbled. "I'm thinking."

A sound made them turn to find Maria's cross-eyed face squished against the glass. The jolt to their tense nerves nearly knocked them over the balcony. The victorious child giggled behind the glass and was gone.

"How's it going with Susan? Is she worth saving or do we feed her to the minions?" Barbara asked after their hearts had quieted.

He snorted a laugh. "Worth saving, but she might not want *me* after this. Likely I'll end up in a padded room talking to an imaginary Jasper."

"If he doesn't get there first," Barbara said. 'Speaking of . . ." She raised an eyebrow.

"No way."

"He wouldn't care. You know that. And if they did something to him, it might be an *improvement*."

"Not funny."

"Think about it. Who would suspect *him*? He is more than capable of holding his own. You saw how he was when those bullies came in for Zeke that day."

"That was years ago."

"Still," she said. "You'd just have to tell him what to expect. With all those beautiful women over there, he definitely won't be looking at their *bruises*."

She was right. He hadn't thought about that. Jasper was incapable of looking at a woman's face. It was his worst quality, but now, perhaps, the most useful. Still, the idea of asking anyone, even Jasper, whom Bill loved in a weird uncle sort of way, wasn't something he was prepared to do.

"*Martin's* the military guy," he said. "Jasper was only posted a few months before they sent him packing. And that was fifty years ago. What if he gets sticky fingers or if he says the wrong thing? You saw how they reacted when we just *looked* at them. I can't imagine what they'd do once his mouth got going. You know how he is." To his own ears, it sounded like he was trying to talk himself out of it. The heat of shame reddened his ears. "Out of the question," he said with a little more conviction.

"What do you think those two codgers would do if they knew what you were thinking? If they knew Luke was in trouble, they'd saw their own arms off to help him."

"Terrible visual." Bill wrinkled his nose.

"You know what I mean."

Barbara stood. She adjusted her shawl, wrapping it around her waist. "I don't think we have much choice. The longer you wait, the greater the danger of that boy becoming whatever those people are. You can pretend you want to book a consultation. One look at Jasper and they won't ask questions."

"I don't know..."

"Diana would've wanted you to do it."

Bill frowned. "That's not fair."

"You're right." She took hold of the door handle and looked back at him. Wind flapped the ends of her shawl against her legs. "It's not fair. None of this is. But I'll tell you something. We wouldn't be sitting here having this conversation if *she* were alive. She would've already dragged those bastards out by their ears and made them promise not to touch that boy." Then Barbara pulled the door open and joined Maria inside.

For a moment he stayed outside, stung by the truth of what Barbara had said. He looked at the darkening sky, wishing for Diana to send him a sign, tell him that everything was okay, assure him that he would come home to their daughter the same man she remembered. He rolled his phone in his trembling hands, then he called Martin and Jasper.

23

Two old men with nothing to do were easy to get going when the boredom of retirement smothered their lonely homes. They had arrived twenty minutes after Bill's call, about five minutes after Barbara took Maria to her apartment. Bill had given them little information, only asked if they were busy and said he needed to speak with them in person. He assured them that the So-Lo hadn't burnt down and that Maria and Luke were okay and that the chili Barbara had bragged about earlier was still warm. The sound of an old war movie being turned off was the last thing Bill heard as Martin said goodbye, as was a toilet flushing as Jasper hung up. The men headed to the apartment, shocked when they faced each other in the hallway.

Martin raised a hand to knock, but it met no resistance when the door suddenly swung open. Bill was already sweating, and Jasper remarked he should have put on a clean shirt if guests were coming.

Martin poked him in the stomach with the handle of his cane. "You're not goddamned royalty. Now smarten up. He's got sot something to say." Jasper grumbled all the way to the kitchen, where he fixed himself a bowl of chili before Bill could wait no longer.

He told them. The story was awkward and unbelievable. More than once he had to stop Jasper from interrupting. As the story unfolded, each revelation more incredible than the last, Bill felt a mixture of relief and embarrassment. By the end, he felt as if he were too insane for even a padded room. Had it been decades earlier, he realized they wouldn't have even put him in a padded room. The kind of crazy he was talking . . . they would have given him a lobotomy instead.

"Excuse me while I shit myself," Jasper said when Bill finished. A splatter of chili sprayed from his mouth. Beside him, Martin calmly took a napkin from the table and wiped his arm.

Martin traced his finger in the air as if sorting through Bill's explanation. "So these . . . things . . . we're not sure what they are and we're not sure what they do. But you think they're killing people or going to kill people and that they might get Luke?"

"You saw it, Jasper," Bill said. "You saw it on Cody right away. Remember?"

Jasper crossed his arms, harrumphing and pulling faces while he worked the problem and retrieved the memory. "Nothing gets by me," he said importantly. "You're damn right I saw it. I thought it was a gang thing, you know how those bums are always messing up their heads. I didn't see the . . . that octopus thing you said he's got with him, but he looked as well as Gilbert did after that chemical explosion. Remember the one at the plant? That Cody fella looked just like him." He pointed to Martin's head. "Pale as all hell, except the side of his face like he's got syphilis." He stopped. "Maybe it's syphilis!"

"I'd ask you how you know what it looks like, but I don't want to know," Martin wrinkled his nose. "It's not syphilis, Jasper. And before you ask, there was a lot of it overseas. The thing on Cody, it looked more like a giant wart to me. Never seen one that big, so I couldn't help being curious. A tumor like that on the side of a guy's head is hard to miss. I thought he covered it up pretty well, but I could still see the edges. Didn't think it was dangerous." He folded his hands behind his neck and leaned his head into them, staring at the ceiling, thinking.

"I don't think the *mark* is dangerous," Bill said. "I think it just means there's something inside whoever has one."

"Like an *I Voted* sticker for aliens?" Martin said without a trace of humor. Jasper snorted.

"Same idea," Bill said. "The bruise, it doesn't seem to do anything but get bigger. Maria said the arm or whatever it was that tried to grab Sully came from near Cody's foot. But the mark never left his face. It just got . . . *gooey*, she said. That makes me think that the thing can move around their bodies but that it has a home base, near the brain where it changes people and feeds off them too." Vocalizing the theory didn't sound as ludicrous as he thought it would. It seemed possible, enough for him to even believe it himself.

"I think it's horseshit," Jasper said. Bill and Martin opened their mouths to shut Jasper down but Jasper smacked the table with his hands. His spoon jangled in his empty bowl. "Before you assholes stuff a rag in my mouth, let me talk." He waited for them to interrupt him but when they didn't, he pushed back from the table and threw his napkin in the bowl. "Now I've listened to you, Bill, I have. And what you told me made no goddamn sense at all. Hear me out before I shove that cane so far up your ass you'll be a tripod for the rest of your life." He thrust a finger at Martin, who sat back down. "It makes no sense, and you both know it, but in all my years knowing you, Bill, since you were no older than Zeke, I've never known you to spin a tale. You're a terrible liar. Always have been. Even those white lies you tell Greta. You know damn well she looks like a horse in those dresses she wears. You have her believing she's a model the way you go on, but her eyes are as bad as those potato sacks. She doesn't see how red you get when you're trying to keep a straight face, but we do. Tell him." He juggled a thumb at Martin.

"You *do* get a bit peachy," Martin said.

"Everyone needs a compliment now and then," Bill said.

"The point is, I know when you're lying, Bill. It's on your face like a hemorrhoid. Can't miss it no matter which way you handle it. That doesn't mean I believe it, mind you, but I believe that *you* believe it and that's enough for me." He folded his arms across his chest, finished.

For a time, Martin was quiet. A sheen of sweat reflected the light over the table, and if one looked close enough, the silhouette of Bill's worried face was discernible on the old man's skin. He said, "If these people are like you say they are, my biggest concern besides not coming back at all is *us* becoming like them. I don't think it's contagious, otherwise we would all have turned out like Cody. Perhaps it's something that's transmissible by blood or saliva. Maybe those marks are from teeth or a stinger we don't recognize. Most people believe that the bubonic plague was eradicated, but that's not the case. There's still a few hundred cases every year. We saw it in India in the nineties. I was part of a group providing air transport for one of the observer headquarter relocations for a few weeks during that time and I tell you I never want those days back. It was on the other side of the country, but I couldn't help but look at every speck of my body and think it was going to rot." His thin finger went to his Adam's Apple. "Even had me looking at this like it was a swollen lymph node. I knew it wasn't, of course, but that didn't stop me from poking it raw."

"I can't promise anything, Martin," Bill said.

"I don't expect you to," Martin replied. "When I joined the military, I was promised a place in the ranks, and I was promised training. That's all. I was never promised a specific role or specific posting. They committed to operate as safely as possible, but they never committed to keeping me alive. They couldn't. Yet here I am. Retired, but never *resigned*. If Luke needs us, I'll do everything I can to help. And I have to admit, you've got me curious enough that I'm willing to spend a perfectly nice evening ruining it with *him*." His humor eddied around them and with its gentle hands lifted their chins to face each other.

They rose. Bill took from the block near the stove a small knife that he wrapped in a dishcloth and stuck in a grocery bag. He offered the pick of the block to Martin and Jasper, but the men shook their heads and pulled small knives of their own from their pockets.

"You carry those around?" Bill asked, looking from Martin to Jasper and Jasper to Martin.

"Beijing Buffet," Martin said simply. "Best buffet in the city, but terrible area. Nothing's ever happened, but it's good to be prepared."

"Francine Stillman's husband came at me with a towel."

"A towel?" Bill said, then he knew. Of course he knew. He shook his head. "You were naked."

Jasper shrugged. "A wet towel whipped on your bare ass feels like a bullet."

"Behave, Jasper. This is the one time in your life that you need to be . . . not like you, okay? Look at anything but their faces, and for God's sake keep your mouth shut."

They left the apartment. Martin and Jasper went to the garage with Bill's keys while Bill went to Barbara's apartment to hug Maria one last time. "I'll be back before you know it," Bill said.

"Are you picking up Luke?" Maria asked.

"I'm going to try."

On the table was a half-colored picture for Luke. She rose from the floor and plucked the finished green, yellow, and blue bracelet off the coffee table next to the picture and pressed it into her father's hands. "This will make him happy, Daddy. If he can't come tonight, this will make him happy until they let him come again."

"I know it will," Bill said, squeezing her until she squealed. He looked over his daughter's head at Barbara.

"If you're not back in an hour, I'm stealing your apartment. You've always had the better view," she said.

"I knew there was a reason you stuck around," he said, and left his whole world coloring a picture for a homecoming that might never happen.

24

Bill pulled the Volkswagen onto the darkened streets. The ride was quiet until the chili hit Jasper's stomach and all four windows had to be rolled down. Then the sounds and better smells of evening hit them. There was music from bistros, laughter from friends and couples walking arm-in-arm, the sizzle of meat hitting outdoor grills not yet put away for winter, and the bark of dogs disquieted by it all. They passed the switchyard. Neither Jasper nor Martin had been to the area since their trip to the Dirty when they'd seen Joe, so they gaped and gawked when the deterioration they'd anticipated didn't materialize.

The once miserable area welcomed them like a grandmother's bosom. Shanties made new with care folded around them. Fairy lights were strung on doorways and balconies, colors of autumn —reds, yellows, oranges—were arranged in planters and in windows and in wreaths on doors. In windows were scarlet maple leaves, bronzed cattails, and willows whose silver puffs dappled indoor forests designed to enchant passersby. And the same doors that had been slammed at the coming of dark as though this were a street in Transylvania were now open and full of people.

Cars lined both sides of the street and for five blocks Bill couldn't find a space to park. He pulled the Volkswagen to the curb outside a new day spa that advertised a brightening seaweed wrap to lighten and reduce unwanted dark spots.

"Now, there's a business that understands supply and demand," Martin said as they stepped onto the sidewalk.

"Stay close," Bill said. "And remember what we talked about. Jasper, you're hard of hearing. Martin, you have bad eyes. I'm ready to elevate and brought two friends who could use a lift too. Sound good?"

The men grunted their agreement. Martin began squinting and Jasper said, "Eh?" "Eh?" and cupped his ear when the two beside him worked at small talk. They were blocks away from the Can-Do, but already they felt eyes on them. They weren't under the microscope yet, as the glances were fleeting and disinterested, but they hoped to keep it that way. More buildings had been renovated since his last visit, and Bill supposed more *people* had been renovated, too. The bruises were bigger now, and there were a great many lumps and bumps where before there had been flat bellies and sculpted bodies. No women were wearing skirts, possibly because of the cool autumn weather, but neither were any of them wearing form-fitting clothing. Their shirts ballooned. Their bottoms tented. The men walked on, ignoring it all.

Outside the Can-Do, a couple was walking. Martin, with his head down and his cane poking around to move himself forward like the half-blind man he pretended be, almost bumped into the couple, but at the last minute his ingrained reflexes jerked him away. The couple stopped walking. Heads tilted, eyes narrowed, the man and the woman turned. Under a cone of lamplight, their bruises showed like tar splatters on canvas. Martin toddled on, perhaps blinder than before. Their eyes bored into him and stayed that way even when Bill led him and Jasper into the white-washed interior of the Can-Do. Not one man looked back to see if the couple was still watching them. They *knew*. Through the glass, they could feel the inspection.

At the counter sat the same woman Bill recognized from before; Elanor, he remembered. She was no longer trim or ageless. Elanor had gone bulky, and her smooth skin had begun to fester like an infected wound. Patches the color of open scabs appeared in clusters above her shirt collar and on the back of her hands. The bruise on the side of her face that once she'd managed to cover was now unmistakably black and seemed to leak toward her chin. She'd covered everything with thick coats of makeup that dried and flaked.

She didn't hear them enter until they were at the counter, when Bill knocked gently. Elanor was working on a cross-stitch pattern on fabric stretched over a small hoop. It displayed a number of birds with golden beaks and deep blue plumage, but as the scene unfolded left to right, the beaks grew rounded and misshapen, then droopy, then nothing resembling beaks at all. The clear demarcation of wings and feathers and tree branches and leaves on one side melded together on the other. Blues sprayed onto oranges, oranges onto browns, and greens onto everything else. Tiny dots of string gave way to intersections of knotted and tangled lengths of material not intended for the art. There was hair and dental floss, the bloodied butcher's twine from an old roast. Yet Elanor had been tugging away at the craft and set it on the counter without a hint of self-consciousness.

Martin and Jasper, still blind and deaf, sidled away from the fiasco.

"May I help you?" Elanor said, blinking rapidly at them as though the circuits to her eyes had been shorted.

Bill avoided recalling their previous meeting in case it caused the same wariness as in the couple still standing outside. He said, "I had a tour a while ago by a man. I can't remember his name." He tugged the whiskers on his chin. "I think it was Charlie, maybe? Or Rory?"

"Cory," Elanor said. Not Cody. But *Cory*.

"Cory," Bill said. "That's right. I was hoping to book a consultation with him for my friends and me." He gestured to Martin and Jasper, adequately stooped beside him.

Elanor looked at them, and for a time Bill thought she was sizing them up, that she had seen through the pretense and was going to summon the stooges outside to come take care of them. Martin and Jasper would be dragged to one of the pods and Bill to another, and they would be held down and made monsters. Her eyelids were open so long they began to lose their shine, but then Elanor's rapid blink returned and her frozen face grew animated once again.

"Cory's not here right now, but another member of—"

Pause.

"—our transportation team can help you."

The woman's confused words, *transportation* instead of *transformation*, *Cory* instead of *Cody*, and the bizarre cross-stitch suggested a deterioration far greater than Cody's. She smiled at the three men. Her Picasso face—drooping here, ascending there—unsettled them to the point that the old men drew in breaths and held them for fear of disturbing whatever lay inside her.

"I'd really like Cory, if possible," Bill insisted.

"Who's Cory?" a man said as he rounded the partition behind Elanor's desk.

He was a good foot taller than Cody but had none of his reasonable disposition. He had cruel eyes and a jutting chin. He left the counter to inspect the three of them. Martin squinted at the man's stomach. Jasper squinted as if to hear better.

"You know Cory," Elanor said, looking at the ceiling, now walls, now floor, picking at the bloodied butcher's twine with a pen.

"You mean *Cody*?" The man frowned at her. He gave them a tight smile then slid Elanor's cross-stitch hoop off the counter where no one could see. "Cody is off right now, but we can set you up with Edwin or Charity, if you'd like."

Bill raised a palm. "Thanks, but a while back Cody gave me a tour. I admit I was skeptical then, but he really was quite convincing, and I see why. You can't question what's right in front of you. And I don't think it's so bad to want a little piece of that magic for yourself. I'm ready now, but I'd like Cody to have a word with my friends. Maybe he can convince them too."

The man—*Terry*, by the name emblazoned on his nametag—drew his head back and peered at Bill through slitted eyes as though he were spying the hole in the top of a needle. He rolled his tongue under his upper lip and exposed a lump in the soft underside of his chin so big that his beard ballooned around it like wilted flowers on a volleyball. It wasn't *jutting*, Bill realized. It was *engulfed*.

"You'll have to come back when he's in on Monday," Terry said, meeting Bill's eyes. He gave him a look that said, *You saw. You saw and you're pretending you didn't.* This seemed to poke Elanor, for her eyes rose from whatever she was doing behind the counter and her weird head tilted, glaring from one man to the next, and back again. Outside the window, the lurking couple put their hands on the glass, watching.

Martin caught it all and groaned. He put his hand to his chest and said, "My. I'd ... like to sit if I may."

He stumbled to the seating area near the window, leaned heavily on his cane, and sat. Inches behind his head, the couple pressed their faces to the glass. Jasper, meanwhile, played at being ancient. He let his mouth droop open as though abandoned by muscles. He squinted to hear, sniffed to see. His old, trembling fingers removed his hat and he wiped his liver-spotted forehead with the back of a curled hand.

"Do you mind leaving Cody a message for me?" Bill asked the glaring man. He considered asking for Cody's phone number but knew they wouldn't give it to him. "Can you tell him that Bill from the So-Lo stopped by? He had a special offer for me, and I'd like to talk to him about it."

"If you tell me what it is, I'll—"

Pause.

"—honor the *deal*." Terry waited. The corner of his mouth flickered up.

"Your guess is as good as mine," Bill said.

"What'd you say?" Jasper croaked.

Bill leaned toward Jasper. "I said I didn't know what the deal was. The guy's not here to tell us."

"You should call him," Jasper wheezed. Near the window, Martin rocked forward and back, forward and back with his cane.

"Cory's at home," Elanor said behind the counter.

"*Cody.*" Terry gritted his teeth.

"I hate to do this to you, but my friends, well, it took a lot to get them here. They heard me talk about Cody and now they want to talk to him too. Would it be too much to ask to give him a quick call?" On cue, Martin began coughing into a tissue. Jasper farted.

Terry scrunched up his nose. He pulled his cellphone from his pocket, dialed a number Bill couldn't see, and put the phone to his ear. Like flowerheads to sunlight, the men raised their eyes, suddenly not old, not infirm, but attentive.

"No answer," Terry said after a while.

The way Terry looked at him, Bill suspected there wouldn't be an answer, no matter how long they waited or how many times Terry called. There wouldn't be an answer because Terry hadn't called Cody. He hadn't called anyone. If he had, it was his own voice mail or that of a business he knew would be closed and therefore wouldn't pick up.

"Is he there?" Jasper grunted. When Terry shook his head, Japer said, "Call him again."

The old man cocked his ear as Terry asked. "Is there a rush?"

"You're goddamn right there's a rush." Jasper scowled. "Look at me. Can't sneeze without pissing myself. You got a fix, and I want it. And I don't want to sell an arm to do it. Bill says we can get a deal and we're not leaving until we get it. Tell us where this Cody fella is and we'll talk to him."

The sudden burst from the old man drew a flicker on Terry's face. His eyes darkened. Behind Martin's head, the couple began tapping the glass. A little louder. A little louder. Elanor took up her cross-stitch hoop and began stabbing it with her pen, never once watching it, but glaring at Jasper, at Bill, at Martin.

Terry said, "You're right. Life's too short to wait for miracles to happen. You know what?" He paused so long they thought he might have died standing up, but then Terry went on. "Any friend of Cody's is a friend of mine. We'll set you up for *free*. All of you. No charge. We can do it right now. What do you say?" He stepped aside and swept an arm toward the partition behind Elanor's desk.

A spot of urine darkened the front of Jasper's pants. Bill swallowed the lump of terror rising in his throat. Behind them, Martin gasped. He clutched his chest and rolled onto his knees, bent over on the floor. "Call . . . call an ambulance," he sputtered.

Elanor went on stabbing the hoop with her pen. Terry did not reach for his phone. The couple behind the glass now had their fists up, pounding them against the window like rabid fans at a hockey game. Jasper tottered toward Martin while Bill made the call. Send *two* ambulances, he told them, watching Jasper wheeze and puff and clutch his own chest in an overdramatic display of similitude.

Not four minutes later, with Bill, Martin, and Jasper clustered on the floor and Elanor and Terry glowering at them from the desk, a firetruck arrived. The men who rushed into the Can-Do weren't marked by tar bruises or ink spots inside their skin, nor did they have any noticeable ball-sized lumps on their bodies. They had long-night puffs under their eyes and thinning hairlines and skin that hadn't seen enough of summer. When the ambulances finally arrived a few minutes after that, the firemen gave the lurking couple a look that suggested they go or a firehose would be lashed upon them. The couple left. Jasper was examined and cleared to leave. Martin was laid on a stretcher and rolled outside with Bill and Jasper following.

But Terry caught the old man's wink to the others before he was lifted into the ambulance. Oh yes, he did.

25

He sat in the dark living room, halfway through a full glass of vodka. The blinds were drawn, the cat was still nowhere to be seen, and Slick was ignoring him so there was no one to talk to. The devil that she was, she refused to let him end his life on his own terms. She slapped away the pills, whipped away the razor blade, rejected his attempts to tie a knot and slip that rope over the banister. But she allowed him alcohol, so here he was, unable to kill himself, yet unable to live with himself, on his way to being blindingly drunk. He thought she might have liked the tickle of alcohol, because he felt not only his own buzz, but hers, fluttering inside and around him like a million butterflies. He supposed he could drink himself to death but knew that with his luck he would puke it all out and Slick would just punish him for their hangover the next day.

He looked at the clock on the cable box. His grandmother would be home in an hour. Thinking of her brought the tingle of tears to his eyes and he wiped them away. She'd begun to decline rapidly in recent weeks, spacing out more than he'd ever seen, losing words and actions, even her own name, of which he'd reminded her several times a day. Once, he'd found her pouring coffee into the cat's water bowl. And just yesterday she'd come out of her bedroom with her legs stuck inside the arms of a blouse. He'd sent her to change, but not before spotting the dark stain of shit on the back of her underwear.

The woman he loved more than anyone on the planet had become an infant, and not because of old age but because of *him*. It would have been better if she'd stayed home and out of sight, but Slick pulled her to the building each day to continue the mission of netting more hosts. And she was happy to do so. Cody sipped his drink, wishing he would choke on it.

Someone banged on the door. Three quick blasts to the aluminum that hurt his head. He sipped some more. Another blast. Then four more. Then Terry's sour voice spitting like venom. "Open up. I know you're in there."

Cody gulped from his glass, lifted himself off the couch, and went to the door. The moment he unlocked the bolt, Terry rushed in. "Your phone fuckin' broken?"

"I'm off, Terry." Cody sighed.

"You're never off. None of us are ever off. You mind telling me who the fuck Bill is?"

"Huh?"

Terry dropped into his grandmother's recliner and thumped his boots onto the coffee table. "Two old guys came in with him, asking—"

Cody waited for the circuits in Terry's brain to reconnect. He thought of bashing Terry over the head with the bottle of vodka, but Terry blinked, and his venom started spewing again.

"—for you. *Cody offered us a deal. We only want to talk to Cody*," Terry whined. "I'll tell you something. Those assholes *knew*, Cody. And I think you fuckin' told them."

"I didn't say anything, Terry," Cody stated flatly. "But if I wanted to, it would be none of your goddamn business. This isn't your show, it's—"

Pause.

"—mine."

"Not for long," Terry said. "And who do you think is going to run it when you're gone? Charity? Edwin? They're just as fucked as you. You need me, man."

"And who's going to replace you?"

"No one. I'm working on an arrangement."

Cody lifted an eyebrow.

"I'm close, man, so don't fuck it up."

Under Cody's shirt, the butterflies fluttered. He finished his glass and sniffed. "You don't get to win, Terry. She won't let you," he said quietly, knowing it was the truth.

Terry shot out of his chair and slapped the empty glass out of Cody's hand. The ball under his chin wobbled like a water balloon. "She won't let *you* win. This is my game now. She made us fucking lords, man, fucking *lords*! And you wasted it." He tapped the long, drippy mark on the side of his head. "You should have used what she put in here to figure it out, but you didn't. You were always too stupid to use what you had, and now you're paying for it. Not me. I've got a plan."

"Which is?" Cody asked.

"Expansion," Terry said, drawing out the word.

The butterflies thrummed with anticipation, but the vodka in Cody's stomach curdled. The sourness of revulsion rose in his throat and he choked it back down. "What do you mean, *expansion*?" Only, Cody knew what it meant. It meant that Slick wasn't going to just stay in Garrett. No. She'd move on to London, Toronto, Montreal, Vancouver, Mexico, Europe. She wouldn't just expand but *conquer*.

"Garrett's too small now, don't you see? She's bigger than that. We take her out, get our networks going, and she'll kill it out there."

His too-real metaphor brought a chill down Cody's spine, but Cody didn't say anything. There was nothing to say. Soon he would be gone and Terry would take over, and there was nothing Cody could do that could stop it. The weight of the situation was heavy like an anvil on his heart. He filled his glass again and drank. "Where did you say those guys were from?"

"That shitty store near those old apartment blocks. The *So-Lo*," Terry said. "One of the old fucks faked a heart attack but a firetruck and ambulance came before we could get them. Either you tell them to stay the fuck away or I'll take care of it." He swiped the bottle off the table and took a swig. Vodka dribbled down his chin and onto his ballooning beard. Then Terry was gone.

Wind rushed in through the door Terry had left open. The grocery flyers on the coffee table rustled. The paper bag from his bottle of vodka blew onto the floor. Cody watched the movement in the house, knowing that soon there would be none. The cat appeared and sat tentatively in the doorway as though debating whether to stay or go. An indoor cat his entire life, Tinker would be unprepared for the jungle of the outside world, but still it would be better than being trapped with Cody and Elanor in their house casket.

"Good luck, buddy," Cody said, tearing now for the cat he'd never adored. Tinker looked back at him, blinked, and disappeared into the night.

For a time, Cody cried. He cried over the cat. Cried over his grandmother. Over Charity and Edwin and Billy and Kade. Eyes red and with vodka slackening his tongue, he clattered around the house until he found Bill Asket's card. He dialed the number, not expecting an answer.

"Hello?" Bill's steady voice said at the other end of the line.

Cody hung up and flung the phone away as though it had burned him.

The phone rang. Cody listened for a while, but each time the ringing stopped, it started again. He knelt and swept his hand under the couch. Then he pulled the trilling phone to his ear and opened the line. He grunted something intelligible.

"Luke, is this you?" Bill Asket said. When Cody didn't answer, Bill continued. "You don't have to say anything if someone's around you. Just sneeze or something so I know you're okay. Can you do that?"

"Luke's that kid, right? The one with your girl?" Cody said, rolling in his foggy head the memory of the teen and the little girl at the So-Lo. "Something happen to him?"

There was silence on the other end until Bill finally said, "Cody?"

Cody burped.

"I need to talk to you."

"Is the old man all right?"

"Martin's fine," Bill said.

"Look who's the actor now, huh?" Cody lay on the couch and closed his eyes, feeling just a touch better to have another human who was not Terry and not tethered speak to him.

Bill grew serious. "Cody, Luke's in trouble. One of you turned his father, and once his mother gets out of the hospital, they're going to turn her too. I don't know exactly what you're up to, but I know it's not good. I see the marks, Cody. It's on everyone down that street and they're starting to come into my store. Good until they're not. It's inhuman."

"It's all human," Cody slurred into the phone. "Anyone ever tell you that humans are shitheads?"

"Humans don't have monsters coming out of their clothes," Bill said. "I know you've got something, Cody. Whether it's on you or in you, I know it's there."

With his thumb and forefinger, Cody formed an invisible gun. He cocked his thumb and fired at the darkened TV. "Bullseye."

Both men were quiet. Cody on one end, relieved to have been caught. Bill on the other, mortified to have been right. "Don't touch Luke's mother. Her name is Ruby. Isabelle Ruby—"

"I got no control," Cody interrupted. "Like you said, I'm—" He paused. His circuits were fine, but his heart was not. "I'm dying, Bill. And when I'm gone, the whole world's going to implode. Pssschhh!" Cody's hands sprang apart, a mini explosion in his grandmother's living room.

"There's got to be something you can do." Bill was pleading now. Even in his drunken state, Cody knew the man had begun to beg.

"That Luke kid. Ruby what's her name. Your girl. Those two old shits. All of you. It's just a matter of time. Didn't want it to happen. Didn't mean for it to happen. But can't do nothing about it now." His mouth was getting dry, so he went to his grandmother's liquor cabinet and took out an unopened bottle of Bristol Cream. He broke the seal, unscrewed the cap, and drank from the bottle. Slick renewed her butterfly tingles. Cody opened his shirt and poured some on her. She vibrated into it like a clitoris to an orgasm.

"Cody?"

"Yeah?

"You're not a bad person, otherwise you wouldn't be talking to me. You can change if you want to," Bill said. "I think you *want* to change. You still have time to do the right thing. Until you're gone, you still have time."

"Can I ask you something?"

"Go ahead."

"Do you think we're already in hell?"

Bill was quiet, then he said, "I think you can *make* your heaven until the Big Guy decides where we're going to go. The things that we do help him decide. You still have time for that, you know."

"You really think that?"

"I do," Bill said, and Cody knew he meant it. People like Bill always did. People like himself, however, people like Terry, or Charity or Edwin, they made their own hell on the way to the real one.

"Goodbye, Bill," Cody said and hung up before Bill could say anything else.

Bill phoned back, over and over while Cody drank until he finally shut off his phone. He looked at the clock on the TV. His grandmother would be home any minute. He didn't want to see her in the state he was in. She wouldn't recognize him, and he was so drunk he wouldn't be able to help her the way she needed to be helped. He took the bottle of Bristol Cream and stumbled out of the house.

26

All four of them were talked out, so they sat at Bill's table cradling cups of chamomile tea that did little to settle their nerves and did less to help Luke. While Bill accompanied Martin to the hospital and Jasper drove the Volkswagen home, Barbara put Maria to bed. Now with the midnight moon high and bright, and only a moderate warning of elevated cholesterol from the hospital, Martin leaned on decades of training when he broke the silence.

"We can't stop this unless we know what it is."

"Shoot the bastards," Jasper said for the hundredth time. "Goddamn shoot them. A bullet will stop them."

"Maybe," Martin said. "But maybe not. And if it did, are *you* going to be the one to pull the trigger? To those who don't understand what's happening, it would look like cold-blooded murder. And it would be. You'd have to shoot hundreds, maybe thousands of people, but the police would take you down way before that."

"There's got to be something we can do," Barbara said. "Try Cody again."

With a lift of his shoulders, Bill said, "He won't answer."

Jasper pushed back his chair. He began banging buttons on the coffee maker until Bill moved him away. Then Bill retrieved the cannister of dark roast, glanced behind him at the puffy eyes surrounding the table, and scooped enough coffee to fill a pot. It began bubbling and spurting almost the moment he set it to brew.

"We should kidnap Luke and drive away. Go hide somewhere," Barbara said. "What about that house of Willie's?" she asked hopefully.

"We're not criminals," Bill said, though he knew that whatever action they took to stop whatever spurge was encroaching on the city *would* be criminal. There was no way around that. You couldn't stop a horde of people who didn't want to be stopped gently or with reason. You had to *make* them stop. He didn't like it, but there it was. And they all knew it.

They drank coffee, debating their options, none that had any promise. It was three a.m. when, resigned that they could do nothing at all, the So-Lo's security alarm sent an alert to Bill's phone. He opened the application and saw on the video screen a body outside the So-Lo's entrance, curled in a fetal position. The person had broken the window just above the kickplate. Bill groaned and deactivated the alarm.

"At least you're awake for it," Barbara said.

Jasper began a diatribe against *those good-for-nothing troublemakers with nothing better to do than get high and wreck what's not theirs* and followed Bill and Martin to the elevator to inspect the damage.

"Don't get close," he said as Bill unlocked the interior deadbolt. "He could stick you with a needle."

The So-Lo's ambient lights were dimmed from nine at night until seven the next day, so the men proceeded in the dimness, able to see enough yet unsettled by the shadows that played around them. They moved forward, stepping as one unit, nerves tight as violin strings, while the immobile body of a man with his back to the kickplate came into view.

"We should call the police," Martin said. He shuffled ahead, lifted his cane, and nudged the man's back with it.

A low, raspy moan vented from the man's mouth.

And then a sickening squeal from somewhere else.

It was the sound of a cat whose tail got slammed in a car door, the hiss of a kicked cockroach, the shriek of an owl hunted by an eagle. They leapt away. The sound gurgled out and died.

Bill looked at the body, looked at the men, and *knew*. "Cody?" he whispered so as not to disturb the beast.

The man did not respond. Bill took the handle of Martin's cane, hooked the man's arm, and pulled it over the kickplate. Cody's face rolled toward them. The black mound on the side of his head, now undisguised, undulated like slow moving water.

"What the holy hell—" Jasper gasped.

The mound hiccupped. Bill nudged it with Martin's cane and a hiss erupted that hurt their ears. In an apartment on the other side of the street, a light came on.

Bill unlocked the adjacent door and used his rear to hold it open. He took hold of Cody's ankles, then remembered what Maria had seen there and dropped them like they were red hot coals. "We need to get him in," Bill said in a low voice, looking to Cody and then to the other men for help.

"You want one of those goddamn things on ya?" Jasper spat. "It's a trick. Touch him and he'll turn you."

Martin and Bill leaned over, hovering close enough to see a trail of vomit down the front of Cody's shirt, but far enough to be able to leap away if the mound lashed out at them.

"He's sick," Martin said.

Bill spotted the empty bottle of Bristol Cream in Cody's other hand. "He's drunk. Help me get him in." He lifted Cody's arm with the tip of his shoe and flung it back outside, then he dashed for the pair of utility gloves he kept behind the counter. He put them on, unsure if they were any protection at all.

"I'm calling the police," Jasper snorted.

"Not yet." Bill hurried back to the entrance.

Jasper grumbled. His face puckered as though cinched with a drawstring through his nose. "I don't like it."

Martin removed his cardigan and tossed it to Bill. "Wrap it around the openings and tie it tight," he said, pointing to Cody's ankles. Bill did. Then he took hold of Cody's feet and dragged him inside while Martin held open the door. Wet burps gushed from Cody's mouth. Little dribbles of goo the color of squished blackberries squirted from the thing on the side of his face, and soon the So-Lo was filled with the malty smell of alcohol. Passing Jasper, the thing reached for his foot, but the limb was limp and fell back before Jasper could kick it.

Bill dragged the man and the monster past the confectionery aisle, down the space between the grocery aisle and the refrigeration units and into his office, where Cody promptly vomited beside Bill's desk. Bill dropped his ankles.

"Cody?" he said. "Can you hear me, Cody? Do you know where you are?"

The undulating mound ticked up as if to respond, then sank down again.

"Holy fart in hell . . . I think they're *both* drunk," Jasper said from the doorway.

For once, Martin agreed with him. His trembling hand went to his head as he considered their predicament. Then his eyes swept over the aisles to the front door, from which anyone could hear them. He spied a stack of flattened boxes between a filing cabinet and the wall in Bill's office and used one of these to close up the window, securing it with a newspaper rack and a cardboard display filled with chocolate bars. He returned to the office.

"Cody?" Bill said again.

The thing squeaked.

Jasper, who not long ago insisted that sticking a finger in a man's eye was the quickest way to see if he was all right, dared not move.

The three men stood cautiously near, squinting down at the broken man and the mewling beast. It was Martin who took the bottle of water from Bill's desk and splashed Cody with it. Cody began hacking and coughing and wheezing for air. Instinctively, he rolled onto his side, whooping up water and whatever was left in his stomach.

Jasper kicked his shoe and hopped back. There was a soft bubbling sound from the creature, and out from the cuff of Cody's shirt uncoiled a long, tendonous limb. It flopped to the floor, limp. It was the same color as the one in Maria's picture.

Cody's eyelids fluttered. He muttered something none of them could understand. His bloodshot eyes shone back at them, focusing first on Jasper, then on Martin, then on Bill. He pulled his hands to the collar of his shirt and fumbled the buttons open.

Their gasp could have awakened every tenant in the building. Jasper's busy tongue went still for the first time in many decades. There, on Cody's small body in Bill's office long after the moon had risen, a dark gelatinous beast sagged heavy over skin and hair. It had twenty arms, now three, now eight, that quivered, now stopped, now slithered out with many snaking fingers, now only one. It was a floppy serpent, the red insides of a man, the pink meat of his brain, everything and nothing at all.

"No... more," Cody rasped.

The beast went to Cody's mouth as if to silence him, but Martin flicked the appendage away with his cane. The beast grabbed at it, took the rubber end into its body, and *chewed* with invisible teeth. Martin tugged, the beast quivered, his cane vibrated. With an effort that left him panting, Martin pulled as hard as he could until the cane came away. Where the end had been was now a jagged mess of aluminum and slime that stretched like hot cheese. The effort seemed to drain the beast, for it bubbled back down and simmered on Cody's body, but they did not doubt that it was watching them. No, they did not doubt that at all.

Cody lifted his head. "I didn't kill him. It was Terry... it wasn't me," he said. His eyes watered and then Cody began to cry. It was a silent cry, no sniffs or catches of his breath, but a slow and steady stream of tears that the beast absorbed indifferently.

Bill moved to comfort him but then thought better of it and kept his distance. "How do we stop this, Cody?"

"M-m-me," Cody stammered. "Stop—" The beast sank into his chest. A burst of blood sprayed from his lips.

"It's killing him," Martin gasped. "It doesn't want him to talk."

Cody closed his bloody mouth. His jaw became rigid and the veins in his neck stuck out. Open, closed, his mouth strained against the beast's control. Finally, he cried, "S-stop me."

The beast coiled around Cody's neck. His eyes bulged. His pale skin went pink, red, purple while the three men looked on. Jasper snatched Martin's broken cane and whacked the limb that had fallen to the floor. The beast released Cody's neck. It hissed and struck out. Jasper smacked the limb away, then he took the business end of the cane and stabbed it. Black liquid oozed onto the floor.

"Stop me," Cody choked again.

Bill fetched the baseball bat he stored behind his desk and tossed it to Martin, then he rushed to the far wall, where a hockey stick that one of his suppliers had given him for a playoff promotion hung above pictures of Maria and Diana. He dashed back, raised his stick...

...and could not bring it down. Not on another man.

"We've got to kill it before it kills him!" Jasper shouted over the beast's shrieks. He jerked the broken cane out of the writhing wet mass and drove it in again. Again. Again.

Three limbs erupted where there had been none and swept Martin off his feet, but the old man was quick. From his knees, he took up his bat and hammered with all his might. "Yaahhh!" he cried, cracking each new extremity until it bled. "Yaahhh!"

Just then, there was a rumbling that shook the floor. It was the sound of freight train blasting through the parking lot, crashing toward the window. Bill looked out his office door, over the aisles he'd maintained since he was a boy himself.

And saw that it was a stampede.

Headed toward the So-Lo.

There were dozens—no—*hundreds* of people. And they were charging to his store. Ten bare-chested men brandished knives as long as their arms. Twenty pajama-clad women wielded hammers raised high. Many had golf clubs. More had crow bars. There were wrenches and fire pokers, axes, nunchucks, bows and arrows, and more than a few guns. Bookending the sides were eight-foot spears. Their battle cry was the cry of the beast, in the office and in every mouth outside.

"He's got me!" Jasper hollered. "Oh, God, he's got me! Get 'im off!" He shook the leg the creature had wrapped around him but its hold tightened.

Martin's bat came down on the limb tethering to Jasper. The beast wailed.

Outside, the throng of minions howled.

A woman slammed into the glass. The dribbly black bruise on the side of her face pulsated against the window. A man smooshed up beside her. Another. Then four children. Then Luke's father, Joe.

"Open up!" Joe shouted into the glass. "Open up or we'll come get you!"

A woman brandishing a rolling pin slammed against him, then a trio of teens with switchblades.

Across the street, lights were beginning to flare from second, third, and fifth-floor apartments. Now the sixth. Now fifth.

"Open up!" Joe pounded the window, breathing hard and heavy as the throng flattened him.

The racks Martin used to secure the window began to shake, and a hand punched out from the edge of the cardboard.

Bill turned to the devil on his floor. Martin and Jasper were spearing and clubbing, but still the thing flailed and shrieked.

"P-please," Cody gasped, and held Bill's stare.

Then Bill Asket, who'd never struck anyone in his life, brought the hockey stick down. He struck with the power of a man who'd reserved all his violence for this one moment. He aimed for the devil and scored.

Hockey stick, cane, and baseball bat descended once more. The front windows began to crack. Jasper stabbed. Martin clubbed. Bill beat. Their target moved. They readjusted midair so as not to strike Cody, but the creature was quick. Whenever a man hit the man, he felt the strike in his own soul. And whenever a man hit the creature, Cody felt the rescue of his.

The cardboard blew inward and the racks toppled over. A woman with a machete scrambled over the kickplate and scented her alpha. Then she charged toward the office. Ten others sped after her.

"P-put me with Kade," Cody said. And with a last thrust of effort, he tore the creature away.

They struck instantly.

Every one of the So-Lo's windows shattered as three hundred people and one creature shrieked.

Then there was silence.

27

Below the glow of dozens of balconies, the moonlight stampede jolted to a stop. Women who ran barefoot and bloodied put down their weapons. Men who raged to the high call of war quieted. Newly awakened children blinked at the parents or strangers around them and sucked their thumbs, wanting the comfort of their mothers. The warriors in the So-Lo looked about the ravaged building, confused and ashamed, and departed the way they had come. Beyond them inside the office, Jasper, Martin, and Bill witnessed the disintegration of evil into the floor.

Inch by inch, Cody's open shirt revealed the damage the creature had done. His parchment-paper skin had decayed to a pitted, sickly grey. And his ribs, under which his baby-bird heart fluttered, had been whittled to the thinness of straws. The creature's phantom face blazed once and not again, leaving Cody in its wake. He was no more alive than Diana, Bill saw with revulsion—and wished Cody a peaceful eternity, wherever his may be.

As if sensing Bill's thoughts, Cody lifted a finger. "T-thank y-y-you," he breathed. The mark on his temple dissipated, and Cody was gone.

28

After leaving flowers in front of the now closed Can-Do, a caravan of two vehicles left Hobson Street while unforgiving wind swept the bouquets away. No matter which stations the radios turned to, the programs in both Volkswagens belabored the weeks-ago sun-burst phenomena, deemed *Nightingale* by local pundits, as an extraordinary once-in-a-millennia event that reinforced the need for emergency preparation, while Garrett's conspiracy radio, *Truth Radio*, urged listeners to line their ball caps and toques with foil, as the head was the aliens' preferred point of entry, if and when they ever returned.

Turning now to the cemetery, the radios were silenced and the seven quieted.

Maria's and Luke's wide eyes swept like dust over the gravestones, resting long enough to read the inscriptions, then on to the next. Beside Luke, Ruby's small frame did not move, but she held her son's hand tightly and looked ahead to the little hill where her husband was buried. Though her fear had died with him in the stampede, so had risen the uncertainty of the future ahead. She and Luke were free and would soon be living in Willie Flinder's modest apartment, once Bill completed the renovations, and she was still getting used to having friends. At Barbara's insistence, Ruby had even begun to contemplate returning to school. The idea terrified and thrilled her.

The cars slowed at the little hill on the north end of the cemetery. Here the stones were small and simple, if there were stones at all. No clusters of families were gathered in death, no rows dedicated to generations of sons and daughters—only single insertions, isolated amongst other castaways. Wind picked at their skin as they exited the vehicles. They lifted their collars and buttoned their jackets and strode to the graves they were here to see.

Martin and Jasper respectfully stayed aside while the others stepped to the wooden cross with the credit-card sized metal plate bearing the name of Joseph Vorlicky. Neither wife nor son wept. Maria took Luke's hand and hugged him, and Bill was reminded of Diana's empathy. He looked up to blink away the wetness in his eyes.

Barbara put an arm around Ruby's shoulders and whispered in her ear, "He was a bastard, though, wasn't he?"

Against her will, Ruby laughed. The sound made her son smile.

They walked on.

A dozen headstones away, they came upon the graves of Cody Dean Clyde and Kade Hart, a boy with no middle name, a boy that had made national headlines when he died in a fire. It was Bill who had put the information together. Cody's deathbed profession prompted another call to Constable Brander, who—eager to make peace since a period of confused existence—

wasted little time in investigating Bill's tip. Terry was named a person of interest almost immediately, but just as quickly the emaciated man stepped into the path of an oncoming transport truck. His body hadn't been flung, as is the case with most pedestrian accidents, but collapsed into itself like a dry, giant bubble. *The skin of a shed snake,* the despondent driver described to a scrupulous reporter, and Bill agreed.

Maria and Luke placed the flowers they'd brought next to the insignificant grave markers. Jasper said an awkward prayer on behalf of all, then they returned to their cars. Wind buffeted the trees but did not carry the flowers on Cody's and Kade's graves away.

Other novels by S.L. LUCK

Redeemer

Interference

Authors need reviews! If you enjoyed this novel, please consider giving an online review at your favorite store.

Many thanks!

Check out my short stories and blog at www.authorsluck.com

Connect with me at:
www.authorsluck.com
Twitter: @Author_SLuck
Instagram: @authorsluck

Manufactured by Amazon.ca
Bolton, ON

22562464R00192